LIQUID COOL

THE CYBERPUNK DETECTIVE SERIES

Crime in a High-Tech, Low-Life World

AUSTIN DRAGON

WELL-TAILORED
BOOKS

Published by Well-Tailored Books, California

These Mean Streets, Darkly
978-0-9909315-6-0 (ebook)

Liquid Cool
(The Cyberpunk Detective Series)
978-1-946590-60-2 (paperback)
978-0-9909315-7-7 (ebook)

http://www.austindragon.com

Book cover design by Whendell Souza

Printed in the United States of America

CONTENTS

THESE MEAN STREETS, DARKLY

A <u>LIQUID COOL</u> PREQUEL / SHORT STORY

The Cyberpunk Detective Series in a High-Tech, Low-Life World

AUSTIN DRAGON

CHAPTER 1

Beware the Rabbit Hole

Metropolis was more. It was an urban megacity that occupied a region nearly twice the size of almost all others in the nation, hence its power. Amateur wordsmiths in the media were always trying to make up new hyphenated words to describe it—omni-city, over-city, super-city. Megacity seemed such an antiquated and ill-suited term. Metropolis was called a megacity way back when it was ten times smaller. All its buildings, both business and government, were larger and taller today. The downtown business district, with City Hall right smack in the middle, towered over the many ethnic neighborhoods, with the only exception being the exclusive, super-rich ones, of course. Everything spiraled out and away to create a concrete maze from the ground to the sky. There were no houses as in the past. Everyone lived as they worked, in mega-skyscrapers. There were no individual storefronts. Businesses were either part of a floor, owned the whole floor, or owned the entire business tower. The dark urban landscape was offset by flashing neon and video signs. Street lampposts hung over nearly every city corner, and lights liberally adorned the surfaces of buildings, usually in some kind of geometric design. If that wasn't enough visual madness, there was the glowing eye-wear of the people themselves. Bright lights scared away the gloom and doom of the dark and cloudy skies—nine out of ten city psychologists said so. This "neon jungle" was filled with fifty-million two-legged animals (humans) living, breathing, and dying beneath the ever-present rain.

Buildings dominated the horizontal space, but the public transportation thoroughfares sprawled out vertically, ultimately circling the entire circumference of the city. All private hovercar traffic was funneled into designated virtual lanes, one above another. The only vehicles that could fly where they pleased were the police, firemen, and garbage trucks. And then there were the megacorporate zeppelins floating through the air, flashing their advertisements for the hour or the day.

There was a system to life that everyone followed from the smallest guy, shuffling along to make a living to the god-like guy, consumed with power and fortune—where to work, where to live, where to play. Public schools, public transportation. Labor and delivery rooms to birth your babies, morgues for the "meat" (dead bodies), and finally, funeral parlors for processing to the crematorium. The cycle of life. That didn't mean that the gray people of the masses had to go about life in the rain without style. In their designer Goodwill wet-wear clothes and glowing shades, they found their own particular way to cope and survive in the drudgery of the world. Know your place, don't upset the order of things, and, though you'd never get Up-Top, make it to retirement to relax free-and-clear for your last decade or two of life. Most accepted this unsaid, universal contract. Most accepted that they were mere automatons in the cosmos, even those not bionic, either working for international or multinational megacorps, the archenemies of Big Brother, or working for uber-governments, the "Man," the archenemy of Big, Bad Business. Metropolis wasn't a bad place, but it wasn't a good one either.

There was another choice, a third choice, as an occupation—the streets. Forgo the legitimate, nine-to-five corporatist or government job for the freedom of the streets. But that was euphemistic talk for the Crime World. There was no money to be made being an off-Grid survivalist. In the criminal world, a bigger criminal or the cops would probably get you eventually, but many didn't mind the side-hustle, the gamble to try to beat the odds. Make—or steal—enough to live like an obscenely rich and famous scenester or wealth-hog, or buy your way Up-Top where Paradise was not a hallucinatory dream, but a real-life, fairytale reality for the masses and not the select few. The ultimate payoff could be huge, which was why the risks were so deadly. Every slippery-shoed hustler, knuckle-dragging thug, and in-bred criminal underboss was in your way, and you were in theirs. There were the streets and then there were the mean streets, which despite the neon lights were dark and dangerous. Mean streets were the places that every legit, Average Joe should stay far away from.

The back streets were truly black—no digital signs, no nearby street lamps, no building strobe lights; only the natural light from the sky, which meant near-darkness. It was a not-so-nice part of town. No smiley faces or smiley people here. Crime never tried to hide here. It happened right in the open on main streets as well as the back-alley corners and the many not-so-respectable establishments. It was Exhibit A of the inevitable dark side of the free-market. Dirty money for dirty products and dirtier services. "Some place in the city has to be zoned for sin," the conventional wisdom said, otherwise the filth would be knocking on everyone's front doors, both respectable and rich alike.

The name of this part of the city was Whiskey Way, and, back in the day, all kinds of illegal things were run through its streets. Can a place be inherently bad so much of the time that it always attracts bad people? No one knew the answer. Whiskey Way was always a crime hot spot and neither City Hall nor any Mayor was ever able to "solve it." On these streets, even if bright and sunny were possible, it would be like looking through a cloudy glass—darkly.

The thin man stood tall in his three-piece suit, though he was actually scared at having to deal with such a person—a crazy thug, who watched him through dark shades. In the dark of day or the pitch-black night, everyone covered their eyes with glasses.

"Did you know that the sky has all kinds of shades of red in all that blackness? Like blood and bruises." Red snickered as he popped another red pill. "What's the name?"

"Easy Chair Charlie."

The Thin Man was already reaching out his hand with a photo.

Red took it with a metallic hand and studied it. "Where?"

"Sweet Street in Old Harlem."

Red reached out from the shadows again. The Thin Man handed him a wet bag of cash.

"It must be serious for you to venture out all by your lonesome to the mean streets, in the rain, through dark alleys, far from your luxurious, upper-floor domicile. Maybe I can be your next-door neighbor one day."

"I much prefer you down here."

"Where I belong, right?"

"Down here you're something sinister. Up in my world, you'd just be a freak in a rabbit mask. I doubt that perception would be good for the psycho business."

Red laughed. "When you're right, you're right." He finished flipping through the money. "You know why I like cold, hard cash? Because that way no one can ever double-cross me. Credit cards can be bugged, traced, tracked, or erased remotely. We couldn't allow that to happen. Don't trust that digital stuff. Gotta remove all temptation from the equation. There're no apples in my garden."

They both went quiet and still. A pedestrian half-ran down the street nearby. Red was invisible in the shadows, but the Thin Man had to pull his black hat down a bit to hide his face. The passerby had neon-blue shades and was an average-looking guy in a suit with a hoodie; obviously trying to get out of the rain, somewhere fast, or both.

"Let's get on with this," the Thin Man said under his breath. "You have the money. I need it done within the hour."

"You know how I do things, right?"

The Thin Man was getting more impatient and looked up at him. There was no neon sign with its blink-blink to pierce the night, but the Thin Man could see him fine with his night-view red spectacles. Red's silly buck-toothed grin, his large floppy ears sprouting from his head like bean stalks, those dark holes for eyes behind the shades, and dressed in a similar suit—though not as dapper.

"I do. So go do it."

Red snickered again. "I'll get a-hoppin'."

The sky was especially menacing today, she thought. A vast expanse of blackish-blue with streaks of red, but there was no accompanying downpour, not even a drizzle—but it was coming. Boy, it was coming hard. She could tell from the rumble above.

This was Metropolis weather. Drizzle, rain, storm, repeat. Old-timers like her actually remember the old places like Seattle. The world was now Seattle—always raining. But the Metropolis didn't care. Its structures were always growing higher into the sky, its technology always expanding with flashier machinery, the throngs of the gray masses always multiplying with more offspring—as if there wasn't enough people packed into the city. But the rain was more powerful. It slowed the pace of human progress to a crawl. If it weren't for the rain, the skyscrapers would have reached Saturn by now, the machines would have become suicidal, and the people would have become homicidal. The rain actually kept the world manageable. You could run, but not too fast. High-tech could progress, but never smother the end-users.

Carol lifted up the collar of her gray slicker, shivering just thinking about the downpour to come. She returned her black gloved hands to her coat's pockets. "We're late, you know," she said.

The little girl, decked out in her trendy gray wet-wear—a hooded, two-piece gray outfit with attached knapsack and soft lunch-box in her hand—continued to skip through the puddles on the sidewalk. Even in a hurricane, she would stay perfectly dry, except for her cute face with blue eyes and a lock of light brown hair dangling out from beneath the top of her hood. With each splash, she watched a hint of some color in the water—maybe a blue or orange or lavender. Her goal was to see every rainbow color for the day. She stopped to glance at her mother with a smile. "Skip with me, Mommy."

"I'm too old for that." She would never tell her daughter that the ground puddle rainbow display was courtesy of the City's nasty 'natural' chemical residue. "And I don't want all that water all over my stockings," she continued. Other than her slicker, Carol wore her plastic head scarf and plastic boots over her shoes. She called herself old, but she had a ways to go before really being old. She was a White female with dark hair and minimal make-up. A mini-umbrella was always clipped to her slicker, but she never used it. The wind loved mini-umbrellas, snatching them right out of human hands to use as a projectile to hit some unsuspecting fool in the head.

"You need frubber leggings like me, Mom." The girl was now posing like a model, sticking out a leg wrapped snuggly in the wet-wear legging, which looked almost exactly like her natural skin. Her mother always wondered if she wore them for style or for boys.

"I'm okay, thank you. I'll buy the fancy clothes for you, and I'll keep my old, boring clothes. That's what parents do. Now, come on. We're late. And the rain will bucket down any minute."

Their weekday walks to her school in the early morning hours always took them through the outskirts of Woodstock Falls, a working-class, multiethnic neighborhood. Nothing crazy or wild ever happened here, and that's exactly how the residents and business owners wanted it. But that didn't mean she was any less vigilant of the surroundings. Even safe neighborhoods were not immune to the occasional undesirable or street punk.

Carol didn't run. She wanted to go at least a full week without slipping and falling on her butt. Her daughter skipped ahead of her, one puddle after another. At this time of morning the streets were virtually empty, except for early morning deliverymen, sweepers, and the ubiquitous trash collectors zipping by in their hovertrucks.

It was their daily ritual Monday to Friday—Carol walking her daughter to school, without fail.

At the other end of the street in the shadows, he watched them. His telescoping goggles automatically adjusted focus to follow the females. He stood quiet, leaning on the corner building under the large black awning. He was too far away and it was dark enough that he could be right across the street from them and they wouldn't see him.

"Digital man killed the analog man..." he hummed the lyrics to himself. The song was barely audible from his old orange headphones.

He stepped forward in his exceedingly comfortable, five-toed, platform shoes to follow them.

The walk wasn't a bad one. Her daughter loved it, because it was that quiet time for her to play unencumbered by any other care in the world. For her mother, it was quiet time too, but far from carefree. While her daughter joyfully skipped along the slick sidewalks, her eyes were constantly roving for trouble. She was a meek woman, except when it came to the safety of her daughter. In that regard she was a vicious, carnivorous tigress. "Freakazoids," she called them. The prowlers and pedophiles that the media liked to report on and scare parents about.

"Let's go this way, Mom."

"Which way?"

"Alien Alley." The girl pointed to the neon sign, wall poster adorned pedestrian-only alley.

"Why? Are you expecting to see some extraterrestrials?"

The girl laughed. "No, Mom. There's no such thing as space aliens."

"Except for the human ones."

"It's a shortcut."

"How many times do I have to tell you—?"

"'There's no shortcut when it comes to safety'," the girl repeated her mother, word for word, before she finished.

"Then you ask me to allow you to walk to and from school by yourself."

The girl sighed, now realizing she had sufficiently wound-up her mother.

"Okay, Mom! No Alien Alley. Pretend I never asked."

"Imagine how many freakazoids are down there. I never even heard of this alley."

"We pass it every day to school, Mom. It's always empty."

"Then why don't they call it Empty Alley?"

"Oh, Mom. Forget it!"

"You don't take safety seriously."

"I do."

"I wish you did."

"I do, Mom."

"Like this instant, there's a damn freakazoid following us."

"What?" The girl stopped skipping and immediately turned around. She stared back down the long, dark street. "Where?"

Her mother just watched her with her hands in her pocket. Her daughter looked at her, then back down the street. She stared for a while, and then the smile returned to her face.

"There's no freakazoids back there, Mom. You're just trying to scare me for nothing."

"Doesn't look like I'm doing a very good job."

"Mom, they've shown us the entire Scared Straight series in school multiple times, including pedestrian street safety."

"Listen to you."

"Mom, I do keep a good look out when you're not here. I promise I do. Just how you taught me. Promise."

Her mother lifted her arm to glance at her large wristband watch. "Let's move it. We'll be late for sure, and I don't want you to get another tardy demerit."

"Let's cut through Alien Alley, Mom. It's empty. We can run. No one can catch us if we run."

"I'll get wet."

"No, Mom. We'll be running too fast for that. And we'll beat the big downpour that's coming, too." The girl looked up to the sky, squinting, as if something was about to fall on her any minute. "You'll be right with me. Let's do it, Mom. Live dangerously, Mom."

Carol stood there, watching her daughter with a half-smile.

Her daughter had already turned back to walk to the alley. "We'll get through the alley lickety-split and to school on time. But we have to run now, Mom."

"Give me a minute." Carol touched her plastic head scarf and bent down to make sure her socks and boots were pulled up. "Old folks have to prepare themselves for childish recklessness. It's not spontaneous anymore for us."

"It is going to bucket down, Mom. You said so yourself."

"Okay, young lady, you can stop now. There is such a thing as overdoing it and losing the sale, when you got it in the bag, by adding one thing too many."

Her daughter grinned at her.

Carol stood up straight and looked back with an oh-so slight grin. "Run!"

Mother and daughter disappeared into Alien Alley with sounds of feet sloshing through water.

CHAPTER 2

Red and Blue Light Show

T he police cruiser glided through the sky thirty-feet above all the normal congested traffic. It was a standard five-seater hovercraft with its two officers in full silver-and-black body-armored uniforms and visored half-helmets. The driver was Officer Break, a Black policeman on the Force for some twelve years. Officer Caps, the White policeman in the passenger seat, joined the Metropolis Police Department a year later. The senior officers had been partners for over seven years now. While most policemen couldn't wait to get off beat work for Homicide, Vice, Sex Crimes, White-Collar, or anything else; they both preferred the grunt work. It meant do your shift and then go home; nothing more. Moving up the ranks meant more paperwork and more headaches. The only headaches they wanted in life were those from restless wives and kids entering puberty.

"Come in Unit 7-8-2-7," a voice echoed through the front speakers.

Officer Caps touched a flashing red button on the dashboard.

"Unit 7-8-2-7. Go ahead, dispatch," he responded.

"2-11 in progress at the Downtown Seven-Eleven on Beat Street. Shots reported by armed suspect. Armed civilian security guard on the scene holding near the main entrance. Code 2."

"10-4 dispatch. Code 2 acknowledged. En route three minutes."

"10-4 Unit 7-8-2-7, back-up units five minutes out. Dispatch out."

"Acknowledged, dispatch. Over and out." He tapped the button again.

"Five minutes?" Officer Break asked matter-of-factly. "We'll have the perp bagged and tagged before the cavalry arrives." He accelerated the cruiser forward on a vector further above the sky traffic.

The Downtown Seven-Eleven on Beat Street was not a huge store like others in the city, but it was on prime real estate on the street corner at the bottom of a parking structure in the city's "capitol." During the work week, the foot traffic was huge. Other times, customers could whip in and out of vehicle parking by hovercraft, hop into the express elevator, exit, shop, pay, and go. Everyone knew the relatively small store was a gold mine for its owners, but no one understood why the occasional robber would try to steal from it with City Hall, Police Central, and Downtown FBI just a few blocks away—mega blocks yes, but still only blocks away.

The robber waved his heater (laser pistol) wildly. "If I see a cop, she's dead!"

Someone watched the human stick figure of a punk yell with his blond mullet hairdo partially hidden under the hood of a jacket. He held the laser pistol to a terrified Asian female store attendant. Mascara tears trailed down her face onto her white-and-red 7-11 uniform—a college kid paying her way through school, but today, in the wrong place at the wrong time. But then the sniper sight, with its yellow lens, was focused on him, not her.

19

The White male punk was pinned inside the convenience store and making up his words and actions as he went along, trying to look tough, covered in tattoos everywhere, even on his face. A lone strip mall security guard had already taken a shot at him once and was now kneeling behind a communications pole across the street—the punk had fired back at him. He smiled, eager for the coming 'excitement.'

The strip mall guard was another college kid, from some East European country, and was as scared of his standard issue gun as he was of the robber. He looked up to see the glow of boot rockets high up in the sky and sighed with relief. The police had arrived.

Downtown Seven-Eleven was like every other one in the world. They were all identical. Only the overall size changed. Row after row of products, and what couldn't be placed on shelves, could easily be fetched from the back by robotic arms and presented to the counter for purchase. The front counter was like a mini neon digital explosion of various advertisements, especially for lottery tickets, as well as scrolling news headlines, the New York and Tokyo Stock Exchange ticker feeds, and "Have you seen this child?" or "Have you seen this criminal?" bulletins.

The punk pulled his human shield back further into the store and around the counter to take better cover behind the register. He watched the outside street closely.

"I should have shot you and that guard and made a break for it. Now we'll have to have the shootout right here. How unlucky for you. No college graduation for you. No twenty-first birthday for me."

"Just let me go. I didn't do you anything," the store attendant said as calmly as she could manage.

"You didn't give me my money."

"It's not your money."

"It's not your money either, so why didn't you just give it up? You think your bosses who aren't here care about a few bucks in the till? A few bucks is nothing to them but a lot to me."

"To do what?"

"None of your business."

"You're holding a gun to my head, so everything about you is my business."

"Feisty, huh, for a hostage who's about to die." He held her closer and repositioned his gun to her temple. "Who do you think is going to kill you first? Me or the cops? You know how many innocent people get accidentally shot by the cops?" He glanced further into the store. "And that goes for the rest of you, too!"

There were thirteen other hostages in the store, all of them lying on the floor as directed earlier, looking up at him with fear.

The large front glass of the store was neon glass and had a tint that changed colors. In an instant, it shattered and cascaded down to the ground. The top of the punk's head was simultaneously blown off and his body collapsed to the ground. The hostage grabbed the sides of her face screaming hysterically.

Officers Break and Caps stepped through the open storefront, their boots crushing the glass on the ground as they walked, long guns in hand. As with all Metropolis police officers, the word "PEACE" in big white letters was prominent on the front and back of their uniforms.

"Ma'am," Officer Break called out.

The woman was in a state of shock, staring at the body of the mangled would-be robber-killer.

"Ma'am!"

She looked at him now.

He put a finger to his lips. "Shh!" She stopped screaming.

Officer Caps touched the call button on his shoulder-communicator. "Dispatch, this is Unit 7-8-2-7. Robbery suspect is dead. Scene secured."

"Unit 7-8-2-7, meat wagon en route. Back-up on scene now," dispatch answered.

From outside the store, through the drizzle, one appeared, then another, then several more silver-and-black police "PEACE" officers appeared—their silent jetpacks with accompanying boot rocket nozzles made them seem like wingless black angels descending from the sky. They stepped through the open storefront into the premises—long guns in hand, visors concealing the top half of their faces. Now the night was illuminated by red-and-blue-siren lights.

"This is the police! All hostages please stand and come forward with your hands in the air," one of the new policemen said with an enhanced, booming voice. He lifted his mouth from his shoulder-microphone to speak normally. "Ladies and gentleman, we'll process you, take statements, and have you home within the hour."

All the store customers on the floor slowly rose to their feet and held up their hands. Officer Break walked to the store's attendant and took her by the shoulder. "Ma'am follow me outside. Ambulance services will take you to Metro General."

She had stifled her screams, but her eyes locked on what remained of the would-be robber on the ground.

"Ma'am, don't look at him. Don't pollute your memories with that human filth. He got what he deserved. Go about your life and don't give another nanosecond of thought to it."

"Thank you...Officer," she managed to say.

Their first call of the day was a silent alarm. The next call was a full-out "red-and-blue siren party" with the lights illuminating the sky for miles around. Office Break peered out his driver's side window as he acknowledged the ground officer directing him down to a patch of sidewalk with a double flash of his high beams. Officer Caps watched the people on his side congregating on their balconies at the nearby hi-rise closest to the scene.

"It's going to be a tight fit," Break said to his partner.

Caps leaned forward to look down to the sidewalk. "I've seen you land this bird on a dime before," he responded.

Officer Break spun the cruiser around, backed it up, situated the craft, and slowly took it down. It touched down and both officers immediately lifted up the doors to step out.

Two White officers walked to them—Boot was the bigger Russian, and Bus was the Italian.

"We heard you two gave some skell a cranial haircut with one shot. That sounds like you, Caps."

"B and B," Officer Caps greeted with a smirk.

"Don't be shy, guys," Officer Boot said. "It's almost month-end and we'll be counting up the kills. If I'm going to be knocked down from my perch at the top, I want to know by who in advance."

"Break drives, I shoot 'em," Caps said. "But this time, it was all Break."

"Break," Officer Boot said. "That means, we're tied up, Caps. You and me."

"I'm not worried. I'll knock you off the kill-hill."

"I don't think so. Only three days left."

"What's going on here?" Break asked them. "A 2-07?"

"Yeah. Little girl, ten years old, snatched right from her mother while walking to school. Pedophile, no doubt."

Break and Caps were visibly disgusted.

"It never stops. These pee-dophiles," Caps said.

"Gentlemen, I nominate whoever this sick perp is for the honor of being next on the kill board," Boot said.

"Deal," Caps said.

"It'll be everyone's pleasure," Officer Bus added.

Break and Caps could see another police officer gesturing to them from behind the police tape.

"Detective Do-Little calls," Break said wryly.

Carol sat on the bare asphalt, the rain pouring down. Her eye make-up ran down her cheeks, not from the rain, but from crying. She looked up and they just kept coming—"PEACE" officers descending from the air via jetpack. Back in the day, it was "POLICE," but many years ago someone somewhere in City Hall wanted to soften law enforcement's image. She always welcomed them, but always wondered about the visual paradox. The entire area was cordoned off by police tape and police cars, flashing red and blue lights everywhere. Police on crowd-control stood on one side of the "POLICE LINE. DO NOT CROSS" tape and crowds of onlookers stood on the other side.

A policewoman stood next to her, dressed the same as the men, just as deadly with her "PEACE" lettering, but a smaller build. "Ma'am, you sure I can't get you an umbrella? You're getting soaked."

She shook her head. The policewoman's face frowned a bit, but it was with compassion.

Another policeman appeared and crouched down next to her, holding an umbrella over her with "DETECTIVE" on the chest and back of his uniform. He flipped up his visor so she could see his eyes.

"Miss," he said, "I know you gave us the preliminary statement, but let me take you down to the station so you can tell us again on the record. The more times you tell the story, the more likely you'll remember an important detail, however small, that can help us find your daughter."

"I can't leave here."

"Miss, you're not leaving. You're simply coming down to the station, which isn't too far away, to give your full statement for the record. We'll find your daughter."

"Ma'am, I'll get you back here personally," the policewoman said. "It'll be okay."

Carol looked at her and then looked at the detective. "But will you find her alive?"

She had a wild look to her eyes and the detective said nothing. She looked down to the ground. He glanced at the female officer.

"Yes, ma'am, we will." The policewoman gave the detective a dirty look.

"Officer, can you get her something warm to drink before we leave for the station?" he said to her.

"Yes, detective."

"And get her out of the rain. There has to be some place warm for her to sit." He turned back to the woman. "Miss, let the officer get you off the ground and some place warm. I'll check with my men to see if there is any new news and then we'll leave."

The female officer leaned down and helped Carol to her feet. The detective handed the umbrella to the female officer.

"I'll take her to the van," she said to the detective, and he nodded.

As he watched the female officer take her to a nearby parked police hovervan, Detective Monitor walked to two of his officers.

He knew the nickname the beat officers had for him. He came from a well-to-do Old North European family; the latter being irrelevant, the former being very relevant, because he made detective in record time.

"What ya got?"

"We'll canvass everywhere, Detective, and then canvass it again and again," Officer Break answered.

"We have the entire Alley blocked, and I'm taking the mother back to Central, so as the senior officers on site, you two run the show for me."

"Yes, Detective," Officer Caps said. "Should we expect the Feds?"

"No, the Feds don't jump anymore unless it's a Red Ball. Too many kidnappings for them to handle anymore, so we get it. Besides, we have more resources in Metropolis than they do."

"Good," Officer Caps said.

"What is this Alien Alley, anyway?" Detective Monitor asked.

"Nothing," Officer Break answered. "The word is that during business hours it's a space fiction nerd hang-out. Extraterrestrial, spaceship, sci-fi alien crap. Just kids. No hard crimes."

"What about off-hours?"

"Apparently, no one goes there off-hours."

"Why?"

"We don't know and no one seems to know."

"What about the street?"

"We'll question the local sidewalk johnnies. They know everything there is to know about every street and alley in the city. We'll put them in the box if they don't talk."

"Don't be fooled by them. They like the box. Warm bed, breakfast, lunch, dinner, running shower, and toilet at taxpayers' expense. Lock-up is exactly where they want to be. Tell them to talk or we *won't* let them stay in the box."

"Yes, Detective."

"Forensics is already here, and I called in the dogs."

"Dogs?" Officer Caps asked. "Won't the rain make any canine search impossible?"

"Try anyway. Police dogs need to earn their pay just like us humans. We may get lucky. We need to get lucky. It's a helpless little girl for Christ's sake. I don't want this one to end up in the morgue. I hate these calls. I'd take a hundred calls of shootouts, robberies, and hijackings if I could avoid these calls. These calls tend to always end badly."

Metropolis Police Central stood at the opposite end of the avenue from City Hall and looked like a cubical fortress. It was also rumored to be deepest building in the world, burrowing endless levels into the ground—a holdover of the Cold War days when nuclear annihilation and civil unrest of a biblical proportion was the daily fear of government bureaucrats. That was long before the megacities and supercities of today, and the rain. Central was home to a 500,000 plus police force—the largest in the nation.

Carol sat in the general waiting room inside the station, which some interior decorator attempted to make as bright and cheery as possible, but it wasn't the opposite of the grimy exterior of the building; it complimented it. With the daily march of police with their combat boots and the steady stream of captured criminals in and out, how else would it look? She sat in her chair quietly, glancing around—there was only an elderly couple seated two rows behind her.

They were actually in the inner waiting room behind the main counter and wall. The outer waiting room was like a massive zoo, with people all over the place waiting their turn to be helped, DMV-style, by counter police. She looked the other way to the bull pen of dual cubicles where the street police sat and worked when not on the beat. Further away, she saw elevated single cubicles where she imagined the detectives sat. Beyond that were the offices for the higher-ups.

She had given her statement—again and then again. Now she waited to be taken home by the same policewoman as promised. All of it seemed surreal. She realized that she hadn't even called her job to tell them she wouldn't be in. Her daughter's school would have already logged another absence for her daughter. She had one already. Three tardies equaled one absence in the system. Carol couldn't remember what she had planned for work that day, but she knew there was something important. She closed her eyes and opened them when she heard voices.

The same female policewoman was standing with the same detective, both listening to a man in dress blues.

"Take her home," the Captain said.

"What do you want me to tell her, sir?" the detective asked.

"It's your case. Tell her whatever you like."

"What are we supposed to do? You won't let me elevate it to a Red Ball, and you won't let me toss it to the Feds."

The captain angrily motioned to him with his finger. "Come here. And you too."

He led them around the corner to the large open room with the Big Board and pointed. Row after row of numbered cases were listed in "Active" status. They were categorized by crimes, noted by two letter abbreviations. Not many cases were in the "Closed" column.

"The Feds won't take it, because they have one hundred missing persons cases on their plate now. We won't elevate it to a Red Ball, because of what's on our plate now. Which one of these mothers do you want us to tell to go to the back of the line with their missing son or daughter? Well? What's your answer, detective?"

"None, sir."

"Work your case, like everyone else. I decide who gets extra resources, not you. There is nothing special about this case. A missing girl in Metropolis is not special. A dead husband in Metropolis is not special. A drive-by shooting in Metropolis is not special. It's routine. Maybe one day you'll learn that. Work your case and get out of my face."

The captain left them where they stood as he walked the other way.

"I'll take her home," the female officer said.

"You can tell her that we'll be in touch if we have any updates," the detective said.

The female officer gave him a dirty look. "I'll come up with a better lie than that."

She turned and left him alone.

"I need a drink," he said to himself and walked to the break room.

Security at Central was formidable—armed police guards, security cameras, armed sentries at the end of the hallways near the elevators, and scanning archways; but that was only for entering. Entering and exiting pedestrian traffic was divided by a solid metal barrier down the middle of the grand hallway. For those exiting, they walked out without any checks whatsoever.

One of the police officers in work blues noticed a man in the crowd on the other side of the barrier, going out.

"'Night, sir," he said as he waved slightly.

"'Night, officer," the man answered.

The Thin Man exited the main entrance.

CHAPTER 3

Frantic

Her first foot hit the puddle, splashing the dirty water on her clothes. Her right foot hit the ground and did the same. None of it mattered. Nothing mattered. Her running was constant now. She had tied her plastic head scarf so tight to her head that there wasn't enough give to allow any rainwater to roll off. Her coat was wrapped around her body so tight that the buttons were about to pop off, with her running through the streets. Carol was a woman mad with grief—her eyes said so. People on the streets instinctively seemed to know this and parted to either side to stay out of her path.

But she didn't need their avoidance. She needed their help— anything would do. Carol was in a city of fifty million people, but it felt like she was a tiny star in the vastness of space with nothing visually around her. The neon jungle blinked and pulsated as it always did, but the emptiness remained.

Carol was not an athletic woman, but in her mindless run through the same street over and over, around and around, there was never a hit of exhaustion in her face. She ran down the adjacent street then up the adjacent street, then back and through....

Ahh!" Carol ran through the streets as if she were being chased. "Where is she? Where is he? I must find him! Give me back my daughter! Give me back my daughter!"

Into Alien Alley she went.

She was worse than a sidewalk sally. They, at least, had some semblance of purpose. Carol had the entrance to Alien Alley staked out and had endlessly wandered around it before her running began. She looked like she hadn't slept or bathed in days; her eyeliner was a combination of dripping and caked-on. Her clothes were the same ones from that fateful day when her daughter was taken.

The police had descended on the Alley like a full battalion in some ancient battlefield, but found nothing. It would be a week or two before normal business returned. In the meantime, during the day there was a smattering of people, and at night, it was a ghost town—except for Carol.

She would stop suddenly from time to time and stare at the crowds, staring right into the faces of the crowd. Gray people. The society had so many phrases for things. The masses in their often gray and black outerwear were called gray people. What's wrong with "the masses?" Why do new words need to be made up for the old words? How many synonyms can a thing have? Carol asked all these questions as she stood and stared.

Most people ignored her. Many more didn't even notice her to begin with. Occasionally, a few would remove their visually-enhanced shades to stare back at her with curiosity or contempt with their natural eyes, or bionic ones.

The rain began again as Carol stood in the middle of street like a statue, blinding her. She couldn't move. In her mind, she could not go away. She had to remain and keep a vigil on Alien Alley. She had to keep watch for the Red Rabbit. It had to be her, and Carol would not leave until she got her daughter back.

She lifted her head up into the rain and was going to scream again as she had done many times before. But Carol fainted to the ground. It was all too much for her.

The Fence stood with his thumbs gripping under the armpits of his bright purple vest, his flowing slicker over it. The man wore no hat. He had bleached-blond hair, but his men—four of them—all wore flapper hats covering their ears. They stood, leaning against the side wall of the burger joint. The smell of fresh cooking beef was becoming unbearable. The long line was solid proof of the quality of their food.

One of the men looked at the Fence with watering eyes. "I'll be quick," he said.

"How? Look at the line. Business first, and then we'll eat after."

"Your treat?"

"My treat."

The men were all smiles.

One of the men pointed into the distance. "The sticky-fingers crew," he said.

Three kids approached—the one in the middle seemed to be the boss, and he immediately recognized the Fence. The kids had tattoos on their arms and necks from what could be seen.

"Why are we meeting here?" the kid asked. The three of them looked around at the line of people and the busyness of the street.

"It's a public place, isn't it?" the Fence responded.

"Yeah, but—"

"But nothing. What do you have for us?"

The kids were clearly nervous.

"This is weird," the lead kid said. "Everyone can see us."

"Exactly."

"My advice to you three jokers," said one of Fence's men, "is do all your business in public. The only thing worse than someone smelling undercover cops is smelling diaper-wearing newbies. You meet in private and someone'll put two taps in your forehead, all of you. Take your lives and take your stuff. You better get wise if you want to play in the crime world. I should charge you for that advice."

The kids were not amused and glared at him.

"Come on, let's get on with it," the Fence said them. "What do you have for me?"

One of the kids reached into his bubble coat pocket, pulled out something wrapped in cloth, and handed it to him. The Fence took it and, with his other hand, put on his special inspection glasses.

"Help me!"

Fence and his men, the kids, and everyone on the streets turned to see the woman come out of the crowd. The criminals froze as the woman ran towards them.

"It's a set-up!" one of the kids yelled and angrily looked at Fence. The boy reached into his jacket for something.

One of Fence's men punched the boy in the face, sending the boy crashing to the wet pavement and his pulse pistol dropping to the ground.

Fence wrapped the item up and threw it back at the lead kid. "Take it and go!"

The kid grabbed it and looked at his partners. One picked him up from the ground, the other grabbed his weapon, and the three ran.

The woman kept yelling as she approached Fence and his men. One of his bodyguards pulled his weapon from his jacket, but Fence smacked his arm.

"You want the cops to kill us, stupid!"

Carol was the center of attention to everyone queued in front of the Burger Joint and the crowds on the street. She stopped her advance and walked slowly to Fence alone. She grabbed his shoulders and he could see the utter desperation in her face.

"Please help me. The police can't find her—my daughter. The Red Rabbit has her. My daughter is all I have. You're a criminal. You can help me. Help me find my daughter. I'll pay anything."

"Fence, let's get out of here!" one of his men yelled.

"Red Rabbit?" Fence turned to his men.

"We can't get involved," another of his men said.

"You know this Red Rabbit?"

"Yeah, Red Rabbit with the red pills. He killed the White Rabbit with the blue pills and took his clients. Let's go," his man pleaded.

"And?"

"Fence, let it alone. We can't get involved. We're small-time. We can't mess around in this."

"I have an idea."

"Fence, we can't get involved. What's wrong with you?"

"We're not."

"Fence."

"It's a mother. Don't any of you lowlifes have mothers?"

"Yeah, mine tried to knife me when I was seven," said one of his men.

"Mine shot my father and tried to shoot my brother and me too," said the other.

"Why am I even talking to you two? Where's the nearest public phone?"

The sound of crows started low, but then began to increase in volume. Flash had two minutes to get out of bed and switch off the alarm before the crowing sounds would start blaring loud enough to shake the room. He rolled out of the bed, literally, to his feet and, without looking, switched off the alarm clock on the side stand. Then he lowered his head and fell back asleep standing up.

Seven minutes later another alarm went off on the opposite side of the bedroom. His head rose just a bit, his eyes squinted, and like some form of zombie, he shuffled across the room to do the same there—turn the damn thing off. His head was about to lower again, when robotic arms descended from the ceilings and drew open the shades to let the natural light into the bedroom. The window magnified the light beams so it looked far brighter outside than it actually was.

Their five-room legacy apartment was on the fifth floor of their complex. The bedroom was far too big for two people, especially as scarcely furnished as it was, with the master bed, side tables, and a couple of couches. No mega-TV on the wall, as was common—they kept that in the family room, and the dresser and standing mirrors were in their dual walk-in closet that, despite all space taken by their ever expanding wardrobe, was still big enough to be categorized as another room.

"Rise and shine! Rise and shine! Rise and shine!"

Flash turned his head and saw the robot standing right next to him, a stupid smile on its metal face, holding out a cup of silk coffee to him. Flash stood in his orange A-shirt and orange-striped black shorts. His robot stood next to him in its purple A-shirt and powder blue striped black shorts.

"Good morning, Master Flash." The humanoid robot was a basic model—over-sized, multi-jointed hands; full swivel socket shoulders, elbows, hips, and knees; rectangular chest, upside-down triangular area under its shorts; and striated, tubular arms and legs. Lots of product design went into the face, but Flash always thought, for all the money and time that went into the machine, it was surprising that all they could come up with was faux-facial muscles that could contort its mouth into a stupid grin, round anime eyes, and a simple ridged nose. He and his friends could make better when they were kids back in kindergarten, without a multimillion dollar budget, only the art crap they could get from the corner general convenience store.

He grunted something and grabbed the cup of coffee from the robot. The robot went back into the apartment home to begin its chores as Flash drank down the coffee and stared out the window. Flash was a light-skinned Black man with a ponytail and the attempt of a goatee.

"Another damn day in this dump." He suddenly yelled out, "Honey, get out of bed!"

His wife stirred beneath the layers of faux-leopard skin blankets. The only thing visible was her tanned toes with bright yellow nail polish sticking out from the bottom.

An hour later was the last, but most important, pre-work chore. Bundle the kids off to school and the wife off to work. He stood with his family at the metro stop. The platform was brimming with rush-hour passengers waiting for the monorail. He made the usual small talk with his family, though none of it was phony. This was quality time as much as the evening family dinner was.

His wife had the same complexion as him, but she wore part of her hair in front of her shoulder and part behind it. Under her gray slicker was her orange, designer Good Will clothes to match her orange-painted finger and toenails. His son was a mini-him and his daughter was a mini-version of his wife—fourteen and twelve, respectively. The daughter dressed just like her mom, but her color of the day was dark blue. His son had the makings of being another mogul like Flash's boss—he had his own style, dressed in a dark suit and tie with a white shirt.

The whistle sounded, and people moved closer to the edge of the platform as they heard the hiss of the coming monorail. Wife and kids instinctively put on their blue eyewear. He kissed his kids on their foreheads and wife on the lips, then held them together as they also moved closer to the platform's edge.

The monorail may have looked futuristic in its day, but now it was just a "gray tubular sardine can" to shovel passengers into. The city's solution to graffiti bandits was to spray paint the entire thing at the end of the night so the lines of cars were uniform in their sickly gray color come morning. The doors opened and the people piled in. Some ran in to the closest open seats, others preferred to stand and grab the handholds dangling from the ceiling. His family got in; his wife raised her hand to grab the closest handhold, and the kids raised their arms to hold onto her. Flash stepped back out of the monorail. There were three successive audible warnings and then the doors slid shut. He waved, and they waved back as the monorail sped away on its track lines.

It took him only five minutes to exit the metro stop, climbing up the long stairs—only fools and tourists attempted to take the public elevators where muggings were a daily occurrence. In a city of this size, there was no possible way the police could be everywhere, but it was getting better.

His was a public transportation family, but he put food on the table by shuttling those around the city who preferred or had the money to avoid it. Flash had been a taxi driver for Let It Ride Enterprises for the last ten years.

He absolutely loved his job.

Metropolis sky lanes were always chaotic. Row above row of hovercraft traffic. Public transportation was supposed to eliminate the hovercar, much like computers were supposed to eliminate paper. In both cases, the opposite was the reality. Only the wealthy, or at least the middle-class, were supposed to be able to even afford a basic model hovercraft, but annual sales were so brisk that the government slapped a surcharge tax on it, like they did with every other successful product or service.

Large hovercraft, like trucks and tankers, were in the bottommost virtual lanes. Buses and RV hovercraft were in the lanes above them. All personal and commercial hovercars were in the main virtual lanes above both. Hoverbikers (who everyone hated) zipped around wherever they wanted.

"It's amazing more of you don't get run down!" Flash yelled at the helmeted driver in a plastic slicker, who descended from the sky on a hot pink hoverbike and cut him off. It disappeared around another vehicle ahead.

He sped up again and kept one eye on the road as he pushed a few buttons on his dashboard computer.

"Where am I picking up my first fare for the day?" he said to himself.

Lights around his dashboard computer flashed yellow.

"Fare!"

He looked in all his side and rearview windows as he signaled and dived.

Dispatch called in new fares, but anyone on the street could take their mobile, point, and manually laser-signal a passing cab for pick-up.

He descended, mainly watching his dashboard computer monitor to stay on the approved virtual path, but glanced frequently out the window at the hovercraft traffic he passed.

He leveled his hovertaxicab with the ground and drove up slowly. With the push of a button on the driver door panel, the driver's side window rolled down. His nose instantly picked up the beautiful organic burger smell, and he almost forgot why he was on the ground. He saw a man standing at a public phone booth, waving to him.

He rolled up his window and sped up, then stopped. The passenger door opened. Another man appeared from nowhere and pushed a woman into the car.

"Hey, what's going on?" Flash asked.

The second man didn't get in but closed the door. Flash watched both men run away.

"What the heck!" He looked at the woman sitting in the back with her clear plastic head scarf and gray slicker coat. "Are you all right, ma'am? Did those men hurt you? Do you need the police?"

"I need to find my daughter!" she said. "He took my daughter!"

"What? Those men took your daughter?" Flash grabbed the handset from his dashboard computer without looking. "Dispatch, I have an emergency!"

There were some industries that hated the cops. Others were neutral. Most welcomed them. Rank-and-file taxicab drivers loved the police. The hovertaxi industry considered themselves to be a sister industry, as they too were out on the streets, often alone. And when those streets got mean, the beat cops were the ones to turn to and the ones to defend your life—besides your hidden weapon under the seat. Cops and taxicab drivers were the industries who got shot at (and killed) the most. When taxicab drivers congregated for lunch, they always did so near a parked police car. When cops needed to get one of their own home from the local police bar, the taxi service would have cabs waiting to do so, gratis.

Flash had been quietly talking to the two beat cops a few yards away from his cab for about ten minutes. The two policemen were in standard silver-and-black uniform with the word "PEACE" emblazoned on their chest and back. They all, occasionally, glanced back at the woman sitting in the cab.

"What should I do?" Flash asked.

The two police officers glanced at the woman in his cab.

"Take her home," one of them said.

"Officer, do you really believe she's going to stay there?"

"That's all there is to do. The officers assigned are working the case hard. No one wants to see a missing child."

"But she feels the force isn't working the case," Flash said.

"No. They're working the murders, sexual assaults, carjackings, hijackings, home invasions, arsons, assaults with a deadly weapon, suicide-homicide—"

"I get the picture."

Flash looked back at the woman again with a very sad face. He couldn't imagine him and his wife in the same situation. The thought of one of their children taken by some street criminal made him shiver.

"We hate the picture too, but we can only do what we can do."

A light sprinkle began to fall again. Flash looked up into the sky and instinctively lifted up his collar around his neck.

"I'll take the woman home." He began to walk to his cab and stopped. "What's her name?" He turned to them.

"Carol Num," the other officer answered.

"Thanks, Officers."

Flash got back into his cab. He sat for a moment in his driver's seat quietly.

"I bet my daughter is already dead."

Flash looked up to see her in his rearview mirror. "Don't say that."

"The police are going to show up at my house to tell me they found her corpse. That's why I can't go home. Waiting means I'm waiting for them to come tell me she's dead. I can't do that. I won't. I stay out here on the streets and there's hope. Even if there really isn't."

"I'm a parent too," Flash spoke up. "You do what you need to do to find her, make them find her. My wife and I would do the same thing."

"Life's always easier when you have help. I wish my husband were here, but the dumb blockhead had to go get himself run down by a garbage truck when Lutty was only two years old. He was always clumsy, but I married him anyway."

"Carol, where do want me to take you?"

"What is Alien Alley? It must be a bad place for bad people to be there to do bad things."

"Bad people are everywhere. Any taxi driver will tell you that. They can get anywhere like roaches. But Alien Alley is nothing. I've never heard of trouble there before. It's one of those in-between streets, between the good streets and the bad streets. People go through it, not to it."

"The cops said something about Roswellians—"

Flash laughed. "That was like fifty years ago. That was some rookie reading from the general database and regurgitating it to his higher-ups without anyone looking at date stamps. All that Roswell stuff was big back then, but again, that's ancient history. But wait..." A determined look came across Flash's face with a slight smile. "My boss will know. He knows the back story for every street in Metropolis. He's better than a computer."

He started to grab his dashboard handset but stopped.

"No, forget that." He looked up at his rear-window. "Ms. Carol, are you game for a ride to see my boss. It'll only be a brief detour."

She smiled slightly and nodded.

Flash felt a new energy as he started up his hovertaxi. "Yes, sir, indeed. My boss will know what we should do. Don't give up hope, Ms. Carol. Dr. King said 'We must accept finite disappointment, but never lose infinite hope.' We have to keep that hope alive."

The hovertaxi rose into the air and jetted into the above sky lane of traffic.

CHAPTER 4

Street Shakedown

Metropolis was an unwieldy monolith of a supercity, but defining it more than anything was mobility. Mobile commerce, mobile services, people constantly in motion. Some said that people had to keep moving, even if they were going nowhere, otherwise the rain would wash them away with all the filth.

The Surf Brothers zipped past in their garbage hovertruck, by every other vehicle in the commercial sky lane. Trash trucks were more plentiful than any other vehicle in the city, government, or corporate. There was a lot of work to be done, and if they didn't do it, it wouldn't be the rain that would be the problem, but the growing blob of garbage from the millions of people living on top of each other.

The Dominican brothers smiled as they neared their target.

"There!" the brother in the passenger seat yelled out.

His brother saw it, too, and abruptly took the trash truck down. Only police and fire services could ignore every traffic law there was on the books.

The brother in the passenger seat had already pushed open the door before his older brother had the truck even ten feet down. He held the door still with one hand while he clung to an exterior vehicle handhold with the other. Trash collectors all wore their standard uniform—white jumpsuits with the word "TRASH" on the back and front. The younger brother had slicked-back, black hair and the makings of a goatee.

His older brother looked almost the same, only heavier, a bit taller, and had a slim mustache. He landed the vehicle as his younger brother jumped to the ground to look at the salvage.

People in the city always did the same thing—no matter if it was the upscale areas, working-class neighborhoods, or the downscale and dangerous areas. They dumped their old furniture on some sidewalk or back-alley. But why wouldn't they? Why would anyone pay the outrageous trash collection fees by the City? The trash industry didn't complain. It meant free money under-the-table straight to their pockets—a lot of free money. People left furniture in every possible condition and size; they left statues, old lighting, dish washers, washers and dryers, trampolines, workout equipment and weights, birdcages, dog cages, cat cages (sometimes with the animals inside), bookshelves and books, and even weapons. Once they found an unexploded bomb! Salvage work wasn't all fun, all the time.

The younger brother inspected the complete living room furniture— three couches, a main glass table and two side coffee tables, and a few lamp posts, all arranged neatly on top of each other.

"Good salvage!" he yelled to his brother.

The older brother jumped out of the truck to help. "Don't mention this to anyone, not even the boss."

"I know."

"I don't want to split it with them, anymore. They're worse than the City."

The younger brother laughed. "We are the City, my brother."

He smiled at him. "Well, we're not for the next...ten minutes."

The two men quickly loaded the salvage furniture into the side of the truck. The men were both five-feet-two, but collecting trash packed serious muscle on them over the years. The older brother closed the side panel door, and the men gave each other a double fist bump.

"That's what I'm talking about," the younger brother said as he jumped to the passenger door with one leap. "Trash is cash, my brother."

The older brother jumped up to the driver's compartment of the truck. "Yes, my brother."

"Hey," the younger brother swung into his passenger seat. "You actually are my brother...my brother."

"Brother by the same mother."

"Now that's a brother."

The brothers laughed as the trash truck flew away and back into the commercial sky lane.

The garbage truck almost clipped their taxicab. The two knucklehead drivers didn't even care, the passenger thought to himself. The air had a faint smell of garbage, even though the truck was long gone, but trash trucks were always flying through the sky, and he could see more in the distance—a main sub-station was only five miles away from this squalid business section of the city.

The cab arrived, and before the man could fully close the door, the cabbie was already flying away from the curb. The man gave him a parting middle finger gesture and proceeded into the lobby of the business building.

The Fat Man could stare at his room-sized aquarium all day and all night long. What he particularly enjoyed was watching his luminescent piranhas feed—little fish, big fish, snakes, rats, whatever he had a mind to throw into the tank to watch the frenzy. He was a very large, pale-skinned man, no muscle, all fat, in his bright lime suit and tie. Every one of his stubby fingers had a gold ring, and his smile was one of all gold teeth. The only hair he had was the short fuzz on his scalp.

The door opened, and a smaller man entered, wearing a purple tie and suit to match his purple shades. "Mr. Ergo. Your four o'clock is here."

He reached into his inside breast pocket for his shades. "Show him in."

The Fat Man forced his blubber into his executive chair behind the fortress of a desk and rested his arms on the armrests. His assistant entered again, leading another man.

"Mr. Box," the Fat Man said, watching him through his tinted yellow glasses. "Peri, pull over a chair for Mr. Box. Mr. Box, I'm eager to see what you found and anxious to conclude our business, as I'm sure you're anxious to get paid."

His assistant grabbed a wheeled chair from the other end of the room and pulled it to the front of his boss's desk. Box sat and crossed his legs.

"I'm curious as to how you found me," he asked. "Or knew to call me without a recommendation."

"Why, Mr. Box, the Yellow Pages." The Fat Man laughed. "They have a sub-category for unscrupulous private eyes. Is it private eye or detective? What's the proper term these days?"

"Makes no difference to me as long as the money is good and on time."

"Of course." The Fat Man interlaced his fingers as he rested them on his belly.

Box noticed the room-sized aquarium taking up the wall adjacent to them and leaned forward.

"My pets," the Fat Man said.

"They really eat anything?" Box asked.

"Anything alive, they can reduce to bones within minutes."

"Cute." Box leaned back in his chair and looked at the Fat Man.

"Do you have it?"

"I do. I'm a detective. I find stuff." Box reached into his jacket and pulled out a round three-inch silver disk. "Not too difficult to put a file together." He leaned forward and placed the disk on the top of the desk.

The Fat Man smiled. "Peri."

The assistant appeared next to him with a small briefcase computer. He picked up the disk and inserted it into a portal at the top of the case. He watched a light flash green on the side of the case before placing it on the desk as he opened it. He stepped back.

The Fat Man's fat fingers scrolled through the file by moving the briefcase computer's embedded trackball.

"Hmm," he said. "Our friend has been a very, very bad...rabbit." The Fat Man began to laugh again.

Box was not amused, but kept it to himself as the assistant reached into his own jacket and pulled out an envelope of cash. He tossed it to the detective. Box caught it with one hand and immediately fingered through it. Satisfied, he pushed it into his inside jacket pocket.

"Thank you, Mr. Box," the Fat Man said. "If I need an unscrupulous detective again, I won't even need the Yellow Pages."

Box stood from his chair.

"Since you've been a straight-up client, Mr. Ergo, let me verbally add something to the report as a bonus. This psycho freak is crazy."

"I imagine all psycho freaks are crazy, Mr. Box."

"Yeah, but he's new and already has a serious rep as a contract killer among certain segments on the street. What I'm saying is, I don't know what you plan to do, and it's none of my business, but be careful with this one."

"Thank you, Mr. Box. As you said, it's none of your business."

Box smiled and nodded. "I'll show myself out."

"And Mr. Box, be careful with taking a cab from this part of town. The cabbies are nothing short of highway robbers with the surcharges they tack on. I'd walk up to Null Street and hop on the monorail from there until you get back to civilization."

"Thanks."

The two men watched the detective walk out of the office and close the door.

"Peri, bring the car around. Let's go find this Red Rabbit." He looked at the piranha in his aquarium. "Now there's a thought. I've never served a live rabbit to my babies." He smiled with his gold teeth.

A black hovercar sat in the rain with the Fat Man in the passenger seat and his assistant at the wheel, waiting. Both were wearing dark shades but could see clearly through the rain and fog as they watched the building entrance about twelve yards away at the end of the street. A sidewalk johnny in a blue slicker coat, holding an umbrella, was right at the main door. He saw something then turned towards them and waved. With that, he ran off.

Red exited the dimly lit elevator and walked down the steps to the big revolving door of the entrance. He came out onto the street with red-tinted shades on, paying no attention to the weather.

"Mr. Red."

The voice made his head jerk to the side from the shadows. Two figures were waiting for him—a fat man and a smaller, shorter man.

"Don't be alarmed, Mr. Red," Mr. Ergo said. "I'm a simple business man. A class of people you are well accustomed to dealing with. Excuse my unorthodox way of seeking you out, but true businessmen make their opportunities. They don't wait for them. That's for losers."

Red was quiet and motionless in the shadow of the building; his rabbit ears stood up straight.

"I'm sure we can arrive at a mutually satisfactory dollar amount," the Fat Man continued.

"For what?" Red snapped.

"Silence, Mr. Red. You see, my assistant and I were in the vicinity of a street by the curious name of Alien Alley at the very hour that some poor child was, shall we say, borrowed away from her mother. The fact that we're here and talking to you should be evidence enough that what I say is true."

"You're shaking me down?" Red's voice was angry.

"Shakedown? No, Mr. Red. A simple business transaction. You should have taken more care not to have been seen when you were doing what you were doing. Quite a busy night for you, I'd say. Kidnapping and shootouts. The police are so overworked these days. They are always asking for tips for one unsolved crime or another. Now the police will pay X for said information, but as a businessman, I wanted to give you the fair chance to pay Y and not take said information to the police."

"Before you think about going psycho, psycho, know that we're heavily armed," the assistant interjected, his hand already holding something inside his jacket.

"Oh, no need to tell him that," the Fat Man cheerily said. "This is a calm discussion among businessmen."

"How much you want?"

"I was thinking about a figure Y, of say, one hundred thousand."

"Who's psycho? I'm not paying that to any shakedown artists."

"Then, give me a figure you think is fair, Mr. Red."

"Where do you get off calling me Red? You're not my friend, and you're not a client."

"No, Mr. Red. I'm a fellow businessman. You can call me Mr. Aquarius, if you like, since we're all using our super hero names today."

"I'd call you Captain Stupid if you think I'm going to give you anything near one hundred big ones."

"Mr. Red, I've done my due diligence," the Fat Man continued. "You make much more than that for an hour's work. And I hear you work all the time. Though I must say, I never see the aftermath of your deeds in the paper. Journalism is not what it used to be. Fifty-thousand by tonight, or do I make an anonymous call to Police Central? And, Mr. Red, we both know the kidnapping of the little girl is a mere incidental. What if the police were tipped off that the kidnapping of the little girl is *connected* to the larger event of the shootout."

"Forty-eight hours."

"Tonight."

"I don't have that kind of cash lying around."

"Tonight, at ten o'clock, I make that call to Police Central, Mr. Red. If you contact me before then, I will not make that call."

"I can't—"

"Mr. Red, this isn't the Middle East. I'm not interested in haggling all day long. Fifty-thousand dollars by ten o'clock. I believe we have arrived at a fair dollar amount to protect your dark deeds from the police authorities. I will leave a few associates in the lobby of your building, and you can pay them before ten o'clock...or not." The Fat Man turned back the way he came, but his associate remained, closely watching the killer. "Pleasure doing business with you, Mr. Red. Don't mind my assistant here. He'll simply wait and watch you until I'm safely in my dry hovercar. I wouldn't want you try to do something unfortunate. That wouldn't be nice of you. Bye-bye, Mr. Red. I've never conducted business with a red rabbit before. But then, all is possible in the city of Metropolis."

"Yeah, bye-bye, Captain Stupid," Red said under his breath.

The Fat Man couldn't stop laughing as he watched. His aquarium piranhas devoured the large white rabbit he tossed into the tank.

"That's how you make rabbit stew!"

He began to walk back to his desk when the corner of his eye caught a shape moving to him. Red came out the shadows into plain view of the ceiling lamp. The Fat Man ran to his desk as he pushed a button on his belt. Red ran up behind him and rabbit-punched him in the back of the head—*Crack!* Ergo's eyeballs popped out of their sockets and his tongue shot out of his mouth.

The alarms screamed from the office. Large footsteps could be heard and the door was kicked open. The assistant ran in with his compact machine-gun. "Mr. Ergo!" he yelled. "You!"

Peri fired at Red, who stood there as the bullets riddled his body, but with no effect. Peri's face was overcome by terror as Red was on him, throwing him across the room. His face slammed against the center aquarium, and he saw it. The Fat Man in the tank, being finished off by the piranhas, gold teeth and gold rings sinking to the bottom.

Peri picked himself up from the ground, yelling hysterically. He started running.

"Wrong way," Red said, grabbing the man by the collar and directing his flight of fear in the opposite direction.

Peri ran right out the window.

Two sidewalk johnnies sat in the brownish couches of the lobby of Red's building.

"Do you suppose this Rabbit guy lives here?"

"How would I know?"

"What is this place? Is it residences?"

"Yeah. Hotel residences. The whole building."

"What a dump."

"We don't have to live here. We're just waiting for a drop-off for a few bucks."

"Do you see these couches we're sitting on? It's like they've been here since the founding of the country. Look at the mildew and muck on these." He wiped his hand on the side of the couch with a look of disgust.

"We don't have to live here, and we don't have to sit here ever again if we don't want to."

"Imagine the rats and roaches this place must have. They must be so big that the landlord can legally charge them rent."

"Hey, is this the guy?"

The other sidewalk johnny looked at the revolving door, too. Red walked through the door with some kind of glowing blue stick.

"What's that in his hand?"

The men stood from the couches in fear.

"Is that some kind of gun?"

Red walked to the men with no shades on his face; only the dark, ominous eyeholes of his mask. They could feel his stare as he cocked the electric rifle.

"Wait a minute, Mister! We were just asked to wait here for a few bucks. We're not involved."

Red's furry head mask turned bright red as he shot the man with a blast of blue energy, sending him sailing through the air and crashing into the elevator doors. The other man ran as fast as he could, crying, before he was shot in the back by another energy blast. Red's mask slowly reverted from red to a reddish white as he walked to the elevator door and pulled the dead johnny away so he could open it. He entered, closed the door behind him, and pushed a button. The elevator began to ascend as the ratty, brownish carpet began to catch fire from the discharges from his electric rifle.

Officer Break and Caps arrived for their first real call of the day. The cruiser set down, and both policemen walked to the scene. The police tape had already been set up to keep everyone out, but this time, all the police were on the other side of the cordon, too. The buildings first few floors were engulfed in flames.

They walked over to another police duo.

"Officers," the policeman said.

"Officers," Break said.

"What do we got?"

"Dead body drop. At least two people."

"Burn down an entire building to cover up a murder."

"Very enterprising of our city's murderers."

A red hovercraft appeared in the sky, above the crowds, with sirens flashing, and police moved the crowds back to allow the craft to land. Everyone still called them fire trucks, even though they became much more than that a long time ago. Police were in silver-and-black. Firemen were in red-and-black gear with the word "FIRE" on the chest and back of their uniforms. Their mechanical uniform enhancements were much more pronounced than the police's and made them appear to be eight-foot tall, muscle-bound giants. The Fireman's Union wouldn't allow one single, solitary fireman—or firewoman—to be replaced by robots, so they did the next logical—and more expensive thing—they merged the two.

The firemen moved into position as high-pressure water fired from their arm and chest nozzles. The drivers of the fire trucks fired water cannons at the blaze.

"How did you get all the building residents out so fast," Officer Break asked.

"We didn't," the policeman answered. "Besides the dead bodies, there wasn't anyone else."

"How is that possible?" Officer Caps asked. "The entire building was empty?"

"The entire building was emptied of all residents three days ago."

"How convenient," Officer Break said.

"We thought so."

"ID on the vics?"

"We couldn't get in for DNA, yet," the other officer answered. "Criminals still don't get that you can't burn away DNA. All you do is make a mess for the fire crews."

"Job security for them," Officer Caps added.

"Job security for us," Officer Break said.

CHAPTER 5

Liquid Cool

Run-Time reclined in the chair behind his desk in his spacious office as he listened to the phone he held to his ear. Flash sat in one chair in front of the desk, and next to him was one of Run-Time's VPs, a finely dressed Lebanese woman. Flash always felt privileged to be in the presence of his boss, the Founder, President, CEO, and COO of Let It Ride Enterprises—taxicab, limousine, and vehicle protection services.

Run-Time wore his slim fit business suits with slim ties. The only casual thing he wore was his trademark flat cap. His parents were from the West Indies, and the Black mogul kept a close haircut, clean-shaven face, and his chestnut complexion pampered with crystal facials and baths once a week.

"Yes, Captain," Run-Time answered. "There's no possible way we can make this into a Red Ball? The woman isn't famous, but what if a famous person were to involve himself in her case."

Flash began to smile and looked at the VP sitting next to him.

"Tell me what you need, Captain, to make this happen. I'm happy to bring in as much or as little media as you need to give you cover with the

Chief's Office. One of my employees knows the woman. Captain, we're both parents so we both understand, in some way this woman's grief. Yes, I understand. Yes. I don't want to add any burden to your fine men and women in silver and black. Yes, I understand. I appreciate your help, Captain. All we want to give this woman is some hope. Yes. Thank you." Run-Time began to chuckle. "Yes, Captain, I do plan to be at the Mayor's Annual Breakfast. You know I am a staunch business supporter of this fine city." Run-Time began to chuckle again. "Captain, my annual contributions to the Police Union's fund is automatic. That way, neither emotions nor politics ever enter into the equation. My check is always in the mail." Run-Time smiled. "Yes, Captain. Thanks for taking my call. I know everyone involved is giving their maximum effort to find this woman's young daughter. Thank you. Bye-bye."

Flash perked up as his boss returned the phone to the receiver.

Run-Time remained quiet for a moment.

"No Red Ball," the VP said.

"Well, we knew that before I made the call," Run-Time answered. He looked at Flash. "The number of missing persons cases in this city is mind boggling. What percentage of those are actually runaways or one divorced parent driving off with the child no one knows."

"She is a widow, and the child did not run away," Flash quickly said.

"Oh, I don't doubt you. But the hands of the police are tied. Red Balls are for high-profile cases. That's how it is, and that's how it will always be. Me jumping in won't elevate it to a Red Ball."

"But if your child were taken, it would," Flash said sadly.

Run-Time reflected for a moment. "We're all adults in this room. People are all equal, but in a city of this size with needs up here,"—he gestured with his hand high above his head—"and resources down here,"—he moved his hand downward to the floor—"some people must be more equal than others. There's no other way to do it, sadly."

"I know," Flash said.

"But that doesn't mean we can't bring our own resources to the party. Where is this woman now?"

"She's waiting for me in my cab."

Run-Time looked at his VP. "Bring her up to the Floral Conference Room, get her a nice meal to eat, and when she's settled in, call me."

Flash stood from his chair. "Thank you, boss." He leaned forward and shook Run-Time's hand.

Run-Time stood too. "No one should be alone in their time of need. What's her first name?"

"Carol," Flash answered.

"Let's get Carol up here."

Carol sat at a glass table alone, sipping her drink with a straw. An empty plate rested in front of her with a knife and fork—she finished the meal almost as soon as it was placed in front of her. Her recent grief had masked the hunger, and she didn't realize that she hadn't eaten in almost two days. The conference room was spacious and had an array of multi-colored flowers on the pastel wallpaper. It was a beautiful room, she thought, complete with its own working mini-waterfall on one side of the room and real potted bamboo trees. She sat at one of five round tables at the back of the room. In front were rows of single chairs, as if a presentation had recently passed, or one was scheduled.

She had sipped the last of her lemonade and sat back to look toward the tinted building window. Her mind was now on the thoughts of Alien Alley. Was her daughter calling out for her at this very moment?

Flash walked into the room and Carol sat upright.

"Hi, Carol. How did you like the food?"

"It was good. It was great."

"Their food is always good. It's a place on the bottom floor of the building. We order from them all the time."

Carol saw a woman hold the door open, and another man entered. Run-Time walked right up to her and extended his hand. "Carol, is it?"

"Yes."

He took her hand. "My name is Run-Time and I'm the Founder, President, CEO and all-around booster for Let It Ride Enterprises. I wanted to, personally, tell you that both you and your daughter are in our prayers. If there is anything in my power that I can do to see the safe return of her to you, I will do it. I speak for everyone in the company, and everyone, here in this room, is a parent."

"Thank you."

"I will not sugarcoat anything, Carol. I tried to get Police Central to add additional resources to this case, but as you probably know—"

"I am one of hundreds," she added. Her eyes drifted from him down to the floor.

"Yes. Sad, but true. However..." Carol looked back at him. "I want you to take this." He handed her a white card. "Flash will take you home, and I do want you to go home. Get a good night's sleep. I know it will be hard, but you have to force yourself to sleep. The police may not be adding additional resources to the case, but they will at least get a call from the Chief of Police, himself, and dozens of officers will be looking at the case, at least for a day, because of my call. Every bit helps. If they find anything new, they will certainly drive to your house to tell you in person."

"Thank you."

"Then, we're going to have you back here at my headquarters tomorrow."

"I'll do it, boss," Flash added.

"Flash will have you back here tomorrow, and I will have you meet with someone. I've known him for a long time, and he's not just a cool cat, but he's a solid operator. Let's see what he can come up with to find your daughter. I've already spoken to him on the phone."

"You have?" Carol's eyes opened wide.

"Yes."

"So it will be home, sleep, and back here to meet my friend. How does that sound as a plan?"

"It sounds great."

"Good."

Run-Time, for the first time, let go of her hand as she stood. He could see the ray of hope in her face. They could all see it. The VP nodded and smiled. "Hang in there, Ms. Carol," she said. Flash walked her out of the room.

The main elevator was already waiting for them—one of the security guards held it for them and he too nodded at Carol.

They got in. Flash felt the hope himself. He was so glad he had come to his boss. He knew he'd find a solution.

Carol stood quietly too. The ride was silent, but they could see the numbers count down in large digital numbers on the door. She almost forgot about it. She looked down at the white card from Mr. Run-Time.

The card read:

LIQUID COOL
Detective Agency
D. Cruz
Private Detective

These Mean Streets, Darkly concludes in the debut novel of the cyberpunk detective series, *Liquid Cool!*

LIQUID COOL

THE CYBERPUNK DETECTIVE SERIES

Crime in a High-Tech, Low-Life World

AUSTIN DRAGON

PART ONE

Shootout on Sweet Street

CHAPTER 1

Easy Chair Charlie

Metropolis.

Everything that was seen or heard, every smell, and almost every feeling belonged to it. Skyscraper monoliths with their side lights rose into the near-perpetual overcast sky one way, blink-blink, and the lukewarm downpour fell onto the neon urban jungle the other, drip-drip. From the ground, looking up, on those days that were as clear as it could ever get, buildings seemed to have their own halos, courtesy of the rooftop lights. On "normal" rainy days, that same illumination gave the sky a faint glow. Also from the vantage of the streets, the city's lighted buildings pulsated in all the many psychologically-tested and focus-group-researched colors to mitigate the street's base griminess, despite the ever-rain. The flashing neon signs screamed every second of every day; their soft-sell, quasi-hypnotic consumerist cons of Big Bad Business and government public service "aggravations" (PSAs) of Big Bad Government. But people were numb to it all, no matter how outrageous or provocative.

The crowds on the streets moving about were like a collective life form. Everyone clad in their gray-toned or black slickers, and for those carrying them, umbrellas with glowing colored handles. Most had their ears covered with headphones, their heads covered with hoods, and everyone had their eyes covered with glowing colored glasses. The masses were in the world, but mentally someplace else—away from it, never a part of it, unless there was a reason, and there rarely was a reason. Tech-tricksters, analog hustlers, and digital gangsters, at least, had purpose. The masses had only one concern—to exist, get to the end of the day unscathed, and then do it all over again the next day. Maybe smile a real smile a time or two in life. Escape was only possible if you could buy or trick your way Up-Top or, of course, when the Grim Reaper came a-knocking. 'Til then, for most, there was plugging the ears into the music, and the eyes (and brain) into the virtual television. For too many others, it was also about jacking the body into the drugs or the mind into the cyber-games. Everything in an attempt to stave off the dark emotions and conventional madness that accompanied the daily grind of life in the 50 million-plus, supercity of Metropolis, and the many, many other metropolises exactly like it, though smaller, on Earth.

"Yo, yo, yo. Easy Chair Charlie! What's the street talk, E.C.?" a voice called out.

If it were not for their glowing colored glasses, the three street kids would have been invisible through the drizzle of the night. Easy Chair Charlie stopped his musically-influenced stroll through the streets, pulling his headphones down around his neck. He wore his favorite embroidered, black slicker that flowed behind his tall, lanky frame. He also had the attached clear hood pulled over his bleached-white spiky hair and wore glowing, dark blue-black shades, but looked out from the top as if they were bifocals.

A neon sign flashed, and he could see the kids clearly—flapper hats and chia-pet bubble-coats—squatting on the corner. "What you playin'?" he asked.

The boys looked like gorillas with the heads of old World War I fighter pilots. The water-resistant, faux-fur of their coats kept them toasty warm in the rain.

"Just a game of street jacks to pass the time, Easy," answered the same boy. "Easy, what's the street talk? You always know the low-down. If we get something, we'll give you a cut like always."

Easy Chair Charlie was a hustler of some distinction. His racket was the numbers, and he had the inside scoop on every professional and amateur, major league and minor league sports game, hovercar race, horse race, dog race, boxing match, or martial arts match there was and every illegal and back-alley one, too. But he was branching out from his old racket, though he still had the touch and threw a tip here and there to the street kids he liked.

"No action now. But I may have something for you later," he said.

"Righteous, Easy. You always come through for us."

"You always come through for me. The street looks out for self."

"You know it, Easy."

"Catch me later."

"You got it, Easy," they said in unison.

Easy Chair Charlie returned his headphones to his ears and strutted away to his tunes. He gave them the thumbs-up as he disappeared into the rain.

Downtown loved to tout the ethnic diversity that was the melting pot of Metropolis. It was true; everyone felt equally miserable, and that they were being melted into a pot—a big wet one. With so many millions in the supercity, there were more ethnicities, nationalities, and languages spoken here than any other place in the world.

In the old days, groups fervently protected their neighborhoods, but legacy housing changed all that, some say, ending the traditional ethnic communities forever. There were still the ethnic enclaves of old, but often, they were not run by the nationalities that originally created them, back when Metropolis was just a city, let alone a mega-city or the supercity center it was today. The suave, hipster Old Harlem, with more historical landmarks than any other part of the city, was run not by Blacks anymore, but Italians. Most of its buildings were not as tall or as massive, but many argued it had the best clubs and restaurants in the city. It was also the center of the cigar aficionado world, one place in particular.

Joe Blows was where Easy Chair Charlie was going—the world famous Joe Blows Smoking Emporium on Sweet Street. He was out of smokes and needed to replenish his stash. It was a lucrative storefront, but also an official historic landmark of the city. In the old days, movie celebrities and megacorporate playboys made up its famous clientele, but though it no longer featured in the papers and trades like back then, everyone knew it as the establishment for all cancer-stick connoisseurs, and people came far and wide for a stash. There wasn't an exotic, classic, or premium cigarette or cigar in the world that they didn't carry. But no narcotics. If you wanted that, any corner dope daddy or drugstore cowboy on speed-dial could get you that. Joe Blows was for those who loved smoke—the taste and feel through the lungs, nose, and mouth. For the true connoisseur, that was the high. It had its main store, but the real action was the adjoining smoking rooms, where old-time smokers sat around chatting it up for hours and doing deals as they smoked and joked over drinks, dinner, poker, or a game of pool with beautiful waitresses around. Joe's was strictly a straight joint—male chauvinists and babes only, though nowadays, a quarter of its clientele were female smokers.

"This is a public service announcement to remind you that the Metropolis Surgeon General says you can double your life expectancy by ceasing the use of all tobacco products," said one of the baby-faced agents in a suit, but without a lick of style.

The government's "cigarette police" would stop by every month or two to pass out anti-smoking flyers, but were met with howling laughter and men stuffing the flyers—in front of the agents—into their butt cracks or in the front of their jock straps. However, today was one of those bad days, and Easy Chair Charlie entered the smoking room as the two meek college kid agents—paid government volunteers—were practically running out as smoking room customers threatened them with obscene gestures, jeers, and curses. The entire establishment was yelling at them to leave.

Easy Chair Charlie chuckled, carrying his two just-purchased boxes—his stash of exotic cigars for the month—from the main store to the sitting rooms.

"Easy Chair Charlie!" a booming voice called out.

Fat Nat, a large pot-bellied man, waved to him as he stood up from a card table of other men. Easy waved back with a smile and then gave him a salute. He walked to the table and set both boxes in the center, on top of the men's cards.

The men grinned at the words on the boxes.

"Havanas, Easy?" a seated man asked. "How the hell can you afford a box of those? One of those is worth a king's ransom, and you got *two* boxes."

"This is Easy Chair Charlie. He knows how to get things, so he can sit back easy-like in his chair," Fat Nat said.

They listened keenly to the sounds. Easy carefully cut the outer plastic wrapping from one cigar box with his switchblade and asked, "May I perchance offer my good comrades a genuine Havana?"

The men stood from their chairs as Easy lifted the lid and then slit the inner plastic covering to allow the aroma of the cigars to rise from the box. Each man pulled a glove from a pants pocket and put it on their right hand. One by one, the four men grabbed a cigar and inhaled deeply as they were passed under their nostrils.

"This, Easy...is what heaven smells like," Fat Nat said.

Easy took one himself. One of the men pulled another chair from a nearby table for him. "Easy, set yourself down in an easy chair." Easy smiled as he and the five men sat. Fat Nat pulled a box of old slow-matches from his chest pocket and struck one. He lit Easy's first and then each friend's cigar with its steady, slow-burning, tiny flame. He left his for last.

"The first puff of the cigar." Easy leaned back in his chair to savor it.

"Easy is like no other." Fat Nat lifted his Japanese whiskey glass. "Here's to Easy and easy living in this wet, rainy, modern, miserable world."

The men drank.

Easy Chair Charlie stifled a slight burp. "Gentlemen, I may have something for you."

The street knew Easy for his take-it-to-the-bank betting tips, but few knew of his new, more lucrative, racket of the acquisition. Not a finder. They only told you where an item you desired was, but Easy found it and delivered it right to you. Acquisition experts, like him, were in high demand and insanely compensated. He could make more with the successful acquisition of an item in one year than his old gambling racket. His specialty was acquisition of items from Up-Top—where the wealthy and powerful of the planet lived. That's where the astronomic cash was to be had.

"Something good?" Fat Nat asked.

Easy did a slow exhale. "If I play my cards right, I'll be able to make it all the way to Up-Top myself. Not just get things. And you know how generous I am to my friends."

The men smiled.

"How Easy?" Fat Nat asked.

Easy Chair Charlie leaned back. "How indeed." He took another draw from his cigar like a king. They all heard a low hum. Easy clenched his cigar gently between his teeth and said, "Excuse me, gentlemen, my pants are vibrating."

A couple of the men grinned as Easy stared down at the display of the mobile phone in his hand. He answered it as he got up from the table and walked outside.

"Something good must be callin'," Fat Nat said to the men.

From the roof of a skyscraper, a silver-and-black body-armored policeman stood with a high-powered binocular attachment over his visored half-helmet, watching. To him, two miles away was turned into five feet away. Easy, Fat Nat, and the boys were back at the card table, laughing and joking.

From the darkened sky, a policeman slowly descended via rocketpack, the yellow flames glowing from the double exhaust nozzles. The word "PEACE" was visible on his black chest body armor. Two more policemen descended from the sky and then another half dozen.

Foot police arrived on the ground, and people crossed the street or double-backed to walk away from them—something bad was about to happen. In mere moments, the busy street was empty, except for the police and an arriving police cruiser that appeared, hovering six feet from the ground in stealth mode.

Joe Blows also had its main bar—a big bar. Members always got their first drink free, and all members, besides their love of smoking products,

68

loved to drink. And Joe Blows only served alcoholic drinks. If you wanted coffee, green tea, or another girly-man non-alcoholic, then you needed to get in your hovercar and go someplace else.

"Hyper, waiting on my drink order!" the waitress yelled out.

The bartender behind the counter seemed to float on air as he moved to her with a tray of clear and colored drinks. She smiled, and he smiled back.

"You're slowing down, Hyper. Normally, you'd have my order before I started my sentence."

"If you say." He continued to get bottles and glasses, pour alcohol into glasses, get trays, and then set drinks on the bar and on trays for pick-up. He moved like a machine.

"I thought you were off tonight—" she began.

A pulse-round of white light exploded her tray of drinks, sending glass and alcohol everywhere. Another blast hit Hyper in the shoulder, knocking him back, and ripped through the wall behind him. The waitress screamed as more rounds whizzed past, hitting the bar counter and the wall. She stood in place, yelling hysterically.

Everyone in the bar dived to the ground for cover.

"Get down, Tab!" Hyper yelled from behind the counter.

Big G was about to throw his card on the table, when a pulse-round blasted through his hand and the cards. Fat Nat kicked the table away and pushed his friend to the ground from the chair. All the men were flat on the ground as the pulse-rounds ripped through the establishment. They could hear screams from patrons and things being blasted apart. One of the old-timers got to his feet and ran to the side entrance.

"Stay on the ground!" Fat Nat yelled.

Another customer jumped up and ran to the main entrance, also in panic; others jumped up, following. A pulse-round ripped through the wall, knocking the left leg off one man's body and grazing the head of another, sending both patrons to the ground in shock.

"'Nuff of this!" Fat Nat bolted away on all fours.

"Nat, where you goin'?"

Tab, the waitress, kept screaming, frozen, as multiple pulse-rounds whizzed closer and closer to her head on their way to blast the front bar area to pieces. Fat Nat appeared from around a corner, crawling fast. He stopped and pulled his piece from his back waistband. The rifle auto-unfolded; he aimed and then fired at her. The waitress fell, crashing to the ground on her back and her screaming never ceasing.

"You want to get killed!" A round hit the wall above his head. "Hyper, you alive?"

"I'm good, boss. Now, I can get that bionic arm I always wanted—for free!"

"Who's shooting my place to hell?" Fat Nat was red with anger and stood to his feet.

"Nat, get your ass to the ground before you get yourself shot in the head!" one of his card buddies hollered as he was crawling into the bar area on all fours.

Fat Nat yelled at the top of his lungs, "Nuke attack!"

"Emergency Nuclear Blast Doors activated," answered the overhead computer voice.

The sound of several-feet thick alloy walls rose from the ground in a slow rumble as they sealed Joe Blows up like a tomb. The barrage of pulse-fire continued, but was just a melody of taps from outside, rather than projectiles of death and destruction.

Fat Nat stood to his feet with a deep frown on his face to survey the damage. He walked to the bar and peeked over the counter. There was the kid, Hyper, lying on the floor, missing an arm, in a puddle of blood, but smiling.

70

"I'm good, boss." He gave a casual salute with his good arm. "The blast cauterized the wound, so there's almost no blood."

"Tab?" Fat Nat yelled.

"Yes, boss."

"What's your disposition?"

"I'm shot and lying on the ground."

"Any major damage?"

"How would I know? You were the one who shot me!"

"Would you have preferred to be shot by me and alive or shot and dead by unknown bastard gunmen because you were too dumb to put face to floor?"

"Is that supposed to be a trick question, boss?"

Fat Nat continued his inspection of his place. His card-mates appeared and joined him.

"What's Big G's disposition?" Fat Nat asked.

"Big G will be needing a new hand."

"Fat Nat, what are you going to do?"

The other men looked at him, and they could see Fat Nat seething as he walked through the establishment—damage, debris, and bodies everywhere.

"Make sure no one's dead," Fat Nat said to his friends.

"What will you be doing, Nat?"

"Nobody shoots up Joe Blows, my place of business, and gets away duty-free. I'll be back."

"No, Fat Nat. Not the Terminator stash. You can't be shooting up the streets with machine guns."

"Nobody shoots up Joe Blows!"

"Nat," said another man. "You can't be running around Old Harlem shooting up bad guys. This is our neighborhood. If it were somebody else's, I'd say give me a piece too, and let's go. But you don't be shooting up your own neighborhood. What's wrong with you?"

There was one loud, muffled metallic knock, then several more pounds from outside. Someone was knocking.

The men looked at each other.

"This is the Police!"

Sweet Street was totally shut down. Thick, neon yellow police tape—POLICE LINE. DO NOT CROSS—cordoned off the entire area and it was a light show of red and blue flashing sirens. People crowded the slick sidewalks and streets outside the tape, while media arrived in force. One hoverambulance after another landed on the scene.

Fat Nat argued with the policeman, but was gently restrained by his smoking buddies.

"I demand to see the body," he yelled again at the policeman.

"Sir, this is now an official crime scene—"

"Yeah, I should know," Fat Nat interrupted. "I was one of the ones inside getting shot at, watching my employees and customers get shot up and my place of business get blasted to hell."

"Sir, I understand you're upset, but we have to maintain the integrity of the crime scene."

"Showing me the body of the supposed one-man, crazy gunman is not going to mess up any crime scene. Let me make it simple. Do you want to show me the body, so I can see who this mook was, or should I shuffle my fat self on over to the media cameras and talk about the deep psychological trauma I'm experiencing—yeah, I can feel it coming on. I might need to call my lawyer or a doctor, or my lawyer and doctor at the same time. Lawsuit settlements come right out of the police budget nowadays, never city hall—"

"Wait here, sir."

The policeman walked over to a superior talking with three other policemen. After a few moments of speaking, one of the policemen gestured to Fat Nat with his index finger: *Come here*.

The white blanket was lifted from the lone gunman, lying dead on the sidewalk.

"Do you know this man?" the policeman asked.

Fat Nat stared at the body for a while. He looked up and said, "Never saw him before."

Fat Nat's smoking buddies also stared at the body.

"What about any of you gentlemen?" the policeman asked.

They all shook their heads.

"We're sorry we were so jerky about this. Sorry we can't identify him for you, either," Fat Nat continued. "So this mook shot up the place with pulse machine guns?"

"High-powered," the policeman added. "He gave us quite the gun battle."

Fat Nat shook his head. "And this is supposed to be a safe neighborhood. Well, I have lots of calls to make—hospital, insurance, and so on. I got to get my place of business made whole. Joe Blows has never been closed in sixty years, and we're not about to start now. I should have the ambulance guys check me out, too."

"Sir, we'll have the shift detectives contact you tomorrow for a full statement," the officer said.

"Thanks, officer. Tell us when you need us at the station." Fat Nat gathered his buddies and led them away towards the crowd.

The policemen watched them.

"Looks like they know more than they're sayin'," said one officer.

"People always know more than they're saying, especially when they're the victims."

Fat Nat and the boys stopped in front of the police-tape line.

"Nat, that was Easy Chair Charlie," one of the men whispered. "Easy Chair Charlie never touched a gun in his life! Those—"

"Shhh!" Fat Nat turned his head briefly.

The policemen were still watching them. Fat Nat smiled at them. They ducked under the neon yellow police tape and disappeared into the crowds as a light rain began again.

PART TWO

Where's Cruz?

CHAPTER 2

Run-Time

R un-Time.
    Middle-school drop-out at eleven years old. Body shop go-fer at twelve. Hovercar mechanic at thirteen. Valet attendant at fourteen. Hovertaxi driver at seventeen. Hovertaxicab owner at nineteen; bought three more at twenty-one. Millionaire at twenty-two. Started *Let It Ride Enterprises* at twenty-five. Mega-multi-millionaire by thirty.

Run-Time was a big deal in Metropolis, a "Who's Who" among the wealthy elite, and he wasn't even forty, yet. But, there was nothing "elite" about him. He was from the streets and kept that sensibility, despite his wealth. He owned all the top car washes, hovercar body shops, hovercar rental shops, hovercycle rental shops, hovertaxicab, and hoverlimousine services in the city. Anything that had to do with private transportation, Run-Time had his hands in it.

But, the operation that surpassed every other line of his businesses was his mobile hovercar security services. The hovercar remained the top luxury item in the city, despite ubiquitous public transportation and commercial hovertaxicab services. With virtually every city resident in some type of legacy housing, it was hovercars that people spent virtually all their discretionary income on. Such an investment demanded some kind of protection, and Run-Time was there to fill the need. Call Let It Ride, and a rep would descend from the sky via jetpack to guard your precious investment hourly, nightly, or daily. No one messed with your car when Let It Ride was protecting it.

Cruz had been a client of Run-Time's for years, one of his premium customers and, long before that, a best friend. Run-Time realized the hard way, the higher up the wealth ladder one went, the smaller the number of people one could genuinely call "friend." In all the years Run-Time had known Cruz, Cruz never once asked for a favor or money.

Run-Time strolled into his headquarters building early. He never wore sweats or hoodies. Monday to Thursday, he wore his slim fit business suits and slim ties, and on casual Fridays and the weekends, if he came in, he left the tie at home. The only casual thing he wore was his trademark flat cap. You'd never see his head without it, and you'd never see him wearing it backwards. He didn't have to work as hard as he did now that he'd "made it"—he could hire people to run his business for him, while he lived the pampered, human vegetable, booshy life, but that wasn't in Run-Time's DNA. He was the hardest worker around, among his fifty-five-thousand plus employee corporation. His people worked hard, and he paid them well for it.

Peacock Hills was one of the premiere business districts in the city. From a distance—a long, long distance—the monolith buildings looked like gargantuan fingers extending into space through the city's rain cloud cover. Each was illuminated in the conservative colors of white, light yellow, and blue. As with most of the city's buildings, the roof lighting of each structure reflected off the sky giving them the appearance of having angelic halos.

Run-Time exited the elevator on the penthouse level, two hundred and fifty floors up, and did as he always did. "Good morning, good ladies," he greeted.

He was not a boss who demanded that staff snap to attention at his arrival. His philosophy was, "if you can't give me a high-five, fist bump, or shake my hand like a normal person, then you're working at the wrong place. I'm just a guy, not a dictator or the Second Coming."

Three women sat at the reception desk, evenly spaced apart from each other. "Good morning, Mr. Run-Time," the receptionists responded in unison.

To look at them, you'd think they coordinated their outfits the day before. The Caucasian woman with the British accent was dressed in yellow, the Asian woman with the Southern accent was dressed in blue, and the Black woman with the West Indian accent was in red.

"Boss, your nine a.m. is here early," one of them added.

"Give me five minutes and bring him up to the office."

"He's almost forty-five minutes early, boss."

He stopped and gave her a look. "What am I thinking right now?"

"We'll send him up in five minutes, boss," she answered.

He took the steps two-by-two to his private second floor of the penthouse level, and to his office at the very end of a long hallway.

Two Japanese men sat facing his spacious, custom-made ivory desk. The older man wore a glowing suit as white as the man's full head of hair and eyebrows. The younger man wore a black suit. Run-Time could tell that the older man was not only in charge, but at the highest level in his mega-company—he wore mere sandals. Oh, his feet were covered in the most expensive silk socks, but wearing sandals meant his feet never touched the public street like the commoners of the world or even his subordinates. Most in the world had to wear at least calf-high boots, but the older man moved from office to hoverlimo to jet plane only. The younger man watched Run-Time with a slight smile, but the older man was stone-faced.

"The Orochi Corporation would humbly request a contract for exclusive services with your company," the younger man continued.

"I'm very flattered, Mr. Ping," Run-Time said. "However, there is the matter of the platinum services that I provide to my clients, who, incidentally, are very dependent on my services. I've spent nearly twenty years building that dependence. Also, if I'm exclusive with you, then who would take my dear, good mother to the library? I have a few relatives that depend on me. I can't withhold my limo services from them—family and friends."

A slight smile flashed on the older Japanese man's face.

"Mr. Run-Time," Mr. Ping said, "we are not talking about immediate family, relatives, or other acquaintances—a simple exemption clause in our exclusivity contract would be acceptable, and expected. Do not allow your desire to retain contracts with the city sabotage a more superior business arrangement. I am sure we could come up with a figure that would...alleviate any discomfort that exclusivity with our corporation might cause you. Your mother would appreciate more the fact that you could buy her her own hovercar with full-time drivers. Maybe, her own private jet with dedicated pilots. Maybe even, a luxury peri-terrestrial space flight from time to time."

Run-Time smiled. "There is a transformational point that any truly successful businessman reaches in his life."

"What would that be, Mr. Run-Time?"

"Money becomes meaningless. I made more in one year than my father, mother, both sets of grandparents, and every one of my known ancestors made in their entire lives, going back as far as the genealogical records can go. Ironically, I became as wealthy as I am, because I don't care about money. *Purpose* for me is being the best at whatever I set my mind to and having the freedom to pursue that quest, to always be reaching and fighting for excellence."

"Money is never meaningless, Mr. Run-Time." Mr. Yo finally spoke. "Soon, after you realize that money is meaningless, you realize something else."

"What is that, sir?"

"That the money you acquire is no longer for you. It is to amass power. For that, there is never enough money."

"I appreciate that advice, Mr. Yo, but for me, it's a principle. I am a man of principle."

"We, as well, Mr. Run-Time. Principle is the bedrock upon which every other part of what truly makes a man a man is built. With the house of his life, one can build upon a foundation of sand or stone. It is an important decision."

"We agree completely. I must say, Mr. Yo, that others have done what you're asking, favoring one side or the other. But I will never become exclusive with the government, nor will I go exclusive with any multinational or megacorp. I cater to all. That's what my business is known for—from Main Street to Money Street to City One. I'm sure you can understand that principle."

"No," the older Japanese man quickly replied. "It means you are not mature enough to enter the halls of real power. You still think small thoughts, have small ambitions. Those are of a child and not an adult."

Run-Time contained his laugh. "I'm close, but I haven't turned forty, yet. I think I have more than enough time to be an adult with big-boy pants, big-boy thoughts, and ambitions."

"That's the other thing you will learn, Mr. Run-Time. Mortal men never have enough time. You think one hundred billion dollars is big because you associate with street people who have no money. Yes, to them that is big money. But, Mr. Run-Time, when your life serves a multi-trillion-dollar company, you see things in their true light. One hundred million dollars is what we spend in one weekend on a party for our executives."

Run-Time was not a man easily offended, but he was annoyed now.

"Sir, I prefer to be proud of my accomplishments in life, thus far. Not bad for a junior high school drop-out without a high school diploma."

The younger Japanese man laughed. "Still peddling that story, Mr. Run-Time? You secretly got yourself a MBA from the same university my nephew attends. Very pricey. Very prestigious. Very elite."

The older man interrupted him. "I am so sorry we can't do business together, Mr. Run-Time. Our CEO demands exclusivity in his business, so we will continue our search."

"I apologize for not being able to serve your needs, Mr. Yo."

"We, as well," the older man responded as he rose from his chair and immediately walked out of the office.

The younger man rose, smiled as he bowed, and followed his boss out of the office.

Run-Time watched the men move down the hall from his chair behind the desk. The two men disappeared around the corner.

His three vice presidents entered the office from an adjoining room—all finely dressed in dark suits. Two female—a tall Lebanese woman and a West Indian woman, and one stout blue-eyed Irishman. Right behind them, a man wearing overalls over his purple suit, holding the handle of a contraption with one hand and a long telescoping wand with the other, entered the office.

They watched as the sweeper did his work, quickly scanning the entire office. In the cut-throat, war-like corporate world, it was common for a visitor to "forget" a listening device or two in someone's office during a meeting.

"It's clean, boss," Bugs said.

Run-Time nodded as the sweeper left the office.

"They can hurt us, boss," one vice president said.

"Badly," said another.

"If you can't handle the capitalist jungle, then you should never have left the baby crib," Run-Time said confidently. "You're good to your customers and they won't abandon you."

"What about politically?" a third VP asked.

Run-Time tapped his fingers on his desk. "However..."

His executives could almost see their boss's mind race.

"I want to know every one of our competitors they approach, and get our research boiler-room ready—hire what we need. If we're going to be in a market-share war, then let's make sure we can launch our strike before they do."

The phone from his desk beeped and he hit the answer button.

"Call on one for you, boss. A China Doll." He pushed the button and could see a face on the phone's small TV screen. "China Doll."

He looked at his VPs as his finger tapped the mute. "And have marketing and communications put together a strategy by lunch time." He picked up the phone receiver. "Full conference meeting at noon." He put the receiver to his ear.

The executives wrote their notes to themselves on electric steno-pads and briskly walked out. One of them stopped and pointed to the door. Run-Time made the gesture to leave it open.

He touched the button labeled VID-PHONE. "Doll. What's shakin'?"

"Where's Cruz?" the female voice asked.

"Haven't seen him."

"He's not picking up his mobile. He's supposed to be having dinner with me at my parents' today. The first time."

"That's a scary thought. No man wants to spend time with the future mother-in-law. That's why he's disappeared."

"It's not funny. You know how he gets after any birthday of his. All morose and anti-social. Where could be?"

"He's fine."

"I'm at work, and I can't go looking for him, but put the word out for me."

"You want him to call or stop by?"

"Call is fine. No—stop by. If he's not here by two, he can just meet me there."

"I'll get him there. Not very many places for him to hide. My man, Cruz, is a creature of habit."

"If he even thinks of standing me up, he'll have another crazy female after him."

"That's a thought. I'll check with her, too."

"Why?"

"She's crazy, but she may have seen him."

"She's a sidewalk sally mental case."

"I'll get him there."

"'Kay."

"See ya."

"Bye."

CHAPTER 3

China Doll

China Doll.

C   She closed the video-phone receiver on her end and walked out of the break room with its psychedelic, flowery wallpaper; her hand brushed aside the multi-colored hanging beads over the doorway.

She was the consummate fashionista with every piece of clothing, every accessory, and every piece of jewelry being the trendiest and the most stylish. Leaving all that aside, they made her look "film quality." Today, she was adorned in a luminescent halter top under a glossy leather jacket, a sapphire blue pearl belt wrapped around her waist, black skin-tight pants, and topped off with black heels, adorned with faux-diamond glitter. Her hair was tied back, with the ponytail carefully resting on one shoulder, always a colored neck scarf—today in basic black—and her makeup was always perfect and never overdone. Every finger had a colored ring, and each wrist had multiple bracelets.

Eye Candy Image Salon was always packed with customers from the time it opened until its late night closing. Women came from every corner of Metropolis to be made to look like movie stars with its "fashion police" of makeup artists, hairdressers, manicurists, pedicurists, skincare techs, tattoo artists, wardrobe stylists, and even dressers to assemble their wardrobe, if needed. The establishment was owned by Prima Donna, the Matron Queen of Metropolis fashion, who still had the magic touch after so many decades and personally tended to their oldest and highest-tipping clients.

China Doll was Prima's number one and was boss in her absence. Like every other fashionista employee, she wasn't some by-the-hour laborer. This was a coveted and highly competitive career, and everyone who worked in the parlor had advanced degrees in beauty and skincare, fashion and style arts, health, and nutrition.

The interior of Eye Candy was designed like a beehive design, and every section was visible, due to its transparent walls, to every other section, except the break room, full body baths, and the bathrooms. Eye Candy was nothing but carefully coordinated chaos—women sitting on chairs getting their hair and makeup done in one section, their nails and toenails in another, facials in another, tattoos in another (always temporary to change according to current fashion trends), skincare consultations in another, and style analysis wardrobing in yet another section.

China Doll walked back into the spacious waiting lobby, filled with eager clients, and looked at the counter computer screen for the next name.

"Mrs. Fancy, come on down and get that cougar self in my chair."

An elderly woman with platinum blonde hair and dressed in a shimmering navy dress hopped up from the waiting chair, smiling. "I'm ready, China."

"No, Mrs. Fancy. You'll be ready when we're done with you, apply your fave au courant perfume, and top it off with a splash of glitter."

She went by China Doll, but women who knew her called her China; men called her Doll. Only her family and Cruz called her by her real name—Dot.

She led Mrs. Fancy past her busy colleagues, working on their customers in the large hive hairdressing section. Busy at work were Cyan, who had a million outfits, but all were the same color of cyan; Pinkie, one of the newer girls, known for her bright pink hair; Goat Girl, another new girl, known for the large ring hanging from her nose septum; and Lipps, who had quite the set of augmented lips. Then there was the boss herself, Prima Donna, decked out in an amazing white and black outfit.

Mrs. Fancy, as a client for over twenty-five years, knew the routine and climbed into the styling chair.

"Found him?" Cyan asked China Doll.

"I have my people on it."

Cyan and the other stylists laughed or smiled.

"Your people?"

"Yeah, my people. I have that kind of juice."

"Listen to her," Pinkie said.

"So, how did that boyfriend of yours get away without your people seeing him?" Cyan asked.

"He's playin' games. The key to tracking Cruz is tracking his hovercar. Find the hovercar, find the man."

"How hard can that be, then? He rides that bright red Pony of his that you can see five miles away, even in the fog and rain."

"He can't get away. We're having dinner with my parents."

The girls began to laugh.

"What?" China asked.

"That explains it," Cyan said.

"Want to see how fast a man can run?" Prima Donna chimed in. "Tell him he has to have a meal with his future parents-in-law. All you'll see is a dust cloud, streaking through the water on the ground. Isn't that right, Mrs. Fancy?"

"That's how it was with all four of my husbands," she said and everyone laughed.

"That's how it was with all five of mine," Prima said, getting more laughs.

"That's not Cruz. He's different."

"Where is he, then?" Cyan asked.

"Maybe he's getting styled up like Mrs. Fancy."

"Oooh. Going to a competitor," Pinkie said. "That's not copacetic."

"No, he wouldn't do that. He's one of those men, who thinks he can do a decent job himself with his clippers, scissors, and a hand mirror. My people will find him. He can't hide."

"Hey, what about our meeting tonight?" Goat Girl asked.

"The meeting goes on as planned. China has a life outside of politicking," Prima said.

"Politicking?" Mrs. Fancy asked.

"Yeah, we're organizing the world against them evil, job-stealing robots," Goat Girl answered.

"It's disgusting what the world has become. How could anyone allow a robot to style their hair or do a manicure? It's unnatural," Mrs. Fancy said. "I'm not talking to any walking toaster for fashion advice."

"You tell 'em, Mrs. Fancy," Goat Girl said.

"I wish everyone was as human-centric as you, Mrs. Fancy," Prima said.

"They want the robots to steal all our jobs," China said.

"Can they really do that?" asked another seated female customer. "Who's going to allow a robot scissor-hands near their head? Not me."

"Oh, it's bad," Goat Girl said. "They got them non-humanoid robots— those helmet-heads and finger-suckers."

The women laughed.

"Oh my, what are those?" Mrs. Fancy asked.

"Goat Girl already named them," Pinkie said.

Prima answered, "You put the 'helmet-head' on. That's what the robot looks like, and it can cut and style your head in ten seconds."

"If it doesn't lobotomize you, first," Pinkie added.

"That's what I'm saying. And the finger-suckers can cut your fingernails and paint them in five seconds. Or your toes, so they say. Robot hands with no fingers, just holes."

"Imagine putting your digits in those nasty holes."

The women laughed again.

"That is so gross, Goat Girl."

"That's the Brave New World," Prima continued. "A world where the humans have no jobs."

"So what about tonight?" Goat Girl asked. "The meeting."

"We're meeting," Prima answered.

"What are you all doing?" another customer asked.

"We're organizing all the hair stylists, manicurists, pedicurists, skin techs, nutri-techs, tattoo artists, fashion consultants, and fashion stylists into a union," China replied. "We're not going to allow robots to steal our jobs."

"Who's behind all this?" Mrs. Fancy asked.

"The two-headed snake. The suck-your-wallet-dry megacorps and our tax-payer funded suck-your-paycheck-dry uber-governments," Prima answers. "We won't let them get away with their schemes on our watch."

"That's right," Goat Girl said. "Hell no on our watch."

"Sounds exciting," Mrs. Fancy said. "Are you going to have supporters?"

"Oh yes, Mrs. Fancy. We're going to need tons. You won't have to be a fashionista or even a client to join and support our union."

"All you have to be is human," Goat Girl interjected.

"Well, I think I'm human." Mrs. Fancy said, laughing. "Well, China? Am I human or a well-kept android?"

"You're the real deal, Mrs. Fancy. One-hundred percent, grade-A human."

"China!" one of the stylists from the back room called out. "Vid-phone."

China Doll looked at her and yelled, "Is it Cruz?"

"Nah, it's one of Run-Time's guys."

China looked at the women. "My people." She looked back at the new stylist. "Tell them to tell you the facts. I'm with a client."

The young woman disappeared through the bead curtains to the break room.

"Oh China, you can take the call if you need to," Mrs. Fancy said.

"But I have people, Mrs. Fancy."

The new stylist came out from the back room and walked to them. "He asked if you know a guy named Phishy?" she said.

"Yeah, I know Phishy. That's one of Cruz's frenemies. Why?"

"He knows where Cruz is at."

"How would he know that?"

The young woman shrugged. "I don't know."

"I'll phone that slider when I have Mrs. Fancy settled in nicely under the hair dryer. How would Phishy know where Cruz is?"

"Here Phishy, Phishy," Cyan joked.

Prima glanced at China. "You put the word out, and they got back to you fast."

"Well, he's not on the other end of my mobile or standing in front of me, yet," China Doll said. "We shall see."

CHAPTER 4

Phishy

Phishy.

Metropolis was not overflowing with life; it was choking on it. Water wasn't a precious commodity here—it was a curse, alternating between always raining or about to rain. It was space that was sacred. People were stacked on top of one another in flashing super-skyscrapers that reached into the dark skies. Hover vehicles buzzed around; jetpackers zipped around; drones gyrated around, all in the airspace above the crowds. The only real open public space was the sidewalks. That was where the spontaneous action happened daily and not from the average masses of automaton-like city citizens, that passed through, going about life. The sidewalks had the real action from the people, who made it the center of their universe.

However, sidewalk life had its problems, too. It was the "real hustle"—scamming and scheming for cash—that created the problem. Homelessness had been eradicated long ago, like polio and cancer; housing was mandatory for all, even for those without a legacy. But sidewalk johnnies were like the weeds you heard about that ruined a man's plush green lawn in the old days. Hanging around, watching trouble, causing trouble, hustling, looking for a hustle, but doing little of anything meaningful. They congregated, watched, chatted it up, sat around, smoked, joked, disappeared to the johns when needed, or disappeared to their sleep shack for a few hours—and repeat. At least, they were harmless. Like a piece of litter—step around it and ignore.

Dope daddies were different, perpetually pushing their "product" on an eager clientele of dope fiends itching for their daily fixes—only the rain was more persistent. Nowadays, the fiends were appropriately called dope roaches. That's what they were: come out to feed (their fix) and disappear back into the darkness. Dope daddies had it down to a science, and for every one of them the cops sent to prison camp, any one of their lookouts, street corner chiefs, low-level pavement pushers, or runners, would readily step up to take their place. An endless cycle of street drug life. The only way to dry up the illegal drug swamp was to get rid of the addicts. The only way to get rid of the addicts was to...get rid of people. But the cops did what they could to maintain, at least, an ordered chaos.

Then there were the in-between situations. Street hustlers, front street freddies, like Phishy. A little non-narcotic running here, a bit of courier work there, whatever scam he could get into to bring in some extra cash. Nothing illegal enough to get him a solid prison stint, but always at the level where if he got caught, he'd get no more than a mere misdemeanor situation—pay the fine and be on his way, not even a blot on the record. Cops and courts couldn't be bothered with street hustlers working non-violent, low money scams. In a vile world, you had to set your priorities properly.

Phishy always wore a dark colored vest and pants, but underneath was always some off-white colored, long-sleeve shirt extravaganza with colored fish all over it. He had a street name to maintain. He strutted down the street, side-stepping the sidewalk johnnies and sallies, saying hello to friends, slapping a high or low five as he went along.

"Yo, Phishy," the food truck guy called to him.

It was Dog Man. Only hovergarbage trucks were more ubiquitous than hoverfood trucks. In Metropolis, you didn't have to go out in the rain on a food-run if you didn't want to; the food would come to you. But most hoverfood trucks staked out their turf either in the air or on the ground.

Dog Man had the perfect corner, with six lanes of pedestrian traffic on the ground, and the same above him in the air. His hovertruck never flew anywhere anymore; it was a permanent fixture on the corner, open twenty-fours a day. Man! He could make a damn good hot dog. His food truck "owned" this street. In other words, he paid a wad of cash to the city to get exclusivity for his main truck here and two more at the other end of two more streets.

"What's up, Dog?" Phishy asked as he neared the truck. The aroma was like a drug itself.

"Do you know where Cruz is, Phishy?"

"What? Why you askin' me?"

"It's not me," Dog said. "Run-Time has the all points out for him."

"I haven't seen him since Wednesday."

"Well, if you see him, call Run-Time. Maybe you can get some cash out of it."

"Hardly." Phishy frowned. "You have to be a customer to get anything from Run-Time. Otherwise, he's as cheap as the Scrooge on Christmas Eve."

"Meaning you tried to scam him, and it didn't go well."

"I try to scam everybody, even my friends. If I didn't, that would be like discriminating."

"If you say so, Phishy. How about a dog?"

"Oh man, Dog Man. You're worse than the dope daddies. You're selling the wiener version of hard narcotics out of this food truck. I get fat, I can't fit into my clothes, and I don't earn enough to get an all new wardrobe."

"Half a dog won't put any fat on them bones. You can skip the sauces."

"You can't have a dog without the sauces, and a beverage to wash it down. That would be just plain wrong." Phishy pointed at him. "Half a dog with my favorite sauce, spicy hot, beverage, and that's it. Put it on my tab."

Dog Man started to get his hot dog. "Phishy, I don't know why you keep using that line. You have no tab with me or anyone else. Pull that cash out that I know you have, and I don't want any wet or dirty bills."

"I told you, I try to scam even my friends." Phishy reached into his vest pocket for his cash.

He could feel his mobile phone vibrate on his belt. He grabbed it.

"Phishy, Phishy, Phishy," he answered.

"Why do you do that?" the voice said. "Are you like two years old?"

"Yo, China Doll."

"Don't 'yo' me. Where's Cruz?"

"Why is everyone asking me about Cruz? I haven't seen him since last Wednesday. Do you have everybody looking for him?"

"Yeah."

"What'd he do?"

"No one can find him."

"Men need their alone time, too. Leave him alone. He'll show up when he shows up."

"I know you know where he is."

"I haven't seen him since last Wednesday. But if I do, I'll tell him he found a great hiding place and keep hiding there."

"Don't make me come down there, Phishy. Tell him he better not even think of not making dinner today. He knows how important it is."

"Dinner?"

"Yeah."

"Can I come in his place? I'll be hungry again."

"Uh...no."

"Why you got to be like that, China Doll? Phishies need food too."

"I'll save some goldfish food for you, then. You know what you have to do. Use those street skills of yours and find him."

"You got Run-Time looking for him. Now me. Did you call the police and national guard?"

"I don't need them. That's what I got people for."

"Do I get a few bills if I find him?"

"No, but you can have the goldfish food. Bye, Phishy."

"Bye, China Doll."

Phishy returned the mobile to his belt. "See how I'm treated, Dog Man."

His mouth watered at the sight of the hot dog on a petite plate in Dog Man's hand.

"You got something for me, Phishy."

"Oh yeah. I was distracted."

Phishy reached back into his vest pocket for his cash. He revealed a bill. "Here doggy-doggy." He slapped the bill down on the food truck service counter.

"I'll assume you're talking about the half hot dog." Dog Man buttered on Phishy's spicy sauce and then handed him the plate. He made change quickly and before Phishy could speak, said, "Beverage coming up." He grabbed a cup, hit the dispenser for ice, and then another for beer. "Know what I'm going to say now?"

Phishy had the entire half dog already stuffed into his mouth. "You're going to give me the other half for free."

"Don't forget about Cruz," Dog Man said. "You get distracted easy. So where is he? If everybody is calling you, then you know where he is."

Phishy kept chewing. "I'm still thinking about it. I'm a man who reacts to incentives."

"Phishy, don't make that girlfriend of his come down here and stomp you into the pavement."

CHAPTER 5

Punch Judy

Punch Judy.

She sat on the mega-steps of the housing complex with a cloud of pink smoke flowing from her mouth and a long-stem cigarette dangling from her fingers. Her short hair was the darkest of crimson. She wore mirrored glasses on her face and had a simulated mole, a dot, above her pinkish lipstick-covered lips. Black leather jacket with a plastic hood, pants, and heeled boots was what she often wore. The jacket hung open to show her holographic, colored top, with the initials "PJ".

Back in the day, Judy was a soldier in the punk-posh gang, Les Enfants Terribles in Neo-Paris, France. Haute-couture designer clothes—the most expensive right off the racks of Goodwill—with fashion-matched combat boots, knuckle-studded, leather, half-gloves, and Devo-style half-helmets on their rainbow colored, punk hair. They were "royalty."

But then, the gang got greedy and it all went wrong. They started to believe their own hype and tried to extend their territory way beyond the French quarters. Posh gangs never do well in direct confrontation with feral gangs of chaos or long-game, Moriarty-planning, brainiac gangs. It was like the Fall of Old Paris all over again. Les Enfants Terribles, The Terrible Children gang, was decimated in mere days by rival (real) gangs in one show of unity. The gang war left many parts of Neo-Paris burning and most of the Les Enfants Terribles dead.

Punch Judy was crazy, even then, when it came to loyalty. She could not let it go and went to war with all of them by herself, tracking key leaders outside of the country. A murderous chase through the streets of Metropolis in her self-made death-mobile led to a horrific accident, pinning her body in a burning wreck, as enemy gang members stood and laughed nearby. Then Cruz happened.

Even if she wasn't an ex-felon, there would be very few jobs available to an ex-gang member, like her, with psych problems. Her days were spent mostly like today—smoking on the stoop, wasting her life away, while watching people walk by, the hovercars fly above, the rain fall from the sky, and counting the raindrops.

"Punch!" She heard the man's voice, but didn't see him.

She lethargically looked up with her mirrored, wet shades to the first apartment window above her. A pudgy man looked down at her from a large, open window. She stared back without a word; she liked to sit in the rain. The feel of the drops made her feel content.

"Are you not going to answer me?" he shouted.

She took a draw from her cigarette.

"No wonder you have no friends."

"I have no friends," she answered in a contemptuous French accent, "because they were all killed."

"How long ago was that? Why do you sit under my window? I'd pay good money to switch with my neighbors not to see you under my window."

"You say the same things every time I see you, you stupid man. What do you want?"

"Don't you carry a mobile?"

"Stop asking me stupid questions you know the answer to, you stupid man."

"Turn it on! People are calling me, like I'm your personal secretary."

"Who is it?"

"I'm not your personal secretary! Turn on your mobile and find out for yourself!"

The man disappeared back into his apartment and slammed the window shut.

She placed her cigarette in the corner of her mouth as she reached into her jacket pocket. As soon as she flipped it on, it rang. She looked at the outside display screen, but didn't recognize the number.

She answered it and saw the tiny face of China Doll on the display.

"How did you get my number?"

"Where's Cruz?"

"Why are you asking me?"

"Maybe, because you're the sidewalk sally who sits in front of his building all day long."

"I am not a sidewalk sally!"

"Where's Cruz?"

"I don't know, and I don't care, and I wouldn't tell you if I did know and care."

"Tell him I'm looking for him."

"No, I won't."

"And call me immediately."

"No."

"As soon as you see him."

"No."

"Now you can go back to doing whatever nothing you were doing, you sidewalk sally."

"I am not a sidewalk sally! I live in this building!"

"Whatever."

"I am—"

It clicked before she could finish. She cursed in French and crushed the mobile phone to pieces with her bionic hand. "Chinese donkey, I hate you!" She threw the pieces of the mobile into the air, showering the steps with fragments everywhere.

"Hey!"

Four of the local sidewalk johnnies watched her.

"I'm sorry," she said to them.

"I thought you were one of us, Punch," one of them said.

One could see the men were dressed decently under their gray slicker coats. It must have been a multi-buy sale, because the slickers were identical and all had their hoods covering their heads. Their faces were another matter. Weathered faces with scraggly mustaches, beards, and heads of hair. This particular crew of sidewalk johnnies wore subtle yellow shades.

"I am one of you," she answered, standing to her feet.

"That's not how it sounded when you were talking on the mobile, Punch. It's like you're ashamed of us," another man said.

"No, that's not true. She was disrespecting you, not me. I'm an adopted sidewalk sally. You know that. I have problems. You know that."

"We all got problems, Punch. Every last person in this city has problems, even the ones who pretend they don't."

"Absolutely true." She walked down the steps towards them and could see in their expressions that they were not happy with her. "No hard feelings. I'm always here with you. We look out for each other. Isn't that true?"

"Yeah, but if you don't want to associate with us anymore—"

"No! I won't hear any more about it. We are the guardians of the streets. We know better than anybody what the street is capable of. We must stay united because the street can get angry. We're the line of defense against that. Besides, you know I say all kinds of things. That's why I try to keep from talking. When I talk, fifty percent of what comes out of mouth will be stupid. Isn't that true?"

The men smiled.

"Okay, Punch. Everyone deserves another chance," one of them answered.

"Exactly. Now help me do something. I need the eyes and ears of the street. Do you know where Cruz is now?"

"I thought you told the person on the mobile you weren't going to look for him."

"I'm not. I'm using my connections to do it, but not for her. It's for me."

The men looked at each other. "We haven't seen Cruz."

"Me, neither."

The other two men shook their heads, too.

"I saw him pull out the place early this morning in his ride, headed east, but that's it," one of them added.

"He goes out. He has to come back," Punch Judy said. "We'll just wait for him."

"Do you think we can get some money out that person on the mobile?" one of the men asked.

She gave him an askance look. "Doubtful. His girl wants to know where he is."

"Oh, China Doll."

"We like her," said another man.

"I hate her. I hate him."

"That's no way to talk, Punch. Cruz is cool."

"He is not cool."

The men laughed.

"Since it's for China Doll, we'll put the word out on the street to find him," one of them said. "Should we bring the 411 to you?"

"No, I don't care."

"We'll get it to China Doll, then."

"We like China Doll," another man said.

"No, tell me too, then."

"Why?"

Punch Judy thought for a moment. "I don't know, but I want to know, too. I'll think of a reason later."

"Okay."

The four sidewalk johnnies scuttled away into the drizzling rain. She turned to walk back up the mega-steps to her sitting spot.

She hated that everyone liked Cruz. But she liked that someone else didn't like Cruz either—Cruz, himself.

PART THREE

I'm Cruz. Watcha Want?

CHAPTER 6

I, Cruz

"I'm Cruz. Whatcha want?" That's how I greeted strangers. Though, I had to admit that it was somewhat of a rude and snarky response, but, hey, I didn't like strangers. I liked my friends, my frenemies, and even my enemies—all of them I knew, but strangers, I had no regard for. My girlfriend, frequently, scolded me on my bad manners, saying "a stranger is a friend you haven't met yet." I had a far less charitable definition of them. Social scientists predicted that the bigger a city gets, the higher the anti-sociability of its people. There was no city bigger than Metropolis, and I was born and raised here, and most of my waking thoughts were about how to get out of here, so I wouldn't die here.

My name is Cruz. My first name is unimportant, because no one ever calls me by it, not even my parents.

Calling Metropolis a city was like calling me a molecule. True, but what exactly did that even mean? Demographers and assorted eggheads had semi-decided on its official classification—supercity, beating out less popular terms, such as omni-city, over-city, and ultra-city. At least everyone agreed that mega-city was inadequate. That's what it was called when it was ten times smaller than it was today. Fifty million people living, breathing, and dying in a rainy supercity in a world of super-skyscrapers.

Metropolis wasn't a bad place, but it wasn't a good one, either.

Here, I sat in my vehicle with my face almost pressed against the driver's side window, looking out at the downpour and watching the rain roll down the glass. Astronomers said it rained diamonds on Jupiter and Saturn. Well, this wasn't there, and even the ladies would tire of a constant diamond downpour; probably would cut every living and inanimate thing to shreds, too. This was Metropolis, where it was always raining or about to rain. The only seasons were variations of the perpetual rain—light rain, heavy rain, or the storm season. There was one month of a break during the year, which would be fine if the year had only two months, but it had twelve.

People said the sky was black, but that wasn't true. The dark clouds above that encased the city only pretended uniformity. If you stared at them long enough, they would let you peek through their facade. It was like gray people on the streets—everyone looked the same from afar in their dark slickers, but they all managed individuality, somehow. I saw the sky's dark blues, purples, dark greens, mustard yellows, and grays, too.

Besides the *pitter-patter* of the rain hitting my vehicle, the only other sounds were from the old monorail line about thirty feet above me. I could hear its hissing rumble every fifteen minutes. I wanted to be left alone to rain-watch and meditate, or whatever I was doing in my head. My vehicle was parked on the ground in an alley and the only people around were the scarce few who walked past the entrance to another alleyway, fifteen feet from me. Other than that, there was no one to bother me—no sidewalk johnnies, no troll moles, no passing garbage hovertrucks, and no juvenile delinquents, skipping school and looking to do crimes.

My mobile phone had been off since last night. Who knows how many messages I had waiting? But I didn't care. I needed my alone time.

Twenty-four hours, seven days, three-hundred-sixty-five or fifty-two weeks or twelve months. The endlessness of it all.

I had been in a funk for the last few days. It happened every year before, on, around, and after my birthday. I was always especially morose during this time. An evil day invented to force you to take stock of the thing called life. I wouldn't want to be around myself, which is why I segregated myself from friend and foe for as long as possible, until the spell passed.

I felt trapped, like a bug in a spider's web. Everybody followed this system of life, from the littlest guy shuffling to and from his nine-to-five, all the way to those god-like guys, living above us all, consumed by their own power and fortune. We all had the same basic concerns, but in the end, we all ended up at the same place—meat at the morgue. The masses did a lot in that in-between time to go about life in the rain with style— designer Goodwill wet-wear clothes and colored neon shades—to blot from the mind the fundamental drudgery of it all. To survive to your ultimate destination, you had to know your place, not upset the order of things. You either worked for the international, multinational megacorps, or you worked for uber-government, the "state," and, though you'd never get Up-Top, you could retire free-and-clear for your last decade or two of life. It was the unsaid, universal contract that most accepted.

But I had tried to make my futile mark on the cosmos with my contrarian self. I avoided umbrellas; instead, I wore my tan fedora. I didn't wear neon shades, and I didn't wear dark-colored slickers; instead, I wore my favorite tan coat. Everyone had dark colored hovercars; I drove a bright red, classic Ford Pony. That's what I did to separate myself from the masses—pathetic and pointless, but did it anyway and could do no different.

What the hell have I even accomplished? If I clocked out of life, what exactly would be my legacy? I hated my birthdays. My parents told me I hated them, even as a kid, the time you're supposed to be the most optimistic in life, even despite all the sweet birthday cakes and presents from every known relative on the planet. My girlfriend said I needed to stop my annual "morose period." "There are people in the world with no food to eat or born with no eyes or limbs or born mentally retarded. What is your complaint?" she'd say to me. "An innocent kid was shot in the head today and will be brain-dead for the rest of his life, or a woman had her kid crushed by a drunk driver in a hovercar," she'd add.

True, I had no serious tragedies to complain about. No great losses. No disabilities. I had all my fingers, toes, limbs, and other natural organs—not a bionic part anywhere. Metropolis hadn't been bad to me.

Everyone simply had to accept it all. I did. But this was an especially bad year of reflection for me, which is why I was here sitting in my red Ford Pony, hiding out on a street I've never been, far from any part of the city I had ever been, so I could just sit, stare at the falling rain, and simmer in my own perennial moroseness and not be bothered by the girlfriend, friends, enemies, frenemies, sidewalk johnnies, hustlers, or any strangers.

The only interruption to the steady rain was the ubiquitous flashing neon and video signs. I paid no attention to the specific ads or messages they were peddling. It was always the same. The corporate ads wanted you to buy something, and the government ads wanted you to do something. The average citizen, in a normal day, was supposedly bombarded by no less than 50 thousand messages in the city. No wonder people were stupid. All those subliminal messages were taking up all the free space in a person's brain—the universe's ultimate disk hardware.

My hiding spot was one of the few less bombarded parts of the neon jungle. The neon signs, video ads, flashing street lights, flashing beacons for sky traffic, and building side lights should have been overwhelming, but we were all born into it—the visual madness. Most even thrived on it. Without the artificial light, all there would be was the dark, rainy, griminess of the city's urban landscape. That's what the colored eyewear that everyone always wore outside was really for—mitigation, being a must-have piece of technology was an after-thought.

I had found a damn good hiding spot. I had set down in the residential alley, in the early morning hours, between two monolith buildings in Silver City—the center of the city's robotic production. I was lucky, because such spaces between super-skyscrapers were not by design, but evidence of a building oversight. Buildings pushed up into the dark sky and sprawled out vertically to cover every inch. With people stacked on top of each other, building by building, space was one of the most important commodities. And here I was, lounging around in the unplanned alleyway, the hovercar equivalent of a sidewalk johnny, staring up at the rain. It was a good hiding spot, and I planned to use it often.

I saw it. The hovertaxicab descended from the uppermost part of the alleyway, on the left, about twenty-five feet or so in the air.

"Damn," I said to myself. It was one of Run-Time's.

I chose Silver City because, since it was so automated, there were far fewer workers here than the rest of the City. Less people meant less public transportation, less hovercars, and less hovertaxis. But they found me anyway.

The hovercab rose back in the air and did a one-eighty to fly away, back the way it must have come.

The cabbie would call dispatch, and dispatch would call Run-Time. If Run-Time was looking for someone, and you were in Metropolis, consider yourself found, unless you were hiding down in the sewers with water rats, "un-killable" jumbo roaches, and whatever roly-poly isopods were lurking and swimming around in the filth. No one did that. I didn't need to check my mobile. I knew people were looking for me. For a nobody, I sure was treated like a somebody.

All I had to do was push a button to start the engine of my classic Ford Pony. High-performance, super-charged, advanced nitro-acceleration hydrogen engine. A sleek, bright red muscle-vehicle coupe to make the average person gawk and the mouths of the genuine hovercar enthusiast and collector hang open.

I had found the shell in a junkyard over fifteen years ago, when I was in middle school and it took me a few years to build and restore it, spare part by spare part. I had been upgrading it ever since. No one believed that I found and built such an expensive muscle hovercar from scratch, but it was true, and I drove it every day. It was considered a true classic and got me solid offers to part with it almost every week, but you don't sell a classic Ford Pony; it's a purchase for life—like a legacy house. My Pony had been featured (without my permission) in so many hovercar magazines that I lost count.

I coasted out of the alleyway without revving the engine. I wanted no more than a purr out of it. If "they" were coming for me, I had to make my getaway quietly. That's what I did. Not even turning on my car lights, I flew out of the alley, waited for my chance, and drove into the empty sky-lane. I'd stay under the monorail line bridge, as long as I could, to avoid Run-Time's taxis. Big Brother government had nothing on Run-Time's civilian surveillance of cabbies throughout the city. They were better than any drone army.

I thought to myself that the refrigerator at home was empty, so I might as well do some grocery shopping. Yes, I had the upcoming Great first dinner with Dot's folks, which probably was the other contributing factor to my post-birthday blues.

At the time, I had no idea that an operator, named Easy Chair Charlie, who had sold me my semi-illegal, nitro-accelerator for my Pony years ago, got himself killed the night before.

CHAPTER 7

The Good Kosher Man

I felt naked parking my vehicle outside on the regular street without any kind of security. I used a guy from Run-Time's service, named Flash, so often, some people felt he came with the vehicle. But if I wanted to hide out, then that was the price. And "hide" was a laughable word to use with a bright red hovercar in a city where everyone's vehicle was gray, black, some shade of blue, or, to be daring, silver. I draped my Pony with the car cover in the trunk and locked it to the car. At least no one would see its shiny red paint from afar.

This was Woodstock Falls, and I gave the street—Graffiti Alley—one more glance in both directions. Despite its name, there wasn't, and never was, a speck of graffiti anywhere, ever. Woodstock Falls was a safe, working-class, multiethnic, but mostly Jewish, neighborhood. Like similar working-class neighborhoods, residents and business owners fiercely kept the trash—human and otherwise—away. The reason why was simple—the residents didn't just work here; they lived here. The bottom half of the monolith skyscrapers were the businesses and all above to the top was residential. No hovercar, taxis, or bullet train needed for them. Transportation for them was a simple stroll down the hallway to the elevator capsule.

Graffiti Alley may have had no graffiti, but it should have. It was secluded and dark, and though it was a main street, had the feel of an out-of-the-way back alley, where bad things were supposed to happen. There was never a lot of traffic, and the foot traffic was always sparse. I wondered how the businesses were able to stay afloat financially.

I wondered that about every business, except one. Good Kosher.

The only reason to go to Graffiti Alley was The Good Kosher Market. After all these years, I couldn't tell you the name of any other business on the street. Good Kosher took up the entire length of the street, and that's saying a lot, since streets were ginormous in Metropolis. Food came in three categories—processed (practically everything sold on the market), organic (supposedly the "healthier" alternative"), and natural—or, as I would say, "straight from the dirt." I never shopped anywhere else. I didn't eat processed and felt the whole "organic" thing was nothing but a scam (by the unholy coupling of government and megacorps) to overcharge people for food. I only ate natural food and Mr. Watts and his five sons had been serving nothing else for more than a century. It was like many generational businesses. I was a devoted customer and member of its select clientele for the last twelve.

Graffiti Alley may have been practically empty, but inside, Good Kosher was packed. I always felt people were teleported into the store by Scotty's grandson, because my words when entering were always, "Where did all these people come from?"

Inside, it looked like an underground football stadium with neon rows of product. People zipped around on hovercarts of all sizes. In traditional markets, the products came to you. Here, you got your own stuff. Other than the hovercarts, there really wasn't any machination of any kind, which was rare for any modern store. But it was a "natural" market, so the presence of robots might clash with the store's image. The sons, however, wore mech-gloves with store inventory displays on the wrist area, and the hand section was telescopic to pull down things from the top shelves, without ever having to get a ladder. The gloves probably had a million other uses, like a Swiss-army knife.

I grabbed a small hovercart near the entrance, sat in the small single seat, and began my spree. The other thing that made the store so popular was precisely because nothing ever changed—fruits and vegetables were on aisle 20, juices and milk products on aisle 15, teas and coffees on aisle 16, meats on 5 and 6, etc. No one needed to ask where anything was, because everyone already knew. Good Kosher was not into anything gimmicky or faddish. Mr. Watts would say, "Nothing gets on my shelves that hasn't been in the general market and people have been eating for at least a thousand years." Funny, but true.

"I'm glad to see you continue to eat good food, young man," he said to me as I leaned on the main counter, opposite him. "More young people need to embrace that. The human body is a machine, and it always needs the best power to be put into it. I'm glad to see your hovercar enthusiasm has shown you the way to live a long life. Good fuel, car lasts forever. Good foods, human body lasts a little less than that."

I nodded. "My favorite power station for my Pony. Good Kosher for me."

"I see a question on your tongue. Mr. Cruz."

Mr. Watts knew me too well. "Is it customary to get a future mother-in-law something? Like flowers?" I asked.

When you were a fixture of a neighborhood for so long, own such a popular business for so long, employ the same workers and cater to the same clientele, it didn't take long for everyone to feel like you truly were family. Every family had a sage—the wise, ol' uncle or wise, ol' grandmother. Mr. Watts was our sage. You did your shopping first, one of his five sons rung up the order at the cash register, and then you spent however long chatting it up with the Good Kosher Man himself.

I didn't know how old Mr. Watts was, but he had to be in his late fifties at least, but there was nothing old about him. He had a full beard and mustache with the hair graying at the temple and the edges of his beard. Like his sons, the uniform was a khaki jumpsuit with a fully-equipped utility belt, beaded strings around the neck, and a pointed Chinese bamboo hat to protect from the constant exposure of the artificial daylight ceiling lamps, which all its indoor natural plant life depended. The skin techs at Eye Candy, where Dot worked, would be proud. He probably had the rare hats shipped directly from the Southeast Asia territories, back when they were affordable. No rice paddies here, but Good Kosher had its own interior gardens in the back and off-limits to customers, growing a wide variety of roses, tulips, and other flowers. Watts and sons would go back into that room, with its steady rain mist falling, and handpick bouquets for customers. Good Kosher was a secret flower shop too, and no one had better—if you wanted real ones and not synthetic "garbage" that everyone else sold that could survive a nuclear blast.

"Mothers-in-law don't get flowers, even if you like them. And even if they did, they surely wouldn't qualify being a future one. The future doesn't exist—there is only the present."

"Are you sure?" I asked, as one of his sons finished ringing up my order and I handed him my cash card. "It's very important I get on their good side."

Mr. Watts made a laughing sound. "They? So it's both the mother and father in-law. I don't envy you. First dinner?"

"Yeah."

"Dress nice and arrive before the arrival time. That's all you can do. Don't talk unless asked a question, even from the girlfriend. Just look cool."

I laughed. "I always look cool."

"Yes, you're a natural. But remember, they'll be watching you like a hawk."

"I'll be as nervous as spaceman flying through a meteor shower. Well, as long as there are no best practices for a thing like this."

"Be yourself," Mr. Watts said. "Don't think about. You think about it, and you'll get nervous. Think about something else."

"Like?"

Mr. Watts stopped and gave me a smirk. "Something appropriate."

I returned the smirk.

"Think about the next modifications to that inappropriately red hovercar of yours."

"Inappropriate?"

"I still say that vehicle is a police magnet."

"I never speed."

He shot me a look.

"On residential streets," I added.

Mr. Watts smiled. "What time is your date with the parents-in-law?"

I took out my vest pocket watch and looked at the digital display. He could hear me sigh.

"As I suspected. You've been stalling for time. You're not going to be dressed well and ahead of time if you're standing here in my store. Exit, stage right, immediately, Mr. Cruz. Assistance with your bags to your vehicle is complimentary."

He gestured, and two of his sons were standing next to me, grinning.

"But, but I don't want to go," I said.

CHAPTER 8

The Wans

Sometimes government passed a law that so radically changed the societal landscape that no one could remember what it was like before it. The landmark Jarvis Laws created, what was now called, Legacy Housing and did more to make the world we lived in than anything even the Founders did. It democratized the power of home ownership for everybody—like the modern mobile phone altered communication and media forever. Once a mortgage was paid off, it could be passed on to family and descendants forever. The politics and legal battles became which descendants would get it next, but the ancient real estate market disappeared with the dinosaurs and Dodo birds. Housing for the rich, poor, and everyone in-between was essentially free. But nothing ever turned out to be as it was intended in this world.

Elysian Heights was definitely "booshy"—the wealthy, bourgeoisie, upper-class of the down-here. The mega-apartment complexes, triple and quadruple the size of a football stadium, were two hundred-story plus into the sky. Each tower was like its own country, with its own dictatorial semi-autonomous residential government, its own paramilitary security force, and its own pleasure world. The only other place people coveted more was Up-Top.

This is the world my girlfriend, China Doll, came from. However, she worked in the Bohemian zone and was at home with working-class regulars, like me. Few knew she was born and raised in Elysian Heights, and fewer would believe it.

The rain was stinging, which I considered an omen of this "special" day. Visibility was bad, and I drove my Pony up to the main checkpoint entrance to the towers. A six-foot-five, musclebound guard walked to my driver's window to take my ID card, while a second one watched me from the guard shack—but it was no "shack." The guard found my name on his clipboard display and handed back my ID card. The massive metal gate began to lower and I watched the signal post off to the side. When it changed from red to green, I drove forward.

The interior streets were huge and empty. They were nothing more than the space between these mega complexes—no people, hovervehicles, or even plant life existed. All life that mattered was in the towers. I drove slowly, never going over the speed limit, and then flew into the open visitor garage for the China Towers. You would never see a sidewalk johnny here.

I felt like a man marching to his execution, as I took the parking elevator capsules up. When buildings are made this massive, elevators are designed more like autonomous, computer-controlled rocket ships. There's no other way to get up and down fast enough; cables would inevitably snap, no matter how well made. Imagine the sorry, sad-sack "pioneers" in the old days, being aboard an old-style elevator with cables unraveling and breaking when you're coming down from the 180th floor. Would you scream yourself to death before your elevator car crashed to become one with Terra Firma? I realized that thinking about elevator deaths was probably not the wisest activity while standing on an elevator now passing the 130th floor.

As I shuffled down the hallways that were better suited for vehicle traffic, because they were so wide, I took out my pocket watch. I was 31 minutes early. Now, if that didn't set me on the right foot with girlfriend and future parents-in-law, then nothing would. I stood at the door and looked at the door knocker in the center and then at the door bell on the side. This must be a psychological test; I was certain of it. Pick the wrong one, and I would be forever tainted in their eyes.

I lifted the door knocker and struck the door twice and rang the doorbell—at the same time!

The door swung open, and there was Dot. I looked at her and she looked at me. She was dressed in a modern blue and white kimono-style dress. I wore my same tan outfit as always, with a white shirt and dark vest, but wore a matching blue and white tie that Dot had bought me and told me to wear, and now I knew why. I guess she figured her parents would say, "Aww, how cute. They even match when they dress." As if it were that easy to win over the parents-in-law.

I could see she was at war within her own head, whether to be mad at me for hiding or glad that I showed up early.

"Oh, no, was it a lunch date with the parents and I'm late? I mixed it up then. I thought it was a dinner date and came early to impress you."

She held back a smile, then it appeared, then it turned to a frown. "You are so skating on thin ice, right now. I'll decide your fate after your performance tonight."

"As long as the three of you don't gang up on me. You know how fragile I am around my birthday."

"I don't want to hear it. I had an all-points bulletin out on you. Run-Time, and even Phishy and that sidewalk sally psycho in your building looking for you."

"Dot! Who dat!" A voice rang out in broken English from within the residence.

"Ma!" Dot yelled back, startling me, followed by a string of Chinese.

She pulled me inside and closed the door. It was my first time inside the Wan residence, and my head was already scanning around.

"Shoes at the door and off with the hat," she said and then continued speaking in Chinese to her parents.

I pulled off the slip-on boots and bent down to set them neatly against the wall near the door. My body seemed to sink an inch into the thick, white carpet. Dot was barefoot, her toenails painted black with a sparkling faux-diamond in the center of each toe. I noticed it was the same with her fingernails. How do women do that?

I hated to take off my hat. It either stayed on or it stayed off. I was not into switching back-and-forth. "I'll just keep it with me," I said to her, holding it in my left hand.

"Just don't set it on the dinner table."

"I'll throw it on this nice, fluffy carpet of yours."

"Let's meet my Ma and Dad."

Everything about the place was palatial—the hallway, the living room, and kitchen.

Dot was actually the spitting image of her father, only female. Mr. Wan was dressed in an almost glowing white shirt, with what looked to be various animals embroidered around the collar and the sleeves. Mrs. Wan was in black pants, but was wearing a beautiful electric blue top. She was shorter than Dot, with shoulder length hair.

I noticed immediately that they were smiling before they looked at me and were not smiling now as they watched me.

"These are my parents."

The only Chinese I knew, courtesy of my vehicle computer, was how to say "hello." I did so, twice— *"Nín hǎo"*—but, no response from the parents.

"My parents don't speak English, but they are very happy to meet you," Dot said.

That was a nice trick. She was translating for them when they weren't even talking. My girlfriend was in the wrong industry. Surely, telepathic translation could be a lucrative occupation.

"Oh, it's okay," I said. "My parents don't speak much English either." A lie.

This was going to be a long night, I thought, as I smiled again at them. They were completely emotionless, watching me.

"Cruz, you'll sit here." Dot took me by the hand and seated me in one of the ivory chairs at a fairly large square dining table.

She left me alone and returned to the kitchen with her parents. I reflexively jumped in my seat as an explosion of non-English yelling erupted from the kitchen. Now, I was glad I didn't speak Chinese. It sounded like the parents were letting her have it, but she was dishing it back at them. I've heard some pretty vicious shouting matches, including in my own Puerto Rican family, but as it continued, there were times I sincerely wondered if a call to the police might be warranted. It was brutal, and then it stopped.

Dot appeared, smiling, with a set of dishes, and her parents appeared, not smiling, with more dishes of food.

"My parents are so excited that we all finally get to meet," Dot said.

I sat quietly and smiled.

The Wans set the dishes on the table. Plates were passed around as they took their seats and then the utensils.

"Cruz eats with chopsticks all the time, Ma," Dot said.

Mrs. Wan gave her a questioning look, but after a combination of grunts and gestures from Dot, she understood. I lifted the chopsticks and smiled at the house matron. Mrs. Wan did not smile back.

Dot was the savior of the evening. She spoke to them in Chinese, then to me, and translated for all. After a while, it was almost fun as I never

119

had to "talk" to the folks. The food was exceptional. I had Chinese food plenty of times before, and it was never bad, but this was gourmet eating. I already made a note to get the recipes from Dot.

Then, darkness fell upon the land.

"I'll be right back," Dot said. "Little girls' room for me."

I watched China Doll walk off and disappear around the corner. I felt the knot in my stomach. My eyes turned to her parents. They hated me. I could see it in their eyes. The father's gaze was a glare. The mother had a snarling frown as she watched me. She leaned forward.

"You are a bum," she said and I was taken aback. "A bum! Why don't you go away? We will never permit our daughter to marry a bum. What are you? A Laborer." The woman knew how to hit below the belt. "That's your occupational title on your ID card. We know all about you. What is that, but a bum? You have no prospects, no job, no career, no future. You offer nothing to our daughter, because you are nothing. We will not permit our daughter to become nothing. Throw away all her hard work, her advanced degrees, her potential, her promising future as a businesswoman, leader, and role model for our community on a bum like you." She pointed her finger at me. "I will poison your food, you bum. You don't go away and leave our daughter be, we'll get you."

The father leaned forward my way and said, "We'll cut you. Cut, cut."

"Poison," the mother repeated. "I spit on your burrito!"

The flush from the bathroom reverberated throughout the house. Dot appeared smiling and looked at me. Obviously, her intention for leaving me alone with her parents was far different than the hell that had transpired.

"We should eat in the living room, and you can see the funny Chinese language TV my parents watch," she said.

I glanced at them—the mother had a slight smile on her face.

"Actually, though this is some of the best Chinese food I've ever eaten in my life, I have to get ready for a new job interview early in the morning."

"You didn't tell me that," Dot said.

"I wanted to surprise you, but...don't let that spoil the evening. This was great. It was nice meeting you, Mr. and Mrs. Wan. I have to turn in early."

"Take some food home with you," Dot said. "I insist."

"Okay."

"I should walk you down, too."

I laughed. "Going from here to the parking lot is like taking a shuttle to the moon. Stay. Don't worry about me."

"Are you sure?"

"I'm positive. Home-cooked meals and family time. You stay."

I didn't even notice the Wans were gone from the dinner table. Dot disappeared into the kitchen again, and there was that rapid-fire Chinese again. She returned with a brown paper bag. I peeked inside.

"Lunch and dinner for at least a few days," I said as I took the bag. "Maybe you can buy them those language tapes, so they can learn English. I'm sure they'd love to say things to me in English."

Dot half-laughed. "I've tried; believe me; I've tried. They're too stubborn."

I looked up, and there were the Wans again, watching me. Dot's back was turned to them, and they glared at me, but when Dot looked back at them, they quickly reverted to sweet, ol' impostors.

Dot walked me to the main door. "Job interview?"

"I'll tell you all about it at lunch tomorrow. Keep your fingers crossed." We stopped at the door. "Good night, Mr. and Mrs. Wan." I waved at them. I could act too.

"I'm going to walk you down."

It was pointless to try to dissuade her.

She did all the talking as we descended in the elevator capsule. My mind was elsewhere. I realized again that matrimony with Dot was a package deal. I get her, and I get them. The burrito crack was to tell me that they had snooped into every crevasse of my life, a full, dive-deep background check on me. I had eaten a burrito once, and it almost killed me. A friend (who ceased to be one after the incident) had spiked it with something I was allergic to, and I spent a month in the hospital. But that was when I was like nine. My future Mother Dearest wanted me to know they really did know everything about me. What must have really galled them was there was nothing to find. No felonies, no misdemeanors, not even an arrest, unlike ninety percent of the world. Most of their booshy Elysian tower-mates probably couldn't boast the same.

Half a comedian's jokes were about evil mothers-in-law, but I had to be lucky and get a real evil one, and an evil father-in-law as a special bonus. They couldn't get me by exposing some hidden, dark, criminal past to Dot, so they had to resort to the last refuge left to them—naked violence. Moms would poison me, and Pops would cut me. How could Dot be fooled by their innocent, old-country, sweetness persona? Nobody gets to an upper-level palatial apartment home in Elysian Heights by being anything other than a bastard. Marriage to Dot could be a very complicated matter in terms of my continued existence among the living. It would be such irony to avoid every street gang, government thug, and corporate knuckle-buster out there, only to be offed by your future parents-in-law. It's happened before.

We exited the elevator capsule, and the building parking bay was lined with black-suit-white-shirt-and-tie uniformed car attendants. There were on duty twenty-four-seven. No need for Run-Time's mobile car security here. Elysian Heights had its own, and they were armed, too.

"You didn't have to walk me all the way down," I said.

"I wanted to," she said.

"Hello, Ms. China Doll," one of the car attendants greeted.

"Hello, Guy. Keep sending me customers to the shop, and we'll keep making you look nice for the ladies."

He laughed. "They say I'm like an Up-Top Don Juan guy, Ms. China Doll."

Dot took my car keys from him and pressed the front door button. I realized that the valet already had my Pony waiting; obviously, the elevators had video surveillance too. She held the door open as I got in. She leaned over and gave me a kiss, but I knew it was a prelude to something else.

"What?"

"If I were to ask you something about my parents, you'd tell me the truth wouldn't you?"

"Of course, truthfulness is the foundation of any good, lasting relationship."

"Can my parents speak English?"

I looked at her for a moment.

"Not a word," I answered.

CHAPTER 9

Run-Time

I planned to drop by my favorite late night eatery, but instead, I just drove the city. I did it occasionally during those times when the Metropolis that never sleeps was at least taking a nap and there wasn't as much hovercar traffic in the sky. It wasn't raining, so I had my moon-roof open to feel the cool breeze zipping by at over a hundred miles an hour in the fast lane. My Pony needed its exercise, too.

It got back to Rabbit City after six o'clock in the morning. This was home. I stayed at the Concrete Mama. Rather than pull into my residential complex, I parked in front of the building with the moon-roof still open. I had picked up a quick, early-morning breakfast snack and sat in the car, munching a churro and drinking my sweet tea.

The hoverlimo that descended from the sky was unmistakable, even before seeing the neon "Let It Ride Enterprises" letters on both sides of the vehicle. It landed, and Mr. Run-Time, himself, exited and, instinctively knowing I was watching, waved.

"I heard that Dot had the cavalry looking for me," I said to him with the driver's side window rolled down and Run-Time half-leaning in.

"And then some. I thought at some point she'd call the police and Feds on you, too."

"That's what I heard."

"You must have found a good hiding place."

"One that I plan to use in the future."

Run-Time laughed. "I have a few myself, so I know how important they are for your alone time."

I nodded as I downed the last of my sweet tea.

"And you got to meet the future parents-in-law."

"I did." I said it with a hint of displeasure.

"What happened?"

"Are the Wans criminal bosses?"

He laughed again. "Dot's parents? If megacorp execs qualify as criminal bosses. They're bean-counters. That's how they made their fortune. Why? What happened?"

"Nothing." I sighed loudly. "All I want out of life is to get ahead and be content with what I've accomplished. All I can say at this stage of my life is that I'm a laborer. That's my listed occupation—laborer. That was my listed occupation when I was in high school, so I've accomplished nothing."

"Cruz, why would you say that?"

"Because it's true. I've been so principled. I wouldn't work for the government or some multinational, sitting in some cubicle. Yeah, and all my friends who did are managers and supervisors, and I sit in my little red vehicle as a laborer. When do I get my break? How long do I have to wait for my one break? I'm getting so tired."

"Cruz, everybody is struggling. Don't be fooled. You want to be them, and they want to be you. Everyone always thinks the grass is greener on the other side. Be patient. Your ticket will come.

"I know it looks nice on my company biography. The 'Run-Time rags-to-riches' story. I didn't drop out of middle school at eleven to begin my path of self-made millionaire. I dropped out, because I realized it was all pointless. Stay in and get good grades and amount to not much, like my father and so many others. Turn to crime like my uncle, and so many others, and end up dead or in jail. Those were my choices, I asked myself. Who makes up these rules? They say you have to be able to figuratively bend a spoon with your mind to make it in Metropolis. Says who? I said there was no spoon. I said the system is rigged, but not by the powerful. It's rigged by the powerless, trapped within it. The power to be either the powerless or the powerful is and has always been in my hands alone. I knew the cards the cosmos had dealt me from birth. This was my path in life, but was it my true destiny? No. That's exactly why I seized the opportunities I did. Because I knew what the future was, so why not make a different one? There's not a single, solitary thing to lose.

"Cruz, keep your nose clean as you always have, and your ticket will come. That much I can promise you. Don't mess it up now. You have too many years invested. You and I both have seen what happens to those who went for the quick-fix or supposed-sure thing, instead of being patient."

I always liked talking to Run-Time. He was a born motivational coach and life counselor. It's why we were friends for all these years. He talked the talk, and he exuded positivity. That's what I needed. I was too much of a glass-half-empty kind of guy. I needed to surround myself with the Run-Times and Dots of the world to pull myself out of the mind gutter.

"Yeah," I agreed soberly. "It's hard to be patient when everyone is passing you by. An endless rat-race, but I'm not getting anywhere."

"You got solid legacy housing, an amazing girlfriend, and a classic car that everyone wants. The housing and the car are just things, but don't discount Dot in your life. You got a lot more going for you in life than you're acknowledging. Here's the thing, Cruz. Just because people are passing you by, doesn't mean they'll finish the race. Just because they're passing you by doesn't mean they're going anywhere. Just remain Cruz, the cool cat that you are, and your ticket will come."

The Concrete Mama was a piece of work—architecturally speaking. It was like a chunk of granite set down on Earth from space. It was a no-frills monolith tower of legacy housing. If there was ever a planetary shockwave from a nuclear blast or an asteroid crash, you could bet the Concrete Mama would still be standing. It was ugly, but it would be here until the end of time in its ugliness. It was also my home for fifteen years.

My legacy housing was willed to me from my maternal grandparents. My parents had their own, so it was passed to me. Those of us who lived in the Concrete Mama were not rich and we weren't the working-class. We were just legacy babies—laborers. We had free housing for life, made a meager living to cover any other incidentals, and nothing more. I hated it here, but free is free.

Unlike modern buildings, you couldn't take the parking elevators directly to your floor. You had to go up to the lobby first and then take the elevator capsules to your floor. The lobby was a cesspool of sidewalk johnnies and looky-lous, all minding your business. I despised it. I exited the parking elevators and walked to the residential elevators as fast as I could, ignoring everyone.

I waited, as I always did, in a huff. The lobby was always a madhouse. Strangers all over the place, watching you, looking to see what you were carrying, and staring at anyone with you, if there was anyone with you. The indignity of it all. Lobby scum. It was like an episode of the Island of Doctor Moreau with animal people crawling around, hopping around, chasing their own tails, and sniffing each other's private parts.

"Did that girl of yours find you?"

I turned and it was Punch Judy. I almost didn't answer her.

"She did."

"Tell her not to call me! I am not your personal secretary!"

The elevator arrived, and I got in and pushed the button to force-close the doors. Punch Judy got mad and proceeded to curse at me in French.

The other thing I hated was that I was halfway up in the building. If I had been even one more floor up, I'd be in the premium section, where the apartments were double the size and almost as good as the penthouse levels. *C'est la vie*, as Punch Judy would say. Such was my unlucky life.

The hallways were always dimly lit, but I never felt uneasy walking to my place. I reached my suite—apartment 9732. With a sigh of relief, I pulled out my key, fastened by a chain to my belt, and unlocked my deadbolt. Immediately, a blast of air and mist enveloped me to eradicate all those external germs (more on that later). I was home now.

I lay on my bed with my right forearm on my forehead. I thought about what Run-Time had said. He was right, of course. You create your own destiny by altering your own perception of things. Maybe, I did over-exaggerate a bit earlier. Besides Punch Judy, there was only three other sidewalk johnnies in the main lobby, and the only sniffing they were doing was from the cigarettes they were smoking. I chose to view the situation as negative, so it was. I always got a little soft before I fell asleep, and it always took me awhile to do that. It was the sounds of pouring rain from my side table radio that always helped me sleep best. The Concrete Mama's walls were so thick that, even if there was a hurricane force rainstorm outside, you wouldn't hear a thing. That's why I had the sounds radio. The rain could always lull me to sleep. Unlike most of the population, I didn't hate it. I hated the lack of sun, but not the rain.

"Capitalize," I heard Run-Time's voice in my mind. "Capitalize on your opportunities, or someone else will."

I guess it was better to focus on a friend's life advice, rather than the fact my future parents-in-law threatened to kill me by poison or knife-attack at the dinner table. But to me opportunities were like the elusive electric butterfly in a video game. You see it, but you can never get to it. It's the programmer's demented idea of a joke. Like the story of Prometheus. Eat all that heavenly food in the temple you want, only a flock of cannibalistic harpies will rip your guts out with their claws afterward. Only a lucky few can ever really capture the real opportunities. This was Metropolis, not fantasy land. Fairy tales are as rare in this city as a full day of direct sunlight.

"Yeah?"

I had answered the phone, with the video off, and was talking, but my conscious mind had not yet engaged. My eyes were still closed and I could have been dreaming, actually.

"Cruz," Run-Time's voice continued. "I need a favor."

"Yeah."

"I need someone to kick around a bit and do some investigating."

"Investigating?"

"Technically, anyone can do it, but I want a third party. Someone reliable with street smarts, who can do things discreetly. I thought of you. You're not on any gigs now, right?"

"Yeah."

"Come on down to the office tomorrow morning."

"Yeah."

"And Cruz."

"Yeah?"

"Take a look at the newspapers before you come in. The story about an Easy Chair Charlie and his ill-advised shootout with the police."

"Yeah."

I was a true vocabulary virtuoso when I was half asleep.

The electric roller coaster of life was about to snatch me.

PART FOUR

A Case or Not?

CHAPTER 10

Fat Nat

Run-Time's business empire, Let It Ride Enterprises, took up most of its monolith tower in the trendy, but wealthy, Peacock Hills on Electric Boulevard. There were the business districts of "old" money, and there were the "new" money business districts, like Peacock Hills. There wasn't a president or CEO of any business on this street over the age of 45.

Let It Ride's clientele was always treated like royalty, whether they were a foreign dignitary or celebrity, or some working stiff who paid for no more than a simple hovertaxi ride from one end of the block to the other. But I was more than clientele today; I was expected by Founder, President, CEO, and COO, Mr. Run-Time, himself.

He had three VPs, and it was the Lebanese female one who escorted me from the lobby after I greeted the reception staff—I was on a first name basis with all three receptionists—straight to the Man's office.

Run-Time greeted me with a handshake and a hug as he did with all his friends. It was always as if it were the first time he ever met you, but that was part of his charm. He only wore slim fit business suits, the expensive kind, with slim ties, along with his trademark flat cap. He had suits to match every color of the natural and synthetic rainbow. Yesterday, when he came to see me, he was in greens; today, it was powder blue.

He led me to his huge ivory desk, exquisite in every possible way. The female VP had already moved a third chair to the front of the executive desk, next to the two other men who were already seated. I recognized them as soon as I was led into the office. Fat Nat of Joe Blows Smoking Emporium was the bigger man. I wasn't a smoker myself, but if you were part of the classic hovercar restoration or racing scene, you would have set foot in his place. Fat Nat was not fat at all, but I guess, Musclebound Nat didn't sound so good. With him was one of his buddies, who I had also seen before, Big G, but you called him G. He actually was fat and had the man-boobs to match. The men stood.

"Fat Nat," I said as I shook his hand. "Mr. G." I shook his hand.

We all took our seats.

"I've seen you before," Fat Nat said.

"Yeah," I answered. "Been to Joe Blows quite a few times. I'm into the hovercar restoration scene, and I've done some racing, just for kicks."

Fat Nat nodded with satisfaction.

"Cruz, did you have a chance to read the news?" Run-Time asked.

I leaned forward in my chair. "Easy Chair Charlie is dead?"

"Shot dead by cops," G said. "Well, shot dead in a shootout with cops."

Fat Nat looked at Run-Time. "I don't mean to be disrespectful, but what can a hovercar hobbyist and some-time sky-racer help us with? We need someone serious on this."

I chose not to be offended. "I may not be as serious as a heart attack, but I've been known to exhibit my share of seriousness."

"Cruz, here, can check around for us," Run-Time defended.

"Why can't it be one of your guys?" Fat Nat asked.

"For the exact same reason you don't want one of your guys involved," Run-Time answered. "None of us can have our names directly connected."

G added, "We need a fall-guy to give us plausible deniability."

"It's not like that," Run-Time interjected. "We need a trusted third-party to poke around discreetly."

"Poke around can mean a lot of things," Fat Nat said. "I still don't know why him?"

"Easy Chair Charlie, a mad gunman?" I looked at the men. "Impossible. Easy Chair Charlie was no gun-toting street gangster. He was a numbers guy. I heard he also got into the acquisition business, too, but nothing hardcore criminal. And a shootout with police? Impossible. He wasn't stupid or crazy."

"You seem very sure of that," Run-Time said.

"I knew him."

Fat Nat and G glanced at each other.

I answered the question before they could even ask. "I was a client of his." I looked at Fat Nat. "You're in the classic smoking business; I'm in the classic hovercar business. Sometimes, you have to be able to get things that aren't available on the local legit market or through regular channels. Someone like Easy Chair Charlie was the guy to get those things for you." I could see Fat Nat nod. "He got me a few hard-to-find and semi-technically-illegal things for my vehicle. Again, nothing hardcore criminal. He was an operator, not a mad gunman. He also was a family man."

G nodded and pointed as if my words were hanging in the air. "Exactly," he said. "A family man. He would never do such a thing."

"But he did," I said. "Or that's what the papers said happened, because that's what the police say happened. What do you say happened?"

I didn't know what to make of these two men staring at me without answering a simple question.

"Am I missing something?" I turned to Run-Time. "You want to hire me to poke around to do what? What is it that you're saying happened that's different from what the papers and the cops are saying?"

"It's nothing mysterious," Run-Time replied calmly. "If he did do what they said, completely contradictory to his nature and good sense, then why? That's what we want you to find out. That's all."

Run-Time placed an envelope on the top of his desk.

"Kick around for a few days and see what you come up with," Run-Time said. "You'll be our detective."

"Is this how they pay detectives? Wad of cash in an envelope?" I asked.

"That's how we're doing it," he continued. "I have a lot of interests with the City, including the police, so I don't want my name anywhere near this. Fat Nat, the same. People got shot up and killed on this thing, so there is also public opinion to contend with. Pro-criminal businesses don't tend to do too well in this city. Fat Nat and I could get hurt bad, business-wise, if any investigation, no matter how logical, were to get back to us. That's why I told Fat Nat you were our man. I wouldn't trust this to anyone else."

I leaned forward and took the envelope. "I appreciate that," I said. "I know how important your business is to you. Okay, I'll poke around. No one will ever know anything. It's not like I'm a real detective."

I could see Fat Nat and G glance at each other.

"For this though, you are," Run-Time said.

"Of course." I realized I shouldn't have added my little commentary at the end. "I'll get started. Should I contact you or Fat Nat?"

"Me," Fat Nat answered.

"I'm only the matchmaker between parties on this one," Run-Time said. "Whenever I can help a friend, I will. And if that help can be provided by another friend, even better."

I stood and the two men shook my hand again. I could see they weren't particularly thrilled at my involvement. Run-Time's female VP returned to the office—I hadn't even noticed she'd disappeared—to escort me to the elevator capsule.

When I left Run-Time's, I hopped into my Pony and went straight to Joe Blows on Sweet Street in Old Harlem. I double-parked on the street and waited until I saw the hovercar appear in the sky, flying into the emporium's parking structure. I not only knew what Fat Nat looked like, but what his hovercar looked like, too.

"Cruz," I said to the front door girls.

"Cruz?" one of them asked.

"Yeah. Tell Fat Nat that Cruz is here to see him. He'll take the meeting."

One of the three girls disappeared from the front desk to go into the back.

"Looks new," I said.

"Oh yeah," the girl said as she raised her cybernetic hand. "I lost my hand in the shootout. I get fitted for the skin next week."

"Congratulations."

"Why, thank you," she said with a smile.

The third girl returned.

She led me to the smoking rooms, and I immediately saw Fat Nat, G, and several other men playing cards, puffing on fat cigars.

"Mr. Cruz," Fat Nat greeted. "You're fast. I'll give you that."

"Can we speak in private?"

Fat Nat was amused by my request and looked at his comrades at the table. "Sure, Mr. Cruz." He looked at the girl. "And you can go back to the front and back to work."

The girl gave him a "whatever" face and walked back the way she came as Fat Nat threw his hand down on the table, delicately held his cigar with a gloved hand, and rose from his seat. "Follow me, Mr. Cruz."

As I followed him, I noticed we were not alone. G and every one of the other men were following like we were little kids following the teacher to the playground. He led us down a long, dark winding hallway to a single door. Fat Nat pushed it open. "After you, Mr. Cruz." I walked into the cluttered office and his merry men filed in.

"What's this about, Mr. Cruz?" Fat Nat said as he sat on the sole desk in the office as his friends stood on either side of him with arms folded. "Not enough money?"

"No, Mr. Nat, I am not here for more money. I'm here for you to level with me before I get started. I came here as a courtesy to you, to talk to you as a man, privately. But since you want to include the Seven Dwarves here, then let's include them. What didn't you tell me at Run-Time's? What was Easy Chair Charlie into that you didn't tell me or Run-Time? What? It would be one thing if you were someplace else and heard about it, but you were here. Your place was shot to hell, and you even had a few customers killed, but the first thing out of you was to say he didn't do it or it was a set-up. The Metropolis Police Department shoots the gunman who shot your place to hell and you side with the gunman and not them. What are you holding back?"

Fat Nat's face had changed different shades of red in my tirade and was now a ball of nervous sweat. He looked at his friends who had turned their folded-arm death-stare to him, not me.

"Uh, guys, can you give me and Mr. Cruz a minute."

The looks on their faces were priceless. G opened the door as the other men filed back out, and he closed the door. The three of us were left in the room. It was when G locked the door that I said to myself, "This can't be good."

"What was Easy Chair Charlie into that you didn't tell us?" I repeated.

Fat Nat was standing now and had picked up a newspaper from the desk to fan himself. After he composed himself and his normal skin color had returned to his face, the Italian sat back on the desk.

"He said he was working on something. In fact, he was close to wrapping it up."

"What something?"

"He said he'd get enough money from the deal to buy his way Up-Top."

I stared at him, then glanced at G. To buy one's way off-surface into the paradisaical Up-Top regions was everyone's dream, even my own.

"Such a thing is only possible for the uber-rich or the uber-criminal. Not even Run-Time is rich enough to buy his way to Up-Top," I said. "Mr. Nat, what are we talking about here?"

"It was a set-up," G added. "One moment he was sitting at our booth enjoying the smokes, then he got a call on his mobile and had to leave. Then all hell broke out."

"Why didn't you say that to the police? Or tell that story to the press?"

"Why?" Nat asked. "Five cops were put in the morgue, one was paralyzed, and another had his pecker shot off. This is a police-friendly establishment. Joe Blows has always been. I'm going to suggest that police purposely set up and gunned down my friend? Not if I want to stay in business."

"Mr. Nat, police are body-cammed up the wazoo, every one of them, from the time their foot steps out of their station or hovercruiser, and the body-cams are not monitored by the police department, but the Police Watch Commission. That's an independent, civilian body, not government."

"How do you know so much about this?" G asked. "Run-Time told us you never were arrested or had any negative involvement with the police."

"I interned at Police Central when I was kid in high school."

"Interned? I never ever heard of any kid interning at the police station."

"I was weird. Do you understand what I'm saying?"

"We're not stupid. He couldn't have been set-up, because the Police Watch watches the Police Department," Fat Nat said. "So you say."

"But Easy Chair Charlie wouldn't get up from a table after he bought a couple boxes of high-quality Havanas, take a simple call on his mobile, and then instantly turn into a gun-crazy maniac and starting shooting at everyone in the place and the cops," G said.

"Where did he get the weapon from?" I asked.

G pointed at me. "Exactly."

"We got a Puerto Rican and two Italians in the room. What are we saying?"

"That this is some serious crap," Fat Nat said.

"I'm a one-time detective here. I'm just a laborer, and I'm not cut out for anything dangerous. The most dangerous thing I'll do is race a hovercar at three hundred miles an hour. That's it. None of us are little boys. Easy Chair Charlie never bragged. If he said he was going to come into that kind of money, then he was coming into that kind of money. He wasn't part of the uber-rich, so we're talking about hardcore criminality to get that kind of cash. I'm not tangling with any Cosa Nostra, Triads, or ninjas."

"Neither are we," Fat Nat added. "Why do you think we went to Run-Time in stealth mode?

"Okay, this is what I'll do. Only because Easy Chair Charlie was a righteous guy and he didn't deserve to go out like that. I'm going to discreetly inquire around and find out if this is something to pursue, meaning turn it over to trustworthy authorities—Run-Time knows them all. Or, we drop this, like Superman dropping a nasty chunk of Kryptonite, and never look back. There are the streets; then there are the mean streets. I don't go near the mean streets. I'm supposed to be getting married. The worst trouble I want in life is my psycho parents-in-law."

"We hear you," Fat Nat said.

"That's the plan. I'll find out what we're dealing with. And let's not even call it a case, and I'm not even a detective. I'm just a guy asking questions."

The men nodded.

"That's the plan," Fat Nat said.

"The plan." Mr. G pointed at me. "Yes."

"Sorry about jumping to wrong conclusions, Mr. Cruz."

"Forget about it, Mr. Nat. It happens to all of us. I got what I needed and we're all agreed. I can get started."

CHAPTER 11

Phishy

I got Fat Nat to promise me to come clean with Run-Time and tell him the whole story with Easy Chair Charlie. I knew Run-Time would want to keep even further away from this whole situation than before. But the worst we could do was keep him in the dark about something this politically explosive; he'd never do that to us. Friendships are hard enough to come by in this city, so never blow one intentionally.

Since I was never a criminal myself and didn't associate with them, I had to find the next closest thing. That would be my frenemy, Phishy. He was the only friend-enemy that I tolerated and still spoke to. I didn't know why I tolerated him, but it definitely wasn't because of his assortment of colored shirts with fishes on them.

I guess it was because he also had an aversion to the hardcore criminal world, every bit as strong as mine, but he maintained a knowledge of the players and, more importantly, he kept his ear to the streets. Anything worth knowing or not knowing, Phishy would know about it or who to go to find out.

"Easy Chair Charlie?" I asked.

Phishy was still spinning around on the sidewalk, doing his chicken dance. This was how he greeted me, with some dance jig. I waited until he had sufficiently amused and tired himself out. There was no point in yelling at him to get serious. Phishy had to be Phishy first, before his brain could interact with others.

"Who ended up finding you?" he asked me, standing at attention with a big smile.

"No one found me. I managed to get to China Doll's all on my own without any of you."

"She had everybody looking for you. I put my sidewalk johnny brigade on it. With Run-Time's people in the air and mine on the ground, we would have found you for sure. Your hiding places are getting better, though. You have to be commended for hiding so long with that bright red hovercar of yours. Are you switching cars? I bet that's how you're doing it."

"Easy Chair Charlie, Phishy."

"What about him?"

"What was he into?"

"You know what he was into. You were a client of his."

"Besides that."

"There was no besides that with Easy."

"Surely, you heard how he died."

"Surely, I did."

"And? You really believe Easy Chair Charlie spontaneously went psycho and shot up his second home, Joe Blows, and go bullet-to-bullet with the cops?"

Phishy started scratching his head. "How would I know? It happens all the time. You read about it all the time in the news. Maybe, Easy was smoking something else besides his fancy cigars."

"There's nothing on the street about him? No gossip or rumors?"

"Like what?"

142

"If I knew, I wouldn't be asking you."

"What do you think Easy was into?"

"Well, this was a waste of time," I said to myself.

"I can ask around if you want."

"No, I don't want you to do that. You go around asking questions, then it gets out that someone is going around asking questions."

"Sorry, I couldn't help you out, Cruz. If I had heard of anything, I would tell you. I'll tell you the first thing I hear, without asking questions."

I nodded, but I could see Phishy was genuinely unhappy he couldn't help me.

"Do you know anything about his wife?" I asked.

Phishy laughed and shook his head. "What's this about, Cruz? Are you like some kind of detective?"

"Detective? Why do you say that?"

"Asking me questions. You're going to ask his wife questions. What's a guy who restores hovercars and does odd job work asking questions for?"

"I've decided to become a curious person. Phishy, don't be telling anybody about my business."

"If you become a detective, can I be like your paid confidential informant?"

"I am not a detective! Don't be starting any rumors. I'm serious, Phishy."

"I won't be telling anybody about your business." I could see Phishy's little rat-brain racing around in his head, thinking about whatever schemes and scams he was formulating.

"Bye, Phishy."

I turned around and walked back to my Pony.

"I'll keep an ear out," he said, following right behind me.

"I'm sure," I said as I opened my car door quickly and got in, trying to keep as much of the falling rain from the vehicle as possible.

I closed the door. Phishy just stood there waving as my vehicle rose up, up into the sky traffic.

Damn. I had asked him about Easy Chair Charlie's wife, but he didn't answer. That was the other thing about Phishy—his scatterbrained tendencies were contagious. You had to focus to keep him focused. It didn't matter.

It wouldn't take me long to get there, and I'd find out for myself.

CHAPTER 12

Mrs. Easy Chair Charlie

I lived in Rabbit City, and it was far from being a working-class or upscale neighborhood, but it wasn't the dumps. Free City was the dumps. A sea of super-slender towers with each level a family residence. It was government housing for the unlucky five percent of the population without legacies. This was the best the government could do for only five percent of the population.

I sat in my Pony in the rain, waiting. It wasn't long before my guy descended from the sky by jetpack. Flash was the guy I used most of the time, when I called Run-Time's Let It Ride for mobile car security. He was a light-skinned Black guy, with a ponytail and a small goatee. Flash was friendly, reliable, and he took his job seriously, whether driving a hovercab or, in this case, car-sitting security. I was not about to leave my Pony unattended and unguarded in Free City. I was sure a thousand boosters were watching me through binoculars and telescopes at that very instant—plotting a try at stealing or trashing my Pony.

"Cruz," he greeted, wearing a yellow jumpsuit over his suit clothes and blue eyewear.

"Hey Flash," I said as I got out my car. "Not sure how long I'll be."

"It's fine."

"And be careful."

"Don't worry, Mr. Cruz. I know Free City well."

He pulled down the zipper of his jumpsuit to show his dual shoulder holsters with guns.

I had been to Free City a few times for some hovercar restoration jobs and once did an unpermitted (yeah, that means illegal) street race through it. It was during the day, so it was okay. The night would have been very, very different—in other words, I wouldn't be here.

Free City didn't have sidewalk johnnies and sallies loitering around. Free City had street punks. They weren't gangs, per se, though they were into all the criminal activities that real gangs were involved in. They were bored delinquents, who staked out sections of sidewalk, waiting for victims. They never bothered residents—they were residents too—they waited for strangers. People like me.

As I neared the tower Easy Chair Charlie's wife was in, I saw a few of them watching me. They were just kids in chia-pet bubble-coats and wearing flapper hats, all with silver shades on. They looked like round gorillas with fighter pilot heads. The buildings had plenty of neon lights and signs, but punks and criminals always found those pockets of darkness to hide in.

The silver-shaded punks came out of their shadowy corners and walked directly towards me down the gray asphalt path.

"Hello, Mister. Can we help you find your way? We're always eager to be the good citizen," one of them said in a sarcastic tone.

Another had his hand in his jacket. He could be bluffing, but bravery was unwise in places like this, especially if you were unarmed.

I flicked a business card right in his face. The punk stopped in his tracks and they let it fall to the ground.

146

"I'd pick that card up and read it, if I were you," I said to them.

They stood there and watched me for a moment. One of them finally picked it up, read it, and showed it to the lead punk, the only one wearing a bandana on his head.

He grinned. The punks turned and disappeared into the shadows.

I stayed away from the real mean streets of the city, so no weapon was necessary. And I wasn't into anything that would ever make the mean streets ever want to reach out and touch me. For the rest of the city, I had a business card for every dark, dank corner I might find myself in, to keep the human vermin away. As long as the human vermin could read, I was fine.

Free City building didn't have elevator capsules—they had elevators. I only had to go to the fortieth floor, but it took forever. Matters were not helped by the elevator car being some damp, moldy, semi-dark tomb. I purposely did not look at the floor. I didn't want to vomit at what I might see.

"My name's Cruz, ma'am."

The woman, who answered the door, peered at me through a screen partition. She was average size, in a one-piece flannel dress with orange hair.

"How did you get here, wearing that hat?" she asked. "And you still have all ten fingers and toes. The ground floor punks let you get up here with that hat?"

"I'm wearing a classic fedora, ma'am, not a hat."

"Well, listen to the booshy talk. I suppose you don't drive a hovercar."

"I don't. I drive a classic Ford Pony. A Pony is not a hovercar; it's a vehicle."

The woman burst out laughing. "Okay, Mr. Cruz. You got a sense of humor, so you're okay."

"Are you Mrs. Easy Chair Charlie?"

"Oh, God no. I'm her sister. Ethel!!!!"

The woman's scream was like someone stabbing me in the eardrums with an ice pick.

"What?" I heard a woman's voice scream from within the residence.

"It's Mr. Cruz!"

"Let him in, then! And who is Mr. Cruz?"

The sister opened the screen door, and I walked past her and her invisible cloud of cheap perfume. My eyes were always scanning my surroundings, whether inside or outdoors. However, I never got that far as my eyes instantly locked on the trio of gremlins before me—three dirty kids in diapers. Nothing struck horror in my heart like the sight of a dirty kid in a diaper, because it meant the diaper was dirty, too. What was a diaper, but strapping an unflushed toilet to your body for the day? I don't use public toilets—ever. All I could see in my mind's eye was the image of some dirty kid in a dirty diaper ripping it off and flinging it at people; people like me. Suddenly, I had an uncontrollable urge to dive out the nearest window.

"What's wrong with you?" the sister asked. "You look like someone kicked you in the stomach."

"No, I'm okay."

"I know our humble residence isn't what you booshy-class are accustomed to, but it's home sweet home to us."

"Mrs...?

"Call me, Sister. Everyone around here does."

"Sister, I've been many things, but booshy has never been one of them."

"What part of the city do you stay at?"

"Rabbit City."

The woman broke out in an "A-ha!" She moved to the three kids. "Where the booshy playboys live."

That was a first for me that someone considered Rabbit City upscale.

"How did you get up here without getting mugged?"

I turned to the new voice. "Mrs. Easy Chair Charlie?"

"Mrs. Easy is fine. Yeah. How did you get up here without a scratch? Did you have some kind of police escort?"

The other woman was a slightly, older version, also in a dark-patterned flannel dress with yellow hair. She walked to me.

"It was a trick I learned when I interned for Police Central as a kid."

She stopped walking to me. "Police Central? You worked for the cops? As a kid? How? You a cop?"

"I'm not a policeman."

"Listen to the booshy playboy," Sister interjected. "Cop! Only booshy say 'police'."

"How'd you get to be a kid copper?"

"I'm not a cop. I said: I interned with the cops as a kid."

"Interned? What's that?"

"In school. Kids go to businesses and hang for a day for extra-credit for class."

"And you went to the cops?"

"Yeah."

"Why'd you do that?"

"I'm a contrarian."

"What's that?"

"I do the opposite of what other people usually do."

"That's for sure," Mrs. Easy said. "What are you then, if not a cop?"

"I'm just a laborer guy who restores classic hovercars..."

"Vehicles, you mean," Sister interrupted.

"... on the side. Not a cop."

"Policeman," Sister interjected.

"Considering the circumstances of your husband's death, I probably shouldn't have—"

"Keep your undershorts on, Mr. Cruz. I'm not about to break down sobbing. Go on with your story. How'd you get up here without a scratch from the ground floor punks?"

"Especially with that hat!"

"Fedora," I corrected Sister, and she laughed. "When I interned for the cops, I had to go into a shady part of the city, and the captain, at the time, wrote on the back of his business card: 'Cruz is my friend. See that nothing happens to him, or you will NOT be my friend, and I will come visiting to show you how much you're NOT my friend.' He told me to throw it at the leader of the local street punk gang. It worked, and I've been using the trick ever since."

"Who did you get to write on a business card for you this time?"

"Someone, here in Free City, whose good graces I know they would want to remain on the right side of. The leader of a much bigger Free City gang than them."

"And why would he write you such a business card message?"

"I restore hovercars. I restored his racing hovercar for him."

"Mr. Cruz, that's a stupid story. Even if it were true, it would only work with brainy criminal class criminals. The animal criminal class would shoot you, even if it means they'd get shot, too. They don't think, they react. What were you packing? I know you stuck a gun in their face. They really are a bunch of cowards. Everyone knows it."

"You caught me, Mrs. Easy. I just flashed the big gun in my jacket."

"I knew it. Wait! You didn't bring your gun up in my place?"

"I left it in my vehicle with my bodyguard."

I suddenly felt a presence behind me and there was the sister scanning me from neck to leg with a pole metal detector. "He's clean," she said.

Smack!

I jumped at the sound and glanced at the three kids. The smallest one with only a couple of teeth in his mouth was holding a large fly swatter in his hand. He cut the air with it and laughed. He found his mark and slammed the swatter down on the floor. His—I think it was a he—two siblings pranced about in a fit of unrestrained laughter, flapping their arms, then one after another, jumped on top of the fly swatter with their bare, dirty feet. "Dead!" "Dead!" Was it too late for me to dive out the window?

"Have a seat, Mr. Cruz, the detective," she said.

Every chair and couch was covered in garbage—toys, clothes, magazines, and papers.

"Sit anywhere. Just throw it on the floor."

I was uncomfortable doing so, but I did. I couldn't believe Easy Chair Charlie lived here, and this was his wife. Easy always presented himself as a class act, and there was nothing classy about this place; I saw a fly buzzing around in the apartment home.

"Wait a minute. Why did you call me a detective?"

"Isn't that what you're doing? Detecting?"

"Yeah, but what made you call me that?"

"Your associate."

"My associate?"

"Mr. Cruz, did you really believe I'd let a strange man come up to my place, with my sister, little nieces, and nephew. Are you crazy? Your associate called ahead and told us you were coming. If he didn't call, you'd still be outside a closed, triple-dead-bolted, electrified door."

"Is the first initial of this associate, Phishy?"

She laughed and her sister appeared and stood behind her, laughing too.

"Don't worry, Mr. Cruz. He said you were undercover."

I did my best to contain my annoyance. Run-Time and Fat Nat hired me to be discreet, and Phishy was going to have the whole world thinking I was some kind of real detective. All I needed was a Metropolis bureaucrat calling to ask me why I'm going around calling myself a detective, when I'm not licensed, and my designated occupation is "LABORER."

"As long as he told you that."

"And he said my husband was friend of yours."

"Yeah. Well, he got a few rare items for my custom vehicle. He was a solid operator. I expected to do business with him for a long time."

"I'm sure a lot of people did. What are your questions then, Mr. Cruz? The police have bothered me a half dozen times with their questions, so I guess one more time won't hurt."

"Do you believe the story? That Easy went psycho and then went on a shooting rampage with the world and the police?"

"Yeah, I do," she answered quickly. "You seemed surprised, Mr. Cruz."

"I am."

"People go psycho all the time. Why not him? He was a human, like the rest of us. But in his case, he'd have an added incentive to go psycho."

"What do you mean?"

"We never had any children, Easy and I, but he could see I wanted that and a better life. Everything he did was to get me to that better life. I know what people say about Free City. No one talks worse about it than my sister and me. Stuck here for all the years we've been. It's no place to live, and certainly no place to raise children. It's worse than a dump. Easy, with his work lifestyle, felt no different. But it was all for me. He loved us. That's why he went psycho. There was no other way for us to escape." She obviously could see my confusion. "You must be new at the detective business, Mr. Cruz. Two words. Life insurance, Mr. Cruz. I'm the sole beneficiary of his life insurance. Suicide disqualifies someone, but not suicide-by-cop. Me, my sister, and the kids are getting out of here as soon as the check comes and clears the bank, which is what my late husband intended."

"We won't be booshy, like you, Mr. Cruz, but we'll be doing okay," Sister added.

CHAPTER 13

China Doll

I watched Flash fly away into the rainy sky as I sat in my Pony.

Wow, I thought. I suck at this detective thing.

Dot's pretty face looked up at me from my video-phone.

"They were happy," she said. "Never did I hear there was any trouble on the domestic front."

Mrs. Easy was also a client of Eye Candy—probably for more years than I was a client of Mr. Easy Chair Charlie.

"You're really going all out with this detective thing," she said, smiling. "Yes, that slider Phishy told me you're a detective, but said you're undercover. I think it's cool. It shows real initiative on your part."

"Really?"

"Yeah. You should do it for real."

"I don't have the money to get a detective license."

"Then save for it and work under-the-table, like everyone else does, until you do."

"I'm not sure I'm suited for it."

"Why not? You hate inside-office work. You hate cubicles. You hate 9-to-7 jobs. You hate same-thing-everyday jobs. Detective work would be the opposite of all that."

"Maybe."

"Maybe? Cruz, you're always complaining about being just a laborer and now you have your chance to be more than that, do something cool, and you're making excuses."

"No, it's not that. I'll try it."

"That's all I'm saying. Try it out and see."

"I just don't know how good I'll be."

"You say that after one day? What's wrong with you? What do you think my skills were like after one day, my first day on the job? Was Run-Time a mogul after one day?"

"Okay, okay. I didn't mean that."

"Cruz, don't flake out on this. An opportunity is sitting in your lap, like a baby. Don't throw the baby out the hovercar window." (Now she's talking about babies.)

"That's an image."

"Imagine if I could tell my parents you were a bona fide detective!"

"Please don't do that."

I suddenly had images of her parents, dressed like gangsters, machine-gunning me in a dark alley.

"I'm going to hold you to it, Cruz. Go be a detective. I don't want to see you moping around or complaining anymore."

"Yes, dear. I'll go be a detective."

I didn't tell her that my glory days as a detective lasted for a sum total of one day. My case fizzled out before I even got started. I thought I was being all sophisticated in Fat Nat's office, worrying about uber-gangsters and cyber ninjas—all to be felled by the great, grand conspiracy of whole life premium insurance.

CHAPTER 14

Run-Time

It was the Irish VP guy, this time, who escorted me into Run-Time's office.

There I sat, giving Run-Time the rundown of the case that was never to be. From here, I would head over to Fat Nat and company.

"I have to admit that it was quite exciting, all of it."

Run-Time was smiling at me. "You believe the wife?"

"I checked in with Dot. She personally does the wife's beauty stuff."

Run-Time laughed out loud. "Beauty stuff? You're going to marry her, so I'd advise you use more precise language than that."

"You know I'll be ready. Well, Dot said there was nothing out of the ordinary with the wife. She never said anything that would make anyone believe she was distressed about anything. Quite the opposite, actually."

Run-Time nodded. "Then Fat Nat and I got our money's worth."

"Run-Time, I can't take all that money for just a few city stops in the Pony."

"Cruz, the money is yours. I'm satisfied. Nat's satisfied. What do you plan to do now?"

"I'm not sure. I have a few construction gigs coming up and a big car restoration job at the end of the month."

"You can still do those. What do you plan to do career-wise?"

"I don't know a thing about being a detective."

"What's to know? It was like asking me what's to know about being a company CEO. You do it and you do it long enough, you become it. And it would seem you already have a head start on the promotion front."

"What do you mean?"

"Who's this guy called Phishy?"

"That Phishy!"

Run-Time laughed. "He could be your marketing genius, so be nice to him."

Run-Time was all about encouraging people to do more in their lives. I had seen him do so a million times, so this was my turn. As a legacy baby, I did have more free time than I knew what to do with.

"I'll give it whirl and see what happens."

"Get some business cards."

"Business cards?"

"Everything becomes real when you have some snazzy business cards. People take you seriously, because serious people, at the very least, have business cards. You know that. Sidewalk johnnies have business cards."

I laughed this time.

"That they do," I said.

I stood from my chair and did a patented Run-Time handshake. Shake the hand, but don't let go until you finish what you have to say.

"I really appreciate your faith in me on this. I know how serious it was and how serious it had the potential to become. I won't forget it. I owe you one."

"You owe me nothing. We've been friends for years and that's what friends do."

I let go of his hand and said no more. He gave me a playful pat on the shoulder, and this time, he walked me to the elevator capsules.

CHAPTER 15

Punch Judy

I t was pouring! Rain, thunder, and lighting—the complete trinity.

The Concrete Mama's residential parking was all subterranean for those of us not blessed to live in the upper half of the tower. The problem with that was, in heavy rain, it would leak virtually everywhere—the ceilings, the walls, and many parts of the floor would flood. My parking stall always turned into a mini-lake. It took me a good forty minutes to get everything I needed from the trunk, towel dry my Pony properly, wrap it in a cloth tarp then in a waterproof, anti-static car case, and finally, set-up a cheap, auto water pump that would shoot any accumulating water out of my stall ten feet away into the drainage ditch.

The ritual began. Into the elevator to the dreaded lobby.

"What did I tell you?"

The annoying French voice greeted me as soon as I came out of the elevator.

"What are you babbling about, PJ?" I asked.

Punch Judy stood there with her bionic arms on her hips.

"So you're a detective now? A fake detective. A stupid detective."

I was going to beat Phishy senseless when I saw him again. I ignored her and walked to the residential elevators.

"Don't you want to know what I mean?" she asked.

"No."

"I am not your secretary!"

"Thank God."

"You're lucky I was here."

"Yes, lucky."

"They knew what floor you're on."

I stopped now and looked back at her.

"What? Who knows what floor I'm on?"

"The men looking for you."

"What men?"

"They wanted to know about the detective asking around about Easy Chair Charlie."

"I am not a detective!"

My outburst startled Punch Judy as much as me.

"And people say I'm crazy. Okay, Mr. Not-a-detective, those men were looking for you, and they went up to your floor."

"What? How can strangers go up to the residential floors?"

"Don't yell at me. I'm not responsible for security in this building. It's not my fault you legacy residents are too stingy to hire building security like every other civilized building."

"I've had it with this building! I swear, no one better have been near my place. What did these men look like?"

"Don't yell at me!"

"What did these men look like?"

"Like that," she said, pointing to an elevator that had just opened.

Two men exited and stopped.

"Mr. Cruz," one of them said. "We hear you're asking a lot of questions around town. We should talk. Detective to detective."

CHAPTER 16

Detective Friendly

"What floor did you just come from?" I asked angrily. "Were you snooping around my place?"

"We were on floor 87, waiting for you, just like your woman said," the man said.

"She's not my woman," I said.

"I am not this stupid man's woman," Punch Judy yelled.

"Yeah, whatever. You two behave like husband and wife. Mr. Cruz, are we going to talk or what?"

"Sure, let's step into my office."

For me to use an umbrella was a major event in itself. I never used umbrellas. With my tan fedora on my head and my tan retro-jacket on my body, I could weather most of the rain Metropolis threw at me. But then, there were storms like these. I stood under one umbrella, and the two men stood under their own separate ones.

"Why are you here?" I asked.

"To compare notes among fellow detectives," the man answered. "We were hired by one of the men's families killed in the shootout."

"Why would you need to talk to me?"

"Motive, Mr. Cruz. It's an open question as to whether it was this Easy Chair Charlie or the cops who killed our client family's loved one. The cops had a righteous motive, of course, but we need to know all about this guy. Is your investigation ongoing? If it is, we'll wait on ours. We told the family we'd consult with the cops and any other parties on the case, meaning any other detectives on the case. There's like twenty of us, all together."

"I didn't know it would be so many."

"When it gets kicked to the civil courts, there'll be tenfold that in lawyers."

"I believe it. Well, I wish I could have saved you a trip. My case is closed. We're all satisfied that it was nothing more than suicide-by-cop."

"He went gun crazy?"

"That's it. I actually wrapped up the case before I arrived."

"Okay, then. That's what we found to be indicated, too, and the same with all the other detectives on the case. Well, thank you, Mr. Cruz, for the help. Hopefully, in the future, we can return the favor."

"No problem. You have a business card?"

The man patted his suit jacket with one hand as the other held the glowing umbrella handle with the other. "Left them in the damn hovercar. Look me up. I'm in the Yellow Pages. Bar is the name."

"Okay. Maybe, one day, I will."

"Thanks again, Mr. Cruz. I'm sure you won't mind my colleague and me getting out of this hurricane storm."

I waved at them with a smile as the men waved back and, looking both ways for any traffic, disappeared into the rain.

CHAPTER 17

Flash

Fat Nat marched through Joe Blows with a single purpose.

"Stop admiring that!" he yelled at the waitress, Tab, now fitted with the skin for her new bionic arm, surrounded by the other waitresses.

They scattered as he walked past them and out the main entrance to a hovering taxicab. He leaned into the open passenger door.

"I didn't call for no taxi," he said.

The driver, Flash, held a mobile phone with the video screen illuminated. "I know," he said and faced the tiny screen to Nat's face.

"Hey, Mr. Nat," I said to him.

"Mr. Cruz." Fat Nat was genuinely surprised.

"I just wanted to let you know I'm not finished with my discreet poking around on the matter we're both familiar with."

"Why would you be doing that?" he asked.

"When two plus two comes out five then you have to wonder what the hell is going on. Maybe nothing, maybe a whole lot of something. I'll poke around some more until I'm satisfied; otherwise, I won't be able to sleep. I need to be able to sleep nights."

"The unscratchable itch," Fat Nat said.

"The unscratchable itch," I repeated.

Fat Nat nodded and gave me a thumbs up. "I won't say a word to no one."

"Next time you see me, it will be either to tell you the last chapter of the book is over, or we're only getting to chapter two."

PART FIVE

The Case of the Guy Who Scratched My Vehicle

CHAPTER 18

The Guy Who Scratched My Vehicle

My Pops always told me the more you pretend to be a thing, the more you become that thing and realize you're not pretending anymore. He used the word "pretend," instead of his more favorite phrase, "work so hard you bleed." No one wanted to hear the "work hard and you'll make it" mantra. Metropolis was stacked to the sky with people working hard, but would never make it.

But pretending to be a detective was not a wise life choice. I had already been looking at Labor statistics. It was categorized by government as a law enforcement occupation. It didn't have the highest percentage of deaths, like cops and firemen, but it was close. It had the leading percentage, by a huge margin, of arrest and incarceration. One of those jobs most likely to make you a jailbird. Dot didn't know these stats and I wasn't about to tell her.

I wondered if my fixation on the whole detective thing was because, for too long, I had nothing at all to fixate on. Idle people got excited at the most mundane. I was a laborer, a gig-worker. No permanent job, just odd job to odd job. I hated it, complained about it, but accepted it, because I did nothing to change my situation. Millions of us sat around in our legacy housing all day, and I was one of them. We were our version of the leisure class, but when you're rich it's acceptable; when you're not, it's pathetic. Aimless was aimless no matter how much or how little cash you had in the bank. I never saw social class; I saw people who had purpose. That's why Phishy didn't annoy me and Punch Judy did. He had purpose with his crazy self, and she didn't. I didn't like her, really, because she was kind of like me.

But I had to get serious. Being a detective was to be a one-time deal. I had no money for a license, no office, and honestly, the job was dangerous. I couldn't play games—I was getting married, assuming my future parents-in-law didn't off me before then.

Yet, here I was, in the public library on 40 Winks Street. There were three left in the City. In the comfort of your own home, you could download any content you wanted to your digital book reader, but frankly, who had time for that. There were a gazillion books out there in cyberspace. Being a librarian was actually a serious profession with value; they had advanced degrees in data mining, sifting, and record compiling. Libraries sifted through all the data garbage, the clutter, the Trojan horse X-rated material, and sub-standard nonsense to present you with what you typed into your search and gave you the best of the best. Yes, libraries were also a major hang-out for the sidewalk johnnies, but they were clean and quiet. Here, I was reading book after book on...the private investigation industry.

There were only a few main categories. The first was the procedural detective books. They went into quite a lot of detail about surveillance, stake-outs, skip tracing, computer-tapping, hard drive cloning, etc. Most of it was very dry or commonsense and I could see why the books didn't sell.

The second category was the best sellers—the Hollywood-style, super detectives. These "true" stories were of gun battles with crime lords, beating up cops, sleeping with clients, secret consultative work with Up-Top multinationals, more gun battles. Entertaining, but all stupid. None of it real.

The book I found myself glued to was not the 1,000 page tomes of the first category or the 400 page page-turners of the second, but this 60-page book titled, *How to be a Great Detective with 100 Rules*. It was written by a guy, who had been a private eye for 70 plus years. In fact, he died only a few years ago at the age of 92 and had worked right up until the end. The book was brilliant. I had read it five times already and was reading it again. The rules seemed basic, but his one paragraph explanation of each was packed with real insight and his own folksy, street-wise expertise. He was the real McCoy—not any fake movie-land detective. You could tell by the way he communicated. He must have led an amazing life. To live 92 years in Metropolis—the things he saw and experienced. It's too bad he didn't write a compilation of his life through his cases.

I put the book on the floor, sat there, and sighed. It was the only book I checked out from the library. Here, I was sitting alone in my legacy residence, reading the accounts of a man who lived a real life, a long life and was quite content with it. I knew that, because he kept at it until he died. Nothing stopped him—the mean streets, the meaner streets, uber-government agencies, megacorporations. He did his thing.

He had a metal heart, but back then, if you had heart disease in your genetic history, the doctors would automatically replace your regular heart with an artificial one to be on the safe side. He had bionic hips and fingers—a fall down stairs had caused the former; a nasty habit of smoking nasty cigarettes caused the latter. But again, he did his thing, his way.

I wished I had met Mr. Wilford G., the 92-year-old private eye. He lived and had a lot less than I had. What was my excuse then?

"Who's it from?"

I had received the video-call first thing in the morning and listened to the man on the other end. I had heard what he said; I couldn't believe what he said. An anonymous person was making a full office, with a reception and waiting area, available to me free of charge. The catch was that I would never know who the anonymous patron was.

I drove to the business district of Buzz Town just before the lunch hour to meet the Realtor man. It wasn't Peacock Hills or Paisley Parish, but it wasn't Free City either. Buzz Town was not the best of areas, but it wasn't the worst—it was one of those in-between places, like Rabbit City, where I lived.

I met him on the 100th floor of the tower on Circuit Circle—some people called it the Circuit; others, the Circle. The Realtor definitely seemed like an Eye Candy client. Not a piece of clothing or hair out of place. Nice suit, matching slicker, nice boots, horn-rimmed glasses. He watched me as I toured the empty office space. The office was very spacious and was as large as the combination reception area and waiting area outside its doors.

"I asked, who's this from?" I repeated.

"The landlord is adamant about remaining anonymous, and it's futile to continue asking. My firm takes such requests extremely seriously. The only question is: Do you want it?"

"I'm not accustomed to accepting gifts without knowing who the gift giver is."

"I suspect you'll get over it."

I looked around again. Was this all a dream? I had been having an internal battle within myself about the whole "detective thing." First, I wanted to punch Phishy for spreading rumors. Now, I searched the Net for all the requirements to be a licensed private investigator in the City. The cost of the license fees was outrageous and far beyond my means, but I was also searching for ways to legally scam my way into it, like calling myself a "consultant," rather than a "detective."

"This is quite a lot to take in all at once."

"I suspect you'll get over that, too. If you take the offer, I can have you sign the paperwork, right here, and you'll have the keys in hand as I leave."

I walked to look at the reception-waiting area again.

"Is it a yes?" he asked.

"I could go down to the City and look up who the office belongs to."

"And you would see that my firm is listed as the landlord by proxy."

"Free?"

"You would be responsible for utilities and any furniture, of course."

"What are the terms? Is this a lifetime thing?"

"Hardly, but it is a legacy space and the landlord-of-record would need to give you at least 90-days' notice for you to vacate. That's more than generous."

Who could it be? I asked myself. Run-Time wouldn't be anonymous. Dot didn't have this kind of money. Who?

"How old is the legacy?"

"Three hundred years."

A mortgage paid off over 300 years ago and exempt from any government taxes ever since.

"Yeah, I'll do it."

"Good." The Realtor lifted his briefcase and opened it.

We used the briefcase as a desk as he had me "sign my life away" on a stack of documents.

"Do you know who the landlord-of-record is?"

"I do." He pointed to another line for me to sign my signature.

"They're not criminals are they?"

"Do you know many criminals, Mr. Cruz?"

"I don't."

"Then it would be unlikely that my client is one. Please don't over-think this, Mr. Cruz. Someone gave you access to free office space for an indefinite period. Based on your surprise from our initial video-call, it is a person who is, at least tangentially, acquainted with your affairs. Since you're not a person of financial means, you can infer that the gesture is a benevolent one. If I were you, I'd count my blessings, furnish it, and start my business. I would not think about the who ever again. Last signature here, please."

He pointed, and I signed on the last dotted line of the last page of the documents. The Realtor took the pen and the documents from me, then returned them to the briefcase. He reached into his jacket pocket and then handed me a folded document and a set of keys.

"Your signed business tenant authorization and three sets of keys. Your official copies of the documents you signed will be delivered tomorrow."

"You knew I was going to accept the offer?"

"Why wouldn't you? The keys are copy-prohibited. If you need new keys, then you have to get a whole new door system. Very expensive."

"Tell him, thank you."

The Realtor smiled. "I never indicated what gender my client is, Mr. Cruz, but nice try."

He left me in the office space, walking out the way we came in. I stood in the main office, still in a daze.

I had a business office!

It was only the next day. I lay on the floor on my back, thinking about all the potential names I had come up with for my soon-to-be-real, one-man detective agency. I had gotten the emergency work blanket from my vehicle's trunk, which was for use if I ever broke down and needed to do work on the Pony—which would never happen, but that's why it was an emergency work blanket. I lay on it on the floor, which was littered with crumbled wads of paper. I had been doing this for the last three hours. The only sound for the longest time was the rain against the tall windows, and then I heard it.

The door opened, and I sat up quickly, looking into the reception area. I realized the door must have been unlocked all this time, which was completely out-of-character for me. I was the OCD guy, who checked the front door to make sure it was locked five separate times before I went bed. Who could it be? Did the Realtor guy return? Was it some street punk? Two people appeared at my open office door.

It was him! The guy who scratched my vehicle!

When you were kids in elementary school, stepping on and scuffing a man's pair of kicks (sneakers) was a fighting offense. But boys grew out of that childishness. They grew to be men, when scratching their hovercar was a fighting offense.

That was easily five years ago, but I had not forgotten his face. Though I never expected to see his ugly mug ever again in my life, I remember the day he scratched my vehicle, almost like it was yesterday.

There were people who drive and then there were drivers. For us real drivers, there was no such thing as an accident that wasn't your fault. It was the core of the defensive driving mindset. You must anticipate any contingency, and if a bad thing happened, the blame resided with you. But I had safely parked my vehicle and was just about to turn it over to my mobile security guy—actually, it was Flash—and go about my day.

This maniac came out of nowhere, going against traffic, dove, turned in a semi-circle, hovering above the road, dipping closer to the ground and stopped, scratching my car and slamming into a concrete parking stall divider.

My mouth hung open in shock.

The guy got out and surveyed the damage to his car, but could not care less about what he had done to mine. My spotless, perfect, immaculate, heavenly red Ford Pony was gouged by a deep blue-gray scratch straight through to the metal. My eyes were bulging with rage.

"Get over here!" I yelled. "You scratched my vehicle!"

The guy was on his mobile and completely ignored me, carrying on a conversation.

I looked at Flash, who probably saw the growing agitation in my face.

"Just call your insurance and get away from me, you plonker," he said.

I lost any bit of composure remaining and ran at the guy. I was going to punch him, push him, whatever. As I neared him, he turned and dropped his mobile to the ground to brace for my attack. Suddenly, someone grabbed me from behind—it was Flash.

"He's not worth it," Flash said. "No, Mr. Cruz. You can't assault him. He'd be able to call the cops, and they'd haul you away."

"You scratched my vehicle!" I yelled again.

"So what!" he yelled back.

"You're going to pay every dime it takes to fix it!"

"All it needs is a paint job with a spray can!"

I went ballistic, and Flash really had to hold me back.

"It's a classic hovervehicle, and they're going to have to strip off all the paint and redo it paint coat by paint coat—fifty at least. You don't touch-up a classic hovercar with a spray can!"

"Screw you! My insurance is not paying for that. Get a spray can from the local market. One coat. I may even have a can in the trunk for you."

I desperately tried to reach for his face and claw it off, but Flash restrained me.

"You touch me, and I'll sue you and take that pile of junk from you!"

My head was throbbing; I was so enraged. It took Flash fifteen minutes, at least, to calm me down but I did, eventually.

His insurance paid, but it was a bargain basement one. All I got was ten percent of the damages. I sued him in small claims court. He never showed up, and I won my judgment, but the clerk said good luck getting him to pay. There would be an arrest warrant filed, but no police would ever act on it with murderers, rapists, and gang members to deal with.

I did all I could do, so I did all that I shouldn't do, channeling all my OCD negative energies at him. I found out where he lived, where he worked, his girlfriend's house, his favorite market, every place he went; I stalked him. I stalked him twenty-four hours a day. And I made sure he saw me.

At the beginning, he laughed at me, throwing a curse or two at me, and an occasional obscene gesture. Then he got angry, especially when I followed him to his girlfriend's or when they went to a restaurant for dinner.

The girlfriend was never amused by me, and one time, she came out to go somewhere—he was still in the residence—and saw me and ran back inside. Soon after, I could see she was getting scared—and so was he.

There was a massive rainstorm, so much so the hovercars were staying out of the sky. But not me. I staked out a spot right across from his place and I could see their silhouettes watching me from the third story. If they were on a higher floor, they would have ignored me, but people who live close to the ground look out their windows to the ground. It's just what you did. And there I was.

They thought they were clever one day and sneaked out of their residence the back way into their hovercar and had gone to another neighborhood, clear across the city. I illegally bugged their car, and I set it to ring my mobile if their hovercar started up.

The looks on their faces when they came out of the restaurant and saw me was priceless. They were *really* scared and bolted away from me. I realized I had reached into my jacket for something and they thought it was for a gun.

The next day, the Guy Who Scratched My Vehicle came out of his residence, his girlfriend standing behind him and watching, and he threw a brown paper bag at me.

"Take it psycho," he said. "You got your money. Count it."

I picked up the bag from the wet ground and opened the bag. I knew they expected me to just take it and go, but I walked a few feet, sat right on the sidewalk, and counted every last bill. They watched me with utter contempt.

When I finished, I got up and left, glancing back one last time to glare at them. I actually didn't gain anything in my episode of madness. I got every dime to fix my car, but the expense in time and money of following them and doing the surveillance on them was all on me. But I felt good, as most fools do.

I never expected to see them ever again, but there was the Guy Who Scratched My Vehicle and the same girlfriend standing in my new detective's office, staring at me with smirks.

"Well, well," he said. "A detective. I should have known."

I had just gotten a basic desk and three chairs for my new office. Basic furniture and delivery was quick and easy. I could feel my blood boiling. Why were they here? How did they find me? I wasn't even looking at them anymore. I sat behind my desk, looked up, and they both were sitting down in front of me, smirking.

"You probably thought you'd never see us again," GW said.

"I kinda thought that's how we left things."

"Were we surprised to hear that you were a detective."

Was this more of Phishy's doing? "Who told you that?"

He smiled. "Yeah, I was told that too. You're a confidential detective."

This had to be Phishy!

"Well," he continued, "the wife and I need a detective. We did some looking in the Yellow Pages, and there's so many in there, it makes your head spin. And when you have no one to recommend someone, you're just playing Russian roulette with your wallet. Then we heard about you. We said, we got personal experience with that psycho. He locks his sights on you, and you're done. He'll never stop till he gets what he wants.

Don't ever be on the opposite end of his sights when he locks on you. The perfect detective. Surprised you didn't do it sooner."

"What makes you think I'd ever take you as a client?"

"People beating down the door to hire you, are they?" his girlfriend-wife quipped.

"You can't still be sore about the incident? I paid you your money. So we're even steven."

"Any man who hurts a man's woman, his kids, his family, his pets, his *vehicle*...you damage a man's vehicle and...he needs to be put down. You scratched my vehicle. I would never work for someone so venal. No way. No how."

The smirks from their faces were gone. They realized that I was *not* over it.

"You really are psycho. Hold a grudge for this long. It was over five years ago. Yeah, you're the right psycho for this, and as the wife said, no one else is beating down the door to hire you."

"Listen here, I have integrity. I have standards. I'm going to pick the clients I work for. That's what I'm going to do. I'm going have solid clients with integrity."

His wife burst out with a laugh.

"Good luck with that, psycho," he said and turned to his wife. "Watch this."

He threw a bag on my desk and leaned back. The smirks had returned to their faces.

I looked at the bag—slightly open, filled with small bills. I looked at them, looked at the bag, stared at it. This was a critical junction in my life—what kind of detective would I be? Principled or just some ratty PI for hire. Starve or have money for bills and food.

I grabbed the bag of cash.

Humble pie. I, of all people, was not one to eat anything I didn't know all the ingredients, and that was apart from friends poisoning me back in grade school. But there had to be an exception to every rule. Humble pie wasn't its real name; it was some kind of natural cross-bred apple—humble pie was apple pie and it was damn good. I had it often, and though I was sitting in an old-style diner in a seedy part of the city, surrounded by other grimy establishments, I was enjoying that pie.

I sat in a faded and stained yellow booth by myself. Other identical booths lined the circular wall of the diner. In the center were four-person square tables—all empty—and both the main counter and open kitchen grill were opposite the main entrance. The counter had old bar stools, each with the butt of a customer seated, eating and drinking whatever. There were only seven other people in the yellow booths lining the wall, sitting solo like me. Seven of us were on one side, and way on the other side was one punkish, mustached guy who had glanced at me more than once since I entered and sat down. Even now, after I had ordered and started stuffing my face with my humble pie, he was pretending not to watch me. Seven of us were male, and one was a female. She was the only female in the place, besides the waitress, and this lone female had also glanced at me more than once.

I was almost to the end. I never licked a plate of food, but I scraped every last morsel of humble pie with the fork. My drink was gone, and I gave off the hint of a customer who was done, satisfied, and ready to get out into the rain to go about their day.

"Hey, Mister." The girl was now standing at my booth—not the waitress. She slid into my booth opposite me. "Can you believe this rain?"

"It's a wet one out there," I said.

"You said it. Wet all around. What are you going to do now?"

I pushed my empty plate away from me and wiped my hands with my napkins. "It's funny you asked. Is that a dove tattoo on your forearm?"

She smiled as she extended her arm over the table. "Yeah, it's sweet, huh?" She admired the design.

I slapped the handcuff on her wrist.

The girl jumped up, first with a look of fear and then came a flash of anger.

"What the..." she yelled.

She pulled her handcuffed arm, but the other end I had handcuffed under the table. The table was old, but it was sturdy enough.

"Help!" she yelled looking at the other customers, but mostly at that seventh man way on the other side.

People barely registered any concern, including the waitress and the cooks behind the counter.

"You should sit down and relax."

"Help!"

I was not about to listen to a screaming fifteen-year-old female delinquent—though she probably had graduated to other criminal designations by now. I reached into my jacket for my mobile and was already dialing the number. It was pressed against my ear.

"I found her," I said into it. "Get down here now. Action Alley. Cafe Fifties is its name." I hung up.

"Who are you talking to?" the girl yelled at me.

"Who do you think?"

"Help!" She repeatedly yanked her handcuffed arm as if she wanted to pull it out of its socket.

"Stop that," I said.

"Help! I'm being kidnapped!"

I stood up.

"Gentlemen, and lady, I am a private detective and was hired by this girl's, if that's what you want to call her, family to find her so they can take her ass off the streets before she gets STD'd or dead, whichever comes first. Please ignore her."

I really didn't need to say anything, because that's what they were already doing—ignoring us.

The girl was going crazy, yanking her arm and screaming. I had enough and got up. I stood at the main entrance, but kept my eye on her—and that seventh guy from the corner of my other eye.

The Guy Who Scratched My Vehicle arrived about fifteen minutes later. How he got to the Cafe so fast, I didn't know. But he wasn't alone. There was a shorter and older man with him—the spitting image of him. It wasn't his twin, but his father. It was freaky how similar they looked. So GW knew exactly what he'd look like in about twenty or so years—all gray and balding. But the star of the show was also with them. A shortish, roundish, fattish woman with a big, fluffy, yellow hairdo. It had to be a wig. These were his parents? The father was wearing some kind of leather tank top, and the mother was wearing a sleeveless dress that came to her knees. Both were wearing white socks, visible just under their knees, with their boots. My God, if I were GW, I would never go out in public with them.

The trio was through the door and staring at me, and I had only to gesture with my chin.

"I handcuffed her, so she couldn't run away. She was yelling and screaming before you came, but now she's hiding under that table doing her impersonation of a ninja."

They walked over to my table, and the mother bent down. Then it erupted. GW was the clone of his father. The mother and daughter were clones, too. Only the girl was the slim as a twig version before her metabolism quit, and she blew up to be a fatty too. The girl, still hiding under the table, cursed simultaneously at the mother, who was

179

screaming her own obscenities. I've heard some cursing, but even I felt I would need to wash out my ears with soap. Finally, the girl came out and was standing almost nose to nose with her mother—both screaming at each other at the top of their lungs. All I could think about was the spit they were showering each other with. I couldn't believe what I then saw. The mother punched the girl in the head, dropping her to the floor. That was the end of the cursing and screaming.

The mother joined father and son, who had been watching the whole exchange like zombies. The trio walked back to me.

GW turned to them. "I told ya, Ma. I found the guy to find her. He's a psycho when it comes to tracking people."

The mother, who had no perception of personal space, was inches from me when she said, "You're a good detective. Those cop bums couldn't find our daughter. No one could. You found her in one day."

"There's more," I said.

"More?" she asked, as her head cocked back like a chicken.

"You don't think your daughter was led into temptation all by herself. The source of her corruption is sitting right behind you over there."

The trio followed where my finger was pointing to the punkish guy, sitting in the booth way over. I almost felt sorry for him as his head shot up in the air when he noticed GW and company's eyes locked on him. I saw their eyes narrow and their mouths contort into snarls. They bolted after him.

The punk jumped out of his booth and over the counter into the kitchen. The cooks yelled at him as he ran through, and I heard what could only be the back door thrown open. GW's mother rolled over the counter after him with GW and father following. She may have been fat compared to their skinniness, but she was twice as fast as them.

I stood there shaking my head. How long was I going to be here? I couldn't just leave the girl handcuffed to the table unconscious. I walked back to the adjacent table and sat. I was tempted to order another piece of humble pie, but I decided to just wait.

The trio returned almost an hour later. I was boiling mad, but kept it to myself. I had to be nice, because I hadn't been paid yet. I would ask (demand) a bonus.

I stood from the table, and now, I really felt sorry for the punk—but only for a couple of seconds. GW had a serious black eye, the father also looked like he had been through a major fist fight, and the mother was scratched up, too.

They were all grinning at me. I hoped I wasn't an accessory to murder.

"You're going to get a good bonus, Mr. Cruz," she said.

"And I want a good business review too," I said as I handed GW the key to the handcuffs.

Then it began again. The girl was standing and cursing again, and the mother, as if by levitation, moved back across to her and was screaming at her with full intensity. I was paying attention, but I still had no idea what they were saying—kind of like Dot and her mother, but they were yelling in another language. This was English, but it wasn't. My brain wasn't comprehending a word of their yelling. Then I saw it. The girl punched her mother in the face KO-style. The mother fell to the floor like a rock. GW and father rushed at her like the dogs.

"I'm out of here," I said to myself and exited the Cafe.

"Hey you!"

I turned to see the Cafe's owner glaring at me.

"Why did you bring these crazy people into my business?" He barely finished his sentence when he spit at me.

I was out of range, but I gave him a dismissive gesture as he ran back into the Cafe. I turned to walk away again.

"Hey you!"

I turned and reflexively ducked as a bowl of rice barely missed my face. The owner ran back into the Cafe.

I would not wait to see what else he had planned.

"Hey you!"

I was quarter way across the street, but turned. The owner was preparing a wind-up throw, like those silly cricket players, and this time, he threw an egg at me. It barely missed as I lurched forward. Were we little children in kindergarten? A grown man was throwing eggs at me.

He prepared another of his winding up throws for me. Since we were in kindergarten, I stood on my tippy toes, as if it was dodge ball—I was ready for him. He threw, but it went wrong. The egg went high up in the air and smashed on the windshield of a passing hovercar that was descending to park. It slammed on its air-brakes, hanging twelve feet in the air. Its passenger door lifted up and a kid crawled from the driver's side to the passenger seat.

"I'm going to kill you!" the kid yelled at him.

I didn't know if it was a full moon or not, but the hovercar driver jumped! I expected he had bionic legs and would land effortlessly, but all I heard was a sickening crack, and the expression on the kid's face was that of someone who been hit in the face with a sledgehammer. The kid was lying on the ground, screaming and crying, while the Cafe owner was laughing and pointing at him.

Then there was a spark from the kid's hovercar, hanging in the air, as something disengaged the air-brake. The hovercar descended diagonally, straight for the cafe owner. The man ran through the doors as the hovercar crashed through the doors after him! All I heard was things breaking, people screaming, and smashing sounds. Then a crash that seemed to shake the ground.

That was it. It was way too much excitement for me. I ran away as fast as I could.

CHAPTER 19

The Guy Who Got Shot In My Office

There was something satisfying about going into the office. I always hated the prospect of being chained to a cubicle or tiny office at some government or corporate job, like ninety percent of the people. I knew, even as a kid, I wouldn't do that, but I had little to show for it with my high principles. And with virtually every last human in the city in legacy housing, it meant people were devolving to the lowest possible denominator. Not having to worry about housing meant I could subsist on very little per month. But that meant all you were doing was existing. That's not really living, but that's what most people were doing. That's why so many people got themselves in trouble on the crime scene. But, it was also why this detective thing was so exhilarating for me.

I stood in my office with my mobile computer on my sole office desk, marveling at the screen. I had reviews!

Trusted Reviews was the bible in customer service. Businesses did everything and anything for solid (good) reviews about their products and services. I think some little old lady started it many years ago, and every Average Joe and Jane went to it first when deciding what service or item to buy. There were all kinds of rackets and scams involved with companies, trying to rig the system, but they were always found out, which was worse, because then companies could get banned. Major players in an industry could brag about having thousands or even millions of reviews. Bottom line was, if you didn't have any reviews, then your company didn't exist, no matter how impressive your physical or virtual storefront on the Net.

I now had three. I couldn't believe it. GW gave me such a glowing review that I couldn't believe it was the same person. Then, there were those from his mother and father. All were lengthy (very good), detailed about finding the sister/daughter (even better), and mentioned me solving the case in a day, when local authorities couldn't close the case in many months (the best).

I couldn't stop reading it and smiling. Maybe I could make this detective thing work. I liked that it gave me purpose. Human beings needed purpose, and it was fun, too.

There was some big commotion going on outside the front door of the reception-waiting area.

Did I forget to lock it again?

I got up and walked to check, but just as I approached, the door swung open and a punk, with his back to me, stood there with a gun. My body jumped as the man was shot once. He yelled, was a shot a second time, and then his gun dropped from his hand as he fell. A third shot rang out, and he crashed to the ground. I had frozen in place, but now, my brain engaged, and I dove back into my office.

I heard one or more people running away.

I lay on the ground, watching the dead man on the ground. My eyes were tearing up. My new career was about to be taken away from me, before it could even get started.

CHAPTER 20

Phishy

There was no possible way I could wait there. My office was a red-and-blue siren party. I couldn't bear it. Now I had a police jacket. Anyone involved with any crime, even as a victim, got a file. People could do a Net search on my business address and see that someone was killed in my office. Would you go to a detective who had someone killed in his office? I was ruined. No one would care about any good reviews.

I went back to my place after giving the same statement to police three times to two different sets of officers. They always did that. Lying people rarely were good enough to keep to the same lie multiple times and to different people, though the professional criminals and psychopaths did so with ease. They let me go my way as they plastered their crime scene tape across the door of my office. I suspected I'd be seeing that Realtor very soon.

Well, I parked my Pony and then just had to take a walk, clear my head, and calm down. I was out for about thirty minutes when I started back to the main entrance of the Concrete Mama.

"Hey, can you help me with directions?"

Someone called out to me as I was walking up the mega-stairs. I turned to look back and blinked when I heard the first shot. I dove to the hard, wet ground as whoever the man was took two more shots at me before running away.

I lay there on the ground, gritting my teeth. I was so enraged that if I had the jaw strength, I would have crushed my own teeth.

As GW said, I was a psycho when I got mad. You didn't want to go there with me. I was indirectly shot at once, and a man was killed. Now, I was shot at—me—in front of my own place.

It was the fourth place I checked to find him. There was Phishy, chatting it up with his sidewalk johnny friends. I tapped my horn to get his attention. All of them looked up at me, as I slowly landed my Pony on the ground. I lifted up my hovercar door as Phishy was already running to me with a big smile, but he saw my face, and he stopped; his smile disappeared.

"What's wrong, Cruz?"

I was standing and slammed my door shut. I never slammed my car door. I could feel my own fumes of anger radiating from my body. I gestured to him to approach and Phishy did so cautiously.

"What happened?"

"What happened is that some stranger got shot to death in my new office. The police yellow-taped the whole thing, so I'm out of business before even starting. Then to top off the day and make it even more exciting, someone tried to gun me down right in front of my place."

"In front of the Concrete Mama?"

"Yeah."

"Oh, wow."

"Oh wow, Phishy? I've never been involved with anything like this before. You know that."

"I know. I know."

"I don't do violence. You know that."

"But you're a detective now, Cruz. You have to expect that sort of thing, now."

"Well, there is no now. I'm out of business."

"No, you're not."

"What do you mean?"

"If the cops yellow-tag you, as long as they don't contact you again in 48 hours, then you're in the free and clear."

"What are you talking about, Phishy?"

"That's how it works. The cops got 48 hours to escalate the case. If they don't or can't, then you can rip down that yellow tape and act like nothing happened."

"The police can prosecute you and send you to jail, Phishy, for ripping it down."

"But only before the 48 hours."

"Are you sure, Phishy?"

"I'm positive, Cruz. I know this stuff. You know that I know this stuff."

I watched him, thinking. Yeah, Phishy would know these things.

"But I'll get a reputation—"

"Reputation?" Phishy interrupted me. "There are hundreds of shootings in this city every day, Cruz. You won't get no reputation. But...was it a client who got shot in your office?"

"No, some punk stumbled into my office door, and he was armed, too."

"See what I mean. A street shootout that spilled into your office. You won't get no rep for that. But what about the other thing?"

"Yeah, the other thing. Someone trying to kill me in front of my own place."

"You know what you need to do."

"What's that?"

"Come on, Cruz. You know."

I knew.

"There's no way around it, Cruz," Phishy said. "You can be a good detective, but you have to have the tools of the trade. You're not a laborer anymore."

"Yeah, everyone seems to know that, thanks to a certain person."

Phishy flashed a smile.

"Who do I talk to, then?"

"Leave it to me, Cruz." Phishy's smile was really back.

"I'm not going to let you rip me off, Phishy."

"Oh no. I'll take care of you."

"Where? I don't want any of this near my place."

"Your favorite coffee place."

"The Wet Cabeza?"

"They have the rental offices on the top floor."

"Yeah. Okay. How do you know that? Never mind. And no scamming, Phishy. I don't like them, but I know guns."

"Yeah, I know. You even killed someone when you were five with one."

I gave him a look.

"I didn't tell anyone."

"Like you didn't tell anyone that I was a detective?"

When I dumped on the cafe I found GW's sister in, it wasn't that I didn't like cafes. I did, but I liked high-end ones, without the high-end prices. The Wet Cabeza was my favorite, and it was one those places I went so often that I knew everyone who worked there and the owners.

I arrived and was greeted by the staff, who I knew on a first name basis. I had a craving for some humble pie, but I resisted. I just had a cup of silk coffee and left it at that while I waited for Phishy.

Inside, the layout of the place was a large, open cafe, all booths and barstools at the kitchen counter, with college-kid waiters and waitresses on hoverroller skates.

Upstairs, they had tiny conference rooms for rent. The Wet Cabeza attracted a business clientele, and offering the meeting rooms was a stroke of genius—why should hotels get all that business? It meant there was another reason to keep butts in the seats and the food and drink orders coming all the time.

It was two days later, and it seemed that he was in the same shirt with fishes, but Phishy was never unkempt or smelly. Technically, he wasn't a sidewalk johnny. He just hung with them. He was an operator. My girlfriend called him a slider, but he wasn't sliding through life; he was only sliding from one scheme or scam to the next. But with Phishy it was never too criminal—always small time, so if he were caught there no real chance of jail time.

Phishy had a big, block briefcase in each hand, and he hopped up the stairs, two at a time, with a big smile. He followed me to the room I reserved, and he marched in as I closed the door. I locked it. Too bad I couldn't remember to do so at my own office.

"Okay, Phishy, I checked out what you said about the 48-hour yellow-tape, and you were right."

"I told you, Cruz. I know these things."

Phishy put the two briefcases on the small conference table and opened both cases. Guns, guns, and more guns.

"How much trouble would we get into if the police raided this room this instant?" I asked.

"None. I'm a licensed gun dealer and none are loaded."

"What? Licensed dealer? I didn't know that. You got a cover for everything."

"I'm Phishy. That's what I do."

I looked at the assortment before me, but he stopped me before I could pick one up.

"I got something special for you."

"Phishy, I'm in no mood for scammin'."

"No. Serious. I got some pieces just for you. You're a real detective now, and you have to start building a rep."

"A rep? Am I a criminal?"

"No, Cruz. Everybody needs a rep. That's how people know if to deal with you or not. And when they do deal with you, how to deal with you."

"A rep does all that?"

"Yeah, it does. Here let me show you. I have a pop-gun."

"Pop-gun?" I said loudly as Phishy pulled out a hidden tray of other guns in one case. "Are we like in kindergarten, Phishy? Pop-guns are what we played with when we were children."

"Not those pop-guns. These are the real thing."

"I never heard of that before."

He handed me what looked to be a metal wand attached to some kind of fabric piece with Velcro.

"What the heck is this? Phishy, I don't want kid's toys. I could have been killed."

"Come on, Cruz. Trust me."

He took my right arm, and before I knew it, the fabric was wrapped around my entire forearm. "You wear long sleeves and jackets all the time, so you'll have the concealment. Okay, let's test it. Just snap your wrist. Pop! Trust me, Cruz. Pop it."

I flicked my arm out and nothing happened.

"You're not doing it right, Cruz. You have to be serious. Snap your forearm out as if you can throw your hand like a projectile."

I did it. *Pop!*

The metal wand contraption extended, and I could see it was some kind of gun barrel.

"You pop it, and it shoots one round—bullet, sonic, or pulse round. Whichever you like. No one will ever sucker shoot you ever again," he said.

My mind was changed, and I stood there admiring my arm weapon. "A pop gun?"

"I had it made just for you. I called in real favors, Cruz."

"Okay, what else you got for me?"

"This one."

He lifted the compartment tray of the other briefcase to reveal more guns. He reached in and handed me the sweetest gun I had ever seen. It was a slim, sleek piece of black metal.

"This, Cruz, is straight from Up-Top."

"Then how did you get it?"

He laughed. "Stolen, of course. Well, I didn't, but someone did, and I'm like fifth in line."

"You're giving me a stolen piece."

"Cruz, no one will know. It's untraceable. They have their database, and we have ours. No one shares. You know that. Besides, someone who could afford a piece like that probably has a ton of them; probably doesn't even miss it or know it's gone. How does it feel in your hand?"

I couldn't lie. "Nice balance."

"See what I mean. That is the weapon of a high-class detective. It even comes with a manual."

"Manual?"

"It will take you a day to read it. And when you do, you'll be smiling, like me."

"Phishy, how much are these going to cost me?"

"Wait, I'm not finished."

He lifted up the gun trays of both briefcases and started pulling out pieces. In a minute, he assembled a shotgun.

"Cruz, nothing causes some serious fear like the cocking of a shotgun."

He did so, and its unmistakable sound was universal and, yes, he was right. You heard that sound, and you stopped whatever you were doing to pay attention.

"All three, and you're set," he said. "The pop gun. The omega-gun—"

"*Omega* gun? You're making that up, Phishy."

"It's the gun to end all private guns. That's what it says in the manual. And the shotgun. Now you're ready for the mean streets. And the omega-gun comes with accessories if you want to use its digital features. There's this cool piece that lights up that you wrap around your leg. You'll see."

"What does that do?"

"You'll see."

"Phishy, how much? They say, if you have to ask the price, you can't afford it. All this seems like something I could never afford in a million years."

"Cruz, we're friends. I'll loan you the weapons, and I'll get a percentage of each of your cases. That seems fair. I know you're just starting out."

I grinned, and he grinned back.

"Phishy, Phishy. Always the angle. I amend the offer. Each percentage I give you...what percentage were you thinking?"

"Uhhh."

"Be careful, Phishy."

"Fifty percent."

"Ten percent of my cases goes toward the total cost of the weapons until, and if, I ever pay off that bill."

"Ten percent?"

"Phishy! I'm sure you won't give me the ammo free, and being a detective is not exactly a no-cash-needed business. There's lots of upfront costs. Like I have to go back to my office and turn it into a fortress, so I never get sucker shot at again. Ten percent is it. We're all going to make out on this deal. I'll even throw in a bonus, if by some miracle I can ever pay it off."

"Bonus?" Phishy said, smiling. "That sounds good, Cruz. We're like partners now."

"Yeah, don't remind me. So we're good?"

"We are, Cruz."

"Get me the total cost of these guns and don't play. You know I'll check. And then we'll lock down the terms of the bonus, now, before anything gets started."

"That sounds like the plan, Cruz. I told you to trust me. Now you got the tools of the trade, like a real high-class detective. Just because we live in a low-life world, doesn't mean we can't be high-class."

"You were right. I have to admit it without qualification." I reached out my hand to him. Phishy almost didn't know what to do, but he shook my hand. "You came through for me, Phishy. I won't forget it."

Phishy was genuinely moved. "You're welcome, Cruz. I knew I could do it for you."

CHAPTER 21

Punch Judy

Sidewalk johnnies and sallies all had a "turf." For most, it was a street, street corner, or alleyway. Many never ventured beyond it. But in a supercity with mega-streets, that was fine.

I knew Punch Judy would be where she always was—near the lobby of the Concrete Mama—either in the lobby or on the main steps.

"Hey!" I yelled as I neared her, marching out like a drill sergeant.

She was sitting on the steps, smoking, saw me and gave me an eye roll.

"I got a proposition for you!"

"Proposition?" That made her stand up, and I could already see the annoyance on her face.

"I need to hire someone."

"Oh, the big detective is hiring."

"I need a secretary."

"Secretary!" she grabbed the cigarette from her mouth. "You stupid man, and sexist, too! Secretary, because I am a woman?"

I was in front of her now, and I just pointed at her face. "I'll remember you said that when I go hire some guy for the job!"

That shut her the hell up. I spun around and stormed back the way I came like a bull. I was mad, and I'm sure my whole presentation was poor, but I didn't care. I had to find a secretary for the office, because I was not about to leave the office reception area unattended. I needed someone who looked nice, but was tough and, if need be, could take down the next unlucky monkey who tried to shoot at me in my own office. I'd be ready this time.

I had arrived at my office and ripped down all that police crime tape in front of the door. Phishy was right; the city police put it up, but never took it down. The community or landlord was supposed to do that. It was a city ordinance of all things.

My office had the same feel as the entire floor—empty, abandoned, uninviting. I wouldn't come here. It looked like you'd get mugged. I wouldn't come to my office. It gave off the same vibe as a morgue. There was a businessman inside of me, after all, because I was thinking the right thoughts if I planned to do this occupation for real. But only if I could address all the security issues.

I lay on the floor on my emergency work blanket from my vehicle. Again, contrary to my germophobic tendencies, right next to the tape outline of the man who got himself shot to death in my office. I had learned he was a low-level street punk. Nothing surprising about how he died. What was surprising was that it didn't happen sooner.

I heard the low knock on the door, followed by two more. Did I forget to lock the door again? Had I been hypnotized against my will not to secure my own office door?

From where I lay, I didn't even need to move. It opened, and there was Punch Judy.

Her demeanor was altogether different. I had never seen Punch Judy look amiable or humble before. She gave me a forced smile and stepped inside and closed the door behind her. She stood there, her eyes darting around, trying to decide what to say,

"Umm. Do you still have the job?"

I looked at her from my supine position on the floor, never once answering her.

"I want the job. I need the job. You caught me off guard. That's why I was rude. More rude than French people normally are. I talked before I used my brains. I want the job. I can't live the way I'm living anymore. I can't get a job at normal places because of my psych profile and criminal record. It's not fair. My record has trapped me. I don't want to be trapped anymore. If you give me the job, I'll do a good job."

She paused, wanting me to say something, but I didn't.

"So I'll come back tomorrow and start. My hours will be nine to six. I looked up the hours for other detective offices. That's the normal hours they have. Okay."

She waited again for me to say something, then opened the door. She stopped.

"What is the name of the detective agency, anyway?"

"Liquid Cool," I answered.

"Oh, good. Very cosmopolitan and hip. I would have hated a stuffy name, or something stupid, like the Cruz Detective Agency. Liquid Cool. Very nice. I start tomorrow at nine AM sharp."

She left and closed the door.

I had a secretary. A secretary with two bionic arms that could punch a three-hundred-pound man through the wall, which she apparently did on more than one occasion, hence her psych record. Hence, her nickname, Punch Judy, rather than just Judy. Unauthorized activities as a cyborg will make you unemployable faster than being outed as a carrier of the Asian flu.

Let someone try to sucker shoot me in my own office, now. We'd be ready for them.

CHAPTER 22

China Doll

"I've killed people with these boots!" was what I heard as I came out of the elevator. It's was Dot's voice, and I knew it was the tone of a highly pissed off China Doll. I didn't need to be a detective to figure out why.

There was Dot, with arms folded, glaring at Punch Judy, with her arms folded. Both in front of my office.

There were those days when no matter what the city had to throw at you, you could keep your spirits up and go about life with a spring in your step. This was not one of those days. I was in a terrible mood, and the Dot-PJ show only soured my mood further.

I looked at Dot and said, "She's my secretary, and that's all there is to it. Deal with it." I turned to PJ. "That's my girlfriend and wife-to-be, so you deal with it. I don't care how you two do it, but do. The feud is over, starting this second. This is about business now, my business. The next time I see the two of you together, all I want to see is smiles and butterflies in the air with a rainbow above you. Do you two know how important this is to me? Do you know how much pressure I'm under? My great detective agency could easily fail. You know how many businesses start and close in this city? Do you know how many detective agencies are out there, and I'm the new kid starting out? I'm so pissed, right now. Since I'm the boss, I'm going back home."

I turned around, walked back down the hall, pushed the button, and got back into the elevator. I never even looked back at them.

PART SIX

The Case of the Nighttime Bionic Parts Thieves

CHAPTER 23

Mr. Smalls and His Boss

It wasn't Peacock Hills, where the city's biggest and best non-tech megacorps were housed (tech corps were all in Silicon Dunes). I was on Fat Street, where the second tier companies were clawing at each other to get into the top echelons of business. It wasn't the Dumps, and there wasn't any real street crime, as it was fairly well-patrolled by police, but still, it was grimier than I preferred. Easy's sister-in-law was probably right—I was a bit booshy.

Today was my first shoe-leather day after almost a week of biz research. GW was my first real client—start to finish—and I had no one else since then, so I was on a mission, doing what all the business books tell you. Get off your butt and find your next client.

"I'm here to see, Mr. Smalls," I said to the lobby receptionist.

"He's expecting you?" she asked.

"Yeah," I replied with a lie. "Here's my card."

She took the card from my hand, read it, and looked up at me.

"Detective?"

"Yes, private detective."

The woman almost seemed frightened. "I'll announce you immediately."

People-Droid had been the seventeenth company or so I visited. I started at the first business tower on the corner and would work my way up each tower, then down the street. This was the first company of the third floor; I had 100 more floors to go, and each had six businesses, on average. I figured my shoe-leather soliciting would take me a few years to complete just this district.

"Mr. Smalls will see you, Mr. Cruz."

I knew I had stumbled into something. Every other business took my card and told me that the person I asked for would call me, meaning they'd throw my card in the garbage the second I left the office. At some point, one of them would undoubtedly call building security on me to have the "solicitor" (me) escorted from the tower.

I followed the woman down one hallway to the first office on the left, which meant either my research was faulty or they purposely had misleading public information. If Mr. Smalls was the president, as their site said, he wouldn't be in the first office in the hallway; he'd be at the last office at the end of the hallway.

She opened the door for me to enter.

A man stood there with an annoyed look on his face.

"Cruz," I said as I extended my arm, and he reluctantly shook my hand.

"The detective?"

"Yes," I answered.

"That was pretty fast. Are your offices outside our doors?"

"I would love to play along, especially if it led to a new client, but you must have me confused with someone else."

"You're not the detective we called?"

"I'm a detective, but no, I'm not the one you called."

"Who are you then?"

LIQUID COOL

"I've been checking in with businesses to see if they could use my services."

"Soliciting is not allowed in this building or any other, Mr. Cruz."

"Talking to a person is allowable on the entire planet, as far as I know. We're just talking."

"We have already called a real detective agency, so we won't be needing you."

"Big firm, are they?"

"One of the largest."

"I can understand that, but I doubt you will be happy with their system."

"System? What system?"

"For the big investigation firms, new clients are considered one-offs, so they will send in their little flunky, entry-level agents who will come in here and do more talking than listening, trying to up-sell you on all kinds of other services you don't need, rather than being interested in the situation you originally called them for. Sole practitioner agencies, like mine—I'm the guy. President, CEO, COO, and detective on the go. I don't pass you on to any flunkies. I handle your business directly, because I want your business. Big firms want clients with ongoing, recurring business. That's what pays for their high overhead and exorbitant salaries. Me, no car payments, legacy office space, one employee—minimal overhead."

"Mr. Cruz, that's all well and good, but I need an established firm to handle this matter."

"I understand, but let me ask you this: Do you remember when you started your career and you were hungry?" I waited for his expression. He tried to maintain his poker face. "That's me now, not some version of myself twenty years later. I do have references, too, if it matters."

"I'm sure your references will not be of the caliber..."

"Let It Ride Enterprises, for instance."

"You've done work for them?"

"Run-Time is a personal friend."

"I don't believe you."

"You can check, but I think you really should compare my presentation to the flunkies they're about to send you. But Mr. Smalls, I understand you need to make the best business decision for your company. Here's my business card—it has my mobile on it—and if you change your mind, I'll get myself back to your office. I want to establish a good clientele of corporate businesses, such as yours."

The man took my card and glanced at it.

"I'll let myself out, but thank you for the opportunity to present."

I left the office.

I didn't expect to ever hear from the man. I just consigned myself to a very, very long day of shoe-leather soliciting. That's all I could do. I had to make my own connections. No one would do it for me. Every business guy and gal I ever met said the same thing: Starting a business is brutal, but once you get your first client, number two is easier, then comes number three, four, and five. Then you reach a critical mass where those first ones start sending you business automatically. But be prepared for the initial orgy of unfiltered, soul-crushing rejection. Well this day was already that, except for the brief chat with Smalls.

I had already done the other offices on the floor, so it was up to the fourth floor. As I exited the elevator, I felt my mobile vibrating.

"Liquid Cool Detective Agency. This is Cruz speaking."

"Mr. Cruz." It was Smalls' voice. "You can return to my office. My boss has decided not to go with the other detective firm we called. We'll give you a chance. When can you get back here?"

"I'll be back there in a few minutes."

GW's case was a missing person. Mr. Smalls' case was corporate espionage. When I returned, I was escorted all the way to the office at the end of the hall. Waiting for me were more people in suits, male and female, than I had ever seen in one room in my entire life. Run-Time had three VPs. This company had like fifty, including Smalls. Probably one of the many reasons they were a second-tier company, rather than a first.

"I'm going to make this brief, Mr. Cruz," Smalls' boss said from his seat at the head of the long conference table. He was a much larger man, in a black pinstripe suit and wearing blue-tinted shades. "I want you to find out who's stealing from our warehouse."

All the VPs were sitting at attention around the long conference table and turned from him to look at me in unison. It was funny to watch.

"Find them and then do what? Police?"

"No police. Notify our internal security," he answered.

I knew what that meant. It meant the internal security would be judge-jury-executioners. I heard all about the world of corporate espionage. Stealing was rampant between the megacorporations and if they used the phrase "internal security" and "espionage," as in the case of stealing, it meant the security were on-the-payroll gangsters, who made people disappear permanently. The corporate world, government, the streets—they were all a bunch of criminals. But as long as they paid me; I had bills to pay.

I nodded. "All I need are the details, and I'll get on it today. If I can recover any of the products stolen, do you want them recovered for an additional fee?"

"Do you even know what products we make, Mr. Cruz?"

"You make cosmetic bionic parts—the best in Metropolis. My fiancée has one of your models—NS model."

"The neck and trapezoid replacement model," one of the female VPs said.

"Yeah. She was in a terrible accident as a teenager, and it saved her life."

It was like a giant arctic cloud had lifted from the room. Suddenly, they were interested in me. Suddenly, they liked me. I realized this is what business was all about. Connections. If you knew someone they knew, went to a school they went to, used their product and had some human interest story to go with it, you were "part of the team." It was so simple. Smalls was more interested in me, because I knew a fellow businessman. Smalls' boss and company were more interested that I knew someone who directly used their bionic (and very expensive) product. No one really seemed to care whether I was any good as a detective.

Smalls said as he glanced at his boss, "I'll get him fully briefed on the situation."

"Mr. Cruz," his boss interrupted. "You're not a mindless solicitor then. You seem to know all about my company. Do you also know about our problem?"

"I do. *And* who's stealing from you."

Smalls and all the other VPs looked at me with surprised expressions.

I said, "The only way for someone like me, a new detective in the industry, to get new clients, beating out established detective firms, is if I'm willing and able to do a lot of work the established firms won't. I have to be able to walk into a business, knowing all about their case before they tell me a thing—basically have the case solved. That's the only way, because the expectation of performance is so much higher for us new guys than the established firms."

"You're a smart man, Mr. Cruz," Smalls' boss said. "Who stole my products?"

"Your neighbor."

"My neighbor?" Smalls' boss looked at the other VPs. They looked at me.

"The Tech-Human company across the hall?" he asked. "Those motherless sons-of-bitches, I knew it."

I leaned forward in my chair and rested my elbows on the table. I looked right into the eyes of Smalls' boss, all the way across the table. "Your *neighbor*," I repeated.

Now, he knew who I meant, and a look of disgust came over his face. The two of us were the only ones in the room who knew what I meant.

Smalls' boss stood from the table. "Cut Mr. Cruz a check for his retainer and have the second one ready for when he concludes the case, and a third for a bonus."

"Yes, sir," Smalls said as he stood too.

All the VPs around the table stood in unison.

"Anything else, Mr. Cruz?"

"If my work is to your satisfaction, I'd like to get a business review, too."

"Fine, fine." He turned to Smalls. "Handle that too."

CHAPTER 24

Mr. Wan

My office was my domain. I did all the decorating, had the furniture moved in, had stupid pictures on the wall to cover it, and all the secret stuff, like hiding my big shotgun underneath my main desk where I could get to it easily.

Punch Judy ruled the reception area. It would be like an ex-posh gang member to have an haute-couture interior design decorating sense. With her punk rock playing in the background on an infinite loop, she had turned the barren space into some hipster, scenester receptionist-waiting room of the stars. Psychedelic posters on the wall, her fancy "modern" glass desk with see-through glass drawers, and a boombox on top along with her own mobile computer. All of her workstation was behind a metal barrier, but it didn't look like a barrier with the decorations. The waiting area had these geometric, purple couches around a glass table on a shimmering, neon powder blue rug. The reception table had French fashion magazines, which I thought was stupid because how could people read them, but then I realized—fashion magazines—so that meant lots and lots of pictures with few words, so it didn't matter, and numerical prices were universal.

Now, she was working on her own do-it-yourself neon light sign. I don't know where she found it, but she was busy at work, making a LIQUID COOL sign for the space she designated right on the wall behind her, outside my office. It would be the first thing people would see. She even had another box in smaller neon letters to make DETECTIVE AGENCY. I was impressed.

There was a knock on the door.

I was glad I had turned over office door security to her. I still didn't know why a paranoid, like me, who checked my car and home doors multiple times with my OCD self, would so carelessly leave my new office door unlocked more than once.

PJ walked to the door and opened it. We hadn't connected the door buzzer yet, because we still had to get the hallway camera.

There he stood. Dot's father, Mr. Wan.

He ignored Punch Judy as he walked past her. His eyes avoided me too as he walked in. He casually held his hands together behind his back as he strolled around. First the reception area, then to PJ's desk, then he walked into my office. PJ and I looked at each other, and then I bolted to my office. Just as I was about to go in, he came out. Mr. Wan strolled to the door, opened it, and closed it behind himself. We looked at each other again.

"That's China Doll's father?" Punch Judy asked.

"Yeah."

"You are not in good standing with him. I would not marry her if I were you. You marry her; you marry him."

"Don't say that. I'm trying not to think about it."

CHAPTER 25

China Doll

"What's in your bathtub?"

I sat with my back to the door as I gazed out the droplet covered window, wearing some new headset gadget PJ got me. Normally, people didn't like talking on the v-phone, unless they could see the other party. Texting was the exception, but you surely didn't conduct business by texting. The video-phone headset was an eyepiece, a metal band around one side of your head, and a small arm attachment with a microfilm thin video screen. Quality was perfect, but I had PJ return it to get a less than perfect model. I didn't want them to see my eyes too clearly, so I could look out the window and they'd not realize it.

"There's a gator in my bathtub?" the woman on the other end of the video-phone said and then started to laugh.

"Why are you calling a private detective? Shouldn't you call Animal Control?"

"I want to hire you to find out who put this gator in my bathtub."

"Maybe it just came up from the sewage pipes."

"Mr. Cruz, this is a seven-foot-long gator."

"Is it a gator or a crocodile?" I asked.

"Very sharp question, Mr. Cruz. I can't remember which is which, so let's stick with gator. Will you take the case?"

"I'd be stealing your money. Believe me, Animal Control will want to find out exactly where a seven-foot gator or croc came from too and how it found its way into your bathtub. They'll do the detecting for you for free. So here's what you do."

"What?"

"Video tape it with your mobile first, send the footage to the local news, and tell them to get there fast before Animal Control. Then, when the camera crew gets there, before you let them in, call Animal Control. You'll be famous for a day and will have the government find out who put that water reptile in your tub."

"Boy, Mr. Cruz. You're so smart. That's exactly what I'll do."

"Liquid Cool is all about helping people. Even when there's no real case for us to take. Now, go do your video-taping."

"Yes, sir."

I hung up the video call and pulled the video call headset off of me. "PJ!"

She appeared at the door laughing.

"I do not want any more crazy calls like that!"

"There's a gator in my bathtub," PJ said with her fake American Free City accent, or what she thought people who live in Free City sounded like, and then she laughed.

I sat at my desk staring out the droplet covered window with my cup of silk coffee in hand. There was no view, but the line of monolith office tower buildings across the street with their tinted windows. However, I had a deep sense of satisfaction. It was almost like a dream I prayed would never end. I was just some laborer, legacy baby one moment, now I was a self-employed, business owner with an employee.

"Surprise!"

I was startled, but the smile never left my face as I turned around to see Dot peeking into the office from the door. She waltzed right in.

"Look at this," she said, looking around my space. "This is cool. You have a real place of business."

I set down my cup as she rushed me, threw her arms around me, and planted a kiss.

"Very impressive, Mr. Cruz," she said as she looked around again, then back at me. "You are a detective now. How do you like it? Wait."

She ran over to my door and closed it.

"I don't want to hear no animal sounds in there!" PJ yelled.

Dot laughed, and I held my laughter in.

"Well, Mr. Cruz?" she asked.

I picked up my cup as I bobbed my head up and down. "Love it."

She was back next to me. "Is it dangerous?"

"Not at all," I replied. "Lot of variety, which I like."

"Oh. Tell me about the corporate case."

"The Case of the Nighttime Bionic Parts Thieves."

"Cruz, that's a stupid name. Your agency is named Liquid Cool. How can you come up with a cool name for your business, but give your cases such pathetic names? What was the name of the case before this one?"

"The Case of the Guy Who Scratched My Vehicle."

We both burst out laughing.

"That's what I mean," she managed to say while still laughing. "Enough! Cool names for all cases going forward."

"Gotcha."

"Tell me what happened."

I had two chairs in front of my desk, but I did like I saw so many other business guys do, like Run-Time and others. In the corner, I had my own arrangement of plush chairs around a glass table, the whole set-up on another neon dark blue rug. Dot and I sat on adjacent chairs.

"It was some case," I started. "This company makes all these high-end bionic parts, but almost monthly, thieves were ripping off their warehouse. They had tons of security, but all their internal security guys couldn't figure out how it was possible. They fired a bunch of security heads over it. It was going on for months."

"How did you solve it then, Mr. Cruz?"

"Well...Mrs. Cruz...since it was the megacorporate world, I knew it had to be an inside job, but I knew they would have checked that right away. So how can a theft be an inside job without being an inside job? Answer. The boss is playing nighttime footsy with his neighbor, who happens to be the VP of his main rival. He thinks he's scammin' her for corporate secrets, while in actuality, she's swiping and copying his access cards while he's sleeping."

"Ohhhh," Dot said.

"Fake trucks, fake uniforms, and all they had to do is drive in and out with a cloned access card."

"Very good, Mr. Cruz. How did you Sherlock Holmes all that? Are you that good?"

"I am, Mrs. Cruz. Oh, let me get my cup." I jumped up to grab my cup from my main desk. "What can I get you? I even have my own mini stash in my office."

The door to my office smashed in as a large man flew past me, knocking the cup from my hand. The thug slammed into the window.

We heard the pulse blast sound from under his jacket. After a second delay, the window shattered as the thug rose from the floor with such a look of menace that I knew that no good was about to come next. The thug glared at me, reached into his jacket, and raised his arm towards me. I didn't consciously notice the gun, until after I already reacted.

Pop!

My pop-gun popped out and the pulse bullet blew through his neck with a cloud of smoke and blood. His face, with a shocked look, fell forward off his body and then his entire body fell back out the window.

PART SEVEN

Intermission

CHAPTER 26

Officers Break and Caps

I ran to the window, or what used to be my window, which was a completely idiotic action. At this height, the wind could have easily sucked me out, but my behavior was on auto-pilot. From the corners of my eyes, I saw Punch Judy was next to me on the left. I would later notice she had a layer of sweat on her face and neck; Dot was on my right.

The whole thing was like the proverbial out-of-body experience. I was quite sickened by my behavior, the "stop for the bad hovercar crash to see if there were any dead bodies" behavior, but that's what I was doing. We wanted to see. Even Dot, who'd ordinarily run the opposite way, was with us, precariously balancing with our legs as we looked out over the edge of the side of the building. Dot, PJ, and I were hanging out to see the aftermath of the carnage. It was the reason people had under-vehicle cameras on their hovercars—not for safety, as was always the claim, but if there was an accident with a return-to-earth crash, they could be an easy spectator, maybe even get to snap a few photos from their mobile.

We barely caught the end of the thug descending to the ground, but at this height and the rain, we would never hear a splat or thud, or whatever our minds were expecting. I felt we were watching an episode of Science Fantastic. Which falls faster, a disembodied head or a decapitated body? Answer: they both hit the ground at the same time!

The tower's alarms screeched and we all grabbed our ears. If this were a real business district, blast doors would have raised or lowered to cover the shattered-out window. We just stepped back.

Damn! I said to myself. The police would be here at my office again!

"Oh!" I realized. "Dot, stay here!" I bolted from the office.

"Where are you going?" I heard her yell, but I was racing down the hallway to the elevators. For once, I wanted them to arrive fast.

I had to get to the ground and check the body. Another sucker shooter in my place of business. I had to get his ID and figure out who he was before the police arrived. Once they did, it all would be inaccessible.

The elevator arrived!

I raced out the main doors of the office tower into the street. People were already encircling the mess that used to be a human being. Besides my germophobia, I had no tolerance for anything disgusting or nasty, which a splattered body definitely was. I pushed through the crowd and held my hand in front of my eyes to shield my delicate sensibilities from the mess. The rain had stopped. Now when it needed to rain, it wasn't.

The man used to be a large man. I couldn't believe I was kneeling in front of the mess, but I had to get his ID. My hand went for his pants pockets and, lucky for me, my fingers found the wallet. I pulled it out and quickly opened it. There was the ID card of my sucker shooter. I pretended my eyes were a camera and I memorized the name, address, phone, and stats.

I paused and felt a wave of panic. The crowd surrounding the body and congregating on the streets was gone. It was like a bad movie where the guy realized he's the only one on the street and wonders why as he looked up to see Godzilla stomping him with his left foot. I looked around, and my gaze stopped at the reason. Two big street cops were watching my every move. I never even saw or heard their hovercruiser.

Officer Break and Officer Caps—Ebony and Ivory I called them (silently). PEACE in big bold white letters on their chests, but they could kill you in an instant, like all police, if you did the wrong thing.

"You a body snatcher, Mr. Cruz?" Officer Break asked.

"No, officer. I was finding his wallet for his ID, so I could see who exactly assaulted my employee and myself."

"Body snatching is a felony, Mr. Cruz. Disturbing a dead body is a felony, Mr. Cruz. Taking items off a dead body is a felony, Mr. Cruz."

"I didn't take anything. You were watching me. I looked at his ID and put it back. That's it."

PJ had arrived on the scene a minute ago and stood next to me with her arms folded. Break looked at his enhanced forearm display screen.

"...says you like to punch people with those bionic arms," he said to PJ.

"No, he attacked me. He punched me. I'm not allowed to punch anybody. It's illegal," Punch Judy said to him.

"But you have done just that at least six times."

"No, I learned my lesson. I'm not going to jail, anymore. I have a job now."

"And Mr. Cruz is your employer?"

"Yes."

"Imagine that," Office Break said. "Two troublemakers. You sure you didn't punch that man out of the window?"

"No, I never punched him. In the struggle, he crashed through the window himself."

"Officers, you can check the body for punch wounds," I said, not trying to be funny.

The officers gave me a look.

"The man takes a header from 100-stories up and is literally spread out on the concrete like peanut butter and jelly jam, and you want us to check the body for bionic punch wounds into his body. How do you suppose we'd do that?" he asked.

"Yeah, sorry," I said.

"How did you lose your arms?" Officer Caps asked PJ.

"They were cut off."

The two policemen looked up. "Cut off? By who?" Officer Caps asked.

"Him," she said, pointing to me.

In an instant, the entire demeanor of the two police officers changed. They went from Officer Friendly-mode to Judge Dredd-pre-killer mode. Their eyes narrowed and focused on me.

"Don't look at me like that," I said. "She was in a terrible accident. Her hovercar crashed, and the entire thing flipped and landed on her. Her arms were crushed and pinned, and the hovercar was on fire. She was already getting cooked alive, and it was leaking fuel so it was going to explode, too. What was I supposed to do? Wait for the ambulance? She'd be burnt alive or blown up. I had a laser cutter in my vehicle, because I do hovercar restoration gigs. I grabbed it and did what had to be done to save her life. Her arms were gone anyway, and it was either them or her life. I did what had to be done. I was as psychologically damaged as she was physically and psychologically damaged, but it had to be done."

All the while I was reciting what happened, Punch Judy was nodding in acknowledgment. The policemen's demeanor reverted back to cordial from their "prepare to open fire" expressions.

"Your boss cut off your arms to save your life, and you punched a perp out the window who was trying to harm him." Office Breaks returned to his line of questioning.

"No, I didn't punch him."

"The thug attacked my secretary, Officers, and she was defending herself, defending her person. It was complete self-defense and it was in her legal place of employment."

The officers grinned.

"Okay, Mr. Cruz," Officer Break said. "The thing about guys who think they can get away with stuff is they always mess up in the end."

"Now, don't blackball me," I said to them. "Look at my jacket. I don't even have a ticket. No arrests. No jail time ever. It's not my fault that private investigation is such a dangerous industry, but I'm the victim. I'm making a legal living."

"You have any weapons in that office, Mr. Cruz?" Officer Break asked.

"No. None," I answered confidently.

"A detective without a gun. You really do think we're dumb doofuses?" Officer Break said.

"You can check..."

"So your secretary didn't punch the man out the window, and you're a detective with no guns? It's okay, Mr. Cruz. We have all the statements we need from you and your secretary. Have a nice day. Two deaths from your office within the span of a month. You may not have been in criminal trouble before, but you are clearly wanting to make up for lost time. You have a very good day, sir."

The officer gestured for us to move off.

I could imagine what PJ and I looked like to them. We were two kids standing in front of a parent. The parent knew we did something wrong, but couldn't prove it. But they knew. And our sheepish "not little ol' us" expressions only confirmed it.

"We're going to add your picture on the POI board, Mr. Cruz. You know what that is? Persons of Interest," Officer Break said to us as we walked back into the office tower.

I was not interested in having the increased police scrutiny.

"You have a good day, Mr. Cruz. We'll be seeing you again."

When I got back to our floor, there was the police wrapping the front of my office with police crime tape—again. Dot was waiting in the hallway and gave me a "you're dead to me" look as she brushed past to the elevators. I was officially in the doghouse.

Danger was always fun when it remained an idea or the stuff of the hottest television shows. When you have to blow some guy's head off (literally) and watch him fall out the side of a building to keep him from blowing your head off, then danger isn't so fun anymore.

Dot was scared; that's all. She needed time to process what just happened, and she didn't even know this was the third incident involving assaults with deadly weapons on me in my new detective life. I also needed to process what just happened, almost happened, for the third time.

This time, the only way I came out on top was because I had a cyborg secretary acting illegally and my own illegal weapon. Was this what being a detective was all about? Being a borderline criminal to do your job, to stay alive?

I had gone my entire life without ever even getting a speeding ticket. No arrests, no jail time, nothing. No trouble with police, ever. Now I had gotten shot at three times in a space of two weeks! I had to get smart fast, or I'd get dead faster. There were no other options. I was in a job industry right on the ground floor of the city's mean streets. The streets obviously didn't like me.

How did that poem go? "These Mean Streets, Darkly. With its Cornucopia of Clients and Villains, Starkly." It was the opening quote in my *How to be a Great Detective with 100 Rules* I had now purchased to be my industry bible on my newly chosen vocation.

I needed to think about all this carefully. This detective life "ain't no joke," as they say. This was a job that immersed you in the grime and crime of the city, and there were no two ways about it. People would shoot at me and I'd have to shoot back at them. There'd be fisticuffs and all kinds of violence.

Mr. Wilford G. was lucky making it to 92. I, as a modern-day detective, better get as mean as the mean streets of Metropolis, or I'd be meat in the morgue. I had to decide fast. Be a detective and embrace the life, or quit it now and forever. Whatever I decided had to be final. Mr. Wilford G. said it in his book. There's nothing glamorous about this life— nothing. Some felt it was fantastic, but then they weren't private eyeing for a living.

I took a deep sigh and made the hard decision. I would quit. I wasn't cut out for this, and I was getting married. Dot wasn't cut out for this life. A lot of people would be disappointed, but I was the one dodging bullets. They like it so much, then they could be the detective. I'd go back to my hovercar restoration gigs.

Wait! I couldn't. I already did the full order for all my business cards—and PJ's too. Oh snaps! And the payment was non-refundable.

CHAPTER 27

Bugs

I knew I didn't have long, so I had to make it count. I didn't go home that night, but stayed in the office and made calls. It's exactly when you're down on the ground that people want to kick you. I would not go out like that. While I camped out in my own office, I must have made almost two dozen calls to contacts all across the city to people I knew. I told them what I wanted, and it was an urgent request.

Recommendations came flowing in and I had a crew knocking on my door before midnight. It was Bugs. He reminded me a lot of the late 92-year-old Mr. Wilford G. The man came in wearing overalls over his purple suit, holding a contraption with one hand and a telescoping wand in the other. He was old-school, which was exactly why he was so much in demand. Listening device detection, motion detection security, intrusion defense security, video surveillance, door and wall defense security, door and lock augmentation, trap door and panic rooms. He did everything that had to do with office security.

Even Run-Time used him, but Bugs wasn't considered an elite clientele operator. He wasn't even listed in the Yellow Pages, but he was always working—all word-of-mouth. Those in the know knew he was the best, and everyone was content with keeping the secret amongst themselves. I knew about him because of Dot's boss, Prima Donna, so I felt comfortable talking to him. I didn't want all my legit referrals to come from Run-Time and not-legit referrals to come from Phishy. I had to build my own Rolodex on my own.

Bugs brought his crew—a two-man team. It would take them until early morning to finish installing all the equipment in the office, outside the office in the hallway, and all the other spots Bugs said were a must for me to take control of my total office security. I was never going to be sucker shot at in my place of business, inside, coming, or going, ever again.

While the men worked, I kept my head buried in the books studying my newfound vocation, specifically, private investigation and the law. I needed to know it as well as criminals knew it when talking to law enforcement. I needed to know where the legal line was, so I could avoid it, or when needed, know when was safe to step over. Technically, I was a borderline criminal anyway, operating as an unlicensed detective with illegal weapons and a cyborg secretary, barred legally from using her bionic arms to sort out any variety of low-lives in her way.

My feet were up on my desk, books stacked up on my desk, and my mobile computer in my lap, when PJ peeked in. Strangely, she was always on time.

"Who are all these men?" PJ never said good morning.

"They'll be finished soon. Have Bugs show you the controls for the buzzer and your workstation has three video monitors now. One for outside the door, one showing the ground floor entrance, and the third shows our elevator."

"You won't have any money left after all this. You better get new clients so you can pay me."

"When I have legit clients coming up here, no punching. The police have us both flagged now. Things they let slide before, they won't now."

"What about metal detectors for the door? These men going to do that?"

"They did that already. Have Bugs show you that, too. And they installed some secret compartments too, for weapons."

"I want to keep my rifle under the desk handy. It will do me no good hiding in a secret compartment. I need it next to my hand for quick-draw situations. I don't have that fancy pop-gun like you."

"Wear long sleeves, and you can have one too."

"I hate long sleeves. Long sleeves are for squares. I got nice arms and they deserved to be shown off. If punks see the muscles, they won't be quick to cause any trouble."

"You want to show off fake arms with fake muscles."

"Ah, you're just jealous. Go get someone to cut off your arms, and you can have cool arms too."

"Have Bugs give you all the entry codes for the door and alarm system. And the bypass code for the metal detector arch. I don't want it going off every time you walk under it."

"What about your girlfriend? She'd set off the metal detector too."

"I got that handled."

"What about cyborgs with that new fancy non-metal metal bionics?"

"The metal detector detects all metals and all alloys. They can't make bionics from wood or glass yet, so we're covered."

"What about plastic? That's what they use Up-Top. I don't expect higher-end clients and criminals to come into this dump, but you might as well get your money's worth."

"Nah, they say it's plastic, but it's an alloy. To be as strong as it has to be, it has to be an alloy, not any cheapie plastic they use for toys and average hovercars. And Up-Top doesn't use bionics, they use biotics. They grow body parts in hospitals."

"We don't have that down here, this cheapskate planet. But it's okay, because bionics is better. Cyborgs are superheroes, not squares like Up-Top."

"Forget Up-Top. Just don't get caught illegally using those bionic arms, or you'll get thrown in jail again. You can't get paid a salary from jail."

It was an hour later when I realized the madness that was Punch Judy and I talking about nothing. Bugs was done and he interrupted us. He led PJ back to her workstation first to show her all the modifications and controls. It took him about forty minutes to show her the full scope of her power over all things security, before Bugs returned to my office.

"Punch!" I yelled as Bugs' eyebrows rose.

"What?" She popped into my office, and I threw the box to her.

"The business cards," I said.

She looked at the box, smiled, and disappeared.

"Sorry about that. We're a shouting office."

Bugs chuckled. "I noticed."

"How does it all look?" I asked.

"You'll be able to hold your own against even a full-scale office invasion."

"That's what I need."

"We're also taking care of all the wire maintenance. This building is centuries old, so we have to bury all the circuitry deep to keep it away from the bundle mess of every other floor, and businesses that don't even exist anymore, but the wires are still there. So keep an eye on that. But only if you see issues with operating performance. You need not do anything else beyond that. You really are spending a lot of cash on all this."

"Don't remind me. Do you need me to walk through everything again?"

"I'll walk you through everything again, and you can tell me if I miss anything for you."

"That'll be fine."

He dug into his pocket and produced a small wooden box. "And I can't forget this."

He handed me the box, and I looked at him. "Do I open it?"

"All the systems I use are analog. I don't trust that Up-Top, digital, supposedly-the-state-of-the-art technology. You want to rob me, then you will have to come right up to my place to do it. Not some hack with you in your underpants from a far, far away land. Do not bring any digital technology into this office. But if you do, use what's in the little box."

"What is it?"

"You'll know when you need to. Throw it in the top drawer of your desk until then. Now, let's do the final walk-through, so I can get home to the wife and kids and then get some sleep."

CHAPTER 28

The Realtor

I was ready. PJ was ready. And thanks to Bugs, my place of business was ready. It wasn't crooks and creeps I was worried about, but the return of one man.

It was an especially rainy day when he returned, three days after my third incident of the violence in my new detective life. PJ knocked once on my office door, before opening it to peek in. She was uncharacteristically professional, which meant she somehow knew the stakes involved. I stood from my desk and PJ gestured the Realtor man in.

He said nothing, but walked to my desk and sat in one of the two chairs.

I sat back down and immediately reached into the top drawer of my desk.

"I was expecting you," I said.

The Realtor man was here again and it wasn't for anything good. I figured he had a document in his jacket to give me my 90 days' notice to get the hell out, but I couldn't let him serve me with that document.

I opened the folder and turned it upside to place in front of him. "I took the initiative in assembling these for you and my unknown patron. A copy of the police report and their findings. The victim, known on the street as Tower Cracker, had a criminal record going back 15 years. Apparently, he had a habit of office-invasion robberies. Unfortunately, for him, he tangled with the wrong people this time. The next page is a photo of my shotgun. Ordinarily, it would be crazy to make a record of the weapons you keep for self-defense, since it's technically illegal, but I thought, in this case, it was necessary, and it's all confidential. This office is anything but defenseless. My secretary can defend herself, me, and the office space. I can defend myself, her, and the office space. Finally, I have the receipts of the modifications I made to the office—video camera outside the office, the elevator, main entrance, even the parking bay."

This was when the Realtor paid attention. I let him sift through the paper receipts and examine each one.

"As you can see, the surveillance and security systems installed are substantial. The last page is a bio of the firm that did the work, and their client list. They are reputable and tops in the industry. I..."

I stopped talking when the Realtor man closed the file. He folded it long ways a few times and put it inside his jacket pocket. For a moment, I glimpsed an envelope already there—I bet that was the eviction papers. He patted his jacket over the spot where the file was in his jacket and stood.

He didn't look at me, this time, but maintained a smirk as he spun around and left the office.

That was the fourth time I dodged a bullet.

I never saw that Realtor man again.

CHAPTER 29

The Government Guy

"Mr. Cruz, a Mr. Stackless is here to see you." Punch Judy was using her professional voice again, which meant that whoever Mr. Stackless was, he was important, in her eyes, at least.

She led a small man with the horn-rimmed glasses into my office and directed him to one of the open chairs in front of my desk then left.

"Mr. Stackless," I said as I shook the man's hand. His hands were clammy and disgusting. I suppressed my germophobic impulse to immediately soak my hand in cleansing acid. "How can I help you?"

The man, from the time he entered my office, was looking around. I didn't like it, and I didn't like him.

"I'm with the government, Mr. Cruz." Now, I had a reason not to like him. He sat in the chair and pulled a small notebook from his jacket. "I understand you're a detective."

"I'm a consultant. You have to be licensed to be a detective in this city."

He stared at me.

"I am not amused by your cleverness, Mr. Cruz. You are passing yourself off as a detective, accepting money as a detective, and getting written up in police reports as a detective."

"I'm a consultant, sir."

"But, I have the proof here," he exclaimed, holding up one of the lobby business cards.

"Can I see that?"

He handed me the card, and I studied it. "So?" I gave it back to him.

"You call yourself a detective."

"That's not what the card says."

He looked at the card again:

LIQUID COOL
Consultant Agency
D. Cruz
Private Consultant

He looked up at me angrily. We stared at each other for a while. Swapping cards like a magician was a trick I learned as a toddler. I was surprised he fell for it.

"I'm going to bust you, Mr. Cruz. I will report you and haul you into court."

I stood from my chair, walked around the desk, and sat in the empty chair next to his.

"Mr. Stackless, you do whatever you like. I'm not some sidewalk johnny, ignorant of the laws of the land. When, and if, you falsely bring a lawsuit against me, as you claim, just remember when it's thrown out of court as frivolous, I will countersue you and win. Metropolis courts have a lot more important things to worry about than business cards. I'm sure the judge will tell you that in colorful language and may even ask why your government division is using its scarce resources on such nonsense. And one more thing, Mr. Stackless."

"Yes," he answered.

"Get the hell out of my office."

I went back behind my main desk and sat. He glared at me as he stood from his chair. PJ opened the door—Bugs had also installed a silent buzzer under my desk, so I could signal when I was finished with a client.

"Judy, escort this bum from my office. Then get our attorney on the line and create a file on this man. He's threatening a frivolous lawsuit, so have the lawyer prep the counter-suit paperwork. Mr. Stackless works for the government."

"Oh, big money damages then." PJ was the best at playing along.

The man stormed out of my office and past her. PJ didn't even follow him, but closed the door behind her.

Some government guy comes in my office, trying to threaten my new livelihood. Shot at three times. Spending a fortune on the best surveillance and security systems, and I had no fortune. No way in hell was I giving up my new occupation now. I was committed for the duration.

CHAPTER 30

Officers Break and Caps

In this city, one of worst things that could happen was to get on the radar of the police. Then, you were a marked person, forever. It was a vicious cycle I had seen growing up. Get in trouble once, and the police would forever look at you as a source of trouble. It was a place you didn't want to be. And that's where I was.

PJ was in her professional mode when she led our "good friends," Officers Break and Caps, into my office. Seeing a "PEACE" officer always made your heart skip a beat, even the hardened thug who pretended not to be scared of anything. They were Metropolis' government soldiers in the never-ending war on crime, and they were, when they had to be, a nasty piece of work, able to obliterate a perp or hovercar single-handedly. They had to be scary. The citizens of Metropolis, including me, demanded it. You couldn't stop the criminals we had with anything less than a police force that was nothing short of hell on earth.

But still, my heart skipping beats wasn't good. The policemen stopped in front of my desk.

"How did I know we would be seeing you again, Mr. Cruz," Officer Break said.

"What did I do this time, officers?" I asked.

"We have a complaint that you attempted to assault a government agent..."

"Oh, Mr. Stackless."

"Yes, Mr. Cruz, Mr. Stackless."

I turned the folder in front of me on the desk and opened it.

"Here are pictures of Mr. Stackless parking his hovercar outside the building, walking up the stairs to the elevator, exiting the elevator, walking into my office." I flipped the photos. "Here is him leaving my office, exiting the elevator, walking down the stairs. Notice his appearance and demeanor. Doesn't seem to match with the state of someone who has been threatened with assault. Oh, here are my personal favorites. Mr. Stackless chatting it up, or is it propositioning, some underage girls..."

"You have a good day, Mr. Cruz," Officer Break said as both officers turned and left.

PJ's head popped into my office.

"I'm going to give Mr. Stackless a visit," I said.

CHAPTER 31

The Government Guy

The Metropolis Office of the City Clerk. It was the depository of the city's database of every micro-business, small to large business, and every multinational megacorporation, current and out-of-business, for hundreds of years. The amount of data they housed must have been staggering, and because of the confidentiality of that much information their offices were more like Fort Knox than anything else. They were insignificant file clerks elevated to super-star status, including their own Metro police building security detail, because of those files.

I had no idea what Mr. Stackless' real title was, but there he was behind the public intake counter as another businessperson registered with him. They had to get their pound of flesh, and their fees, anyway they could. Mr. Stackless, undoubtedly, had jurisdiction over my area, and I was an illegal, unregistered business in his eyes. Many people used the "I'm only a consultant" line to circumvent the laws. It never worked, but it could buy you time until you got the means to get the required licenses.

He never saw me enter the Clerk's office and take my seat in the waiting room, after taking a number from the bright dispenser by the door. The waiting room was packed when I arrived, and it was packed with over seventy people, two hours later, when my number was called.

"140!" Stackless yelled out.

He still didn't notice who I was until I was standing inches from him on the opposite side of his counter.

First, his face turned bright red, as he knew I wasn't there to register. He stared at me, not knowing what to do. He couldn't run, but he could call out to the big policeman outside the doors standing guard. The first move was mine.

"Your plan to jack me up with the police failed, so this is what you're going to do," I said to him in a hushed, but unpleasant tone. "You've tried to upset my business twice. Do you know what it's like to be the little guy in a supercity trying to get something going? Or have you been a government worker troll all your life and have never made an honest day's living? I don't have a cushy government job or a cushy corporate one, but you don't see me complaining. You don't see me hanging out on the street, like a sidewalk johnny. I'm trying to make things happen. So this is what you will do. I've solved a corporate case, and I've solved a case from an Average Joe. I need a case from a government guy to round out my virtual storefront reviews." I pointed at him. "You're going to get me that client for being an insufferable bum and to redeem yourself. I want and expect that referral from you. So what's it going to be?"

While I was talking, the redness of his face subsided. He was fully relaxed when I finished.

"Do detectives make payoffs for people?"

"Payoffs?" I asked.

"Yes...if someone's being...blackmailed. And they want someone to make the payoff for them."

"Yeah. We do that."

CHAPTER 32

Phishy

"Here, Phishy Phishy." I'm sure that was the playground tease Phishy had to endure as a child, but I never once joked about his name. I never teased anyone about their name. It was beneath me. It felt like childish stuff, and I didn't do childish stuff. I'm sure that's one reason Phishy always wanted to hang with me. I treated everyone the same, no matter the title or status. He appreciated that. And now I was partners with the crazy cat.

"Phishy!" I yelled and threw the wad of cash at him.

He was hanging on the street with his crew of sidewalk johnnies, like he always did, planning a scam, talking about a scam, or whatever. Phishy jumped in the air and snatched that wad of cash as if he had a bionic hand of steel. Then he transformed before my eyes and had a look. It was like when I threw a piece of chicken to this feral cat as a kid. The cat pounced on that piece of meat as if it had never eaten before and had this look, accompanied by a low, guttural growl. The piece of chicken was in a death-lock in its mouth, and if anything came near it, even its mother, it would scratch its eyes out. Phishy's face looked like that.

I stood there, watching him for a moment, until Phishy's psychotic mood passed.

"Oh." His smile returned. "I'm okay."

"You didn't look okay," I said.

He turned around and was fiddling with the groin area of his pants—I assumed the zipper.

"What the hell are you doing over there?" I yelled.

His sidewalk johnny buddies were in a laughing uproar. Phishy was jumping up and down, his back to me, fiddling with his pants. He stopped, did something, and then looked to pull up his zipper. By this point, his crew was rolling on the wet ground laughing so hysterically I thought for sure they'd have heart attacks.

Phishy turned around to face me. The wad of cash was gone from his hands.

"I'm really okay now," he said.

"Don't even tell me you did what I think you did."

He laughed.

"Girls hide it up there," he said, rubbing his chest. "We put it down there."

"Phishy, it's called a wallet, and it goes in your pants pocket or your jacket pocket. What's wrong with you?"

"Nah, you get robbed that way. No one's going to reach in there. Not even the police."

"Okay, enough Phishy, I don't even want to hear about your personal body security measures."

"Give us a handshake," he said jokingly as he walked to me like a zombie with his hand outstretched.

"Get away from me, Phishy."

He kept coming, and I ran away.

CHAPTER 33

The Wans

When I was a kid in school, I never got into fights. There were plenty of bullies, but my world never really intersected with theirs. Actually, I was too busy with all my off-school hobbies and interning to care much about anyone or anything at school. Run-Time was the same, which is why we became such good friends early on. School was a pit stop on the road of life and an insignificant one, at that.

However, as you grow older, one's style starts to take form. That's when I started wearing fedoras. Back then, elaborate hair-styles were the rage, so it was unthinkable to cover your hair with a hat, which was exactly why my contrarian-self did it. And that's when I became a target of the bullies. They did the unthinkable—they tried to snatch my hat. It was a mistake they didn't make ever again, because I beat up the first three so badly, even my few school friends, like Run-Time, were shocked. I think he started wearing his flat caps sometime after I got the reputation in school, "Don't touch Cruz's hat. He'll go psycho on your ass." My rep was so widely known that local gangs came all the way to school to try to recruit me as an enforcer, which made me laugh. "I'm a germophobe, so hitting strangers with all that blood and sweatiness is nasty," I told them. I thought my logical explanation had kept the gangs away only to learn, many years later, that it was the Principal and my Pops who "went after them" and made it crystal clear never to come to the school again for me or to recruit any other kids.

Don't touch my hat. Don't grab my hat. Only I had the power to remove it and place it on my head. Any transgressions relating to my hat would evoke psycho behavior, very similar to my response for scratching my vehicle. It was a place you didn't want to go.

Speaking of psychos, Dot's father, Mr. "I'll cut you" Wan came to my new office, and I wanted to know why. I could have ignored it, but I felt if I ignored it, he and Mrs. "I'll poison you" Wan would feel they could stop by anytime they liked. My future parents-in-law had to know there were boundaries, and the only way to do that was to visit their business. Fair is fair.

The Wans were ridiculously rich, like anyone else who lived in Elysian Heights. I did my own research on them, though not as thorough as I'm sure they did on me. They made their fortune in computers, but now dabbled in practically everything, which seemed was to give themselves something to do, rather than making money. I would never have guessed it, but they owned one of the major Chinese food chains in Metropolis. They owned tons of businesses, but a Chinese food chain? It seemed so...beneath them. All the good Chinese food chains were owned by Jamaicans. In all my life, did I ever eat Chinese food from a Chinese food store owned by Chinese? I don't think so.

I was playing real detective. I had tracked them from one business to the other until I got to their Fantasia Chinese Food Take-Out and Restaurant chain store. I even parked in the same parking lot they did and, waiting until they were out-of-sight, headed for the elevators. Neon Blues was a working class mixed-use business and residential district like Woodstock Falls, but again, the rich didn't frequent working class neighborhoods, only other rich ones or richer ones. Besides, since I was still in the doghouse with Dot, the time was right for a potential confrontation with her parents.

It was my luck I picked the day that it was raining heavier than normal to tail them around the city. I didn't do umbrellas, but with my fedora and my jacket, I always kept dry underneath. A little moisture on the face was healthy as far as I was concerned. Fantasias were all alike— restaurants with their donut style tables with stools around them and benches along the storefront so people could sit and eat, looking out the main street. You saw one and you saw them all, ground-level food establishment.

Because of the rain, my head was tilted further down than it normally would have been as I walked to the store, and then it happened. A man burst out the establishment and crashed into me. Both of us fell onto the wet pavement. He fell back; I had braced my fall with my hands. The brown-haired man with a goatee was in a shiny-black, trench coat slicker. There I was, in a push-up position to keep my entire body from touching the wet asphalt ground. Then he did it. The stranger grabbed my hat from my head and ran away!

"What!" I jumped up to my feet.

I was about to run after him when someone else bolted out of the store and crashed into me. We fell to the wet ground. It was Mr. Wan.

"He stole my hat!" I yelled.

"He stole my money!" Mr. Wan yelled, and he grabbed the gun that fell from his hand.

Another figure came out of the store. It was Mrs. Wan.

"Get up! He's getting away." She was also armed.

The three of us looked at each other.

"That bastard stole my hat, and he's mine."

"Go away, you bum!" Mrs. Wan yelled at me. "He has our money. He's ours."

"You have no gun, so go away, bum for my daughter's boyfriend."

"That's fiancé to you!" I pulled my gun from my jacket—surprising the heck out of them—and ran after the robber.

People don't run through the streets. Criminals run away. Gang members run after each other. Normal people walk. But I don't suppose I or the Wans were normal. We were going to get that robber. I could chase him forever with my OCD-self. I suspected the Wans were made of the same DNA. That robber was in serious trouble and didn't even know it. Besides, he wasn't armed, but we were.

I was only ahead of the Wans, because I surprised them and dashed away first, but they were right on my heels. Crowds of gray or black slickered pedestrians were everywhere; we had to dodge people and umbrellas. He was like a wild rabbit as he went around the corner, with us in hot pursuit. I was gaining on him, and he glanced back. Then he suddenly stopped, turned, and took a knee. That meant only one thing: he was armed and, of course, shot at me.

I didn't stop, duck, or dodge. But the next shot made me slide to a stop as I fought to keep my balance. I had a choice. Shoot at him and fall into a massive dank puddle of water or keep from falling altogether. That puddle was nasty, so my choice was made for me. I didn't even realize the consequences of the choice I made. The robber aimed at me again. A shot came from right next to my ear. Mrs. Wan blasted my hat right off his head.

"My hat!" I yelled.

The robber jumped up and ran when Mr. Wan shot him right in the butt. In grabbing his backside, he dropped his gun.

This time, the Wans ran first after him, and I stopped briefly to pick up my undamaged, but damp, hat. I wasn't putting it back on my head now that it touched the ground.

"That is the last time I'm getting shot at by a stranger!" I yelled and continued the chase.

LIQUID COOL

The three of us chasing this robber down the city streets was mad. My parents couldn't run like the Wans were after this robber. I think he knew they were going to assassinate him if they ever caught up to him. But now, another sneaking feeling came over me. The robber wasn't running away from us. He was running *to* some place. Where? What was he planning? People die every day in Metropolis. I had a new mission with getting my hat back. I had to keep the three of us alive. Dot couldn't come home after a long day and have a peace officer waiting for her at home to tell her that her parents and boyfriend-fiancé were gunned down chasing some fast-finger freddie robber.

The robber ducked into a storefront.

"Don't follow him!" I yelled at Dot's parents.

They either didn't hear me or ignored me and ran right into the dark place after him. I had no choice, but to follow.

If I knew what was waiting for me on the other side, I'm not sure I would have crossed that threshold. It was obvious as soon as my eyes adjusted to the dim light; we had run right into some gang den. The Wans had their guns pointed at the robber. The patrons of whatever the heck this place was, maybe a bar, were pointing guns at them. They saw me and turned. I was sick of being shot at it. So I went gun crazy.

I shot at them until there were no more bullets, and the Wans did the same. Incredibly, the robber ran out the back as his comrades got shot full of holes. How was this robber getting away after getting butt-shot? Everyone not shot by us were running out of the establishment, like a stampede. I looked and the Wans were gone out the back. I wanted to run with the crowd out of the place, but I had to see this through and ran out the back after the Wans, because they were out of rounds, too.

From madness in a darkened bar to madness in a back-alley with pouring rain. The robber was beating the Wans with some metal pipe! He didn't see me as I charged at him and smashed him against the wall. He tried to get up to hit me with the pipe, but I remembered what I did

243

when those bullies tried to take my hat in school. I could fight dirty-vicious and kicked him, not in the head—I kicked him in the eye, the nose, the front of his teeth, in his left eardrum. He dropped the metal pipe and realized I was the one he should be scared of and was smart enough to block my kicks.

But then, the Wans jumped him, and he did the incredible.

"Help! I'm being robbed! They're going to kill me! Help!"

The robber was yelling for police on us! Real life can just be so wrong. We were going to pound this guy until his body parts pushed through the ground, the center of the Earth, through the hot magma, until he pushed through the other side of the planet in China. But then we froze as the spotlights beamed down on us.

"THIS IS THE POLICE! Put your hands up or be fired upon and killed!"

I had never been so scared in my life. The words from the police, as they descended from the dark rainy sky, made my blood freeze. I had gone my entire adult life, until this day, not hearing those words. I hadn't ever gotten a speeding ticket in my life, but now I was in a holding cell in the furthest corner at the front with my face pressed between the bars. Mr. Wan and I were in jail. But we were in jail with a *lot* of other guys. I was like a big, wet rat trying to squeeze through the bars. My mind was flooded with all those stories you heard growing up about what happens to people who go to jail. "News at 11. Six-foot-tall, three-hundred-pound Navy Seal sent to jail was found dead and stuffed in his coffee mug." "News at 12. Man named Butch was sent to prison and came out as a woman, named Sally. Authorities say they only left him unattended for five minutes, so they don't know how it happened." I could barely keep from shaking, because I had a quick glance at the other guys in the cell with us before I pressed my face against the cell bars. Every last one of them looked like multiple-murderers in their prime.

Mr. Wan, God Bless him, was yelling at them in Chinese a mile a minute. They hadn't jumped us yet, because they were still trying to figure out if he was cursing at them or casting a voodoo spell on them or reciting the best recipes for an authentic Chinese meal. We must have been so funny to them, a real live sitcom before their eyes.

He turned toward the police outside. We couldn't see them, but they were there. "That criminal stole my money!" Mr. Wan yelled. "I should let criminals steal my money? I should let criminals steal the shirt off my back? Here, take the shirt off my back!" He proceeded with ripping off his fancy dress shirt and then pulled off his T-shirt. He bundled them together, snapped the jail cell bars like a whip and continued to yell at the two police who walked into view. "Here, take the shirt off my back!"

The prisoners were getting such a good show, and one of the serial killer looking guys laughed so hard at the agitated Mr. Wan, he collapsed to the floor. It didn't stop there as Mr. Wan yelled, "Here, take my pants too." He undid his pants.

"Hold on there, sir," one of the officers yelled. "We are not interested in a strip show from the likes of you!"

He began to furiously slap the cell bars with his shirt and T-shirt, yelling at them in Chinese. Then we heard an eruption of yelling in Chinese from Mrs. Wan in the holding cells from around the corner. The cops just looked at each other, not knowing what to do.

"Here take my shirt! Take my pants! You the criminals!" Mr. Wan yelled at them.

"Shut up, or we'll stun you!" one police officer yelled.

"Stun me!" Mr. Wan yelled and whipped the bars with his clothes.

"Shut up!" the policeman yelled.

"Stun me!" he yelled again.

"Shut up, both of you!"

"Stun me!"

The Wans' screaming in Chinese and English was relentless. The only reason I wasn't trying to dig out my own eardrums was because my mind was someplace else. It was the reason I was pressed at the outer edge of the cell. Germs! My germophobia wasn't an off-again-on-again figment of my imagination. It was real. At one point in my childhood, my parents had considered putting me in those bubble communities—hermetically sealed communal communities for those with no physical immune system to live in the natural world or those, like me, who psychologically were the equivalent. What had saved me was a nice child therapist lady, who taught me how, in a self-hypnotic Zen way, to re-order my mind. Unfortunately, the technique only worked if my mind didn't cross into that "zone." It was too late—my jitters had started. All I could think about was all the reports of how trash offices are cleaner than the local jail, and how the average prisoner carries ten times the unhealthy microbes than the average person. My mind was fixating on Ebola and every other contagious disease known to man. Then images of the Nose Chunk Flu came into my mind. I could feel my legs giving way. I closed my eyes and tried to summon every nano-unit of composure I had left in me.

Then the Wans stopped yelling, suddenly. I opened my eyes. *There was Dot!*

The topless—and pantless—Mr. Wan was frozen. I was already frozen, wedged between the two cell bars. Mrs. Wan was silent.

Dot looked at the main officer and said, "Are they being arrested?"

"We had to hold them until we verified their story, which we have, but they wouldn't behave, so we left them in there."

"So I can leave them here?"

"If it were anyone else, I'd leave them there. But I don't think I can take any more of their antics, so I will have to ask you to take them with you now."

Dot turned her back to us and whispered to the officer. He listened and then nodded. With that, she walked out of the station.

It must have been another hour or two before the officers opened the cell door and escorted Mr. Wan and me out. Mrs. Wan appeared with a female officer. The three of us were lifted up by full silver-and-gray peace officers and pushed out of the station into the pouring rain.

"If I ever see you three again, you won't be held pending investigation. You will be arrested, booked, convicted, and jailed for real," one police officer said. "I pity that young lady having any relation to the likes of the three of you. The three of you are definitely cut from the exact cloth. I'm sure we'll see you all again in some capacity. Until then, get out of our sight!"

We stood there in the rain looking at each other. There was no Scotty from the Enterprise to beam me up and away from my parents-in-law, so I did the only thing I could do, short of teleportation. I ran away as fast as I could.

My first stop would be the main Disease Control center to sterilize my clothes and give me a full anti-biohazard shower. It was something the average citizen didn't know about, but it was all covered by medical insurance.

CHAPTER 34

Compstat Connie

I would put myself in the "box". It wasn't a real box, and it wasn't even a physical thing. It was what I called completely separating yourself from people and any possible distractions to get some major life task done. It was like going off to a secluded island, but you could go anywhere, even your own place. The key was unplugging from everyone and everything to create your own "fortress of solitude" for an indefinite period.

But I found out there was another group of people, who liked to put themselves in a "box" away from the outside world and all possible distractions to sit and assimilate a set of knowledge like a machine—gazillionaires. All these CEO, founders, and innovative genius scientists of the greatest corporations seem to do it in their quest to come up with the next "big thing." Unlike normal people, they had island retreats, lunar strongholds, or personal flying cities to go to, but it was the same concept—cut yourself off from humanity with a ton of books and no access to the Net.

So, the original idea was not my own. Monks did that long before the Greeks invented money and there could be gazillionaires. Solitude was a must, and often, some quasi-fasting was involved. There was absolutely no answering the video-phone, texts, or emails. For the hardcore, nakedness sometimes was also involved. They said the purpose of all this was to get to your most primal state, so your "inner child" would not only emerge, but go wild. Well, I wasn't doing the complete full monty nakedness in my place. No clothes except for my boxers was what I did.

Regular eating and sleeping also went out the window. When this primitive process of hyper-knowledge consumption was over, they had a flurry of new ideas for their next robot, machine, computer system or program, vehicle, or spaceship. I couldn't knock the process when it worked for me, too.

I had done it before when I was much younger, when I wanted to know everything there was about classic hovercars and restoring them. I don't think I left my place for three whole months, as I consumed every piece of data about hovercars, the technology to make them, the technology to keep them running, and all those ninja tactics that would set me above anyone else doing what I was doing. I was in my twenties and was in all the top classic hovercar clubs in my neighborhood and beyond. Every other member of those clubs was at least in their fifties, so I was the "child prodigy". But I wasn't a genius. I simply channeled my OCD tendencies into something productive.

So I was about to do this for my new vocation. I needed to, because I was about to jump right back into the Easy Chair Charlie case, and the client was me. Easy never touched guns, so the notion he went gun-crazy one night was...crazy. I was also still checking around on the Guy Who Got Shot in My Office and the guy PJ threw through the door and I blasted out the window with my pop-gun. Then yesterday, someone showed up at the office main entrance, and he looked a lot like the sucker shooter who tried to gun me down in front of my place. Thank

God for remote video surveillance. He sniffed around (literally) and then left.

Random violence happened in Metropolis all too often. But this wasn't random. I couldn't prove it yet, but the bigger question was— why? I would learn everything possible, and impossible, there was to know about that night of the crime. So, before I went into the "box", I had to visit Compstat Connie. She was like the female version of Wilford G. Megacorporations had machines that knew all there was to know worth knowing. The City had Connie and, lucky for me, I first met her when I was a police intern kid in school. So that, not my business card, was my introduction to her.

City Hall looked different because of its white marble interior, flecks of embedded black paint, with huge columns from ceiling to ground throughout. But it was ruined by the video displays everywhere that showed the Mayor and City Hall meetings, department meetings, committee meetings, ad infinitum.

This was the second time I had business at the city in the space of a few days. Based on all the referrals the Government Guy gave me, I would be here a lot more often.

Downtown Metropolis was the nerve center of the city. I would never say the brain, because that implies intelligence. The city was not that and never would be; it was what controlled the brain. Its monolith towers were no bigger or taller than any other in the city, but they always looked different when I flew by in my vehicle. Some said it was its historic architecture of lighter colored paint for its exterior in contrast to the dark hues of the surrounding towers. But really, in the dark rainy skies, no one notices. It had to be a state of mind. You knew it was the center of power, so you intuitively saw that in its buildings when, in reality, it was the same as everywhere else.

While the City Clerk's office was in a prominent place in the main city towers, the Crime Information Center (CIC) of the Police Department was in what could only be called the basement levels. The Clerk's office had guards and other visible security; CIC had nothing.

Compstat Connie had to be in her late seventies, and she ran the multi-hundreds-of-millions-of-dollars division, but when I entered the subterranean offices, she was at the counter sorting through papers, like she was an entry level worker. It was the same with the Government Guy, who was at a counter doing his own work. It seemed in government, unlike the corporate world, you may get the title and the salary, but you did the same grunt work you did as when you were first hired.

It was still unbelievable, because it was such an important office for the police higher-ups. CompStat (Computer Statistics) was all the crime data collected in the city. That was her division, and it drove everything that the police did—deployment, budgets, resources, and personnel. The stats made it into every government press conference, including all the way to the mayor.

"Why do you look familiar?" she said, watching me from the counter. It seemed like there was no one else in the office, with row-after-row of shelves to the ceiling with file boxes.

We were now sitting in her tiny office. I handed her the "graduation" picture from the last day of my police internship—students and police personnel.

"Well, look at that," she said holding the picture. "Back when my hair had color, other than white. Cruz, isn't it?"

I was amazed. "There's absolutely no way you'd remember me from all those years ago." I laughed. "I wasn't memorable, and there were like fifty other interns running around."

"No, I remember you. I may be old, but I have a great memory. You hung around my division."

"I interned for you."

"And the uniformed officers, too."

251

"You do remember me."

"I told you. What can I do for you?"

"I want to become the male version of you."

She laughed. "Meaning what?"

"It was the talk you gave to us."

"I remember people, but I can't remember one of all those silly presentations I gave back then. I couldn't remember it, even if it were yesterday. It's always off the cuff, spur of the moment, when I give presentations."

"You told us how everything is connected, and your division looks at all the data, and after it absorbs every data point, it can see the connections, the trends, and patterns. That's the ultimate in crime-fighting tools—those connections."

"I said that?"

"You did."

"And you remember it?"

"I do."

"Why would a high school kid remember a speech like that? Were you going to be a cop?"

"No, but it helped me with other occupations. Seeing connections where other people didn't. That's why I'm visiting. I want to do that for one specific day."

"A specific day? What day?"

I knew the day and time like my own birthday.

Compstat Connie reached behind the counter for her mobile computer and started typing.

"What stands out to you about the day?" I asked.

There was a specific reason I asked the question, and if Compstat Connie was the same casual human computer she was before, she'd basically do my work for me—cutting off hours, maybe days, from me being in the "box."

She stared at her screen. "That was the night of the big shootout at Joe Blows." She read more. "And the kidnapping of a little girl at Alien Alley. All the rest of your standard car-jacks, armed robberies, rapes, office invasions, murders."

"But why did you mention those two specific incidents first?"

"They're anomalies. All the rest is normal fare in the city."

"That's what I mean," I said to her. "I need to be able to see anomalies and understand how your mind gets you there. How long will it take you to teach me?"

"Do you have five decades to spare?"

I laughed. "No, but I'll give the time I need to give. Think of me as your returning intern, two decades later."

"I thought you were some kind of hovercar guy."

"I have a new occupation, but don't tell the Clerk's Office."

She chuckled.

"I'm like a private detective."

"Now that intrigues me."

CHAPTER 35

Trash Boss

Who was the most powerful of them all? One government agency to rule them all. It wasn't transportation, energy, health services, or even the police; it was garbage—Trash Services.

One reason I didn't mind the rain, like most people, was because the alternative would be far worse. Imagine this world as a smoky, humid hot-house. We'd all kill ourselves. People forgot that no matter how sophisticated and advanced we thought ourselves to be, any populated city has two things, no matter what: people and waste. Waste services was one of the many gray words people created for polite conversation. Wet, smelly, dirty, venal garbage. You could work yourself into a psychosis, simply imagining how much garbage flowed through a city of 50 million people on top of each other by the day, hour, or minute. Nasty! If the power ever went out, it wasn't the cessation of food to the markets that terrified me. If we ever had an Extinction Level Event, it would be that no toilets would flush, and there'd be no one to pick up the trash. My own borderline clinical germophobia would be unrestrained to a point beyond any ability to manage.

The filth is what I feared, and so did everyone else, which was why trashmen were treated with the respect they got. Everyone knew what would happen in mere hours if there were no City Trash and Waste Services. A reporter did an exposé and said the city could survive a few days without food, a week without water, without the Net for about ten days max, because of how many critical systems were manned by only machines. But the absence of trash and waste services would render the supercity unlivable within six hours. I once had to beat myself up to stop thinking about it, because a severe germophobic panic attack had gripped me and I felt my sanity slipping away. I think that was why people truncated their official name from Trash and Waste to just Trash Services.

One thing about being involved, even tangentially, with the hovercar racing scene, as I had been, was you saw places of the city no one else had seen. These secret thruways and back alleys no one ever went made you firmly aware of the secret underground world of trash. On the main streets, trash was picked up quickly, never being allowed to pile up for too long. In secluded lots and alleys, that was not so, as the many amateur (and illegal) hovercar street races had shown me.

It was at one of these secret, amateur races, a few years back I met the Surf Brothers. The brothers were also into classic hovercars, so we hit it off and talked for hours about the scene whenever we met. It was through them I met their boss, Mr. Pyle.

I had heard of him before, when I was a police intern kid. People didn't just throw garbage in the garbage. At Metro Police Central, I got an earful at one presentation about all the weapons, body parts, and full human bodies thrown into the trash. In fact, Trash Services and the Metro Police worked together on cases far more than anyone could imagine, which was why the Director of Trash Services had a dotted line report to the Chief of Police. If you're a criminal and want to get rid of the evidence, don't throw it in the trash. They'll find it.

I drove out to Nil Point early in the morning. The rain was coming down hard, but I paid it no mind. Rain or no rain, no matter what time of day, hovercar traffic would be awful.

Nil Point was where the official offices of Trash Services were located—way out, away from the real main city. It was where all the garbage hovertrucks were always flying to and from. The skies around their building headquarters were thick with their vehicles, almost like swarming bees.

I was surprised that I didn't smell much as I approached the public parking area. What did I expect, open rivers of sewage?

The public parking lot was huge. Trash Headquarters was the center, then a circle around it for government employee parking and the handicapped, then the outer rings for everyone else. There were public hovershuttles that also buzzed around the parking lot, small pods made for the driver, and one or two passengers. They were old, beat-up, and I didn't even want to know the condition of the public seats in the back. I smiled at the driver, who hovered near me, and waved him off. I pulled down my fedora, pulled up my collar, and buttoned my coat. I was used to walking, since I always parked my vehicle away from everyone else, like every owner of a classic vehicle did. The rain was bad, but then, it often was.

I was happy to arrive at the main building if only to get the hell out of the rain. There, I saw the metal detector arch with a policeman on either side.

"Oh," I said out loud. "I forgot my papers." I spun around and went back into the rain.

Was this the crap criminals had to go through?

I walked all the way back to my vehicle in the rain, got in, unloaded all my illegal weapons, got out, and trudged all way back through the even heavier downpour to walk back inside. The two police officers were standing there laughing hysterically at me. They weren't stupid.

As I walked to the arch, one of them said, "Sure you got all of them?" They burst out laughing again.

I ignored them and proceeded through. "Can you point me to Mr. Pyle's office?" I asked.

"Penthouse floor, of course," one of them answered.

Pyle knew he was an important man in the government; everyone knew it, and he made sure those who didn't, knew it too. I met him only once before hanging out with the Surf Brothers. I didn't like him then; I didn't like him now.

He was one man but had seven full-time secretaries, and though I had made an appointment and was early, I still waited fifteen minutes past the time. My rule is, if I'm late, cancel the appointment on my ass. But if I'm early or on time, I don't expect to be waiting. One of his secretaries led me into his office, and I walked in with an obviously annoyed look on my face.

"I hope I'm not inconveniencing your schedule," I said before I reached his desk.

He knew I was irritated, but didn't care as he shook with a vice grip handshake. All trashmen had biceps of steel. "I was on the phone with the Mayor."

I didn't believe him, but I let it go.

"Thanks for taking the time," I said as he gestured to take a seat in the very wide and plush chair in front of his desk. He sat, too.

"How can I help you, Mr. Cruz? I understand you're a detective?"

"Well, since my licensing is on the distant horizon, I'm a consultant."

He chuckled and my little admission—government non-compliance—seemed to be an asset in his eyes.

"How can I help, Mr. Cruz, the consultant?" Another man came from behind, rolling up another chair next to me. "This is my Chief of Staff."

The trash boss needed a chief of staff? That's silly, I thought.

"Mr. Cruz," he greeted me, too.

He sat and opened up a digital notepad with one hand as he held a stylus pen with the other.

"How can I help you, Mr. Cruz?" Trash Boss repeated. "The Surf Brothers told me you've known them for years."

"They have a couple of very nice classic vehicles. I helped restore them. Well, Mr. Pyle, to get right to it, I need access to some video tapes." I leaned forward in my chair. "Is this conversation subject to public record?"

"Listen to him," the Trash Boss said to his chief and then turned to me. "You sound like a lawyer. No, it's private. What video are you talking about?"

"Back in the day, when I was interning for the police in school, I learned a little known fact. I'd say secret. I learned that your office had a dotted line report to the Chief of Police. Something like that sticks in the mind of a kid. How is it that the trashman is partners with the policeman? I learned that one reason was that your people in the field often come across weapons, contraband, and bodies obviously of interest to the police. But the other reason is because all those garbage hovertrucks out there, every last one, like every police and fire vehicle, is also a flying camera and is always recording."

The two men watched me quietly.

"Who told you that?" the chief of staff man asked me. "Because it's not true. Some vehicles have surveillance for insurance and safety purposes, but they are not part of some city surveillance network as you seem to be saying."

I glanced at the chief with a look of annoyance and returned my focus to the Trash Boss. "Can you help me out, Mr. Pyle?" I reached into my pocket and placed a highlighted report on his desk. "It's obvious I can keep a secret. I've already demonstrated that for almost twenty years. I know your people don't even know their vehicles are rigged for public surveillance, and I'm not interested in them finding out. With so many involved in off-the-record, off-the-books salvage, you'd have a full-scale mutiny. But I'm sure you could get a video to me. The highlight on the report has to do with a woman, who had her daughter kidnapped."

The annoying chief of staff said, "There's a kidnapping every hour in the city."

I gave him another of my "shut up" looks, then returned my attention to Trash boss. "What do you say?"

"Mr. Cruz, unfortunately, the information you were given is completely incorrect. My fleet is not rigged for surveillance. The union would have my scalp if we ever did, especially secretly, as you're suggesting. I like my job and want to keep it. What makes this one kidnapping so important, anyway? My Chief of Staff is right; kidnappings happen every day. Think about the consequences of what you're asking, even if it were true."

"Yeah, it would be tied up in the courts forever on privacy grounds. I don't care about that. I have a specific range of times and specific areas I'm interested in. I'll sit through all the video myself."

"No such tapes exist, Mr. Cruz."

"Oh, did you hear about the reward being offered? I'll split it with you."

"Sorry, we can't help you."

"Oh, I'm sorry I wasted your time, Mr. Pyle. And your chief of staff. Umm. Who's Mr. Dyer?"

The men gave me dirty looks.

"You know exactly who the president of the Trash and Waste Services Union is, Mr. Cruz."

CHAPTER 36

Just Me

The review from the Corporate Guy was like gold in getting in front of other people in the corporate world. I had PJ print a ton of intro cards with their reviews prominently displayed on the back. None of them cared about me or my credentials. All that mattered was that I was referred by a fellow corporatist. The review for the Government Guy had the same effect within government circles. I wanted to make sure I established myself as a generalist detective, right from the start. The Guy Who Scratched My Vehicle and family were the icing on the cake in telling people I worked for the Average Joe too. I had the business trifecta—corporate, government, and the people.

Clients were fine, but in the end, could they pay me?

When I called PJ into my office, she had her normal Punch Judy swagger that said "whatcha want?" like I often did when I was in my moods. After I tossed her a wad of bills—her bionic hand made sure not to drop it—she couldn't stop smiling.

"How do you know what secretaries earn in salary?"

"I looked it up on the Net."

"Are you paying me below market or above market?"

"Above market. Liquid Cool is a classy joint with a reputation."

She stuffed the wad of cash into her bra. I had told Phishy women don't do that in real life.

"I really didn't need to see that," I said.

The rest of the day would be her telling me, or talking to herself—I couldn't tell which, about all the shoes and new dresses and jewelry she was going to buy with her first official paycheck.

For me, I sat behind my desk, leaning back in the chair with my feet on my desk and hands interlaced, cradling the back of my head. I wasn't playing detective; I was one. I had an office, one employee, slick weapons, the business cards to prove I was real, and clients that paid me with checks that didn't bounce. As the saying went, Life was good, and even I had a hard time suppressing a smile.

But Wilford G.'s *How to be a Great Detective with 100 Rules* warned me. "The quickest way to go from being a working private eye to being a dead one was being content. Contentment was the devil. It makes you stupid and slow. If you caught yourself smiling, slap yourself. If you're feeling good, get off your butt and go get another client, because you clearly have too much free time. Never forget that the working detective is an endangered species. A wide variety of punks want to do bodily violence to you. They want to put you in the morgue meat market. You want contentment? Go be a monk on Xanadu Pleasure Colony. You want to be a working detective, never smile. There're a lot of grinning dead detectives in the morgue. Keep your hand on the trigger of your favorite piece, and your head always in the game. Be the hero, even if it hurts. Then maybe, possibly, a small chance, you'll live as long as me, with some cash to rub together."

I think that's what endeared me to Wilford G. immediately. He embraced the word, hero. He said forget all that anti-hero, psychobabble, fake suave crap. Never buy into that "fight the System," "fight the

Man," "fight the Power" nonsense. Stay away from the politics, leave the cosmic brooding behind, and stay away from the negative, victim mentality stuff. "A true detective cannot and can never be a victim. We fight the odds, the system, and bad guys. That's why we get hired." "People want a champion in their corner." "The societal scientist, Isaac Asimov, invented three laws for the robot that we still use today. I have three laws for the modern urban detective. What is your number one?

"If 'helping people' or some like phrase isn't Number One, then get out now. If you're in this racket for anything else, then you have no chance. You're going to have to do a lot of bad to do good, and it better be bad things against bad people. If your motives are not pure to begin with, then forget it. You're either a criminal or about to become one— you're one of the bad guys. Close my damn book! My book is for good guys."

I remember, I laughed out loud when I read that. The other thing he said that stuck with me was his answer to why he was a detective for so long. "Why? Because it's an adventure, and danger is the price of admission, and I wouldn't have it any other way." The passage calmed me down after my first sucker shooter at my place.

I had all the ingredients necessary to make it as a private investigator in this crazy supercity of Metropolis. As I heard the launch control say so often, prior to any manned space flight, "All systems were a go." Figuratively speaking, it was up to me to make sure my rocket ship didn't get blown up in space, crash into a star, or get sucked into a black hole. Wilford G. had many sayings, and I had mine. "Being a detective ain't no joke."

Waiting for me at my place was a ton of files, courtesy of Compstat Connie, all from the night Easy Chair Charlie got himself killed. I would leave PJ in charge of the office for two weeks, have Phishy look in on her and do some associated errands for me, and give Dot some away-time (since I was still technically in the "doghouse" with her after the shooting the man out of the window incident), while I locked myself in the "box" at my place, clad in boxers alone. I wouldn't emerge from the Concrete Mama until I assimilated every bit of that data with my OCD self.

The next time this office saw me would be for the real beginning of the Liquid Cool Detective Agency.

PART EIGHT

Formerly Known as The Easy Chair Charlie Case

CHAPTER 37

Phishy

Two weeks ago, it began. I parked my Pony, went up to my place, and locked the door behind me. But before I did all that, I had to do one thing with a former-frenemy before I walked through the door to see another former-frenemy. Before I entered my Box, there were two words I had to say:

"Shoot me," I said.

Phishy had a pained expression on his face. There were many nooks and crannies in Metropolis one could find to do bad things in. We were in an above-ground, unused aqueduct. I stood at one end and Phishy was three yards away facing me.

"Cruz, this is the craziest thing you've ever done. You're supposed to avoid getting shot."

"I'm subconsciously scared of getting shot."

"What's wrong with that? All normal people are. I'm scared of getting shot."

"You don't understand. When I was a kid and we were playing dumb soccer on the field, I was the goalie, and I was really good. I stopped everything that came at me. But one day, one of the bigger boys kicked the ball so hard, purposely below the waistline. The ball almost hit me in the nuts. From that day forward, I was useless. Every kick from anyone I imagined was going to hit me in the nuts. I had to stop being goalie. I was scared, and everyone knew it. I was defeated by my mind, not the actual thing. Big boy had found my Achilles heel, and mentally, I could never get around it.

"But I'm not a kid anymore. You defeat your fears by tackling them head-on. Scared of heights? Go skydiving. Scared of deep water? Become a scuba diver. I can't be a detective if I am afraid of getting shot and get all wobbly in the knees at the possibility," I said.

"But fear keeps you from being shot."

"Phishy, I've already been shot at three times in less than a month of being a detective. What do you imagine will happen in the years to come? I can't be afraid. Fear and reflexes will keep me from getting killed, but I can't be paralyzed by the fear of getting shot. The only way to overcome my fear is...to get shot. After that, my mind will be at ease. It will say, 'self, I'm not afraid of getting shot. Because I already have.'"

"Cruz, that's some pretty bad logic to me."

"I know my OCD mind, and it makes perfect sense. Phishy, you're not killing me, I'm wearing a vest!"

"Bulletproof vests are not force fields. You're going to hurt bad and the blast will...why are you doing this now?"

"Phishy, don't shoot me in the face! Keep the red laser-sight where it's supposed to be!"

"What ever happened to your Box?"

"It starts tomorrow. Two weeks locked in my place. Recovering from the pain will also help me focus my mind when I assimilate all the data I need."

"You'll be black and blue."

"That'll heal."

"It'll knock the wind out of your lungs."

"My lungs will suck it all back in. We're not in outer space."

I braced my body in my nice coat and hat. I looked around and realized if this put me on my back, I'd be in the water and muck of this tunnel. My germophobic self wouldn't allow me to put any piece of my clothing on ever again, no matter how many times they were dry-cleaned.

"Wait." I had the emergency work blanket and spread it out behind where I was standing. But then, I realized I had no clue where I'd fall back. It was possible I would fall to one knee or fall forward. "Damn!" My trunk blanket was already on the muck. I was over-thinking again. Well, I was overdue for some shopping, I thought, as I walked back to where I was standing.

"Phishy, let's get on with it."

"Are you really, really sure?"

"No, but it's the best way I can think of."

"Getting shot isn't fun."

"I already know that, Phishy; let's go."

"Okay. On a count of three. One. Two. Three."

Phishy shot me with the shotgun center mass in my chest. All I remember was the pain, as if a hovercar crashed into my chest and sent me flying back. I can't remember if I cried out like a girl, but then most people would cry out like a girl, male or female, with a blast of pain like that.

I remembered smiling though, because with my fear of getting shot being taken away (by being shot), when I walked back into my Liquid Cool office in two weeks, I would be ready to be one badass detective.

CHAPTER 38

Punch Judy

When I walked back into my offices fifteen days later, I didn't quite know what to expect. Half a month was a long time for the principal of a new business to be absent. They say when you start a new company you're a slave to it for at least ten years, no time off and no vacations. Maybe so, but I did what I had to.

The door was open, and there was Punch Judy with her arms folded with a smile.

"Well, look what came in from the rain," she said. "Is that a new hat?"

"New hat, new coat," I answered.

"When you get new things they're supposed to be different than the old ones."

"I like the colors I had. All I needed was some modifications."

I felt different, and it was more than the new clothes. PJ could manage the office without me for a while. I was impressed.

"You look rested, too," she said. "Was that the first time you ever slept? Did you ever leave your place?"

"Not even once. Defeats the purpose of the Box."

"Box? What is the Box? You locked yourself in your place for two weeks like a house mouse. All these fancy phrases and concepts for simple things. So when I sat on the steps of our building, was I in the Box?"

"No. You were sidewalk sallying it. The Box is doing something specific without anyone to bother you."

"What did you do in your box?"

"Planned out my destiny to be the greatest detective in Metropolis."

"That's what I like to hear," PJ proclaimed. "You need to go into the Box more often. You are too negative most of the time. People don't like to hire negative people. Keep talking like that, and you'll have all the clients. Speaking of clients, when am I getting more money?"

"Before all that, what suspicious people were around the office?"

"No one."

"No one?"

"Just that stupid man, Phishy. Why do you associate with him? He kept coming by and tried to get into your office, but I wasn't allowing that."

"As I knew you would do."

"He kept trying to tell me he was your partner, the stupid man. The liar."

"He's another employee, but on retainer."

"Good. I know who to call when we need lunch pick-up."

"Like that shotgun you have under your desk? Phishy."

"So he's a criminal."

"Says my felon employee. So no one came up here besides Phishy in two weeks?"

"No one."

"Well...good."

"When you look at your messages on your desk, the ones on the top are the ones you call first."

"Why is that?"

"They're the easiest to solve. So quick money."

"Why do you need money? What were you doing when you were sidewalk sallying it, living on the gov's dime?"

"That was then, and I took no money from the government. All my side money came from the dividends of my accident settlement, which you know about."

"Dividend and legacy, baby."

"Just like you."

"No cash nest egg for me. All side-gigs."

"But now we have real jobs."

"That's the rumor. I question your definition of an easy case."

"Easy. Quick to solve. Quick to pay. Quick to pay me."

"Which means, they're either not worth my time or super-dangerous, but I'll look at them. While I look at the messages, I want you to research everything on a Detective Box."

"All this box talk. Who's he?"

"Someone I plan to visit when I go back out in 30 minutes. All the good, bad, and ugly on him."

"Is he going to be a paying client?"

"He may lead me to some leads for an existing client."

"You have clients, now? I thought you solved all of them."

"Detective Box," I repeated as I walked to my office.

PJ ran to her desk and shook her mobile computer to activate it, then her bionic fingers typed faster than the speed of light.

I walked to my office and opened the door. It was a bit musty, but everything was as I'd left it. And, the window that sucker shooter thug fell out of to become one with the surface was still boarded up by steel. How long would it take to fix and how much more money was I going to have to spend to do it? I simply put the whole thing out of my mind.

"What's been going on?" I asked as I took off my tan slicker and draped it over my main desk.

"The phones were nonstop," she said. "You have a serious backlog. I have all the calls ready for you." PJ was holding her electronic notepad, scrolling down her messages on the display. "So you better get to it. I need to get paid again."

"You sure no one was snooping around?"

"You expected snoopers?"

"I did."

"Well, I didn't see any or funny looking people, except for Phishy. Besides him, I saw no one else not supposed to be in the building."

When I was hiding out, post-my birthday, I told no one, not even Dot. So everybody was looking for me. This time, when I exiled myself to the "Box," I told everyone. I was in a working retreat in my place, and no one was to call or come by, ever, not even if an asteroid was coming to blow up the planet.

I stopped what I was doing and walked back out into the reception-waiting area. PJ was busy again with her interior design.

"Is there anything remaining from the paint that was here two weeks ago?"

I tossed some new hovercar and racing magazines on the lobby table. All the fashion mags might make men think they weren't welcome. A grinning PJ said, "No."

I smirked and walked back into my office.

"Oh, you can't throw your wet coat on your desk like that," she yelled at me. "I'll order a coat rack. One of those germ-killing, anti-body odor, fabric drying ones."

"I'm not sure how to respond to that, since my coat doesn't stink."

"That's why you need this coat rack, so your new coat doesn't become stinky. You can't have clients seeing you without a proper coat rack. They'll think you're cheap and won't hire you. Did I tell you I have all your messages organized and prioritized, so you can start making calls?"

"And you need to get paid."

"Good, you were listening to me."

"Detective Friendly," I said, looking at him on my video-phone. "I didn't think I'd be hearing from you again."

"We detectives have to stick together, you know. I rang for you a couple of times and your secretary said you were away for two weeks. Glad you're back. I wanted to check in and see if you heard anything new on the Easy Chair Charlie case."

"No, why?"

"You know how legal stuff can be. You want to make sure all loose ends are tied up or the whole legal stuff can take forever. My firm doesn't get paid until the case, criminally and civilly, is closed."

"Is that so?"

"You'll soon find that out if you're getting into the biz."

"Well, I was done with the Charlie case like four weeks ago. You're the only one who has brought it up since then. Should I be looking into it again?"

"No, no, no. Forget I called. I only wanted to check in."

"How did you know I was back?"

"I didn't. It's a Monday, so I took a chance."

"Okay."

"Thanks for taking my call."

"Don't mention it."

I hung up the video-phone.

"PJ!"

"He called every Monday you were gone."

"Why? What did he say?"

"He wanted to know if I knew where you were."

"And?"

"I told him you were out of town."

"He's obviously watching the offices."

"Why do you say that? He's called every Monday."

"No detective does what he does. Checking in with me. Keeping tabs on me is what he's doing."

"Why?"

"Tell me about Box. What did your research show?"

"How do you find these people? Box is a scumbag. How can he have a detective license with his record? What do you want with him? He does work for bad people."

"Then, I'll be going to visit Mr. Box."

"What about the messages?"

"I'll make calls from the road. If it's promising, I'll call you, and you can have them come into the office."

"Okay, because we need some paying clients in here. I need my money."

"You weren't getting money before."

"I wasn't employed before. When you are employed, you get money. I'm French. We like to shop, so get the paying clients, so you can pay me. But don't get shot before you do it."

CHAPTER 39

China Doll

There were pockets in the city that had vortexes—that's what everyone called them. Wherever the rain came down between two heat vents, these spiraling circles of water would be created that were fun to look at. Kids loved to run through them, pretending to pass through dimensions or time, like in sci-fi movies.

Well, there was one right in front of Eye Candy. I came through the vortex with my new tan coat flapping, my new tan fedora pulled down just right on my head, and I could see Dot and the ladies had already seen me. Damn, I knew I looked cool. I opened the door and stepped inside. Dot, her boss Prima Donna, and her fellow fashionistas were standing there, like a pack, grinning at me.

The real reason for my swagger was the post-Phishy-shooting-me perception exercise, which was a secret I'd take to the grave, when it came to Dot. I felt that my chest was made out of steel. Though, I wished I had a darker complexion like Run-Time or the Good Kosher Man, because that area of my chest was still red and tender, but that was easy enough to hide.

"Well, look at you," Prima said. "We were starting to wonder if you had gone off-world and left your fiancée behind."

"I knew where he was," Dot interjected. "So you're finished with the box?" she asked me.

"I'm finished," I answered.

"And?"

"And nothing. Other than...tonight is date night."

The women laughed.

"Date night?" Dot asked incredulously. "You lock yourself up in your place for over two weeks, show up at my job trying to look suave, and now it's date night all of a sudden."

"Well...yeah," I answered. "The hovercab is waiting."

Prima glanced at Dot.

"He's got spunk, China," Goat Girl said, half-laughing. "Gotta give him that."

"China Doll, you are excused for date night," Prima said to Dot.

"Are you sure? Because I'm not sure I'm sure."

"She's sure," I said. "Guess where we're going?" It wasn't just the ladies, but all the customers within earshot wanted to know. "The Booty Shaker."

Dot let out a yell, jumped up, and ran to the back room.

"Why doesn't my man take me to classy dance joints?" Pinkie asked aloud.

"I don't know," Cyan answered. "Mine doesn't either. I'm thinking we got the wrong kind of man. Hey, Cruz, you got any male friends of the hetero persuasion, like you, and single? Pinkie and I need to trade up."

"Me too," Goat Girl added.

"I'll put the word out," I said.

Dot reappeared with her purse, which, as always, matched her outfit exactly. "Let's go," she said to me.

Getting a hovertaxi was like playing Russian roulette. You never knew what you'd get. Would you get a driver who knew the city and would get you where you wanted fast? Would you get a scammer, who'd take the longest possible way to charge you absolutely the most he could get away with? Would you get the idiot newbie, who had no clue where he was going? Dot and I got none of that; we got the rudest bum possible.

Why didn't I call Run-Time? One of my corporate clients (who paid his bill promptly) had an uncle. The uncle owned this hovercab company, and it was part of my arrangement to get a good review and more referrals. So here, Dot and I were—the first and last time.

"Driver," I said.

Dot didn't see it, but I did. There was no reason we should have been in the sky-lane we were in. The guy was either lost or trying to gouge us on fares. We were heading for a bridge and I knew if I didn't get control of the situation fast, things were going to get very bad.

"Driver," I repeated. "I need you to slow down and pull to the side."

The driver either was ignoring me or had music playing in his ears.

Dot saw the approaching bridge and screamed out. The driver reacted and glanced back at us.

"Pull the cab to the side and stop!" I yelled.

"What's happening?" he yelled back.

Dot's eyes were closed tight, her teeth were clenched, and she was in the beginning stages of a violent fit.

"Pull the cab to the side!"

"Why? What's happening?"

My anger took me, and I pulled my piece from my jacket and pounded on the glass partition between the driver and the passenger seats. I grabbed it and slid it to the right, so the only thing separating us was his seat. In the rearview mirror, I saw the driver's eyes had opened to the size of baseballs, as he knew what I was about to do. He jerked the steering wheel to the right and took the hovercab out of the main sky-lane to the side and stopped, just as I was about to yank his head back through the space between the front and back.

"Move into the passenger seat!" I yelled.

"Are you crazy? We're three hundred feet in the air..."

"Put it in park!"

He continued to protest, but I had already opened the passenger door and was out, my foot on the side steps. I clung to the hovercab as I looked down, then kept moving. We were over thirty stories up, hovering in the air, as every kind of hovercar and van whipped past us. I opened the driver side and was ready to pummel him, but he was already in the passenger seat.

"Don't shoot me, mister. You can have the hovercab."

I jumped into the driver seat and fastened the seat belt. "You bum! Why didn't you do what I said?"

"I'm sorry."

"I should shoot you."

"You can take it."

"I own a classic Ford Pony, free and clear. Why would I want your dirty ol' hovercab!"

"You can take it."

I disengaged the air-brake, looked into traffic, and pushed the cab into drive. I took the cab down to the lowest sky-lane—one story up, then moved to practically touching the ground.

"Dot!"

The driver looked at me and then to the backseat, where Dot was fighting a complete mental collapse.

"It's okay. We stopped and we're close to the ground. We're close to the club, so it makes no sense to turn around now. Come up to the front and get in your position." I leaned towards the driver with menace and yelled, "Get in the back!"

The driver leaped out of the seat and climbed over the seat into the back.

Dot took awhile to calm down and slowly come out of it. Finally, she opened her eyes and looked around. The driver was quiet as a mouse, but watched both of us. Dot climbed into the passenger seat next to me and reclined it as far back as it would go, as the dumb driver moved behind my seat.

"It's okay," I said. "I'm putting it in drive, but I'll go slow."

The one thing drivers in this city hated more than hoverbikers was slow drivers. They hated them with a passion. They'd shoot them out of the sky or have someone else do it if they could legally get away with it. We were the slow driver. I never exceeded fifty miles an hour with an uproar of honking hovercars all around us. We were far from the fast lane, but it didn't matter. We were a moving hazard.

As we passed under the bridge, Dot closed her eyes again and gripped the armrests with all her might. We were under, through, and out. Dot's eyes opened slightly, and her breathing started to get back to normal. When we were far enough away, I put it in gear, and we were off. I was up and into the fast lane. We made it to Booty Shakers in no time.

Booty Shakers wasn't just a dance club. It was one of the platinum dance clubs, and you didn't set foot inside, unless you planned to dance all night long nonstop and have obscene amounts of fun. No one ever left there unsatisfied and when you did, you were ten to twenty pounds lighter from all that sweating on the dance floor.

I pulled up to their valet service, self-park was not allowed, and immediately got out before the valet could get to the drivers' side and opened the back passenger door. I yanked the driver out.

"Please don't shoot me. You can take it."

I leaned close to him. "When my girlfriend was a little girl, she was a go-cart champion. Won races all over the country. At one of those races, they had this brand new course, the hardest course ever for the kiddies.

One of the obstacles was a path that went under a bridge. Well, you can see where I'm going with this story. Those kiddies were going around the course at 80 miles per hour. My girlfriend was in the lead, but she had to win and pushed her go-cart to 100 miles per hour. Her go-cart hit a bump and jumped the course, just as she went under the bridge. She was decapitated. Lucky for her and me, there was a medical team right there, and they were able to save her. Her neck and all down to her shoulder is bionic. So you can imagine what such a trauma like that would do to a child, especially when you clearly remember your head lying on the ground and your entire body in the go-cart ten feet away from you. You can imagine what going under any bridge as an adult could do to you. You could imagine what a driver not stopping his dirty hovercab and ignoring her boyfriend's call to pull to the side and stop could do."

"Mister, your point has been made in the clearest possible way. There's no charge for the fare."

Dot didn't want to go in the club, and she was in no mood for dancing or any kind of fun.

"Let's just go inside and call another cab," I said.

"Cruz, I'm not going to fall for it. I'm not dancing. I want to go home."

"I understand. Let's go inside, and I'll call Flash. He has a spotless cab, and he's probably on duty now."

"Cruz, it's not going to work. I'm not dancing."

"Yeah, I know. We'll go in and call Flash."

"Where's your mobile?"

"I left it at home. It's date night. Where's yours?"

"I'm not falling for it, Cruz. I'm not dancin' and I want to go home."

"Let's call Flash then."

We walked inside, and I immediately told the bouncers we were only going inside to make a call. They were fine with that, as long as we paid full price. I handed them my pre-paid tickets, and we were in. Booty Shakers first got you with the beat. The music was so loud the sound waves practically levitated you up in the air, and the beat forced your feet to move whether you wanted to or not.

Dot and I were dancing maniacs. We each had our own separate hobbies, but this was our hobby as a couple and we were good at it. My Pops always said that couples last longer when there is something that they can do together (besides the obvious one). Not something that either does separately, but that you do together, prefer to do together, something fun. For Dot and I, it was ripping up the dance floor.

Dot had forgotten she was not going to dance. The music had transported us to the dance floor with the hundreds of other people on one of their many football stadium-sized floors. Through the night, we got to display our dance prowess with all our favorite moves: the Cold Lampin, the Dead Woman's Hips, the Flava Wave, the Peter Perfect, the Perfect Peter, the Honey Dipper, the Sucka Sipper, the Big Dippa, the Gettin' Busy... We could do the Booty Rumble, the Swing Slide, the Mad Robot, the Beat Box, the Devo, the Michael Moon Walker, even the Tango Terminator—old and new. We knew them all.

This was how I passed my first night out of the box, with my girl, China Doll.

CHAPTER 40

Box

When I was in the box, I did more than just assimilate data. I had to think big picture. Thinking about being different is far different from being different. I couldn't yell "oh, snaps" one day and ask to do life all over. It was a commitment, and I intended to be the best detective out there—I had to be that internally arrogant—as I had done with restoring classic hovercars. I could only do that by knowing more and doing more than the other guy. Strangely, the two professions were similar in that way. It was about knowledge. Knowing those factoids that no one else knew. Being able to see connections that not even a computer could see. As a kid, I learned every relevant and irrelevant factoid about hovercars, beyond what could possibly be known, which is why my name was always bandied about in the same breath when people asked, "Who'd you recommend for my hovercar restoration gig?" Like me or hate me, everyone agreed on one thing: I knew my hovercars. I had to get to that level with this profession.

That's why I visited Compstat Connie. She was a true data Einstein—could see the higher cosmic mathematics, but couldn't do the basic arithmetic. Well, that myth about Einstein was never true. He could do basic math just fine. And Compstat Connie could balance her checkbook just fine, but she possessed the ability to see through the data and even she admitted, if she wasn't careful, she'd end up as one of those sidewalk sallies, talking to herself on the corner. The human mind craves order. It seeks it out, even when there is none. It swears by it even when it is an illusion. That's why those optical illusion tricks work; your mind wants order. Connie could see the real connections in the data and that's why I visited. She solved my whole case in five minutes and didn't even know it. My two weeks in the box was to figure *how* she made those connections. She did it in five minutes. It took me ten days to figure it out, but I did.

Here I was. It was funny; I called my little mini-isolation retreat in my own place, the Box, and came across my first step in my Easy Chair Charlie case by the revelation of a scumbag detective, named Box.

It may never have been sunny in Metropolis, but sometimes, the bright neon lights were as bright as the direct sunlight as you came around certain sky-lanes. I zipped along the fast lane in my red Pony, this time wearing my open knuckle driving gloves. I wore them when I wanted to be especially serious about my driving. I wore them to keep me in the right frame of mind, when I needed to do some real hovercar driving. Sometimes, my instincts whispered in my ear I was being followed, so I accepted it was true. With the madness of hovertraffic, someone could tail you for hours, and you would never know. It wasn't like in ancient days when cars were on the ground, and there was two-way traffic—maybe multiple two-way traffic lanes. Now, it was the equivalent of going from a regular chessboard to tri-dimensional chess. You could hide and follow someone from above them or below them, besides just following directly behind. Only the government and corporatists had the means to pay for fancy anti-tailing security. For the Average Joe, you were on your own.

Whiskey Way was where I was going. Another low-end, high-crime town I would have preferred not to go anywhere near.

Before I decorated my own offices, I did a tour of all the detective firms in the city. They all fell into two categories: the high-end, one-hundred man firms that looked and smelled like a high-end legal practice, and the bottom-end, small firms that always seemed to share space with some bail bonds outfit. There seemed to be no in-between, and I immediately planned to establish myself in that space, along with taking all kinds of clients—private persons, government, and corporate. Those two things were to make me unique, and I desperately needed to be unique in this industry to have any chance to survive.

Box was a one-man outfit, nothing to stand out from any other in the Yellow Pages, but he had a reputation as a licensed private eye, who'd do any job you wanted, as long as the price was right. "Any job" was code for illegal. Those who knew the detective biz called him a "scumbag." I had no reason to doubt them.

His offices were on the fifth floor of a business tower in Whiskey Way. Across the hall was a bail bonds office, and as a result, there were the smelliest, grungiest place with people hanging around. Since it was a common set-up for low-enders, it must have been a mutually beneficial situation for all involved.

I pushed open the front door to enter; the interior was dim and dank. Box's office was not even an office, but a half-office. The other half he shared with some other detective firm. I could see a haze of cigarette smoke hanging near the ceiling.

"What do you want?" a male voice asked.

My eyes finally made out the figure of a man, standing at a file cabinet, who turned and was looking at me.

"Looking for Box," I answered.

"You got an appointment?"

"Do I need one?"

"That didn't answer my question."

"I'll go to another detective then, where the customer service is a bit more customer-friendly."

"Don't do that. Wait there."

The man closed the file cabinet and disappeared, or I couldn't see him anymore, as I stood there continuing to glance around.

"He'll see you." The man had returned.

I stepped forward, even though I had no clue where I was going; it was that dark.

"The office in the back with the light on," the man said.

This was some kind of office. It seemed the lack of light was to hide all the unsightly clutter. I walked back to the only place that had light. I stopped and peeked into the office. There, seated behind a desk, was Box.

"Box?" I asked, even though I knew it was him, but he didn't know I had been checking up on him.

"You know it's me, so why are you asking?"

I stepped inside and didn't ask as I took a seat.

He cracked his knuckles, then put one hand on his desk, while the other hand was out of sight behind the desk. I put both of my hands on the desk.

"I came to hire you for information."

"Information? I'm a detective. I don't give information. Who are you?"

"I'm a detective," I said.

His unfriendly face turned to a solid frown.

"Why are you here?"

"I need a bunch of information from you, and I'm happy to pay for the information if I have to."

"What information?"

I held my left wrist to my face and looked at the electronic wrist pad strapped to my inside forearm. "A Mr. Ergot and his assistant, a Mr. Peri."

I looked up, and Box's frown was now accompanied by the squinting of his eyes.

"What did they hire you for?" I asked.

"Detectives don't reveal any details about clients."

"Since both of them are dead, murdered, they won't mind," I said.

Box watched me closely. I could see his scumbag mind racing around trying to figure out how much I really knew.

"I don't know those names."

"Never meet with them?"

"No."

"Never talked to them?"

"No."

"They didn't hire you?"

"No."

"You didn't take a taxi to Mr. Ergot's office in The Wharf District?"

"No."

"You didn't deposit a check from Mr. Ergot in your bank account?"

"No."

"You weren't at the scene of Mr. Ergot's murder? Where someone fed him to his own piranhas."

"No."

"And threw his assistant, Mr. Peri, to become one with the pavement after a sixty-story fall."

"No."

"You didn't receive a call from a..." I looked at my electric notepad, "Red Rabbit?"

"How the hell do you know that?" Box sat up straight. "Mr. Cruz, I don't know what you're talking about."

I smiled. "So, you do know who I am."

"Get out of here."

"I want that information. How much money do you want?"

"Nothing from you."

"Why do you have to be like that?"

"You can't spend money if you're dead."

"Did you tell Mr. Ergot and Mr. Peri to be especially careful around this Red Rabbit character?"

"I got paid."

"I knew it! You got my brother killed!"

The voice behind us startled us so completely that we both jumped up from our chairs and turned. A man in a white suit fired at Box. I dived to see Box collapse to the ground and turned to see the stranger pointing his gun at me.

By this time, it was all reflex. I flicked my wrist. *Pop!* The shot hit him in the face.

The man in the white suit fell back out of the office, his gun flying from his left hand. He stopped his fall, snatched his gun in mid-air with his right hand, and fired at me.

Oww!

I can't remember if I screamed out loud, like a girl, or if it was my inner voice, but the blast brushed past my cheek.

I was mad now! Four times I was shot at! Enough!

I rolled away from the doorway as I grabbed my own piece from my jacket and jumped up. Now, it was my turn. I fired multiple times and heard a male scream and then footsteps running away. I shot out the light in the office and ducked to the floor. All I heard was more shots and then the footsteps running further away.

I waited, crouched on the ground. More shots flew into the room. Then, I heard a beep and feet running again. The elevator had arrived, and the man in the white suit ducked into it. With these old towers, there was only one elevator, and undoubtedly thought he was getting away scot-free, but I knew something he didn't.

I had psychologically prepared myself to get shot. I didn't prep myself to get grazed by laser blasts. It was like someone took a dull razor and tried to slash the side of my face with it. It hurt bad. But that wasn't why I was mad as I found the exit window. I was thinking about Box. He was a scumbag, but that didn't mean he deserved to get killed. I saw the body of the guy who "greeted" me in his rude way on the ground, motionless. He didn't deserve to be dead either. Being a scumbag or rude was not a reason to get killed. Maybe they weren't dead, but I gave chase under the assumption they were. That man in the white suit was mine. I knew I shot him in the face, so I don't how he was walking around. For all I knew, he had an inorganic face with no nerve endings from some freak accident. So many people had so many inorganic and bionic parts they weren't born with. You could never tell these days.

Old towers like this had maintenance sections on the lower floors. It's where the technicians did their communications, cybernet, power, and any other electrical work that needed to be done. It also had back entrances, straight to the street.

I burst out into the rain and got my bearings. He would come out of the main entrance, and I would be ready for him. I didn't just have a new hat and coat, but I bought myself some snazzy aqua-shoes, specifically for sneaking up or running like a cheetah through the streets without falling on my butt because of the wet ground. I was about ten feet from the corner when he appeared, and he instantly saw me. He aimed and fired. But again, I wasn't hit. The victim was an old man next to me. He was hit in the chest and fell to the ground with a look of pain and terror. His eyes closed, but then fluttered wildly to match the shaking his body was doing.

"Hold him down and help me," I called out, but people moved away from us in their black and gray slickers. Some even pretended they had seen nothing.

I was even madder now. I searched the man for his mobile and pressed the emergency button.

"This is 9-11. What is the emergency?" the computer voice said.

I put the mobile back in the old man's pocket and stood up. Most people didn't know that when you called the emergency, you didn't even need to say a word; police would automatically be dispatched. Was he a third man that the man in the white suit killed?

My piece was in my right hand and I ran. No, I sprinted around the corner after him. As soon as I came around, I immediately saw him about twenty feet away. His nice clothes weren't so nice anymore, but muddied—he had fallen. He wasn't running, but trying to speed-walk away. He saw me and tried to run again and immediately slipped and fell face first to the pavement.

I approached him like a rocket. He picked himself off the ground and turned. I shot him once in the chest and the second time in the shoulder. He cried out, but again, didn't fall. He turned back around and tried to run. Why wasn't this guy falling down? I flipped the switch on my gun, aimed, and fired one round after the other.

People jumped away, ducked, dove into stores, pressed themselves to the wall. I was running through the streets of Metropolis, in public, shooting at another person. If any policeperson saw me, they could legally just shoot me dead on sight.

The man had disappeared around the corner and I was there. He was finally on the ground, lying flat on his back. His gun wasn't in his hand anymore, but on the ground next to him. I slowly walked to him with my gun pointed. He started up at me, his eyelids flickering as the light rain fell.

"You killed three people," I yelled and aimed at his head.

He closed his eyes as he turned his head from me.

"He killed my brother," he said, then coughed.

I leaned forward and his face had an unnatural look to it.

This was a mess. People all around the streets were filming me with their mobiles, so really, there was no point in running. I could make up a plausible story if I stayed; I couldn't if I fled the scene. But if I stayed, there would be a strong possibility I'd be going to jail for the first time in my life—for the second time. Yes, I couldn't forget about my "bonding" moment with my future parents-in-law.

CHAPTER 41

Detective Monitor

The police arrived in force. Three separate crime scenes, but all connected—to me. I sat on the wet sidewalk in handcuffs, waiting. One male and one female officer stood there, watching me with their hands on their weapon belts.

Another officer arrived, not with the standard half-helmet, but a simple black baseball cap. "Is this him?" he asked as he approached.

The two officers nodded.

The police detective took my ID from them and studied it.

"Mr. Cruz, is it?"

"Yeah," I answered.

"Two casualties in an office. One casualty around the corner. One casualty here. Did you shoot all these people, Mr. Cruz?"

"I only shot the man here. He was the active shooter."

"Was he now?"

"Yeah, and I know you did the ballistic test already, or I'd be in the jail now. When do you unhandcuff me and let me go about my day?"

"And the gun my officers took off of you was the weapon?"

"Yeah. I got it off one of the men shot, a detective named Box."

"Are you licensed to carry a firearm, Mr. Cruz?"

"I don't need to be licensed to fire a gun when I'm firing at an active shooter in self-defense. He shot three people and would have shot more if I hadn't shot him."

"Active shooter, huh?"

"What phrase should I use?" I asked. "Unfriendly person?"

"Maybe he wouldn't have shot anyone if you weren't chasing him with a gun."

"I took Box's gun when he came in and started shooting at us. And he already shot the other guy in the office before that. You know, why don't we ask that old man or his family? Should I have shot the guy who shot you or let him get away? Are you going to unhandcuff me? You have my statement and all the guns involved."

"Do we have all the guns involved, Mr. Cruz? 'Cause I think the gun you say was Box's is actually your throwaway gun, and you hid your real gun."

"Did you find another gun?"

"Not yet."

"Are you going to arrest me? I have rights, you know."

"We're thinking about it."

"I'm allowed to defend myself."

"Not as an unlicensed civilian."

"If I didn't have a gun to protect myself, I'd be dead and maybe a lot of other innocent bystanders would be, too. Police can carry guns, but the people can't?"

"Mr. Cruz, you can carry whatever toy gun, bullet gun, or laser gun you like, as long as it's registered, and you're licensed. Mine is licensed. My officers' guns are licensed. What about you? I hear you're a clever one. You can weasel out of using someone else's gun for self-defense, but to avoid arrest and adjudication at a trial, you need to be licensed to use a gun. That's why you're supposed to stay and call the police."

"It was exigent circumstances."

The three laughed.

"Are you a lawyer, Mr. Cruz?" the detective asked.

"No. And my license is in my wallet. For your inspection."

They looked at each other. I could see it in the detective's face: I was not supposed to be licensed. They took my wallet from my jacket and opened it.

"You got a counterfeit gun license, Mr. Cruz?" the detective asked.

The officers handed it to the detective. I could see the anger on his face as he studied it.

"How did you get a federal license, Mr. Cruz?"

"I can't remember."

The detective held the license in his hand, trying to think of something. He held the gun license in front of the officers. It wasn't for them to see; it was for the body cams to scan it. Someone was talking into his earbud. After a moment, the detective handed the license back to one of the officers, one of them returned it to my jacket, and both lifted me to my feet and unhandcuffed me.

"You think you're clever, Mr. Cruz," the detective said. "I'm pretty clever, too."

"Then why do the street cops call you Detective Do-Little?" I asked.

"What did you say?" The detective angrily snapped back.

"Nothing," I said.

I could see the two officers were biting their lips not to smile.

"I want him cited," the detective said to them.

"For what, exactly, Detective Monitor."

"Discharging a weapon in public."

"That was self-defense," I said.

"This is what, your fourth contact with the police in 30 days? Cite him as a possible person of interest to appear before a judge. You're only allowed three contacts with the police in a month, or you're sent before a judge. You think I'm a pain. They'll have you in those mandatory "how not to be a criminal" classes for 72 hours. I hear people purposely try to harm themselves to get out of those classes."

"You said I had to be licensed, then I show you my license, and you're punishing me. For the damn one-millionth time, an active shooter came into a private office and started shooting people. I get to protect myself, you know, and not allow myself or other innocent people to get killed."

By this time, I was pissed.

"I'm citing you anyway, and you will go to an anti-criminality class."

"That 'how not to be a criminal' weekend class is nothing but an act of unmitigated cruelty to humankind." The street officers laughed, but the detective was unmoved.

"Is this how you treat the pro-police community? Review the file, the real file and not the summary, and you'll see it was not my fault. Seriously. Also, if you look at my jacket, you'll see I've never had a contact, arrest, citation, warning, ever in my life. I was even a police intern."

"Police intern? What's that?"

"When I was in high school, I interned at Police Central."

"No way."

"Yes way. It's true."

"I don't know, Mr. Cruz. We can't prove it, but I know the gun we retrieved was your throwaway gun. Someone who thinks he's more clever than the police will soon have delusions of grandeur and want to do other things, believe they are a master criminal genius."

"Detective, all I was thinking of was the innocent people the shooter killed."

"Who got killed?"

"The people."

Detective Monitor shook his head. "That old man is fine. The two guys in the office are alive, though one is in serious condition. And even the active shooter of yours you claim did the evil deeds is alive in serious condition."

Box was not dead! "What hospital are they at?"

"Why do you need to know the hospital?"

"Box was the guy I was meeting with when we were attacked. Why wouldn't I want to know where he is to visit him?"

The detective ignored him. "Cite him and sign him up for the anti-criminality class."

"That class is torture. Everybody says that."

"Good, you'll be able to experience it firsthand and not have to go by secondhand accounts."

I shook my head as the female officer handed me the citation with a smile.

"Thanks a lot for nothing, detective."

"Think of me when you're sitting in the class," he said sarcastically.

"Oh yeah, I'll be thinking about you, all right," I said.

Detective Monitor blew a kiss at me.

I needed to get to hospital. They didn't need to tell me which one. I already knew.

CHAPTER 42

Box and Rexx

I was always of two minds inside a hospital. On one hand, it was a shining example of society's amazing technology, which was for nothing less than to make people whole and save lives. But on the other hand, since anyone off the street was sent here first, it was a breeding ground of nastiness: germs, bacteria, viruses, and disease—a place only slightly better than the meat morgue.

I took out a bottle from my pocket and sprayed a shot up each nostril when no one was looking. The immune system booster product probably was a complete waste of my money, but it made me feel better, since I couldn't put on a full biohazard suit.

Metro General Hospital was where everyone was taken, unless you were wealthy or politically connected. I had some familiarity with the place from my hovercar racing days. More than a few drivers crashed into a communications or light pole, and this is where the ambulance took them.

Always hectic, Metro General did not have the best specialists, but it was the largest and in the center of the city. I sat in the waiting area of

Floor 76. Box was out of surgery and was taken here...and so was our active shooter friend, who, based on his last sentence to us, I figured out was the brother of one of the two murdered men I confronted Box about. Knowing that, I needed both men to stay alive. I knew most of the pieces to my little puzzle—otherwise known as the Easy Chair Charlie Case— but it was all speculation. I needed to fill in the blanks with facts, corroborate my good detective reasoning with facts.

I had decided, as soon as the police told me that neither man was dead, that I would stay with these men like a parasite on a wet rat, until I had my chance to speak with them. I didn't know why they even had doors to the recovery room, because hospital staff was running back and forth with patients on hovergurneys nonstop. There were only a few other average-looking people in the waiting room besides me, but I was the only one sitting in the last row with my back touching the wall. I wanted no one behind me, and I wanted to eye everyone in front of me.

I was one person who could sit and wait forever, something the Guy Who Scratched My Vehicle and his lady found out the hard way. It was something I could do. I was a natural for stakeouts. That's what I considered it, because I needed to talk to those two men, and I felt...nervous. Sometimes, you had a premonition that something bad could be coming. That's what I was feeling, and I wasn't having any of it.

A head peeked out from the hallway into the waiting area, smiling at me. I gestured to the sidewalk johnny, and he came around with two of his friends.

"Hey, Cruz," the first one said. All of them in poncho-style slickers over their jeans and boots, and all looking like shaving was an off-and-on-again weekly routine.

"Hey," I answered.

"Phishy said to thank you for asking for his help. And we thank you too for giving us a gig."

"Yeah. Well, here's the job."

"Is it dangerous?" asked the other johnny. "I mean, you're a legit detective now."

"It's not dangerous at all."

"But...we're in a hospital."

"You watch too many movies. The job is simple. One of you will sit in the waiting room at the other end of the hall and watch the elevators for anyone suspicious coming my way, and the other will do the same at the other end of the hallway. The third man..."

"Will hang here with you," one of them interrupted.

"Will hang in the waiting area right next to the main elevators. Anyone suspicious coming my way, I want to know."

"You expecting suspicious people, Mr. Cruz?"

"Dangerous people, Mr. Cruz?"

"I have no idea what to expect. That's why I need you. Okay, that's the job. Go, get to your places."

"Yeah, that would be funny if a whole bunch of suspicious people came up here at the same time, while we're standing here talking about suspicious people."

The three sidewalk johnnies laughed.

"I can see why you're Phishy's friends. Okay, get to your places." I shooed them away, and two went one way and the third went the other way down the hallway.

They were gone, and I could see the three other people in the waiting area looking at me.

"You a detective?" a man asked.

"Yeah," I answered.

"You got a card."

"Yeah."

I had to remember that I was a businessman now, and that meant "good customer service." I got up, whipped a card from my jacket, and handed it to him.

The woman sitting next to him leaned to look at it, too.

"That's a cool name," she said. "Liquid Cool. You must have paid a whole bunch of money to get that name."

"I came up with it on my own, sitting in my office with several empty pads, a pen, and a few hours."

I was about to return to my seat when the other man in the waiting area reached out his hand for a card. I gave him one and returned to my spot.

With all my sitting and watching, I pieced together who among the hospital staff were in charge. The head nurse came out from the doors, and it was the one time she wasn't surrounded by other staff. I jumped up from my chair and ran after her.

"Excuse me," I said.

She stopped and turned.

"Is a Mr. Jim Box or Mr. Petrov Rexx able to see visitors?"

"Who are you?"

"Family."

"Of?"

"Mr. Box."

"Why are you asking about Petrov Rexx, then?"

"They were...shot at the same incident. I understand though. I'm sure they have an officer posted, which is why you're asking me the additional questions."

"Go to the nurses' station, and you can see Mr. Box, but as for Mr. Rexx, you need to take that up with the policeman."

"Thank you. Nurses' station?"

She pointed the way.

Box looked like hell. Laid up in the hospital bed with wires and electrodes attached to his head and chest, and an IV from his right arm.

His eyes were half-closed, when I entered his room, and opened slightly more with a groggy expression.

"You told them you were family?" he asked.

"Of course," I said and sat down. "Here's your chance to return the favor by answering all my questions."

"You didn't take any bullets for me. What favor am I returning?"

"For calling the police and not leaving you to bleed out in your dark, dank, dungeon office."

"I bet someone else did that, and you're trying to take credit for it. You're a detective. Detectives lie."

"I got the guy who shot you," I said emphatically.

"I don't believe you."

"Chased him, shot him down, and he's lying one door down from you. So will you return that favor?"

"What's his name?"

"Petrov Rexx. Mr. Peri's brother."

"Christ, it was him?"

"You know him, then."

"He called me on the phone last week to tell me he was coming to kill me for getting his brother killed."

"Well, he almost did just that. So does that earn me a favor?"

"You have all the makings of a real low-life detective."

"Coming from the likes of you, I'm not sure how to take that. Peri worked for Ergot, and Mr. Ergot hired you to do what?"

"Why do you want to know? Why are you even involved in this? You're just a car guy."

"I was never a car guy. I was...I am a classic hovercar restorer."

"If you say so. Why are you involved in this? I don't understand you. Were you bored with life? You won't be bored anymore. And you probably won't be alive too much longer either, if you keep involved in all this."

"Involved in all what? What am I involved in?"

"Leave me alone. I'm not telling you nothing."

He turned his head away from me, lying on the bed, and closed his eyes. I knew he was done with me...unless I reset the situation.

"Well, if that's how you want it," I said.

"That's how I want it."

"Okay."

I watched him, then slowly walked out the room.

Box was wide-eyed when I appeared again, pushing in the hoverbed of Mr. Rexx. He glared at Box with such an intensity; if eyes were lasers, Box would have been vaporized.

"What the hell are you doing?" Box yelled at me.

When I had Rexx situated, I closed the double doors. "I thought it would be nice if the three of us could sit and chat awhile. Three detectives shooting the breeze, together."

"He's a detective?" Box said.

Rexx glared at Box with the look of murder.

"This is the guy who shot you, and I shot him. As I said before, that earns me a favor from you."

"And you roll him into my room?" Box yelled.

"You killed my brother!" Rexx yelled out.

"I told you on the phone. I did no such thing. That crazy rabbit did."

"I don't even know what that means. You did it!"

Rexx was about to throw his urine bag at him when I intervened. "Okay, we won't be flinging bags of urine at people we tried to murder, today. Gentlemen, if we can talk calmly and clearly, we can figure this all out."

"I've figured it out, and you're dead!" Rexx pointed at Box with the arm hooked up to the IV.

"Based on the fact that everyone you shot is still alive, your threats don't worry me none."

I walked closer to Box. "Will you answer my questions?"

"Why? Why are you involved in this, car guy? Who's your client?"

"I am the client! It might be hard for you to understand, but I liked Easy Chair Charlie. I can't say he was a friend, any more than you can say the guy at the food market or the mail delivery guy is a friend, but I'd be pissed if I found out someone gunned them down in the street."

"He wasn't gunned down in the street. Easy shot it out with the cops. Everyone knows that, detective. People go gun-crazy all the time."

I leaned forward to him. "Stop treating me like I'm stupid. People who go gun-crazy bring their own guns to the mayhem. The only thing Easy had with him was two boxes of fine cigars."

"He must have stashed the weapons in his hovercar outside."

"He didn't have a car," I said, "He walked or took public transportation wherever he went. But you know that, Box. Are you going to answer my questions? Mr. Rexx may be busy with the courts and jail for a while, but you and I both know that when he's done, he'll be back at you. So answer the question and clear yourself. What's the harm in that? Your clients are dead." I turned to Rexx and said, "No offense."

"No offense taken. You didn't kill them."

"So?"

I stared at Box. Rexx stared at him. He tried to resist, but he wavered. "You two should be cops. All I'm missing is the beat down."

"Police don't beat down people, anymore."

"Yeah, yeah, yeah. They're body-cammed up every which way, with the friendly Police Watch Commission watching on the other end for the good of people. You believe that, and you are nothing but a doofus."

"Mr. Ergot, Box!" I yelled.

He gave in. "Ergot hired me to find out all about this guy, known on the street, as Red Rabbit."

301

"What the hell is a Red Rabbit?" Rexx blurted out.

"A member of one of those animal gangs, or I should say, in this case, one of the made men in the Animal Farm Crime Syndicate."

"Animal gangs?" Rexx asked and chuckled.

It was my turn to jump in. "There are all kinds of criminal gangs. Think of dogs. There are a 1001 different dogs from a Chihuahua to a Great Dane. There are 1001 different kinds of gangs. Go on, Box. It's your story."

"These animal gangs wear these stupid animal masks—cats, dogs, pigs, monkeys. Rabbits. All kinds of animals. If they weren't so dangerous, it would be funny. Red is obviously with the rabbit gangs. He runs their crew. He got to run their crew by killing their leader, Follow the White Rabbit, and putting Blue Pill Rabbit in a coma."

Rexx chuckled again. "You're not serious. This sounds like a bunch of nonsense. Rabbit gangs. Animal gangs. White Rabbit. Blue Rabbit. Red Rabbit. Are we little kiddies?" Rexx shook his head, incredulously. "Is this how things go, in your low-class city?"

"There's nothing kiddie about these animal gangs. And this Red Rabbit is a real psycho. He likes to kill people, even his own people. He's nothing but violence."

"Why is he called Red Rabbit?" I asked.

"His favorite weapon is some kind of laser lightning rifle. Supposedly, before it discharges, his rabbit mask turns red. The saying is, 'You see red, then you're dead.' I told Ergot and your brother Peri not to mess with this guy. Supposedly, his entire body is cyborg. You can shoot him 'til hell freezes, and he'll still keep ticking."

"Why did Ergot hire you to investigate a gang leader?" I asked.

"I don't know."

"Box, you've already told most of the story, why not finish it? Remember, I tracked you down."

"Yeah, how did you find me?"

"Maybe, if you weren't so busy trying to also find out why Ergot was interested in this gang leader, you wouldn't have been seen. I know you know."

"He didn't say, but I knew why. He was going to blackmail him."

"Blackmail?" Rexx asked. "What did he have on a gang criminal to blackmail him with?"

"Exactly," Box said. "That's what I wanted to know, so I did some poking around."

"And?" I asked.

"I didn't find anything. All I knew was Ergot ended up stuffed into his own office piranha fish tank, half-eaten, with his eyeballs hanging out of his head and his main guy thrown out the window. Then, I heard that two sidewalk johnnies were nearly vaporized at the scene of some building lobby fire. I knew it was all Red's work. Violence follows that guy wherever he hops."

"Lobby fire?" I asked. "Then I rephrase my question," I said. "What do you think Ergot was trying to blackmail him over?"

"I don't know."

"Yes, you do. It had something to do with the night Easy supposedly went gun-crazy."

"If you know, why ask me?"

I ignored him. "Red was there that night?"

"I believe so."

"Based on what?"

"A guy wearing a rabbit mask with big pointy ears tends to get noticed, even in this city."

"How far away was he from the scene?" I asked.

"A hop and a skip away."

"He was there," I said.

"He was," Box said. "But he wasn't seen with Easy, so I don't know what the blackmail could have been about."

"Someone did see him with Easy," I said.

"Who?"

"Never mind. That person has been made to disappear. Where's Red now?"

"Why?" Box asked. "Are you going to trade carrots with him? Cruz, I'll tell you the same thing I told Ergot and Peri; stay far away from this psycho. No good will come from any encounter with him. He shoots you, and you're dead. You won't get the luxury of being able to lie in a bed like me and him."

I looked at Peri's brother, who was listening intently.

"I'd listen to him if I were you," he said.

"So you and Box are friends, now?" I asked.

"My brother was no slouch, so if someone offed him, then they had a decent amount of skills. And no offense pal, but you look like you'd be more concerned about getting a speck of mud on your nancy-boy tan coat and hat."

"My hat and coat are cool," I said to him, "like my classic Ford Pony. But..." I turned back to Box. "I have no intention of getting killed anytime this century, especially by a gang member in a rabbit mask."

"Don't laugh. These animal gangs are animals."

"I know," I said. "I need to know where this Red is hanging out, now."

"You're not going to listen, are you?" Box said.

"I may not have pointy rabbit ears, but I'm listening. I really don't want to know where he hangs out, but I have to. Did you track him to his...?"

"Lair," Box answered. "I'll tell you, but before I do, I'll tell you why I'm going to tell you. You may be a car-guy detective, but you seem to have decent skills, and I want no more competition out there than necessary. I'll tell you, and you'll go there, and you'll find Red, and he'll bunny-stop you or blast you to death and then no more competition."

"Box, did anyone ever tell you that you're a scumbag detective?"

"All the time, but I can pay my bills every month."

"Where is he?"

"Where most of the Animal Farm Crime Syndicate is. You can find him in Mad Heights."

CHAPTER 43

Run-Time

This was my third pass around the streets surrounding Alien Alley. But I had walked it only once. Back in the day, when I was a new hovercar racer, I had gotten into the junk I was driving, and I felt something was off. It kept bothering me, and eventually, I pulled myself out of the race and gave the hovercar a complete inspection. It had a major separation in one of the feeder junctions to the engine. It could have shorted and crashed to the ground from twenty stories up, and there would be no Cruz or Liquid Cool Detective Agency. I listened to my instincts, even if they were wrong. This Alien Alley was off, but I didn't know why. It was in Woodstock Falls, so it wasn't a bad part of the city. However, I did one walk through, and I was done. I would only survey it from the safety of my Pony.

This was the scene of the crime. The kidnapping of a little girl as her mother walked her to school. It was the other anomaly the human computer, known as Compstat Connie, mentioned and I agreed. The crime took place at or before the shoot-out on Sweet Street that ended with the death of Easy Chair Charlie. To a normal person, both events would be unconnected; the fact that they occurred on the same night would mean nothing. But now that I was here and walked the alley, I felt otherwise. The end of the alley, where the daughter and mother would have emerged, had a view. It was a view unobstructed by monolith towers as one would expect, based on a quick glance of a street map on one's mobile. Woodstock Falls was a neighborhood of hills, and the neighboring Old Harlem was not. From Alien Alley in Woodstock Falls was a clear view, across the way, of Joe Blows Smoking Emporium, with all its flashing neon lights on Sweet Street.

Was the little girl just kidnapped at random? Or was it because she saw something or someone she wasn't supposed to see? And now that I confirmed from Box that the someone was a cyborg psycho, named Red Rabbit, the connections were coming together. The events not only happened in close proximity, but they happened on top of each other. I cared about my Easy Chair Charlie Case, but it coincided with the Lutty Girl Kidnapping Case. I had no proof at all, but they were connected.

Those were the "whats" of the cases. It was the "how" and "why" of my Easy Chair Charlie Case I needed. I kept babbling to myself. I'll cross that bridge when I get to it, I said to myself.

Mad Heights.

I was stalling for time, and I knew it. For damn good reason.

When I came through my office door, PJ was fiddling with a new purple mobile computer on her desk.

"Look what I got," she said.

"What happened to the old one?"

"Oh, I burned the keys out on that one."

"Just replace the keyboard."

"It costs the same to replace the keyboard as it does to get a whole new mobile computer. So I got a new one."

"You should get one of those auxiliary keyboards, so all you have to do is replace those."

She smiled. "You do come up with good ideas every so often."

"That's what I've been told. Visitors?"

"None."

"Calls?"

"A ton. All on your desk."

"What about the window? I don't why it took so long to fix. How can it take three weeks to fix a window? Don't throw any more people out my window."

"I didn't throw anyone out. You shot him out the window."

"What about the window, then?"

"Fixed and as good as new, but we can't keep shooting it out. Do you have any new clients? The paying kind?"

I walked away into my personal office.

We all needed to get paid. I was burning through money like a billion-sheet roll of toilet paper in the center of the sun. I could see the words flash in my brain: "Most businesses fail because of lack of adequate start-up capital."

"You Cruz?" the man on my video-phone asked.

"I, Cruz."

"You detective?"

"I detective."

"Good, I need you to shoot someone."

"Shoot wounded or shoot dead?"

"Shoot dead."

"My firm doesn't offer that as a service yet, but I'll refer you."

"Oh, good."

"Do you have something to write on?"

"Hold on...Got it."

"Nine."

"Nine."

"One."

"One."

"One."

"One."

"That's two ones after the nine. Call that express line and ask for the same thing, and they'll help you."

"Oh, good."

"It has to be a detective?"

"Oh yes. You can cover up your tracks, so the cops don't catch you."

"You're a real, live genius."

"Oh, I not all that, but I is smart."

"Hiring a detective to kill someone. That's like hiring a fireman to do an arson job for you. You smart."

"Oh yes. I try."

"Call that number and hire your guy. But don't mention my name, or they'll jack up the price on you."

"Okay. Thanks detective."

"Happy to help."

I disconnected my video-phone. "PJ!" I yelled.

The call came in when I was hunched over my desk re-prioritizing my messages. I had the "hot" pile, the "hold" pile, the "hell no" pile, and a few other miscellaneous ones.

"Line one." PJ's voice came through my video-phone intercom.

I thought it funny to hear PJ say "line one" when all I had was one line.

Run-Time appeared on the video display with his trademark flat cap.

"How are you, sir?" I said.

"I'm blessed, and I hear you've been too."

"I wouldn't go that far, but I've had a good start, aside from a few unpleasantries."

"Unpleasantries are a fact of life. Are you officially back from your vacation? The Box is what I was told you call it."

"I'm back with a new hat, new coat, and new attitude to make things happen. I'm back."

"Good. I have another client for you."

"What's her name?"

"Carol Num..."

"The mother of the kidnapped girl."

Run-Time stopped a beat. "You know her?"

"I heard about it when I was poking around for Fat Nat."

"She's in a bad way, and Flash asked me to intervene."

"Flash is always the knight in shining armor to the rescue."

"I'm going to see her tomorrow, and I'd like to have a solution for her. Maybe, if I could say a detective friend would take a look."

"I'll take it. The case."

"Just like that?"

"Sure. I told you, I'm back."

"She's very fragile, and my police friends say there's nothing happening with the case."

"When do you want me to come by to meet her?"

"Tomorrow. One of my VPs'll call you and confirm."

"I'll clear my schedule."

CHAPTER 44

Carol Num

I made good time to Let It Ride Enterprises headquarters in Peacock Hills. However, all the extra time I thought I had was eaten up by the awful Electric Blvd. hovertraffic. Valet took my Pony—I never allowed valet to touch my vehicle anywhere else, but I knew all of Run-Time's people, so it was okay—and I got in the elevator capsule.

"Mr. Cruz." His Lebanese VP was waiting for me, and after I replied with a greeting, she led me up to Run-Time's executive office.

"Cruz." Run-Time's smile was always infectious. We greeted each other, and he gestured me to an empty seat in his inner sitting area.

There she was—Carol Num, a Caucasian female with dark hair, still wearing her gray slicker with a mini-umbrella clipped to the waist. I shook her hand and sat across from her. Run-Time and his VP sat in their facing chairs. We were all sitting on one side of a cube design. I could see in her eyes this was no ordinary meeting with a client. In her eyes, I was her last hope. I had to be very careful what I said. She was on the edge of sanity. The police had done nothing, in her mind, and no one else had either.

"Should I call you, Mrs. Num?"

"No, please call me Carol."

"Carol, I'm going to apologize right at the start."

"For what?" I could see the hope in her eyes preparing itself to die.

"Because I'm about to speak to you in a somewhat unfriendly, accusatory way that victims in your situation do not deserve."

"I don't understand."

"I need you to tell me the truth, not the story you've been telling the police or my friend here."

Carol's head jerked back in total shock. "I don't know what you mean. I have only told the truth. My daughter was taken from me."

"That's probably the only true part of the story, but I want to know the part before and the part after, but only the truth."

"I did say the truth!" Carol jumped from her seat, her eyes tearing up.

The VP stood quickly and took her hand and, though I didn't look at him, Run-Time was giving me a look I had never seen from him in all the years we'd known each other—anger.

I stood slowly from my chair. "Carol, I'm sorry, but I won't be able to help you. If you can't give me the whole truth, then how am I supposed to go after the kidnapper? I'm sorry."

I stepped away from my chair and walked to the office door—slowly. Carol, the VP, and even Run-Time stood there with their mouths hanging open.

"Wait!" Carol yelled.

I stopped and looked back at her.

"How did you know I wasn't telling the truth?" she asked.

The look on both the VPs' and Run-Time's faces. They did a double-take and stared at her.

"Well, for one, I looked into your background and found that you owned a plasma gun. That is a serious gun, and you got it four years ago, so it was just before you started walking your daughter to school. That meant you carried it whenever you walked her to school for protection, that night, too. You were armed that night and there's no way you would let some guy in a rabbit mask get your daughter without a shot.

"Then I heard you were wandering the streets and happened to come across some low-level street punk corner king. Everyone said it was random. Bull. Among other things, he's a weapons dealer on the street. This kidnapper, supposedly, has a very unique kind of gun. You were going to the only person you knew who would know that. Meaning, you must have bought at least one illegal gun from the guy. Meaning, you must have also seen his gun that night when he kidnapped your daughter. Mrs. Num, I don't have time for games. This kidnapper is a gang member called Red Rabbit, but there isn't anything funny about him. How am I going to find his Animal Farm Crime Syndicate that he's a part of, find their hide-out, rescue your daughter...how can I do all that successfully without the whole truth and nothing but? Your daughter could be getting killed right now, while we're playing games."

That did it. Carol broke down into a sobbing mess.

"She ran ahead of me. We were both running down the alley, but you know kids, and I'm no spring chicken anymore. She sprinted way past me. When she got to other end of the alley, she stopped and went around the corner, and I couldn't see her. I ran as fast as I could."

We were all back in our chairs as Carol recounted the real story.

"When I got around the corner, there was this man wearing a rabbit mask on his head, and his arms were metallic, and he was trying to grab my Lutty. He was holding some kind of machine gadget in his other hand. That's the only way my Lutty was able to fight him off. I heard gunfire in the distance. I jumped on him and started punching his head, but it was solid...like padded metal. He threw me off and grabbed my Lutty by the collar and ran off with her!"

The VP had to calm her down.

313

Her face turned mean. "Before he grabbed her, though, I pulled out my gun and shot him, over and over, but nothing happened. He laughed and told me that if he had a third arm, he'd show me what a real scary gun looked like. That he'd vaporize me and I'd find out why he was called Red." She got quiet as she lowered her head. "Then he ran off with her."

My mannerism was to lean forward when I wanted to have a pointed conversation. With Run-Time, it was the opposite. He leaned all the way back in his chair, and he looked at Carol angrily.

"Carol, why didn't you tell me the truth. Why did you do this? Cruz is right. Your own daughter could be getting killed. Why wouldn't you have told the police this before?"

She hesitated for what seemed like forever. "I did."

"What?" he asked. "What do you mean?"

"I did tell the police what happened." We looked at her, confused. "They were right there at the scene. I told them everything, and then they threatened me and said the city police would arrive and told me what to say to them and anyone who asked. They said if I didn't do what they said, they'd arrest me and lock me up forever, and I would never get my daughter back."

"The Feds?" Run-Time asked, which is what I thought, too. "The Feds told you to do this?"

When Carol shook her head "no," it was the first time I had ever seen Run-Time scared. Because he was scared, his VP was scared, and they glanced at me.

"I don't get it," I said. "Not the Feds? If not the Metro police and not the Feds, then who? What other police are there?"

"Cruz, let's talk privately for a minute," Run-Time said and stood from his chair.

"It's over," he said.

He had led me out of his office, down the hall, and into a side conference room. The room was not as big as his office, but huge nonetheless.

"What do you mean, it's over?"

"Cruz, stop investigating the case. You'll be paid for your time."

"Forget about that. What about her daughter?"

Run-Time paused.

"That is why you called me down here."

"Can you really find the daughter?"

"I can. I'm sure I can. But..."

"But what?"

"It's going to be extremely dangerous."

"Then the police have to be brought in."

"What police are not the Feds and not the city police? You might as well tell me now, because you know I won't let it go."

"You have to let it go."

"Tell me."

"Interpol."

I gave him a confused look. "Interpol? You mean international police?"

"I guess they were international in the beginning. When cars drove on wheels on the ground. But the Feds, nowadays, are international."

"I'm not following."

"The Interspace Police."

Now I understood. "The police from Up-Top."

"Their authority includes not only off-world, but supersedes the city police *and* the Feds on Earth."

"I take it this is a bad thing."

"They could come down and blow up City Hall, and there wouldn't be anything the Mayor, Metro Police, or the Feds could do about. Their power is global, in the truthful, nonmetaphorical sense."

"Then I have to go after the girl."

"If you know where she is, let's tell the police and let them handle it. That's the only play we have. You do not want to be involved with Interpol. This isn't a request, Cruz."

"Run-Time, the girl."

I could see the battle in Run-Time's mind. "Cruz, no megacorp, no criminal cartel, no elected official—the Mayor, the City Council President, the Director of the Feds...none have the kind of power these people have."

"I understand."

"You get on their bad side, and they can jam up everyone you know. You understand what I'm saying?"

"You."

"Yes, me, but that's not the everybody I'm talking about."

"Yeah," I said, softly.

"Marriages don't work out so well when one or both parties are in a space station prison."

"Okay, we do it your way, but I can still try to get the girl. I never was one for the political stuff. That's your specialty. Whatever is going on shouldn't include a little girl being kidnapped and held against her will."

"Why do you think the girl is alive? Even I think she's dead and, especially now, that I've heard Carol's real story."

"It's better I don't answer that, until we see how this all plays out."

"Cruz, do not say anything about what Carol said. It would put her in danger."

"I wouldn't do that. The only thing on my mind is getting her daughter. She's had enough danger for a lifetime."

CHAPTER 45

Blue Pill Rabbit

I was man enough to admit it. I was scared.

No, this wasn't me after I spoke with Run-Time in his offices, and we went back to see Carol on her way. This was me two days earlier after I left my three detective pow-wow with Box and Rexx. Red Rabbit was in Mad Heights. That's where I was going. The reason I could promise Run-Time I'd lay low was because I had done all my dangerous detecting stuff the day before. Of course, I didn't tell Run-Time that.

When you live in a big city, such as Metropolis, you learn your place. You knew where your people hung out—working class, wealthy class, sidewalk johnnies, skaters, hackers, speed racers, etc. You learned where the city-crawl dancers, the biker enthusiasts, historical societies, etc. hung out. Then there were the mean streets, and all the groups that hung out there. You learned where you could go and where you couldn't go in the city, if you didn't want a beat-down or wanted to stay alive.

Like in Hell, the criminal world had levels of bad, then you got to the really bad, then to true evil; beyond that, you didn't even want to know.

Mad Heights wasn't the hangout for the truly evil, but it was for the truly bad and the truly violent.

When we were kids, growing up, was the first time we ever heard about Mad Heights. When I was on the race circuit, albeit brief, one part of our illegal hovercar race passed through the area. It was a big scandal. The guy who organized the race was killed. The rumor was that he was killed by Mad Heights gangs, because he didn't pay for passage through their turf. That talk made adults run away chicken. Imagine what we did as kids. You even mentioned Mad Heights, and we'd want to run and leave town.

And now I was going there.

I was tempted to bring Punch Judy into it, but I couldn't do that for many reasons. One, she was a felon, and I couldn't put her into that situation. She needed to stay far away from that world for her own personal mental sanity. I was her second chance at a normal life, and I couldn't be the one to ruin it. Second, she was a gang member. True, most people didn't consider posh gangs to be real gangs, but if I took her into such a situation, and we were confronted by trouble, she'd revert to her old gang instincts. Guns, gangs, cyborgs. Not good. Posh gangs were at the bottom of the totem pole of criminal gangs, along with white-collar, couch-potato gangs doing crime via mobile computer alone, so that would make PJ more violent in dealing with another gang.

The Animal Farm Crime Syndicate was a real criminal organization, born out of pop culture, and evolved from hooliganism. Back in the day, packs of deranged juvenile delinquents congregated around rugby, American football, international football, and especially—known for their ultra-violence—hoverhockey stadium games, to cause all kinds of mayhem. These hooligans evolved, all right. These delinquent punks roamed their part of the neon jungle in complete control of its criminal life—drugs, prostitution, gun-running, contract killing, and illegal gambling were their main scores. Gangs always needed something to mark themselves. For some, it was tattoos or chopping off a particular finger, but for the new animal gangs, it became wearing their animal masks.

The animal gang I had to find was the Rabbits. They'd have some kind of adjective before their name, but since I wasn't wise to gang life at all, avoiding it like the plague all my life, I wouldn't know much about their habits and turf. The Animal Farm Crime Syndicate wasn't the most powerful or smartest of criminal cartels; there were just so damn many of them, which is what made them formidable.

Back to what I was saying before—I was scared. Under no circumstances was I going to drive my Ford Pony into that place. A hovertaxi was also not an option. I needed to hire a guide and bodyguard all in one. What I was quickly realizing is that I didn't know people who knew people who knew criminals. Phishy and Punch Judy didn't count; he was a slider, and she was an ex-posh gang member from another country. I couldn't hire someone to go into Mad Heights to protect me. I had to hire someone who already lived in Mad Heights to protect me.

"I'd like to start this month's evening meeting of the Metropolis Soldier of Fortune Meet-Up Club by everyone going around the room and giving us your name and a little something about yourself. It's customary that first-time visitors go first. Any volunteers?" he asked. The man looked like his skin had been cooked over an open flame. Survivor of a war? Or victim of a bad plastic skin job?

I raised my hand.

"Thank you, young man. Tell us about yourself."

I stood from my chair. "My name is Cruz, and I'm a detective, new to the biz, in fact. I didn't know where else to go, so I came here. I'm going into Mad Heights, and as many of you know, it's not the nicest part of the city. But I have a real case that forces me to go there and track down members of a particular, and particularly deranged animal gang. But you don't go into Mad Heights without bodyguard protection. I bet with all the law enforcement, military, and mercenary experience in this room, there's got to be at least one person who could help a young guy, like me, starting out. I'm so inexperienced at this that I don't even know people who know criminals or anything about that world."

"Then you're in the wrong business, sonny," one man said and the room erupted in laughter.

"Probably true, but it's too late now. I already have my business cards." My quip got additional laughter.

"You can hire them you know," a man said in the back on the other side of the room.

"Hire who?" I asked.

"You can hire animal gang members as bodyguards. Anybody can."

"How do you do that?"

"Call 'em."

"Where?"

"They advertise in the Club's cybernet magazine, along with every other criminal in the city. Between body armor and bombs— bodyguards," the man said.

Once I started this, there was no turning back. It was like boarding a lunar flight and then panicking and wanting off the spaceship. Tough! You were sealed into the craft and were along for the ride, and there was nothing you could do about it.

That's how I felt when my hovervehicle of bodyguards arrived. Again, I was burning though money like I was made of it, and it was worrying me, but I put it out of mind. It was a hovervan plus, and the door opened, and the first one jumped out. The man was huge! On his head was a hippo mask. I had hired four members of the Hypernova Hippos as my bodyguards for the night. Back in the day, the Horses and Pigs ran the show, but not for a long time. The man was a cyborg, but the technology interface was just plain awful. Oversized arms, fat pot belly, fat legs with cables and wires half sticking out from their clothes. I didn't like it, but I couldn't back out now. I walked past him and jumped into the van's second seat.

The man got back into the passenger seat and slid the door closed. The only illumination inside the hovervehicle was from the front window. There were two Hippos in the front, and there two sitting behind me in the rear seats. They all just sat there quiet.

"What's the job?"

"Before I answer that question, since you refused to talk to me on the video-phone, what's the Hippos relationship with the Rabbits?"

"Relationship?" the Hippo in the passenger seat responded. "The Hypernova Hippos think the Riot Gear Rabbits are the dirt between our toes."

"That's a very nice image. The job is I need to find one, question him, and get the hell out of there when I'm done. That's it. You are here for insurance. If someone tries to mess with me, you come in and stop them."

"Why do you want to talk to a Rabbit?"

"I told you all I'm telling you about the job. Do you want it or not?"

The Hippo chuckled. "Why? Are you going to find someone else? We don't take the job; you're up the creek without a boat."

"You're right. I have no back-up plan."

"Let's up the price then, since we have no competitors."

"Let's not, because I'm paying what we agreed, but if the Hypernova Hippos are dishonest, like the Jackals..."

"Hey! We're not the Jupiter Jackals. Price as agreed but you pay before we lift off."

"Half now, half when we return."

"All now."

"I was born at night, but not last night. I pay all now; you throw me out of the van. And just so you know, I shot my first man dead when I was five years old. I prefer talk only, but I'm capable of a lot more. I may not be a Mad Heights man, and you're here as my reinforcements, but I'm not some Chicken Little scared of his own shadow. More than your protection, I need your expertise. You are Mad Heights men. Half now, half when we get back. We can even go to the bank and do an escrow account if you like."

"Give over the half then. And forget the bank. We don't do banks."

"We get back, I'll make the call and have one of my sidewalk johnny friends bring up the bag with the other half of the money."

"Mr. Cruz, you know what it feels like to have your ribcage crushed in by a Hippo death hug?"

"Is that what Hippo cyborgs do? No, I don't know and don't expect to know what that feels like, ever. Do the job I'm hiring you for, or I have a few threats up my sleeve, too."

"You have nothing you can threaten us with."

"Do you want to exchange threats or do you want to do a job and get paid for it."

The Hippo in the passenger seat turned to look back at me.

"Money."

I gave him the bag I had inside my jacket pocket. He didn't even count it, but threw it to his feet. The driver started up the hovervan, and within moments, we were flying into the sky traffic.

As I sat there, sandwiched between the two animal gang members, I realized there was another hole in my new career as a detective—I would need muscle. I hated strangers, but I had no choice with this Hippo crew. That didn't mean that, after this excursion into Mad Heights, I wouldn't start putting together a list of people I could trust to back me up when needed.

When we flew into Mad Heights airspace, I felt my chest tighten. I had seen it from the air from this angle before on television. There was a legitimate reason it was called Mad Heights, besides it now being a madhouse of crime. The neighborhood was old and existed before the building codes were formalized in the city. It looked like a mad group of builders had put the town together. There were skinny towers next to monolith towers, twenty foot towers next to two hundred foot ones. It all looked...mad. If a construction crew was high on drugs and could do whatever popped into their minds, Mad Heights was what they would have come up with. Adding to the madness were the neon signs of all sizes and shapes—no standard like other towns.

Our hovervan departed from the sky-lane and every second that went by the neon signs got fewer and fewer.

"We're going to set down in a back-alley," the Hippo in the passenger seat said, turning his head back. "You're not afraid to walk in the rain?"

"I do it all the time," I answered. "That why I wear my hat."

It was not just a back-alley. They chose an alley so secluded I wondered if it was even part of the city. The only light was from a street lamp yards away. The Hippos piled out of their hovervan, and I jumped out too, immediately being splashed by muddy water and realizing I had jumped right into a puddle. The Hippos chuckled.

I wondered when they would do so. Two Hippos stood and took off their ridiculous hippo masks. When I saw their ugly faces, I almost said out loud for them to pull the masks back on. The fat, pudgy faces stared at me with beady little eyes. They'd airbrushed their face from their foreheads to their noses to give that better effect with their masks on. Their hair was a crew cut, except for the edges, which were tied and cut in a style to, I guess, look like hippo ears. The hairdo looked stupid, but when you're a criminal, who can effortlessly pound someone to death, you can look stupid.

As we walked away, I realized two Hippos were not following, but waited with the hovervan. I was about to protest as I thought I had hired four bodyguards, but stopped myself. Would I leave my vehicle unattended in this place? Why would I expect them to? And Let It Ride Enterprises wasn't sending any of their mobile car security guards anywhere near this armpit of the city.

It was probably part of their gang code, too. With masks off guarding me, it meant it wasn't a gang op, but masks on, guarding their vehicle meant, if you messed with it, you were messing with the entire Hypernova Hippo gang. The more I thought about it, the more I didn't like what it suggested in terms of their protection of me. I had only 50% of the crew I hired.

The street was dark and flooded. Most of the time, I wore clear overboots up to my knees. They were virtually invisible, and I was glad I had them on this time, because the water in the street came up to my calves. The Hippos seemed to enjoy sloshing through the muddy water.

"Turn up there," one of the Hippos said.

When we turned up the street, it was like someone opened a door, and we had passed right through a vortex into another world. For the first time in my life, I was walking down the streets of Mad Heights. It was as noisy and flashy as I had expected. Here, they didn't have sidewalk johnnies; they had sidewalk hustlers, who stood with their backs against the wall in their neon suits and outfits, watching everyone who passed by. I knew what they were looking for—someone like me. Newbies, visitor virgins, people clearly not from here. I could pretend to be as tough as I wanted to be, but they could smell a mark from miles away.

I tried to envision what were the real differences, from a street viewpoint, between here and working class neighborhoods, like my Rabbit City or Woodstock Falls, and upscale ones, like Peacock Hills or Silicon Dunes. Bad neighborhoods just had more of everything in a gratuitous and venal way. The smell of perfume or cologne in the air was too much and sickly, the clothes worn under their dark slickers were too bright, the tech was too gaudy along with their jewelry, their haircuts were too over-the-top, and the muscle on the men and cleavage on the woman was just too much. Rich neighborhoods were perfect in their presentation. Working neighborhoods were decent in theirs. Mad Heights and every mean street neighborhood like it, were just outrageous. It was as if this was what crime felt it had to do to stand out in a noisy, 50-million supercity like Metropolis.

The mean streets had its eye on me. I could see one street hustler smile at his partner next to him, and their eyes locked on me, like a laser-guided missile, even though I had turned my head and was watching them peripherally. One of the Hippos grabbed my shoulder, and the three of us stopped. The two Hippos stared at the approaching sidewalk hustlers, who did an immediate about-face and went back the way they came. As I stared at the Hippos' backs, I could see these cyborgs had massive pile-driver arms. Punch Judy with her cybernetic arms could throw a 300-pound guy through a reinforced window. The arm of one of these Hippos was like six PJ arms—they could throw an entire truck with two 300-pound guys through a reinforced window. The Hippo let go of my shoulder—and I was glad he did, because his hand alone felt like it weighed 500 pounds. We continued walking.

The only equivalent I could think of was models walking the runway with fans, media, and industry people gawking at them. If I hadn't had a Hippo bodyguard on either side of me, I wouldn't have made it. I knew that now. Everyone was watching me. Did I smell funny? How could they know I wasn't a Mad Heights guy? Phishy told me that street people had a sixth sense and could pick out people who didn't belong on the street, and in the bad neighborhoods, it was even sharper. I guessed it had to be if your life was about preying on marks for your livelihood, and spotting police and rival gangs meant the difference between prison or death.

I also didn't trust the Hippos. It was good I had bodyguards, but what was the point if I was scared they'd mug me and leave me in some alleyway, just for the fun of it, despite being paid. Well, something was better than nothing, but I definitely needed my own personal bodyguard service. But again, this was better than nothing.

This was also not the place for an inherent germophobe. I controlled it, most of the time, and hid it from most people, but certain situations made it flare up. I never went near public bathrooms. I'd rather die. I stayed in my own ordered world. However, this wasn't my world. I stood there, staring at the general clinic in front of me, but my foot wouldn't move. There were more dope roaches—drug addicts—around the place than a free drug giveaway in Tijuana. All of them looked like aged zombies, morbidly skinny, scales and sores, bad hair, and bad teeth. The clinic building looked like it had been hit by multiple bomb blasts. Then there were the neon signs: "General Clinic," "Free Needles" "Free Exams" "All Medical Accepted" "Cash Only." When I read "One Finger Body Exams" I was about to run right out of there, but a Hippo grabbed me.

"Are you going in?"

They could see my expression and chuckled.

"Do you have an extra hippo mask?"

They laughed louder.

"Seventh floor," the Hippo said when he returned. "I'd take the stairs if I were you."

Inside the clinic was nasty! The waiting room was overflowing with zombie-looking walk-in patients. People were leaning against the walls and sprawled out on the dirty floor. My skin was crawling. Then I noticed water flies buzzing around. I had to stand there for a moment to compose myself and fight my feet from running out of there. It was nasty!

As with everything in the city, there was no such thing as small. The clinic was on the bottom of a tower, but it was still at least seventeen stories. The bottom levels were the intake waiting rooms and clinics. I was going nowhere near the elevators in this place, so I approached the stairs, and a door opened and a doctor or nurse, whichever, popped out with one bloody white glove on one hand and one dripping brown white glove on the other. I shut my eyes so tightly there was a chance they would never open again. I could not cope with this nastiness. I realized quickly that no good would come from prolonged exposure to this facility. Find my person, question him, and get out.

The Hippos also educated me on the state of Rabbit gangs. There was a coup within the Riot Gear Rabbit gang. The leader, White Rabbit, was killed, and his number two in command, Blue Pill Rabbit, was sent here—barely alive. There were now two separate Rabbit gangs, and they were at full-scale war with each other.

This was supposed to be a clinic, but I had seen only one medic—unlikely for a facility of this huge size. I felt there was something I was missing, and as the outsider, the joke was on me. As I neared the top of the stairs to the seventh floor, there were four watching me, skinny punks with rabbit masks on their heads. Two were barefoot, and that made me want to vomit. Barefoot on this nasty floor?

"Where's Blue Pill?" I asked with authority.

"You part of the Hippo crew?" one asked.

Criminals always had look-outs, even if you never saw them.

"No, I hired them as muscle. I'm not part of any gang. I'm a detective on the outside."

"Why you want Blue Pill then, square?"

"Take me to Blue Pill, so I can ask him my questions directly. Tell him I need to know everything there is to know about Red, so I can take him down. Blue Pill can take him down here. I can take him down on the outside. Blue Pill and I are going to be temporary friends, because we have a mutual enemy."

"Red Rabbit is dead!" one of them said.

The four rabbit gang members were riling themselves up, repeating the same thing, but even I could tell, without seeing their faces, they were scared to death of him.

The entire seventh floor was filled with rabbit-masked gang members, armed with guns, knives, swords, and rifles. If I got into trouble here, my body would be cold and in pieces long before either of my Hippo bodyguards got to me. They both conveniently told me they'd wait at the door for me—I had no say in the matter.

The recovery room where the gang leader, Blue Pill, lay was also overflowing with other rabbit gang members, but these had their masks off. Caucasian Rastafarians! That's what the Riot Gear Rabbits were—White guys with dreadlocks.

Blue Pill lay on his bed, dressed in a hospital gown, with tubes and wires attached all over his body. There was also a tube in his mouth, and I wasn't a doctor, but his arms and legs were burnt horribly.

One of the rabbit gang members, who was furthest away, pushed through the others to stand about two inches from my face. "You don't look like a Hippo."

"I'm from the outside."

"Everybody knows that. Why are you on the inside, inside here?"

"I need Blue Pill's help."

"Why?"

"Because Red Rabbit is a psycho and needs to be taken down."

"Why? That don't tell us anything. Why do you want to take him down?"

"He orchestrated a friend of mine getting killed by the police. You may have heard of it. That shootout on Sweet Street."

"We heard."

"How this Red did it, I'd also like to know, because my friend would never have done it voluntarily. He never even touched a gun, then he goes gun-crazy, and all these weapons magically appear in his hands."

"Maybe Red told him to do it, and if he didn't, he'd hop over to the guy's family and brutally rabbit-kick them to death. Maybe he used drugs on him. Maybe he used machines. Red seems to have many Up-Top machines in his possession, besides his lightning rifle. You seem to want everything wrapped up in a nice little bow for you. Sometimes, you don't get all the answers, and that's life."

"Then, since you don't seem to know, that's another reason to find and take him down. He may make you go gun-crazy against your will and take down your own men or even your boss, Blue Pill, here," I said. "Red Rabbit is our public enemy number one."

All I knew about this Red was what Box had told me, but from the look of the rabbit gang members' faces, they agreed with what I had just said.

"How can we help?" he asked. "As you can see, Blue Pill isn't a conversationalist anymore because of Red."

I looked at Blue Pill and said, "I only have a few questions. Then, I'll get out of here, so you can rest. Third degree burns ain't no joke."

Blue Pill blinked his eyes to acknowledge me. I looked back at his main man.

"Why is Red still alive?"

The question surprised him, and he looked at Blue Pill for a moment. The rabbit gang members in the room were waiting for an answer, and that's why he was nervous, so I decided to help him.

"I ask, because I know you're getting everything ready to finish him off for good, but I don't want to get in between any gang war."

"He's protected."

"Protected?" I asked.

"We don't know how, but he's protected by the Feds."

"How do you know?"

"We have sources everywhere."

"Where did Red come from? Who is he?"

"He was a Rabbit years ago. Always a hothead and untrustworthy. He tried to take control of the gang back then, but White set him straight. Sent Blue Pill after him, so he could 'see things as they really are'." His way to describe the violence.

"Set him straight, how?"

"Broke every bone in his arms, legs, and neck," the main man said with pride. I had to remember I was among vicious human animals.

"You turned him into a cyborg," I said.

The fact didn't please any of them.

"How long was he gone?"

"Seven years."

"Do you know where he was all that time?"

"He disappeared. We never expected to see him again. Then he returns. He wasn't Red back then, but he is Red, now. And connected with the Feds. We don't how he did that."

"He's an informant for them?"

"That's what protected by the Feds means."

"Why would he do that?" I asked. "How big is the Rabbit gang that he controls?"

A sore subject for them. "He controls all of it, except for us. We're loyal to Blue Pill, and we don't care if he has a hit out on us by other Rabbit crew members. There's going to be Red blood in the streets. I can promise you that."

"If you know he's a police informant, then wouldn't his Rabbit crew members know that? Why would they follow him?"

"Yeah. Why?" the main man asked.

My head was trying to make sense of what made no sense, but I wouldn't figure it out here, as my eyes caught the glimpse of a jumbo roach crawling on the ground in the corner.

"My last question—where does Red stay in Mad Heights?"

"Only outsiders call it Mad Heights. You should at least pretend to be an insider. We can tell you where to find him, but it won't make any difference."

"Why?"

"His lair is so fortified that you'd never get to his front door alive. We can't, and we're after him."

"And he's protected by the Feds."

"That only means he'll never be arrested, but that doesn't mean we can't use whatever means to take him out. Isn't that what you said you wanted to do?"

"It is. After I do one thing, first."

"What's that?"

"Rescue the little girl the psycho kidnapped."

"Red is psycho, but no way he'd do something like that. Not his style. He kills things. He doesn't kidnap them and keep them around. Your intel is faulty."

"It's in the news or don't you read."

"The news. All the lies fit to print. That's faulty, too."

"Tell me where he is, and I'll go see for myself."

"Then you're going to need a lot more than good intentions and a couple of fat Hippos to get into Red's lair. Did you pay them yet, your Hippo bodyguards?"

"Why?" I asked.

"You know they're going to leave you behind to die, right?" the Rabbit said with a grin.

They were grinning at me, even half-dead Blue Pill in his bed—with their stupid, oversized rabbit buck-teeth.

CHAPTER 46

Chief Hub

Finally, I could get the hell out of that nasty place. It was interesting how, in one part of the world, people went about their day with water flies flittering around, and in another region, the mere sight of a baby jumbo roach or puddle slug meant a work stoppage. I was proud to be in the latter group. Everyone in the clinic, obviously, was born in a barn—if such places existed on the planet anymore.

I made my way down the stairs, going straight down the center of people sitting and smoking or sleeping on either side. I moved as quickly as my legs would allow, without tripping and falling. Then, dashed though the clinic waiting room, because I could see no more nastiness. I was too fragile. Out the main entrance, I sighed a deep sigh of relief as I looked up to the cloudy sky.

Sometimes, in life, you are cosmically drawn to a place or person, but you can never articulate why. My eyes shifted to a third floor corner window in the building directly across me. There stood, watching from the open window, a rabbit-masked guy. But somehow, I knew it wasn't a Blue Rabbit look-out. I knew it was Red Rabbit; I'd swear to it.

If Red was here, it could only mean one thing. I couldn't be so lucky that on the same day I was associating with real known gang members (Punch Judy didn't count) that I was about to get caught in the middle of a gang war.

He was watching me, and I knew what he was thinking: why am I staring at him with a look of recognition. Yes, we had never laid eyes on each other before. Then he receded into the darkness of the room, and I couldn't see him anymore.

I snapped out of my vigil and looked to see that my two Hippo bodyguards were nowhere near the main entrance. They were gone! I quickly scanned the crowds and glimpsed the two fat Hippos about a dozen feet away.

"Hey!" I yelled at them.

They knew who was yelling at them, and they looked back at me with smirks. They would seriously ditch me in the middle of Mad Heights unprotected.

For a brief second, I was on the exact page of everyone on the streets; I was running. Then, I realized that I was running one way and everyone else was running the other. It was like a twisted game of musical chairs where everyone knew what to do, except for me.

I looked ahead and saw them, dozens of young men with black airbrush paint around their eyes—a tell-tale sign of an animal gang member—and their matted dreadlocks. Just as I noticed it, the Caucasian Rastafarians donned their rabbit masks in unison and ran at me, drawing weapons.

Casually, I moved out of the way. I knew they weren't after me. The Red Rabbit Gang was here to wipe out the remnants of the Blue Pill Rabbit Gang. A final showdown. Above me, I heard sounds I had never heard before and looked up. A hovervan was firing at the seventh floor with laser-cannons! I couldn't believe what I was seeing. Immediately, I heard glass breaking, and laser rounds showered the attacking hovervan from the sixth and eighth floors.

My eye noticed something dive off the roof of the tower. I couldn't tell what the black shape was. It looked like a giant, black hockey puck. It descended like a stone and crashed on the roof of the attacking hovervan. A second later, the vehicle exploded. The hovervan was a ball of fire, with burning bodies falling to the ground with chunks and fragments of the vehicle. I was not interested in being under metal rain.

Fortunately, I had an impeccable sense of direction and decided I could run to the Hippo hovervan before they could lift off and ditch me. So, I ran. Something told me to look behind me, and I did. Running right after me were the two street punks my Hippo bodyguards had previously scared off. But now, I was alone.

I had no idea what these two planned to do to me. Mug me? I wasn't about to stop to find out, so I turned into the alley the Hippos took me through to get from the dark back alleys to the main streets. I double-timed to the end of the alley, just as the two appeared and started after me.

When I was a police intern, I remember one of the instructors saying to us, in one of their many, boring classes, "It is never permissible to shoot first and ask questions later." Hell with that! I pulled my piece and shot the first one in the leg. The punk collapsed, and the other grabbed and dragged him back the other way and around the corner. Then, I heard yelling, but I couldn't make out their words.

Behind me was the dim streetlight, the only thing that pierced the darkness. I needed to move closer to see if the hovervan was still there. I turned back to look up the alley, and a dozen men appeared, all shooting. One shot barely missed my ear. I pulled myself back and shot around the corner wildly. I heard yells, grunts, and splashing on the wet ground. I then sent another volley of gunfire their way and ran to that streetlight.

Since it was not my lucky day, the Hippo hovervan was long gone. I was so screwed, and all I could think to do was step back directly out of the light. What was I going to do, now?

As I stood there trying to think, I had a very strange sensation. I felt I wasn't alone in the secluded dark back-alley. It was more than that. I felt I was surrounded by people—lots of people. It was weird, because I couldn't see or hear anything, but the feeling was overpowering.

I couldn't ignore it. I flipped my pop-gun into the dark. The brief second that the pop-gun blast fired, showed me that my instincts were terribly right. Three men were hit by the pop-gun blast and fell back with grunts. They were all wearing some kind of leather outfit that covered even their heads.

I fired my piece all around me, like I was mad, because I was going mad. Every random shot in the dark was hitting someone! Who were all these people?! I kept firing. I had no idea how many people there were, but they were all around me.

A spotlight turned on above me, and these dark alley people scattered into the night, but I kept shooting at them. I would never shoot someone in the back, but I ignored my rule. A message had to be sent loud and clear: Don't mess with me.

It was the Hippo hovervan. The side door opened, and one of them grabbed me and threw me into the middle seat. The door closed, and the vehicle jetted away into the night sky.

When you called a woman a hot mess, it meant one thing. When you used the phrase for a man, it meant something different. I was a hot mess, sitting there, stewing in my own anger and germophobia. Five words repeated over and over in my head: "I want to go home." I did not want to say or do anything else. But life would not allow any such peace.

We drove until they illegally air-braked the hovercar to the side. I had seen more criminality and violence in this single day than I had in almost 20 adult years of life. No wonder those in the crime world had such a short shelf life. It was amazing they lasted as long as they did. The two Hippos in the front seat turned around.

"You owe us the other half of the money," the one in the passenger seat said.

Here we were, hovering twenty or more stories in the air. They'd pitch me out of the hovervan if they had even an inkling they wouldn't get the rest of their payment. They didn't care that they gave me only half the bodyguards I hired and left me behind to get killed by three different groups. But they would say quickly, "We came back for ya, didn't we? You're alive, aren't ya?"

"You know where to go," I answered. "The video-booth. I call for your money there."

The Hippos watched me before turning back around. The hovervan lurched and dipped a few feet before flying forward. I heard a shotgun cock in the seat behind me. If it was meant to scare me, it worked, but I kept my composure.

We arrived in Wharf City and pulled up alongside a line of public video-phone booths. I got out; three Hippos got out, too, and walked with me. But instead of picking up a phone receiver, I just raised my arm.

A sidewalk johnny nervously appeared from behind the booths with a bag in hand. He threw the bag to me, and I threw the bag to one of the miserable, fat cyborgs. The sidewalk johnny backed away. I stood there and watched them with a big frown on my face. One of the Hippos shook the bag as if he could really tell if it was all there with a simple shake.

"Nice doing business with ya," the main Hippo said.

I knew any words out of my mouth, with the mood I was in, would most likely get me killed. I kept my mouth shut, noticing that my sidewalk johnny "friend" had vanished already. The three of them chuckled and hopped back into their hovervan and sped away into the sky traffic.

I ran.

My sidewalk johnny's other job was to keep a pre-paid hovertaxi waiting and ready, which he did. I ran to it and jumped inside quickly. We arrived at the Concrete Mama, and I ran inside, past all the lobby johnnies to the elevator. I ran out of the elevator to my apartment— 9732. When I was in, with all the locks locked, I could feel my normalcy returning.

When you have a city in a region with more water than the oceans, the government wants you to waste water. "Take five showers a day." "Take a shower every hour." I still couldn't grasp that there were still people in this city, who showered only once a week, not even daily. I was not into soaking in body detergent, anti-bacterial, anti-germ suds. Whatever filth it dissolved off your skin, you'd be sitting right in the middle of it. I never understood the bath thing. My fave was a super shower of lukewarm water, shooting out of the main floor and ceiling vents, and side nozzles, blasting out waves of hot steam. My super sauna shower. I knew I'd be in my bathroom for at least 90 minutes.

Was I being a big baby? Or was the danger of the day not to be taken lightly, and I was right to be unnerved? That was the internal debate I had to resolve. I was a detective now, so I had to expect to frequent bad places, like Mad Heights, occasionally, on a case. I couldn't melt each time.

Who were those leather-suited people in the dark attacking me?

The question popped into my head. I had never experienced something so crazy. All these people standing in the dark around me. What the hell! I had to find out who or what they were, or it would bug me forever. Phishy would know.

My beautiful shower was over, and I got into the nicest, cleanest, fluffiest white clothes, and then I glided over to my bed. I dove in and pulled my super-fluffy comforters over me, and that was it. I was in for the day. I was not leaving this bed. I was traumatized, and I needed time to regenerate, as the saying goes.

Turn off the video-phone!

I jumped out of the bed and ran to it. It rang.

The call was one of Run-Time's VPs—the West Indian one. Run-Time's Carol Num meeting was on. Suddenly, my planned day had been re-planned.

I wouldn't know until much later that my mad time in Mad Heights put me further ahead in the story than anybody else.

At Let It Ride headquarters, Carol revealed what she revealed, and Run-Time revealed what he did, especially by not saying things directly. One of Run-Time's VPs would take Carol home. The other would take me to Metro Police with part of the Run-Time entourage.

"Mr. Run-Time will meet us there," his West Indian VP said.

It was me, her, and four other people who loaded into a waiting Let It Ride Enterprises hoverlimo that seemed longer than my own apartment. We got comfortable; the VP sat across from me. All of them were sitting across from me.

"Mr. Cruz, if I may, and I don't want to offend you..."

"What is it?" I asked the VP.

"If you could let Mr. Run-Time do the talking?"

"Who are we going to talk to?"

"It will be a private meeting of the Chief of Police, his top aides, and the Mayor's liaison will be there, too."

"What about the police detectives handling Carol's case?"

"They won't be there."

"Why not?"

"They've briefed their superiors."

"That makes me very uncomfortable," I said. "When I was a police intern, back in the day, I quickly learned the only thing the superiors do is sit at a desk, laugh at the Police Chief's jokes, and stand behind him when he gives a press conference. What's different today?"

The VP smiled ever so diplomatically, and the other guys looked on quietly.

"The street detectives are doing the work and have the answers. Why again, won't they be there?" I asked.

"We'll relay your discomfort to Mr. Run-Time," the VP said, as she unflipped her mobile and typed.

"Thank you."

As soon as we walked into the swanky executive conference room of the Metro Police on their ground level, I looked for them. Not a police officer in silver and black to be found. Only a sea of police majors, captains, lieutenants, and deputies. There were even a few ranks I never saw before. I bit my lip and stayed quiet as I was led by Run-Time's people.

Then the Feds came in, dressed in black suits, with a group as large as the waiting police. Then, there was a commotion and in came the Mayor with an even bigger entourage. I found the whole thing annoying.

As the three groups approached each other, I noticed Run-Time standing in the back with one of his other VPs, the Lebanese one, and a few other people. The greeting of the police, Feds, and the Mayor's group was something out of a sitcom and took forever. When they were done, the accusations could commence.

"There were no Feds on the scene," one of the federal agents said.

"We have on good authority that the identified kidnapper of this girl was purposely allowed to escape the scene," a police deputy said.

"Feds allowed a kidnapper to get away? Why would we do that? Anyway, we were not on that scene."

"Our officers in the field say there were Feds on the scene."

"We were not there?"

"So, my officers are liars?"

"We're saying it wasn't the Federal Police, and we don't know who was there that you claim was there."

The back-and-forth was becoming more heated.

"What are we planning to do to rescue this girl?" I asked out loud.

The West Indian shot a look at me, and the entire conference room went quiet. Everybody was staring at me.

"Do I need to repeat the question?" I asked.

"No, you don't," said one of the police majors as he approached. "Who exactly are you, and why are you here?"

"I'm the consultant on the case for the mother."

"Consultant? You mean like a pretend detective?"

"There's nothing pretend about a kidnapped child."

"Do you have any children, Mr. Cruz?"

"So, you do know who I am. Then you know the answer to that question. I'm sorry, but does one have to have children to want children not to be kidnapped, or when they are, for them to be rescued."

"I got six, Mr. Cruz, so I think I can empathize with the situation a hell of a lot more than you."

"Do you empathize more than the mother who has been driving herself crazy, trying to find her daughter, because you are doing nothing?"

"Nothing? My officers are doing plenty!"

"Then why aren't they in this room, instead of you!"

"Because I'm the boss, Mr. Cruz."

I was about to snap back at him when a hand rested on my shoulder. It was Run-Time.

"Mr. Cruz has identified the kidnapper."

The revelation caused an uproar as officers and agents drew near.

"Who is the kidnapper," a Fed asked.

"This is still our case," Chief Hub said to him and he turned to me.

"I can tell you the name, but there's a problem," I said.

"What problem is that?"

"He's a Fed C.I." I could feel Run-Time's death stare as I was playing with political fire—telling half-truths. But if it got them to act, I would never repeat Carol's revelation.

"What did you say? We don't have any C.I.s working that area and none that would kidnap a girl. That is a fat lie," a Fed said.

"Red Rabbit is the gang leader's name."

"Red Rabbit?" a police lieutenant laughed.

"As the law enforcement of the city of Metropolis, you surely know about animal gangs and their increasing presence and violence in parts of the city." That quieted the chuckling. "This Red Rabbit is extremely dangerous, and has killed multiple people," I said. "And we know where he is."

"Chief Hub," Run-Time said calmly. "We're here, because we believe this information should be given to you personally, so a clear, effective attack and rescue plan can be formulated."

Chief Hub nodded. "Exactly." He turned to his deputies. "Get a white board in here." He looked at me then at the Feds.

"We sure as hell don't have any C.I.s who are animal gang members in rabbit masks," the lead Fed said.

"Then why did the kid say that?" a police captain asked.

"I don't know. Why don't you ask him?"

Chief Hub walked up to Run-Time, who remained at my side. "Run-Time, thank you for bringing the information to us. You can let Ms. Num know we'll take it from here, but she shouldn't have unrealistic hopes."

"I understand."

Chief Hub looked at me. "Run-Time, this is the first time I met a friend of yours that I strongly disliked. But, there is a first for everything."

I chose not to respond.

I remembered the man when we first came in, because he was the only one wearing dark glasses. He was obviously some agent type from the comm-device in his ear, but he wasn't standing with the cops, and he was there before the Feds and the Mayor and his people came in. Who was he?

Chief Hub was getting ready to scribble on his white board when the room began to shake, and the red emergency lights flashed. That same lone agent man held up his hands and said, "Please be calm ladies and gentleman. There is no danger here."

No danger? The entire building was shaking. Monolith towers were the muscle-bound, steroid-fed version of skyscrapers. Earthquakes didn't shake them. They were built to withstand an asteroid hit or nuclear blast. Police One was shaking, and then we all saw it from the window—a massive shape was descending from the sky.

Every cop, agent, and aide was on their mobiles as the spaceship stopped its descent to hover above the Police One and City Hall towers.

That man walked up to the Mayor and showed him what looked like a badge. He showed it to Chief Hub and the lead Fed, too. Then, we all waited. People were looking at each other, but the Mayor stood silent and still with his eyes fixed on the door.

They came in—Interpol. Back in the day, the International Crime Police Organization (they dropped the Criminal from their name after a major scandal) was always handicapped, because they could never supersede the authority of any country and had to be asked in. But when humans launched off Earth to populate space stations and lunar colonies, Interpol became the Interspace Police Organization, and somehow, their authority superseded any local, state, or national authority. We had hovervehicles; they had real spaceships. We had lasers; they could vaporize your building with a laser blast from orbit.

They were all dressed in white suit uniforms and identified themselves to the Mayor, Chief Hub, and the Fed agent-in-charge. The lead Interpol man talked quietly with the three of them for a moment and then stepped back.

Chief Hub stepped forward and, with a displeased look, said to the room, "We have been informed by Interpol that the principals involved in this case fall into their jurisdiction, and as such, we will cease all operations involving this matter."

"Meaning what?" I asked out loud, and all eyes were on me again.

"Meaning what I said," Hub replied, angrily.

"We have a kidnapped girl or have you forgotten!"

The Interpol man stepped up. "We have that under control, but more importantly, we're in the middle of a major operation involving thousands of agents here on Earth and Up-Top at the highest of security levels. We're dealing with the safeguarding of billions of lives, not simply one person."

"Says who?" I asked.

Now the Interpol guy was mad at me. "Says the planet Earth."

"The planet Earth all convened and gave you the authority to forsake a kidnapped girl?"

"Mr. Cruz, the real world is so much more complex than black-and-white absolutists, like you, want to accept."

"Oh, so you know who I am, too. I wonder what that's all about, then? I know you came down here in your fancy spaceship, but on planet Earth, we don't let child kidnappers go scot-free. If you like these animal gangsters so much, take them and all the other criminal scum off the planet, and they can all live with you Up-Top."

343

"Mr. Cruz, I'm didn't come here to debate you, and I have no reason at all to acknowledge your existence."

"It is true. The Feds were right. The Red Rabbit kidnapper terrorist is not their C.I.; he's yours. That's why you're here. Why are you coming down to our planet to plant kidnapping terrorists here, spaceman?"

My comments caused an uproar in the room.

"Terrorist, Mr. Cruz?" the Mayor jumped in. "I can see you're very passionate about this victim, but let's be respectful until the facts are in."

"The facts are in. The kidnapper is named Red Rabbit, and he's an Interpol informant. That's why they're here to stop us. And the Red Rabbit is a terrorist."

"He is certainly not," the Interpol man snapped back at me.

"He certainly is."

"You have proof of that?" he asked.

"Firing at medical clinics with innocent civilians from hovercars, using laser cannons is a terrorist act." I stepped closer. "Oh, you didn't know there was a witness to that incident. Yes, I was there. What about lobbing bombs off of tower rooftops? That's terrorism, too."

The Interpol man walked right up to me. "By being in this room, you are subject to the Secrets Act, like everyone else. This is a classified meeting, and if you reveal it to anyone...anyone...you will be arrested, convicted, and imprisoned. Unlike city and federal law, we can and will confiscate all your legacy properties. Are we making sense to you now?"

"I bet if the victim was an Up-Top girl, you wouldn't be doing this."

"Are we making sense to you now, Mr. Cruz?" he asked again.

"He understands completely," Run-Time said for me.

The Interpol man and I glared at each other. I decided then and there that I hated him.

"I'm going to the men's room," I said angrily.

"You do that and cool off." Chief Hub was standing next to the Interpol man now. "As I said before, you should never have been here."

I stormed out of the room as they all watched me in conversation. As soon as I came out of the door, I stopped and let it close after me. Then I ran, not for the men's room, but for the elevators.

CHAPTER 47

Mrs. Easy Chair Charlie

I had been a busy bee. Besides being in Mad Heights, there was one other place I had been that they didn't know about. Before I went to the Soldier of Fortune Meet-Up meeting, I had made one other stop—back to the Free City apartment of Mrs. Easy Chair Charlie.

My day may have ended with gangster punks (Mad Heights), but it began with them, too. I strolled into Free City, and I knew the Free City gangs would try to jack me up again and no business card would stop them this time. As I approached the tower of Easy Chair's widow, they appeared. It was the same kids; one after another they walked to me.

"It's the detective again," one said.

"I didn't think he was dumb enough to come back a second time," said another.

I was in no mood.

"Get away from me," I said.

"That's it, Mr. Detective? You got no more fake business cards to show us?"

I really was in no mood for this.

"Guess where I'm going after this?" I asked.

"Why?" one of the punks responded.

"Mad Heights."

They all laughed. "You're not going to no Mad City, you square."

"When you go to a place like that, you have to be prepared to do what needs to be done. I should practice."

Instantly, the expressions changed on their faces. They knew where I was going.

The first mistake was drawing their weapons on me. The second mistake they made was not firing at me immediately. I pulled my omega-gun the same time they did, but I didn't hesitate. My mind was set to shoot them, not kill them—they were still young enough that they had a chance to get on the right path in life; however, I would torture them, viciously. Medium-yield plasma discharge rounds. I needed something to practice on to see their effectiveness. The mayhem commenced. Lucky for them, it was not set to kill; unlucky for them, they would be showered with burning, excruciating painful rounds. The punks were all reduced to whimpering wrecks, bundles on the ground. They cried and begged for me to stop.

"She hired us!"

"Who?"

"She told us to stop you from coming up to her place, no matter what!" one of the punks yelled at me.

"Who?!"

As I approached Easy Chair's place, people were watching me from the windows. I couldn't tell if they approved or not of what I did to their resident juvenile delinquents.

Then I saw them. Two high-tech robo-dogs optically targeted me, their metal teeth extended out, and they raced at me. You never wanted to be attacked by a robo-dog, and these were pit-bull models, which were among the most lethal (along with Doberman and German Shepherd models).

Every city, even super-cities like Metropolis, were inseparable from their automation and machines—never use the word "robot" around my fiancée, Dot. Machines and technology were built to last, and last a long time, and that's exactly what they did. Even the technology infrastructure of the nouveau-rich Peacock Hills had existed for centuries. Everything only looked new, including the robots you saw. But these robot dogs were straight-out-of-the-box new. They were genuinely something to behold. The flawless, shiny-silver metal parts, the supple plastic connector pieces, the blue-metal, razor teeth and retractable front-paw claws. You wouldn't find such beautiful mechanical specimens in any tower mansion in uber-rich Silicon Dunes, but the two killer machines were coming at me in low-life, no-money, Free City.

The robot pit bulls were fast! I was faster. The beauty of my gun was that I could switch its setting with a flick of a thumb. I shot them, and the robots wobbled around and then blew up. I shielded myself from the debris with my coat and angrily kicked the door, but it was already bolted back. There I stood, locked out. I sat on the ground next to the apartment door as I took out my mobile.

The video-phone answered, and Mrs. Easy Chair Charlie was glaring at me. "How did you get my number?"

"Open the door!"

"No!"

"Where did you get the money to buy expensive security robot dogs, pit-bull models, like that?"

"My life insurance! I told you that before."

"Oh, so we're sticking with that story?"

"It's not a story. It's the truth."

"What was Easy going to acquire that was going give him such a payday that he was going to get you and him Up-Top?"

"I don't know what you're talking about."

"People who can afford those kind of robots shouldn't be in Free City. I'm going to report you to the government. Free City is for people without legacies and no money. You have enough money to buy not one, but two, fancy security robot dogs you would find in Silicon Dunes." I stood up from the ground.

"No, don't do that."

"Don't do what? Stand up from the ground or report you to city services?"

"Why don't you go away? Leave me alone."

"Seems like I care more about your husband than you do!"

"That is not true!"

"Jumping in with his murderers."

"That's not true!" She suddenly broke down and sobbed. "Will you please go away and leave me alone?"

"When you tell me what Easy was into that got him killed that night, I will."

"He wasn't killed. He was shot by the police righteously."

"I don't how it was done yet, but he was murdered. I don't know if they shot up the police and then threw him out there, or what, but I'll find out how. And when I do, I'll say you were in on it."

"That's not true! I had nothing to do with it!"

"You're spending your dead husband's life insurance, even though to this day, you never even filed the claim. Where's the money coming from?!"

She erupted into a bawling mess.

"I'm not leaving here, until you let me in and tell me what Easy was into. I got past your Free City gang punks you hired to keep me out, and I got past your robot dogs. You think hiding in there crying is going to stop me?"

She disappeared from the video screen on my mobile. In a minute or two, I heard the locks unlocking, and the door was opening.

That's where I went before Mad Heights. And I went to an even more dangerous place when I ran out of Police One, instead of the men's room. I wasn't eager to do so, and I surely wasn't brave. It was my OCD-self, locking on one singular purpose, and pushing every other thought and fear out of my mind—I would rescue that girl, and no deranged punk in a rabbit mask would stop me.

CHAPTER 48

Red

The two hulks stood at their posts, smoking drug joints. I stood about a couple feet from them, pretending to smoke an e-cigarette.

There really wasn't any such thing as a small building in Metropolis, but this was a twenty-story auxiliary corner building, and the only light on the street was the tall lamp the three of us were standing under with an accompanying drizzle of rain.

The first bald man must have been 350 pounds, easy. Plenty of fat, but unfortunately, plenty of muscle, too. His leathery face had pierced eyebrows, a pierced lower lip, a pierced nose, and ears with multiple piercings. He was covered in tattoos, right up to an imaginary line under his nose, and was topped off with his glowing midnight blue shades. His outfit was all black except for the bright gold buckle he held with his joint-free muscled hand.

His partner had shoulder-length blond hair, tattooed-up arms only, and his shades of choice were glowing black. He sported a goatee and Fu Manchu mustache, meaning it ran down either side of the corners of his mouth.

"Who are you?" the first man asked.

"Johnny," I answered.

"Johnny?"

"Yeah, like sidewalk johnny."

"You're a sidewalk johnny named Johnny?"

"Yeah."

"Why are you here?"

"I'm standing on the sidewalk. That's what sidewalk johnnies do."

"We've never seen you before."

"I'm new."

"From where?"

"Dog Town."

"They got skater slacker and hackers there."

"Yeah."

"Why come here?"

"I was chased off by the gangs and the cops. I'm tired, so I came here. This sidewalk is as good as any."

"You better find another sidewalk to hang at."

"What's wrong with this one? It's big enough for three of us."

"It's only made for two. And two ain't you."

"Why you gotta be like that?"

"I'm being like that, so get away from here."

"Is this building dangerous?"

"Why you say that?" the second man asked me.

"I saw cops patrolling."

"Where?"

"Couple of blocks down. That's why I came here. They're congregating or something."

The two thugs looked at each other. I pointed behind me.

"Back there a block. That's why I asked if this building is dangerous, because if it is, then I'll move to another sidewalk. But if it's empty, then I should go inside and dry my feet."

The first thug put his joint in his mouth and pointed at me. "You're not drying your feet in there. Who are you? Get out of here, you sidewalk johnny bum."

"My name is Johnny. I told you that already. You two smoke too much dope. You're getting stupid."

"I'm about to stupidly punch you. Who are you? Get out of here!"

"All right, all right."

I marched around them to the door they were guarding, opened it, and closed it behind me.

I peeked through the peephole of the door, and the two thugs just stood there looking at each other.

"What did he just do?" asked the first one.

"He walked right past us and went inside."

"How did he do that?"

"I don't know."

I leaned back and locked the other locks; each made a loud noise. I looked through the peephole again.

"Why did he do that?"

"I don't know."

"He locked us out."

"I know."

I shook my head. I spent two hours pretending to be a doofus with them, but they were doofuses of the dope kind.

Inside was dimly lit. The ceiling had low ambient light, but the long hallway was pitch black. At the end, I knew someone was there. I had my night glasses on. I only wore glasses in the dark and I saw him—Red.

"I see you," I said.

"I see you," Red said, sitting in the dark on a stool against the wall at the far end of the hallway. His voice slightly echoed.

There was banging on the front door.

"Open the door!" said one of the two dope doofuses.

"You were out there quite a while with them," Red said.

"I have no interest in you or your two playmates outside."

"They're not my playmates. They're the hired help. Good help is so hard to find, nowadays. That's why I have to do all my work myself. So it's done right."

"They have employment agencies you know—even for criminals."

"Do they now? Any good workers?"

"I wouldn't know. I'm not a girl-kidnapping criminal."

"There it is. You should have played it out longer."

"You try standing out in the rain with a couple of doofuses and see how long your patience lasts."

"You got a point there."

"Give me the little girl, and I'll be out of here like mice on ice."

"Nah, I don't like that plan."

"Why not?"

"I kidnapped her for a reason."

"Is the reason worth dying for?"

"Who's going to kill me? You?" Red laughed.

"That's not nice. Laughing."

Red forced another bout of laughing.

"Very not nice," I said.

I didn't wait as I could see the fur of his rabbit head mask glow a light red. I had dived just as a blast of blue energy went past. All I heard were screams and shattering. I wasn't even prone on the ground for two seconds, when I leapt up and fired my gun at him. Two shots, two misses. The crazy Red had dived out of view.

I leaned back out of the path of the hallway and saw outside the building. The door was vaporized and the two thugs were dead on the sidewalk. The police drilled that rule into me as an intern. "Never stand in front of a closed door at a strange building."

My eyes closed as another flash of blue lighting went past, but much, much closer. They say life should be electric, but this was not what they had in mind when they came up with the saying. The energy blast heated the very air it passed through, and though it had missed me, my skin was warm. Red's weapon was so many variations of illegal.

I instinctively fired back a volley of four rounds this time, hitting the wall. I only needed to distract him for a moment. Inside my inner coat pocket, my left hand went and out came my Mexican jumping beans. I was sure, when I wrote my detective memoir, like good ol' Wilford G. had, people would chuckle, but sometimes, the silly can be the most profound and the most unexpected.

I threw them in front of me, counted to three, and there they went. I fired one more shot and bolted. The jumping beans started to pop. Unlike firecrackers, there was nothing to light and there were no sparks. They sounded like gunshots.

It sounded like I was firing at him and Red fired back at me. As I scurried away, all I saw was the entire area light up in blue, accompanied by the shattering of another piece of the wall structure.

Blast after blast was all I heard, though the sounds were getting lower as I moved further into the building. I reached a hallway with a row of ceiling lamps, and I waited a moment. I hadn't seen one other punk anywhere. It struck me as impossible that Red would have no one else here, but the two doofuses, to stand watch outside the main entrance. I was missing something, but I had to move forward.

I had reached the basement level. I saw no one and heard nothing, so I moved down the stairs, ninja-like. I stayed very close to the edge of the wall and stopped at the foot of stairs. My eyes locked in on a particular door—it had a padlock on it.

I walked up to the door, standing to the side, put my ear as close to it without touching it. I leaned back, pointed, and shot the lock off. I threw the pieces to the ground and swung the door open slowly, my body to the side. A single ceiling light illuminated the dim room. There she was, the little girl Lutty, curled up in a cot in the corner with wide blue eyes watching me. She was in a two-piece gray outfit with matching frubber leggings, her hood tightly around her head.

"Do you know a woman named Carol?"

The girl nodded.

"She's the one who sent me. I'm a private detective. Do you know what that is?"

The girl nodded.

"Now, have you ever watched American football? Not that other thing. The real football where you actually score points in a game. You know that football?"

The girl nodded.

"I am definitely not carrying you so you have to get up and follow me. Not too close, but close. I'll be your running back and you're running to the end zone for the touchdown. Here, the touchdown is getting the hell out of here, so we can get to your mother and the police. As the running back, I won't be tackling, but shooting them. Are we ready?"

She nodded and then slowly got up off the cot. My ears perked up as I held my gun and switched it to another setting. There was no more shooting from upstairs.

She could see I was worried, which was absolutely the worst thing to do in front of her. I glanced at her and could see all the bravery she had mustered was slipping away.

"Don't back down now," I said. "We got to get outside to your Mom and the police. We're going to run—"

356

My head reflexively ducked as something came at me from the corner of my eye. A few of my Mexican jumping beans hit the ground and popped. The girl screamed. I pushed her back and behind me as I fired into the darkness of the hall. All I saw was a red glow, and I kicked the door of the room shut. The blue energy blasted the door to smithereens as I pushed the girl to the side.

I heard the crazy rabbit laughing.

"Was this your plan?" he yelled from the dark. "Doesn't look like too good of a plan. One man coming in here, all alone."

"Tell me something Red, why are you in here alone? Where's your gang? Why aren't they back yet? Why aren't you laughing about that?"

There was only silence.

"I'll tell you why they're not here, Red," I said. "Because they've been snatched up. But not by the police. No, Red, you're big time. No, not from the Feds. You're bigger than that. Interpol has had it with you. You've gone too far. You're one cooked rabbit on a spit. Why aren't you laughing about that?"

While I was taunting the psycho, I had put away my piece. It was a nice weapon but wholly inadequate for this situation. When you want to smash something, you don't use a precision instrument, you use a big bad sledgehammer. I had unfolded my shotgun while Lutty watched me. All I needed was to cock it and shoot. I was already aiming.

"Why so quiet, Red?"

"How did you find me?" he asked from the darkness.

"I'm a detective, Red. And I just followed the breadcrumbs you left me with the trail of madness you left behind. But I'll make you a deal. If you tell me why you got Easy Chair Charlie killed, I know it was you, then I'll tell you how I found you."

"No!"

Red's voice wasn't outside in the darkness anymore but right in front of me. He thought he had tricked me. He thought I would watch for the

357

red glow before he blasted his illegal electric rifle, but I had been watching his shadow tiptoe to me—yes, he was actually tip-toeing. We both had night-vision, but he didn't see my shades on my face or the new weapon in my hands. I didn't just bring silly Mexican jumping beans; I had brought with me a barrel attachment for my shotgun as super-illegal as his electric rifle.

He fired his weapon, but I fired mine too, after the nanosecond I took to cock it. The blue blast came so close to the right side of my face and shoulder that a few inches more, and I would have been vaporized. Lutty screamed as she threw herself down to the damp concrete ground. Not smart on my part to leave it to the little girl to dodge the blast by herself, but kids are resilient. She could throw herself out of the way better than I could. Kids are nimble and fast, not like adults, where our bigness and superiority can get in the way. Red, however, got shot point blank in his rabbit head mask by my shotgun.

I had seen the light switch when I shot off the padlock to the room and flipped it on. There was Red, standing in the doorway, with his weapon hanging down to the floor. He was in silhouette, but by his labored breathing, I knew his head wound was bad—very bad. He dropped his electric rifle to the ground, and that's when I had an urge to cover, not the kid's eyes, but my own. I didn't do blood and guts; I tended to pass out from that sort of thing.

Red Rabbit reached for his mask with his metallic arms and just...ripped it off. I stared at it for a moment, not knowing what the hell I was seeing. The silhouette was a head, but the sight of it showed the top part of a robot head and the bottom half a scrunched up human head with eyes, nose, and mouth. There was no way my shotgun had done that. There was a spark—my shotgun *had* done that. Red was a retard with a mechanically-augmented head.

He jumped at me and grabbed my neck with his cybernetic arms. Instinct would have made me drop the shotgun, but I ignored instinct. It was even worse than I could imagine. His deformed head wasn't augmented by machine. His brain was *part machine*, and he stared at me with his freakish face and the snarl of his tiny, deformed mouth. He wanted to choke me, but all his hands did was hold my neck. I was sure the message from his brain was to crush my neck like an empty plastic cup, but the six-inch hole in the machine part of his brain-head made that impossible.

I kicked him, and he fell over like a mannequin. Lying on the ground with his arms flailing around, his freakish face was disoriented. It was pointless to question him. Red wasn't there anymore. I could tell he didn't recognize me. He didn't know who he was or where he was. He was agitated and panicking at the same time. Even if he was put together, there was no way the police, Feds, Interpol, or anyone else would ever let me near him again. I did all I could do. I took his mobile from his jacket.

"Lutty," I said.

"Yes?"

"Let's go see your Mom." I reached out to her, and she held my hand.

We left Red there on the ground as his hysterical head-jerking and hand and leg movements became more violent with every second. He kept yelling, but not at us. His body was unplugged from reality and didn't know what else to do.

CHAPTER 49

Carol and Lutty

All that madness: from Mrs. Easy Chair Charlie to Mad Heights to Run-Time's to Police One to here. I learned that I was entirely too good at the violence thing. I had surprised myself. I never got to have my nap in my fluffy white sleep clothes after my super-shower. I needed a vacation because my new detective life was absolutely no joke. I also realized that I was probably not going to get a dime in cash for my time and multiple attempts on my life. How stupid was that? I had been detective, who had himself as the client—a fool.

But there I was holding the hand of a missing little girl, exiting the bowels of some criminal den. It was surreal—dozens of police cruisers in the air, Metro and Feds, but much more than that was the media. They were swarming around us—on the ground, hovering right above us via jetpack, or hanging out of their hovervans for wide-angle filming. You would've thought I was a rock star by all the attention.

I instinctively shielded the girl from them. She wanted nothing to do with them, and we both ignored their barrage of questions. I kept my focus on leading her through the media gauntlet to get her to my awaiting vehicle if we could even get there. I decided it was better to keep walking away from them; the direction and destination were irrelevant.

As if on cue, our prayers were answered; police officers descended from the sky by jetpack and created a circle around us. I recognized Officers Break and Caps immediately among them and couldn't help but smile.

"They're going to shield us, so we can get to your Mom," I said to Lutty. The girl looked up at them and smiled, too.

But the media were not the only ghouls waiting for me. Behind them was all of the law enforcement brass. They stood there, sullen, and a few were glaring at me. I had embarrassed them, and I knew I had made enemies for life. But so what? The bastards were going to let the little girl die because of their own arbitrary rules on what should and should not be done in the cosmos of life. It's never okay for the bad to get off scot-free and allow an innocent to die in the ditch, in my book.

With our police escort, I could watch the law enforcement higher-ups. The rain started again, and my new enemies melted into the dark downpour, but I'd be crossing paths with them again.

Officer Break gestured to an overhead police cruiser, and the hovercar descended. "Why don't we get away from the rain and reporters and get moving on the family reunion," Officer Break said. "What do you think?" he asked Lutty.

She nodded. "I want my Mom."

The cruiser landed, and the police pushed the pack of reporters away, who were merciless in their desperation for us to answer their questions.

"Mr. Cruz, do you think this child kidnapping case will make you the leading detective in the city?"

I could feel every employee of the Office of the City Clerk watching my response carefully, but that aside, I would not be goaded into a response.

I kept my mouth shut and climbed into the cruiser after Lutty. Officer Break closed the door, and he and his partner got into the tertiary seats in the back.

Officer Caps looked at me. "Don't get used to it," he said. "That could, of course, mean a few things when it comes to you."

Lutty was now looking at me funny.

"Back when I was your age, I was an intern at Metro Police. I went on ride-alongs and rode in a police cruiser a few times," I said to her.

"Ever arrested for real?" she asked me with an askance look.

"No way. That's for criminals."

"Okay." She was satisfied.

The policemen uttered none of the wisecracks that I'm sure was on the tips of their tongues.

"What about that Rabbit man?" she asked with a look of fear.

"He's done for, and he'll never come at you or your Mom again," I said and leaned forward to her. "What did he think you did?"

"I ran ahead of my Mom down Alien Alley, and he thought I saw him doing something bad. But I didn't. I didn't see him, then he attacked us."

"I know you didn't see him doing anything bad. As long as you didn't tell him what you saw, it's all over now. No one will bother you again with it. Isn't that right, officers?"

I leaned back and watched my Ebony and Ivory "friends" squirm in their seats.

"That's right. No one will bother you about it ever again," Officer Break answered reluctantly.

"Your Mom will be very proud of how brave you were against that bad Rabbit man. I'll tell her all about it and how courageous you were when I rescued you. You know what courageous means?"

She nodded.

"That was you."

"And when Mr. Cruz stays behind to tell your Mom how courageous you were when he rescued you, we're going to be there, standing right beside him. He's a very popular detective, and there are so many people who want to talk with him. We're going to make sure he gets to see them all," said Officer Break.

The officers grinned at me.

This was exactly the situation grown men who purported to be cool avoided at all costs. We arrived at the apartment tower of Carol Num, and if I thought the media reception at Red's hideout was bad, this was like tenfold the rock star-like gathering. The cruiser set down right in front of the main entrance where Carol stood—I saw the eager anticipation in her face; her eyes were already tearing up. Run-Time was on one side and there, yes, the Mayor of Metropolis, himself, on the other.

Lutty couldn't wait to get out of the police cruiser, and as soon as it popped open, she bolted from her seat into her mother's outstretched arms.

It was one of those Hallmark card pictures you always thought was fake—staged by actors, but here was a real one, right in front of me and everyone else on the planet who would see it. The media madness was directed at the mother and daughter, but even they had the smarts to know you don't interrupt a life moment, like this one. Carol's arms were wrapped around her daughter's shoulders, and the daughter had her arms wrapped around her mother's waist. Both were balls of weeping energy.

I stood there as quietly as I could, with Officers Break and Caps standing next to me, and the other two officers in the cruiser behind us.

Who would break the dignity of this beautiful moment? Even the rain had the decency to stop.

"Come on over here, Mr. Cruz," the Mayor said, his hand beckoning.

There were moments in a person's life when time really froze. I didn't know what disturbed me more, the fact that the Mayor of the city knew exactly who I was and by name or that seemingly millions of camera crews turned to focus their attention to me in unison. My life, as the saying goes, was over as I knew it.

I felt a slight nudge to my back—it was Officer Break—and I slowly trudged over to the mother and daughter. Carol opened her weepy eyes to notice me and she smiled. Lutty lifted her head from her mother's chest to look at me too. They pulled me in, and there I was, locked in their embrace. Exactly what I didn't want to happen happened, as the emotions got me. Now, I was fighting my own facial muscles to keep from bawling like a little baby. The war of the tears was over and flowed down my face.

The media ate up the images.

Of course, the Mayor stepped to us and placed his hand on my shoulder. Why *my* shoulder? Why not the mother? Unhand me, man, and be off with you, I said to myself. This was Carol's and Lutty's moment. No one and no force could spoil it. The moment was theirs; I was just along for the ride.

CHAPTER 50

Deputy Doohickey

Mayor Likegate had been Metropolis' mayor for five years and had just started his second term. The typical slickster-in-a-suit—black hair, clean-shaven—but he seemed popular. I didn't know politics, care about it, or had any intention of caring about it ever, like most Metropolitans. But I recognized power, and the Mayor was every bit a power-player like any megacorp CEO.

I found myself being posed by his staff as he shook my hand for photos and stood next to me as Carol hugged me for photos. Now, we had entered the silly season. Carol was as uncomfortable by the whole thing as I was, but just like me, she went with it. Thank God for Run-Time, because after a few minutes, his people came in and whisked Carol and daughter away. Media tried to follow them, but Let It Ride security was already in place and stopped the reporters and their camera crews in their tracks.

The Mayor was in front of me, again, with his entourage of staffers and aides.

"Mr. Cruz, you've done the great city of Metropolis a great service by finding that little girl. The city won't forget what you did," he said to me as he shook my hand again.

Thank goodness politicians had a short attention span. The Mayor and his entourage were off, into their government hoverlimos and in the sky in mere minutes. The media was following his lead and scattered. Both parties got what they wanted—photos and video footage.

I looked around and realized all the police were already gone, even my "friends" Ebony and Ivory. Run-Time walked up to me, smiling, with another man following. Run-Time gave me a long handshake.

"You did it," he said, smiling.

"I did."

Run-Time kept nodding his head. "This is Mr. Frame. He's one of the Mayor's deputies. You two should get to know each other."

The man stepped forward and shook my hand, too. For a slim man, he had the grip of a Mexican wrestler.

"Mr. Run-Time has been telling me about your progress. Looks like your Easy Chair Charlie case is all wrapped up."

"Oh, you know about Easy Chair Charlie, too?" I said. "Why do you say that?"

"Well, whether voluntarily or not, this Easy Chair Charlie and the criminal Red were working together in the Sweet Street shootout. The little girl saw them together, or the criminal Red alone, and he kidnapped her."

"Wow, that is a very snazzy encapsulation of the case," I said.

"I try to," the deputy said, smiling.

"Sounds like your case is wrapped up neatly and solved."

"My case?" the deputy asked. "What do you mean my case? Your case is solved."

"My case isn't solved," I answered. "The case of the missing little girl is solved. The case of the Red Rabbit is solved. But my case of Easy Chair Charlie is not solved."

"How do you mean?" the deputy asked. "The criminal kidnapped the girl, and he was the one who got Easy Chair Charlie shot by the police."

"You know what my problem is right now?"

"What, Mr. Cruz?"

"Why does the deputy of the largest supercity in the world know with such granular detail about the case of some newbie detective consultant? How many detectives must there be in this city? How many kidnap victims must there be who are little girls? But you know mine so intimately. Why is that? Don't answer. The criminal Red didn't get Easy Chair Charlie to shoot up Sweet Street. Red murdered Easy Chair Charlie. He just found a unique way to do it, using cops. But Red wasn't acting on his own. He was hired. The thug who tried to kill me outside of my own place was hired. The thug who barged into my office to kill me was hired. Like I said, Mr. Frame, *your* case is solved. Mine is far from over."

The deputy's face looked like I had gut-kicked him. Yeah, Deputy Doohickey, as I called him, was not happy, which meant his boss would not be happy, which meant this whole mess was tied to the Mayor's office, which meant that Run-Time knew much more, which meant some serious trouble was coming for me.

CHAPTER 51

Punch Judy

I went into my office and saw her interior design handy work had turned the reception-waiting area into a shrine...to me. There were pictures, already framed, hanging on the wall of me with Carol, me with both Carol and her daughter, and me with the Mayor. My first reaction was not a positive one, but then, I looked at PJ with an approving nod. I could see many a future client waiting for an appointment and staring at those pictures. I had to be a legit detective, they'd say. I was shaking hands with the mayor of the damn city, no less.

"You're faster than hyper-space," I said, turning away from the pictures to glance back at her, smiling, behind her reception area.

"I downloaded those pictures while you were still on the TV screen."

"You and Phishy are something. In fact, get Phishy in here. I need more ammo."

"More shootouts with bad guys."

"You can say that. Tell Phishy I don't want replacement ammo. I want extra ammo."

"And they say I have the criminal streak. Are you expecting more visitors?"

I pointed to her newly hung pictures on the wall. "What do you think?"

"Don't want you shooting our potential clients. You're going to have more clients than you can handle. Don't shoot any of them!"

"I'm not going to shoot the clients, just the criminals. We haven't seen all the bad guys involved in this case, yet. Not by a long shot."

"Good, because I need to get paid. Okay, I'll call Phishy."

"That's what I need."

I walked into my office after I pushed open the door. I closed it immediately. At the desk, PJ had all my messages in priority order. The ones that would be the quickest to solve first and, therefore, the quickest potential payment. But those were always the most boring and of no interest to me. As I scanned the printed message from her electronic notepad, I realized something, and touched one of the messages. The message I touched wasn't one message; it was a stack of messages, one under the other. I didn't have five-by-five rows of messages. I had five stacks of messages by five stacks of messages. Not twenty-five, but much, much more. This was insane. I'd need to hire someone else just to read all these messages.

I got up from my desk, opened the door, and walked to PJ's desk. Her silly French-language punk music was playing and there she was sitting, with her feet on her desk, waiting for me. She stood up and handed me three folders. I opened one and inside were more messages, and it was only one folder! I couldn't believe it.

"They all came in within the last hour," she said.

I shook my head.

"Don't answer the phone anymore for today. Let the voice recorder catch them all."

"The one we have doesn't have the disk space."

"Go out and buy one that we need then. Then come back here," I said and threw the folder back on her desk, "and figure out a better way to prioritize."

"That's what I did."

"Do you want me sitting at my desk going through messages all day or out solving cases? Which do want?"

"You need to hire another secretary."

"No."

"A part-time assistant."

"No. You are my only employee. In fact, you're making more than me."

"Cruz, you're a famous detective, now. I can't man the front area, answer the phones, and prioritize messages. Impossible. How am I supposed to do all that? I need help!"

I covered my ears, so I couldn't hear her voice anymore and said, "Call Phishy. Ammo." Then I walked back into my office. "Front of the office is your job. That's why I hired you. Detective work is my job. Your job allows me to do my job or no money."

I reflexively dove for the floor as the hovercar outside my window beamed a bright light into my office.

CHAPTER 52

Phishy

It could have been reporters, but I was taking no chances. I stood at my desk, loading the bullets into my magazine. PJ was sitting on one of my inner office lounge area chairs, loading up her two shotguns.

I may have had guns now and had a natural aptitude for shooting, but I was no gun person. And PJ was an ex-posh gang member, so she definitely wasn't a gun person. You didn't take good ammo out of your weapon and then load up new ammo, just because new boxes of ammo came in. But we did it anyway, because it's "fresh" ammo straight out of the box, right?

Phishy glanced back and forth between us as if he were watching a tennis match.

"Why don't you load up too, Phishy?" PJ said to him.

"Oh no. Phishy is a lover not a fighter." He smiled at her.

"A dead lover or a live fighter. Hmm. What is better for me and my life?" PJ said as she cocked one of her rifles.

"Phishy, I want more ammo," I said.

"Cruz, you're getting a bit obsessive about the safety."

"How many gun battles have I been in now? People trying to sucker shoot me all over the place. I had a major shootout before leaving to rescue the little girl and then another shootout trying to rescue the little girl. Phishy, this isn't a matter of perspective. We need more boxes of ammo."

"But isn't a detective supposed to think his way out of battles?" Phishy sincerely asked.

PJ burst out laughing.

"You stupid man," she snapped at him.

"More boxes of ammo, Phishy," I said. "The hovercar was flying right outside my window with a spotlight."

"Oh, okay. I'll get more. But Cruz, this isn't cheap stuff."

I walked to my desk and opened the front drawer. His eyes opened wide as he saw the wad of cash.

"If you even think of hiding this cash the way you did the last time, I'll ban you from my office."

"Where's my cash?" PJ said standing from the couch.

I ignored her. "Did you hear me?" I asked Phishy.

"I'll do it outside."

I threw the cash at him, and he caught it with ease. "Get out of here and bring me more ammo."

Phishy ran out of my office, smiling. We heard the reception door close, and I just shook my head.

"Where's my cash?"

"Why would I give you any cash when you can't even prioritize my messages, so I know what cases to take on? Maybe I should waste my time talking to more ladies with the gators in their bathtubs."

"That wouldn't be a good use of your time. You need to go out there and solve cases and bring back the money. You're famous now. How hard can that be?"

The voice of a man at my office doorway so startled us, I reflexively dropped my box of ammo to the ground to reach for my gun; the bullets bounced up and down on the hardwood floor. PJ had let go of her shotgun; it hit the rugged floor, and it discharged. The blast blew out my window (again) and sucked all the messages that were neatly stacked at the edge of my desk, out into the sky.

CHAPTER 53

The Mick

PJ ran back out of my office to her desk, and when she appeared an instant later, she literally flew out the window—100 stories up! We watched as Punch Judy went after every slip of paper fluttering down to the ground below. I wasn't sure if she was trying to impress me to get money, or if each of those messages represented dollar signs to her, which again, meant getting money.

"Who are you?" I asked the man standing next to me, both of us watching the jetpacked PJ flying around outside, like a super heroine.

"I'm here to fetch you and bring you to a private cafe to meet a mutual friend."

"Who's the mutual friend?"

"I believe you call him The Mick."

I actually never knew his name. Run-Time had three executive vice presidents—the two nice and female ones; one Lebanese and the other West Indian; and the one big Irish male, who wasn't nice. If you dealt with the female ones, then you were in Run-Time's good graces, which is why I never spoke two words to The Mick in all the many years I was friends with Run-Time. Since I didn't know what I could possibly have done to warrant a meeting with The Mick, I was intrigued.

"Okay."

"I hope you're not as trigger happy in public places as your secretary."

"How did you get in here, anyway?"

"I believe it's called walking through the front door."

"We're still working out the kinks with our external security measures."

"I see you have a ways to go. Shall we go?"

"Let my secretary fly back in here first."

Just as I uttered the words, PJ flew into the office, almost hitting the ceiling, and landed. A wad of messages was clutched in her hand.

"I got all the messages," she proclaimed.

"And you blew out my window."

"So, we're even now. You blew it out first, and now I have. Even."

"But I'm the one who has to pay the bill to fix it each time."

She shook her hand holding the messages. "Get some clients in here. I'll make the calls if you're busy."

"Your boss has a client call to go on now," the man said.

"Oh," PJ said. "Go on then," she said. "I'll take care of the window."

"And," I said, "show me how to do that super girl with the jetpack thing, because I hear, all the time, people doing that and splatting on the pavement."

"Oh, because they're stupid," PJ said. "They jump out the window and then push the button on their jetpack. They watch too much fake television. We have hover technology, not anti-gravity. Anti-gravity is fantasy fake stuff. No jetpack can stop your fall after the fact. You never see base-jumpers do that or acrobats. No jetpack engine is more powerful than Earth's gravity. You start your jetpack, while you're standing still, and then you can fly. That's how you do it."

"Well, you can show me when I get back. And figure out why the door..."

"And I'll figure out why the door was open for this man to walk in like that."

"I'm sorry," the man said. "I didn't mean to walk into your place of business."

"Let's go," I said to him.

The man took me to some hole-in-the-wall eatery I had never been to before. An awaiting hovercar with its own driver took us there. I never saw the name of the place, but I knew it was on the edges of the city of Neon Blues.

The man led me into a virtually empty, diner-style establishment. The Mick was at the furthest booth away from us, facing us with his back to the wall. As we approached, I could see he was sipping something from a coffee cup.

"Mr. Cruz, have a seat." He motioned to the space opposite him.

The man, who led me in, nodded at the VP and walked back the way he came. I sat down.

"Want anything to drink, alcoholic or not, your choice," he said.

"No thanks. I'm good. Well, are you here on Run-Time's behalf or yours?" I asked The Mick. "'Cause I don't think we've ever talked before."

"We haven't. But then, you weren't a detective before. And you hadn't involved yourself in...delicate matters."

"I remind you; it was Run-Time who brought me into this case, both of them."

"Mr. Cruz, you are precisely right, which is why I'm here. My boss wants to hire you again."

"For?"

"He wants to hire you not to proceed with the case any further."

"You mean the Easy Chair Charlie case?"

"Is there another?"

I hesitated. "Well, the Carol case is concluded, so no."

I wasn't offended that Run-Time sent The Mick to tell me this, rather than do so directly at his offices. Run-Time wanted nothing to do with this, and I noticed that everyone seemed to know who I was—the Mayor, police, Feds, and Interpol, even—which meant I was being monitored. I didn't forget that Run-Time was scared—an emotion I never saw on his face, ever. He had to keep his distance from me, but still had to communicate with me.

"Mr. Cruz, let's not play games. I don't like to play games, but you seem to."

"I don't like games either."

"I think you do. You're obviously put off by my boss' request, so tell me what we need to do for you to comply with what he's asking you to do. My boss does nothing without a good reason, and if he's asking you not to investigate this any further, then there is a very good reason, even if you don't know what it is."

"I don't like secrets."

"Why? You have secrets. I have them. My boss does. The entire city does. What's wrong with secrets? Every question of the universe can't be known. I ask the question again; what do we need to do or how much do I need to pay you to proceed no further?"

"Run-Time's a friend, so you don't have to pay me anything. My only question is, am I going to be brought in on this secret at some point?"

The Mick hesitated. "Maybe."

"Maybe."

"Mr. Cruz, let it be, and my boss will bring you in if necessary. You say you're a friend. You've known him longer than I have. Has he ever left you out in the cold before?"

He never had. "Okay, you've convinced me. I'll leave it alone, but that doesn't mean that others out there will leave me alone."

"Which is why my boss may have to bring you in. Things will be monitored, and we'll be in touch. I'm sure as a now-famous detective, you can find other cases to occupy your time."

"I'm sure."

"Good."

The big Irishman got out from the booth and stood. Rather than shake my hand, his arms hung at his side, and he gave me a slight bow, Japanese-style, to say goodbye. He walked out of the place, leaving me alone at the table.

I looked at his empty cup on the table and realized I didn't even have enough cash to pay for a cup of coffee for myself. If I was a now-famous detective, why was I less than broke?

CHAPTER 54

The Mayor

I was treated like a celebrity from the moment I got out of the city hoverlimo that picked me up at my office and flew me to City Hall. Aides were fawning over me and a couple of reporters were following us, as I was led from the lobby, to the general offices, to the elevator capsules, and finally, outside the Mayor's office. There, aides turned over escort duty to the deputies.

A tall man opened the door and gestured me in. Run-Time's office was ridiculously huge. The Mayor's office was double that size. It was like a major trans-continental excursion to walk from the entrance to the Mayor's desk—no Mayor to be seen—but four others were waiting. Chief Hub, the Interpol man, and two other suits. They all were as stone-faced as stone. The tall deputy stood behind me—much too close for my comfort—as I waited.

The Mayor waltzed in with two other aides following him. He had a big smile on his face.

"Mr. Cruz," he called out and vigorously shook my hand. "Thanks for coming by. Please take a seat."

I sat in the chair in front of the desk. As soon as I sat in it, I realized I was dealing with deranged children. The chair was a kid's chair, and from the Mayor's vantage point, all he saw was my head.

"Mr. Cruz, the reason I asked you to come by is I wanted to tell you how things were going to go for you in my city going forward. You will *not* be getting a detective license. I'm, personally, going to make sure no one in government or any business that does business with the city will do business with you. If you are ever caught referring to yourself as a detective, it will be deemed as illegal misrepresentation of being a member of the law enforcement industry, and you will be prosecuted and fined. You can apply all the times you want, but it will never be approved. Your gun license, which you've apparently had a long time, has been revoked. You get caught with a weapon outside of your residence, and that will be a felony, which you will be vigorously prosecuted for. I'll find out who's given you that legacy office of yours, and they will quickly find out what it's like to be on the wrong side of this office. You are not welcome in this city. You can bask in your media limelight, for now, but public attention is such a fleeting thing. The reporters will disappear, everyone will forget your name, and then you'll be a bum again, like you've always been. That's when I'm going to get you. You think we will allow an insignificant civilian to embarrass this office, my police department, and the Interspace Police? You're finished, Mr. Cruz, in this city, finished."

The Mayor should have consulted with the Guy Who Scratched My Vehicle before he said what he said to me.

I got up from their kiddie chair and left his office with my security escort.

CHAPTER 55

Holly Live

"Now to our breaking bombshell exclusive from ace investigative reporter, Holly Live." The newsman in his virtual reality studio didn't stop smiling for a second.

"Thank you, Max. Yes, Metropolis, I've been in the news business for nearly twenty years, and the word scandal is used so often that even I roll my eyes when I hear it, but this story is a scandal that will rock the foundations of this supercity to the ground. Earlier today, at a secret location, I spoke to my inside informant, who asked us to conceal his identity for fear of criminal threats to his very life. The story he told us is of that magnitude..."

The broadcast cut to Holly Live, sitting across from her "secret informant," who was computer-silhouetted, but the tan fedora and coat was unmistakable. The voice was computer-modified, but everyone who knew would know it could be no other person.

I said with my computer-enhanced voice, "About a month ago, a man by the name of Easy Chair Charlie, supposedly, got up from his table in Old Harlem, went outside, pulled the most sophisticated weapons out of thin air, and started shooting at everyone and everything at the town's premiere smoking joint."

"Yes, the Sweet Street Shootout at Joe Blows," the reporter interjected. "This channel was first on the scene."

"That man was soon killed in the shootout by police. Those were the reports on the news. But that is not what happened.

"That shootout was a well-orchestrated murder of which Easy Chair Charlie was the least of the victims. Up-Top agents illegally came to our planet and allowed a psychopathic gang leader, on their payroll, to kill five Metropolis police officers, leaving behind five sets of spouses and children, and kidnap a child witness—"

"The Lutty girl kidnapping case," the reporter interjected again.

"Yes, your station was there. Well, the entire op was done with the full knowledge and consent of Metropolis' police chief and its Mayor."

Holly Live cut in, "You know what's going to happen. People will say this is the wild rantings of a disgruntled person with a score to settle."

"You're right, Holly. That's what they'll say. But then, you say back to them... 'No, go to the surviving widows and widowers and families of these slain officers and ask their union rep, too, to demand all body-cam video footage of that night from all officers and cruisers on scene and see what happens."

"What will happen?" Holly was genuinely asking me.

"Thirty police cruisers and fifty-seven officers, responding to the shootout. *They will tell you; there are no tapes.*"

CHAPTER 56

The Peanut Gallery

In all the pictures you've seen of mass protests or riots, were there ever any in the pouring rain? Never. People were not interested in exercising their right to civil protest in inclement weather. However, I heard something from one of the Concrete Mama sidewalk johnnies that made me think barricading myself in my own place was not such a safe prospect. *I heard that the police were rioting at City Hall.* There were 500,000 police in Metropolis!

We had left the real world and had entered the world of surreality.

"I don't know where you live," I said to Punch Judy.

"We've lived in the same building for over ten years. How can you not know where I live?"

"I just don't."

PJ's place was going to be my safe house. While my place had a meager helping of furniture, every square inch of her place had a piece of modern deco, neon, or fancy something. She may have been an ex-posh gang member, but she was still all posh.

She had turned her living room into a version of her Liquid Cool work-area. Thankfully, she hadn't forwarded the phones, but she had to check, listen, and clear out the voice mail every half hour, or we'd completely run out of message storage. It was crazy. She could barely keep up.

One of her guest rooms was my space. I had locked myself in there, going on day two, sleeping. I purposely chose the smallest room she had. It was a decent size with no outside windows. It was more of a closet than anything. I had destroyed my mobile—they can track you with that. Before my fateful "secret" interview, I had Flash load my Pony into a hovercar transport and ship it out of the City.

PJ didn't watch the news. She only read it on her mobile computer. I know she was always reading it, but she said nothing to me about any of it.

Phishy, with his crazy self, had every sidewalk johnny friend he knew and all their friends descend on the Concrete Mama, like a swarm of ants. They had the lobby and PJ's floor filled to the rim with people— my own civilian security force. Too bad none of them were armed, but it was the gesture that mattered.

"Cruz!"

I told her not to yell, but just knock on the door when she wanted me. When I opened the door, there was Dot. That put a smile on my face. Her parents were with her. That took the smile off my face. I came out of my sanctuary, anyway.

"How are you holding up?" she asked as she gave me a hug.

"Me, I'm fine. I have no idea what's happening out there, but that's good. I'm in here, safe and comfortable."

There was a knock on PJ's front door. If I hadn't seen what I saw, I would have thought I was dreaming. Mr. Wan pulled a .357 magnum shooter from his jacket and Mrs. Wan pulled a smaller version with a silencer from her purse. Did all it take for my psycho parents-in-law to be on my side was our joint stay at the local jail?

Dot yelled at her parents in Chinese, and they yelled something back, but kept their eyes on the door. PJ approached the door, carrying her favorite shotgun. She pressed the button on the door display and gave out a huff as she turned to all of us. "It's stupid man." She opened the door, and there was Phishy, smiling.

Dot's parents put away their guns after PJ closed and locked the door again. Phishy strolled to me.

"It's crazy out there, Cruz."

I held up my hand. "I don't want to know. For me, ignorance is bliss."

"You need to know what's going on," Dot said.

"I can't do anything about anything, so why know? Wait, did something happen at Eye Candy?"

"No, everything is fine. The reporters leaked that I was your girlfriend, and then so many people showed up there, looking for me, I had to leave. I couldn't work with all those people and reporters staring at me through the windows."

"I'm sorry."

"Why are you sorry? It's great. Prima Donna is signing up everyone as clients, and Goat Girl and Cyan are signing up everyone for our new anti-robot union. Everybody is happy. And Prima Donna says thank you."

"She's welcome."

"What's the plan?" she asked.

They had all encircled me, now, PJ too.

"Plan? We wait it out."

"This could go on for weeks or months," Dot said. "You really don't know what's going on."

"No."

"Then how can you have a plan?"

"The last I heard was the police were rioting at City Hall. That's it."

Dot's parents started shaking their heads, along with PJ. Phishy was grinning. "It's a lot more than that," Dot said.

"More than rioting?"

"Cruz, you're not an ostrich. Get your head out of the dirty mud, look up, and know what's going on around you."

"As long as they leave you, my Pony, and my place alone, I'm good."

"And the office!" PJ interjected.

"And the office."

"You listed me ahead of the Pony, so I guess I'm good."

I smiled at her.

Now there was frantic knocking at the door. Both PJ and Phishy ran to the door.

"Don't touch my door," PJ yelled at him as she grabbed her shotgun again. "Okay."

Phishy pushed the display button.

"Phishy," one of the sidewalk johnnies said, standing in front of the door.

"You can't be in and out of my place," PJ scolded Phishy.

"I may need to come back in after I see what they want."

She unlocked the door for him. "No. Stay out."

The door opened, and Phishy stuck his head out. He pulled it back in and ran to me.

"Cruz, there are police downstairs."

"Where?"

"They're pushing their way into the lobby. A lot of them."

"Oh no," Dot said with a scared look.

Her parents had their weapons drawn again.

"Cruz, get your guns," PJ commanded.

"I can't," I said. "They took away my gun license, and I can only use them in my place, not someone else's."

"Stop being foolish," she said. "They're coming for you."

I ran into my room for my gun case.

"Phishy!"

As I pulled my gun case from under the bed and opened it, I asked when he appeared, "You know places like Mad Heights?"

"Mad City? What about it?"

"They got those animal gangs there."

"And lots more, too. Much more dangerous."

"Are there people who just hang around in the darkness?"

"Darkness where?"

"Like in the back alleys."

"Ghouls? How do you know about them?"

"What are they?"

"Night people. They're gangs that hang in the dark with their night-sight."

"What do they do? Just hang out in the dark?"

"No, they get people."

"What does that mean?"

"How do you know about them?"

"Never mind. We'll talk about this later."

"Cruz, your parents are here!" Phishy peeked in the door to tell me.

"What? My parents? Where? Here or on the mobile?"

"Here!"

The notion that my parents would fly all the way to Metropolis made little sense to me, but it was them. My mother came in, holding her little purse in front of her, like she always did. This one was dark brown; she had others. Both had matching black slicker coats and black boots over their pants, instead of under. She smiled at me. She never wore much make-up, but had a perfect complexion; her black hair was always pulled back in a braided ponytail. They were practically the same height—shorter than me by an inch or so. My Pops came in, his graying mustache

387

and beard, wearing a fedora that looked suspiciously like my own, but he hated hats. In his hand was a sheathed sword. Now, I knew it was really him. My father was a prime example of the negative effect of Japanese samurai culture on the general public. He carried that sword everywhere.

"Ma, what are you doing here?" I stopped myself, did the son thing, and gave her a hug and a kiss.

"Pops," I gave him a hug. "When did you get here? How did you get here? It's dangerous out there. You shouldn't have come here."

My mother smiled and spoke in Spanish.

"Yes, Ma, but it's even more dangerous out there than usual."

My Pops had unsheathed his sword and was swinging it around.

"And no sword is going to scare away any street punk, or whoever it is after me. Put that away, Pops, before you put your eye out."

There was a bang at the door, and everyone jumped.

"Who's banging my door?" PJ yelled and pointed her rifle at it.

The Wans were poised with their weapons. My Pops was looking at the door, holding the samurai sword, as if it was a bat, and he was about to swing, and my Mom...

"Mom! Why is your hand in that little purse of yours?"

She looked at me sheepishly.

"I know you're reaching for a piece of that candy and not for some concealed weapon, right?"

She smiled at me and nodded.

I looked at Dot; we both shook our heads.

"I say, we elope and leave the four of them, and everyone else, behind."

"I agree," she said and then yelled something at her parents in Chinese. They just smiled at her, and she threw up her hands.

There was a knock at the door. This time, PJ went to look at the door-cam. My Pops was swirling his sword around, again, with one hand.

"Pops! You're going to put your eye out. And what are you going to do with that? Someone shoots at you, you'll whack the bullet back at them?"

The door opened, and there was a bunch of sidewalk johnnies there. A man behind them pushed through them.

"Cruz!"

He fired a gun at me!

My father swung at the laser blast and hit it back right at the gunman. The round hit him in his face, and he yelled out as one of his eye sockets began to illuminate. Every sidewalk johnny in the hall jumped him and took him down to the floor. Phishy was in the hall, too, and reached to close the door, but PJ just kicked it closed.

"Why are strangers always trying to shoot me?" I yelled out. I looked at my Pops. "You whacked that laser bullet back at that guy."

He grinned and twirled the sword around.

"You've been tricking me all these years, Pops."

My Ma pointed at him and said in Spanish-accented English, "Kendo master."

"Oh, snaps," I yelled out. "Phishy!"

I ran to the door, and everyone followed me.

"What's wrong?" PJ asked.

The door opened and Phishy peeked in. We could see the sidewalk johnnies kicking the stuffings out of the downed gunman on the hallway floor.

"Phishy, a gunman got right up to me! I thought you had the place secured. I thought all these were your guys."

"Cruz, I'm taking care of it. We're checking everyone now."

"Phishy, I got my parents in here."

"I know."

"Dot and her parents are here."

"I know, I know."

"Stupid man," PJ said to him.

"Phishy, I need your A game."

"I know. I got it covered."

He disappeared out the door and began to close it.

"Wait," I yelled.

He popped back in.

"What's he wearing?"

I pointed to one of the sidewalk johnnies, who stopped his kicking and stood up straight. Under his jacket, he was wearing a T-shirt of me! My face and wearing my tan fedora.

"What's that?" I asked.

"That's you," the johnny said, beaming. "Cruz, the People's Detective. The Detective of the Revolution. Liquid Cool Rules Metropolis!"

All I began to say was, "What the—"

When I got back inside, my Pops opened his jacket, and he was wearing a T-shirt of me. My Ma had one in her little purse. Even the Wans opened their jackets to reveal they had them on, too.

"What the heck."

"They're selling them in the lobby and on the street in front of the building," Dot said.

"I'm being franchised." I looked up. "Phishy!" I looked at PJ.

"Don't look at me, boss," she said. "It's exactly what he would do. You're a public figure, now, so you better get used to it."

"Public figure? I am not a public figure. They can't franchise me."

"Oh, *non*. We're stupid!" PJ ran to her mobile computer. "We need to be franchising you, too. I'll have a shopping portal up on our virtual storefront in five minutes. We'll sell the official Liquid Cool T-shirts and hats, too. I need to get paid, so this will bring in a steady income stream."

"How are people franchising me? What's going on? I'm a private person."

My parents and Dot's parents burst out laughing.

"Why am I being laughed at? Laughed at by even my own parents."

"You need to catch up on the news," Dot said.

I shook my head.

"Boss!"

"What?" I yelled back.

I walked over to PJ's home workstation and she pointed to her mobile computer.

"Wait, what did you just have on the screen?"

"Nothing."

"I saw 'Le Liquid Cool.' What's that?"

"It my on-screen translator."

"It's not 'Le Liquid Cool' or 'El Liquid Cool' or anything else in front of it. It's Liquid Cool."

"Boss, forget that. Here's what I'm showing you."

I looked and looked again. "What the—"

Above Metro Police One and City Hall were five spaceships! It was just like you'd see in a classic sci-fi movie, only this was very real, and there was nothing cool about it.

I had held up my hand and turned my head. First, I was told the city's police, not the people, were rioting in the streets. Then I was seeing Up-Top spaceships hovering above the city's seat of power. Now, the police were in Concrete Mama's lobby, ostensibly to get me. I just walked back to my guest room.

The door was shut only for a few minutes, before there was a knock. I opened it, and there was my Pops.

"Where you going?" he asked.

I didn't answer.

"You can't hide in here. Once the toothpaste is out of the toothpaste tube, you have to brush your teeth, even if you already did."

I laughed. "What does that even mean?" He joined in. "You are a Kendo master and philosopher, all of a sudden. Who are you? What did you do with my Pops?"

"Boss!"

PJ's yell made us both look out in her direction.

Phishy was back inside and standing with her. From their faces and everyone else's—Dot, my Ma, the Wans—it was not to be good news.

"What now?"

"The good news is that you've sold 50,000 Cruz T-shirts in 30 minutes from your new Liquid Cool virtual merchandise market."

"Why did you call me?"

"The police are here," Phishy answered.

"We know that already! The police are here. To do what?"

"They want to see you."

"Phishy, are you insane?"

"No cops in my place!" PJ yelled.

"I already had one guy try to shoot me."

"It's their union leader. He says it's urgent."

"You want me to meet with him?"

"Yes," Phishy replied.

"You don't like police. Why would you want me to meet with them? They're here to arrest me. The Mayor and the Police Chief said they'd get me, and that's why they're here."

"Cruz, you need to see the news," Dot said.

"Yes," PJ said. "*Toute suite.*"

"Yes," Dot said. "*Toute suite.*"

"What's *toute suite*?" Phishy asked.

"Phishy, focus. No, I'm not doing that. There is no way, no how I'm meeting them."

"They're on our side," Dot said.

"What are you talking about?"

"They're rioting at City Hall, but they're not with the Mayor or the Police Chief."

"They're on the people's side," PJ said.

I had a splitting headache at this point.

"Their union leader is waiting for you. His name is Wilford G. Jr."

I stopped. "Wilford G.?"

"Yes, why?"

"It couldn't be," I said to myself.

"Wilford G. was your father?"

The police officer was escorted to PJ's place by dozens of johnnies. I had my own sidewalk johnny army at my disposal, courtesy of Phishy, all of them wearing fedoras. My Pops stood on one side of me, with his sword, my parents-in-law from hell stood on the other side. PJ had her rifle, and my Ma was standing behind me, so I couldn't see her hands, but I knew she was packing. I thought the detective industry turned me into a quasi-criminal, but it seemed like it turned everyone around me into quasi-gangsters.

The man was forty-ish and in his dress blues.

"Yes, he was. Died at 92."

"He didn't mention anything about family."

"You mean his books?" The man smiled. "He never did. He kept us private when it came to his work. Never even had pictures of us in his office after seventy years of work. You read his book?"

"I own his book."

"Oh, you're the *one* purchaser. How to be...." The emotions were welling up inside of him, and his eyes teared up. "Yeah, we miss him. Best there ever was."

My attitude towards him was different now. He was the son of my adopted mentor.

"I'm not sure I can be of any help, though. As you can see, I'm trying to hide out."

"Too late for that," he said. "The revolution is in full swing."

"Revolution?"

"Well, that's what it's being called. There's not one police person on the streets. The criminals have free reign."

"Then, your men have to get back out there."

"My men?" He grinned. "I'm the union president; that's all. Not one of us is moving until the Mayor and Chief are gone. And they're not going. We were going to rush Police One, but then, the Up-Top spaceships came in to provide them with protection. They have about 10,000 Interspace police. Numerically, nothing compared to us, but their digital technology is far more advanced than our analog tech. My faction that wants to wait is growing weaker. At some point, we'll take our chances and attack. Whoever wins, it will be a bloodbath and, ultimately, that means the criminals win, and the people lose."

"What do you want to talk to me for then? This is beyond me. I'm just one guy who read your dad's book and thinks he can play detective."

"I think you're doing far better than that, but I just have one question before I answer yours. The allegations you made on that interview show. How did you know there were no tapes? How could you possibly know that?"

"I reasoned it out. The police were out in force for the shootout, and the kidnapping of that girl was within range of your body-cams. You all would have seen the kidnapping happen and the kidnapper. You wouldn't have sat on that footage, so I took a guess there was no footage to sit on. Which meant some kind of conspiracy was going on."

"That was a big, big gamble on your part."

"Not really. Just logical reasoning with my bit of knowledge of procedure. Also, I was at the CIC, myself. They keep the originals of all body-cam footage, not Police One. Most people don't know that. All the footage of the incident was not there, none of it."

"Conspiracy, indeed. Only two people would have the authority to quarantine the footage." Wilford G. Jr. clenched his teeth in anger. "That cuts it. We're going in to get the Mayor and the Chief, today."

"Can I ask another question?"

"What?"

"Are all police...?" I stopped and looked at everyone. They were all hanging on my every word. "Maybe we should talk private."

"No!" everyone yelled out. They had a front seat to the biggest conversation in the City.

"Just ask the question."

"Police body-cams. They are always recording?"

"Always recording?"

"And it's monitored live?"

"Yes. Everyone knows that."

He stopped. He realized what I was saying.

"Oh my God," Wilford G. Jr. yelled out. "They're all in on the conspiracy that killed our officers!"

PART NINE

Monkeys, Spaceships, and the Watch Conspiracy

CHAPTER 57

Run-Time

When you approach your forties and can say you knew someone when you were both barely out diapers, then that's a hell of a long time. You've known them forever.

My Pops was right. Hiding time was over. I put Dot in charge of parent protection, PJ in charge of keeping everyone in her apartment, and Phishy in charge of Concrete Mama security, which was greatly aided by Wilford G. Jr. stationing fifteen police cruisers around the building. I left PJ's place with Wilford G. Jr., and we were joined by several police waiting outside.

Wilford Jr. was a seething mass waiting to explode with the information I revealed. He only promised me that he'd keep it from the rank-and-file, because I convinced him that before we set the city on fire, we owed the people of Metropolis to find out, for certain, everyone involved in the conspiracy and cover-up. I would be the detective and he, the police officer, and we'd investigate the crimes to a conclusion. I got him to agree to that.

Like clockwork, a video-call was routed to our police cruiser, and we postponed my visit with the widows and widower of the fallen police officers, who wanted to meet me. We flew to Let It Ride Enterprises, where Run-Time was waiting for me. On the way, I caught up on the news I had tried to avoid. I wanted to hurt the Mayor and the Chief, but set in motion a chain of events that no one could predict. Who knew how many people had been and would be victims of criminal punks, because there were no police on the streets, because of me. Within an hour of my "performance" on Holly Live's news interview show, the Police Chief's inner circle confronted him in a private meeting. During that meeting, the Police Chief was fatally shot, and two other captains were shot. That same day, police officers walked off the job, taking their police cruisers and weapons with them. By nightfall, all 500,000 had quit and had surrounded Metro Police One.

In the old days, you could set a building on fire, but it was a world of monolith towers that couldn't burn so the police dumped enough trash around the building and set it ablaze. They also barricaded the Mayor and staff in City Hall. The Mayor called a state of emergency, which was unprecedented in itself, but went a step further—he called in Interpol, who agreed to take control of the City and arrest the police. That started a war, and now, there was a stalemate with five Interpol spaceships hovering above City Hall to protect the buildings and the Mayor, who had not been out of the tower in five days. The City was holding its breath.

Run-Time looked like he hadn't slept in five days. "Let me ask you," he began, "do you understand what has been set in motion?"

"You mean, what I started."

"You said it."

Run-Time warned me, but I didn't listen. I acknowledged that he understood the politics of things better than I ever would. However, I knew that fact profoundly, now. I was the cause of the chaos. All because of ego. Would I ever be able to sleep if people died because of my ego?

"The Mayor and the Chief were going to destroy my life. They were going to let a kidnap victim die. They were going to let a psycho cyborg criminal get away to kill more people and do more violence."

Run-Time shook his head. "You don't know that."

"Is this one of those 'see the big picture' speeches? Run-Time, you've known me practically all my life. I don't care and never have cared about the 'big picture.' I'm a simple guy. Did you scratch my car or not? I don't care about the socio-economic forces that led to your father losing his job and your parents turning to a life of crime and beating you up and you becoming a bad person. I don't care. Did you scratch my car or not? Did you kill that old man or not? Did you run down that girl in your hovercar and flee the scene of the crime or not? If people spent more time with the 'little picture,' then the 'big picture' wouldn't be so screwed up."

Run-Time was always Mr. Optimism, even as a child. But the man who stood in front of me was so far from that, it scared me. He stayed quiet for a moment. I don't know if he was trying to think of the best response or was just plain tired.

"I'd like you to meet someone."

"Run-Time, they want me to meet some police widows and widowers."

"I know, but this is important. The big picture shouldn't trump little pictures, but the little pictures shouldn't destroy the big picture either. Where will we be if Metropolis goes up in flames? You and I live here, you know."

"Who do you want me to meet with?"

"The Vice President of the Police Watch Commission."

"Ah," I said. "The people who probably orchestrated the murder of Easy Chair Charlie, but definitely, the cover-up."

CHAPTER 58

Exe

Run-Time ignored my comment. For a second, I wondered if he had even heard me.

I was now in a foul mood. The least of which was the fact that a lifelong friendship was on the verge of dissolution. Friends were hard to come by in Metropolis, and friends you could count on were even more rare. Losing Run-Time's friendship would be a serious blow. However, I couldn't quite figure out what his involvement was in this whole thing. As a businessman, he had to be friends with everyone—uber-governments, megacorporations, multinationals, the Average Joe and Jane—that's how you not only grew your business in the City, but kept it. But there was a deeper level of involvement here behind the scenes. He didn't tell me, and I couldn't guess. That was what annoyed me. Obviously, he'd have friends in the city that I hated. That was life, but some of the players in the city would try to destroy my life. That's what gave me pause. How friendly was Run-Time with them? Was he going to allow them to crush me?

His third VP, Mr. "Mick," joined us. I figured I'd be seeing a lot more of him and a lot less of the Lebanese and West Indian female VPs, going forward, if Run-Time and I continued any relationship. The Mick had refreshments brought in, and Run-Time and I moved to the lounge area of his office to wait for our guest.

Exe (pronounced EX-EE) was brought in fairly soon afterward. She wore a crimson pants suit and matching beret on her head, with a sheer white and yellow scarf around her neck. She had been a member of the Metropolis Police Watch Commission for decades. The lead members rotated through the official titles, and this term, she was the Vice President of the body. She had been its President before and would be again. She was a very gregarious woman and greeted me with a vigorous handshake and small talk as if we had been friends for ages. I don't think I ever saw her before, and surely, I wouldn't recognize any Police Watch member by sight.

The Metropolis Police Department was the largest and most powerful in the world, but the civilian Police Watch Commission kept them in check. Supposedly, they were the ones who monitored every single transaction of the police with the public, suspects, and criminals.

It was a strange fact, because they were powerful civilian members of government. Technically, they weren't part of the government at all. But who were we fooling? You hang out with government for so long, even as watchdogs, no matter how aggressive or antagonistic, you become de-facto part of the government yourself.

Exe was one of those natural story-teller personalities. They could sit and entrance you with a tale for hours, and you wouldn't once look at a timepiece.

"I remember saying 'shoot him.' I was very disturbed by my feelings, later on. Spit, curse, then spit and curse again. This big, burly crew-cut cop told me, 'Oh, it's nothing. People do that all the time. Would we talk that way to the public? Never, even if we were in a rotten mood. The disrespect is all one way. Towards us. But we see it as a game. Their one time to feel as if they have power over the system; talking crap to us, because we're the only part of the system that they can do that to and get away with it.' Wow, I said. Someone spat at me or called me a name, I'd beat them ugly, no matter how many cameras were watching. At that moment, I realized what my late mum meant by her crack, all those years ago, when she started calling me 9-1-1, when I first joined the Citizen's Police Oversight Commission, which became the Police Watch Commission. I was a rabble-rouser, back then. I had an afro to the sky, and I was going to get those police brutality, po-lice goose-steppin', black booters. You think you know so much from outside of the system, but then, you get inside, and you see things how they really are. My late mum didn't think I would become a sell-out. But she knew, long before I did, what would happen. You sit there in the Watch Room, hour after hour, day after day, and year after year. You see what they have to go through on the streets to protect the City. Someone, like me, never goes from not loving the people and the community, but after a while, you get to not liking a lot of them. The community and the police organized into one force. We merged into one entity. They weren't the police anymore. They were my people, and I wouldn't hesitate to protect every last one. And they would do the same for us. Cops say, 'I got the community on my shoulder and watching my back.'

"Wow. Metro Police were so violently opposed to body-cams and Police Watch. I remember. We thought we'd get assassinated. We were scared." She laughed. "All our 'Power to the People' rhetoric, and we were actually hiding under our beds, because we were that scared. Now, we've gone full circle. The community says, "You low-life criminal punks better not mess with our cops, or we'll stomp your teeth in and down to your ankles. Now the cops say, 'We won't go into the field on the streets, unless we're body-cammed with the Police Watch watching our backs.' Full-circle. Before us, nearly 100% of the police brutality cases against the City were settled unfavorably, because they knew, if any got to trial, the payout could be a thousand times more. Now? You have to go back thirty, forty years to find a police brutality case that got a penny. Actually, I think that was the actual settlement—one penny." She laughed again.

"The trial lawyers were also our very best friends, back then, and all for body-cams. Now, they hate our guts. Body-cams ended their gravy train forever. You gotta laugh. I remember when the trial lawyers tried to sue us—the Police Watch Commission—for encouraging police brutality. Us, the people.

"You see, Mr. Cruz, I was one of those pioneers in creating this coalition of community and police against the criminals. The City is far from crime-free, and many parts are extremely dangerous, and there are plenty of gangs, psychos, and cartels out there. But, I was alive, back then, when you could have ten thousand murders in one weekend. The Average Joe and Jane can't even imagine the level of violence on the streets, back then. We ended that all with our community coalition of the people and the cops. But all coalitions are fragile, as these past days have shown us. Police rioting, with people backing them up, against the Mayor and City Hall. We could even have a war—damn, we haven't used that word in centuries—a war against Earth and Up-Top. That's how it's being spun. Accomplishments are oh so fragile. Mr. Cruz, that's where we are. Run-Time told me what you said to him. Based on the look I got from the Police Union leader earlier today, it seems you've been sharing. All I ask is that you give me a chance to prove you wrong; a couple of days is all I need, before you make up your mind. I have a legacy that I can't bear to see shredded before my eyes and more importantly, if such a thing were to get out, and people were to believe it, the damage would be catastrophic to the city. It would be a return to those ten-thousand-killed-in-a-weekend days, trial lawyers getting the most vicious criminals off, victims and their families getting no justice, judges afraid to convict crime bosses, people refusing to serve on juries..."

Exe had weaved a very, very bleak story for me. How was it I was in this situation? The fate of Metropolis was in my hands? I was a small-time, newbie private detective. How was this even happening? If I could have seen the future to this point, even with all my business cards printed, I would have chosen a different path. At least, I think I would have.

"What do you say, Mr. Cruz?" she asked.

"Are civilians allowed to visit the Watch Room?"

"I don't see why not."

"Why don't I see what goes on in this Watch Room and meet all your colleagues at the same time. We can shoot two birds with one laser."

"Excellent," Exe said with a broad smile.

CHAPTER 59

Flash

As The Mick escorted me from Run-Time's office—Run-Time and Exe remained behind to talk. I hoped they weren't afraid of me. Not me, specifically, but what I could do. The only problem was I didn't know what I would do. I was not pleased with the situation I found myself in.

"Our limo is yours for the day," The Mick said, when we exited the elevator capsule.

"Thank you," I said. "Who's driving?"

"Flash. I believe you know him."

I managed a smile, which I hadn't done in, I couldn't remember, how long. "Flash is good people. Thanks."

"You're quite welcome. However Let It Ride Enterprises can help a friend."

I wasn't sure if his use of the word "friend" had some special meaning. That's what sucked about politics—people never meant what they said and were always playing an angle. However, I had to admit it was no different than dealing with anyone in Metropolis. "Everything is politics," Run-Time once told me. Maybe that's why I was content being a house mouse for so long in the Concrete Mama.

Flash was waiting at a hoverlimo in their landing bay. He saw me and immediately opened a door for me. "Thanks, Flash." I hopped in, and he closed the door. Flash was my main guy at Let It Ride. He had guarded my Pony so often that I requested him by name and arranged my own personal schedule for him whenever I ordered mobile hovercar security services.

"They've moved you up to limo duty," I said.

He drove the hoverlimo out of the bay and, in moments, we were ascending into sky traffic. "I told them there was no way you were going to drive your vehicle anywhere with all this madness going on. I told them I was on permanent on-call status for you."

"I appreciate that, Flash."

"You've given me a lot of business, so this was the time to give back."

"What is the madness going on out there? I've tried to avoid as much news as possible."

"Do you know anything?"

"Cops rioting around Metro Police One, and they have all walked off the job. The Police Chief met with top generals, and it ended in a shootout. Interpol spaceships are stationed above City Hall. Is that basically it?"

"You got the main points, but there's a lot more."

I leaned forward as I moved my hoverseat closer to his compartment. "You can never have too much street intel. How do you see the situation?"

"I did something I never thought I'd do. I got my lady a piece of her own, and we've kept the kids home from school."

"It can't be that bad."

"It is. There's no police. The entire 9-1-1 system is down."

"I just thought that buildings would band together and protect their own until the crisis is over."

"We're banding together, but so are the gangs. They're consolidating to exploit the situation, so that means they're killing each other. I have never seen the level of intra-gang violence going on. All of us, taxi drivers, are talking about it. A lot of us are not driving most of the city. Once the intra-gang violence is over, then the gang violence against us begins."

"This will all be over before that happens."

"Mr. Cruz, I've known you a long time, not as long as Mr. Run-Time, but a long time. I've never known you to be an optimist."

He was right. I wasn't one. It made me realize that it wasn't optimism; it was avoidance. I was the cause of all the chaos.

"Mr. Cruz, can I be a bit forward with some advice. I never tell a client his business, but..."

"Sure, why not. It's the times we're in."

"Mr. Cruz, I'm not passing judgment, but you started this chaos with that interview, and only you can bring us back to order. Only you. You may not want to hear that or accept it. You're saying 'Hey, I'm a private detective just scraping by in life,' but you need to get wise to the reality fast, because a lot of other people already have."

"What others?"

"The cops, the politicians. Up-Top. The gangs."

"The gangs?" I was nervous now. "Why would they care about me?"

"They all know your name, Mr. Cruz."

"Yeah, but why would they care about me?"

"Because you're the only guy who can bring Metropolis back to order."

Now I was scared.

"What do you think they'll do?"

"If I were them," Flash said. "I'd kill you any way I could."

CHAPTER 60

Monkey Baker

I had three stops to make. PJ was back at the real office, and apparently, we had both civilian and police security everywhere, so according to her, it was safe. She told me I had some "high-level" clients waiting. I didn't know what "high-level" meant, and she wouldn't tell me on the video-phone. Then I had to meet with the cops, courtesy of Wilford G. Jr. Then, it was to the Watch Room to meet the city's Police Watch Commission.

But there was a cloud over me. Would gangs really want to hurt me? I was in Flash's hoverlimo. No one in the public knew I was inside, so at least, for the day, I would be safe. Then, Flash told me that the hoverlimo was bullet and laser-proof. Good.

Flash and I realized that if we flew up in the hoverlimo and I got out, it wouldn't take long for the media and everyone else to know how I was traveling around the city. Everyone was looking for my red Ford Pony, not a Let It Ride hoverlimo. We did a combat-drop two miles away—he dove above the ground, I jumped out with a black hooded slicker over my clothes, and he flew away.

I walked through the rain towards my office with my head down and my hands in my pockets, but neither hand was empty. I had my main piece in my right hand and my back-up piece in the other. I had been shot at so many times, that I was betting on it happening today. Surprisingly, I wasn't as nervous about walking through the streets with no bodyguards. It was raining hard, and I blended in with the crowds.

Across from my office tower was another tower, fifty stories taller. I stood on the roof, wearing Punch Judy's jetpack, started it up, and let it lift me up, hovering. I was up and over. On the roof of my building, I could see the army of sidewalk johnnies. One of them pointed at me as I flew near, and then they all were looking. I could tell they were Phishy's people—all of them were wearing fedoras. Good grief! Now Phishy, the franchiser, would have everyone wearing my trademark fedora.

I landed, removed the jetpack with their help, and quickly made it to the roof-top exits, with a bunch of johnnies following me.

"They're waiting," she said as I walked through the door.

"My high-level clients?"

"Take advantage of the pandemonium. Get all the paying clients in now. I've been offering a free official Liquid Cool t-shirt for all new clients."

I threw the jetpack and my slicker on the floor. "I don't want to hear about it. Take care of these for me."

My sidewalk johnny escorts were shooed out of the office by PJ as she closed the door. I walked in and opened my office door.

Him!

I instinctively drew my piece and pointed at his head. The seven other police officers around him drew their guns and pointed them at me.

"No, boss!" PJ yelled. "This is your client!"

"What? He's my client?"

"Yes."

I looked at him again.

"Lower your weapons," Police Chief Hub directed.

His men complied, and I did the same.

"I could have shot you!" I yelled.

"I couldn't say his name on the open video-phone," PJ said. "He has the entire cop police force looking for him."

"And you invite him into my office?"

"I didn't invite. He came."

"Why didn't you tell him to leave?"

"He wouldn't leave!"

"Why didn't you throw him out? You have two bionic arms. Use them!"

I realized why she let him stay.

"How much?" I asked.

"What?"

"How much did he pay?"

"He paid the standard retainer, and I gave him a free T-shirt."

I threw up my hands.

"Do I get to talk now?" Chief Hub asked.

"I'm not talking to you, and I'm not going to even be seen with you."

"I think, if you let me talk, you will change your mind."

"Who are these other officers with you? I thought the rank-and-file want you in the meat morgue."

"They do, thanks to you. These are my sons."

"Your sons. You have seven sons."

"I do. All law enforcement."

"How lucky for you. Wait, weren't you shot? They said you were in the hospital."

410

"I was shot, thanks to you. But it was a minor wound, and we used the incident to craft a cover story that was a lot worse, including I was bedridden, so I could move around freely."

"How's your boss doing?" I asked with a sneer.

"My boss isn't doing too well either, thanks to you. But he's not talking to me, and I'm not talking to him, ever since he brought in those Up-Top bottom-feeders. Am I going to be allowed to talk about what I came to talk about?"

"Aren't we talking?"

"Not what I came to talk about."

"Then do so and leave. I have to go visit the widows and widowers of fallen cops."

"You're a real jerk muncher!" one of his sons yelled, pointing at me. "My dad had nothing to do with police getting killed, you lying skell."

"I'm on the side of the cops. What about you?"

Chief Hub held back his oldest son. "Stop it! All of you, wait in the hallway. I'll be out in a minute."

"He's not worth it," the son yelled. "Let him get killed."

"If he gets killed, then how will I clear my name? All people will remember is his lying prime-time interview."

Chief Hub pushed all his sons out of the offices and closed the door.

"Who's going to kill me?" I asked.

"Yes, who?" PJ asked. "If it's you, then I want my free T-shirt back."

"For such a clever guy, Mr. Cruz, you're a dummy. You're a marked man, Mr. Cruz. Metropolis is on the brink of collapse. Who wants that?"

"Your Up-Top friends," I answered.

"They are not my friends! They're the Mayor's friends. Weren't you listening? I'm not on speaking terms with the Mayor anymore. No, Mr. Cruz. The gangs want the chaos to continue, so they can carve up Metropolis into nice manageable slices. It's the gangs."

"Yeah, I've heard that already. I'm already ahead of you, as usual, so you can go."

"No," the Chief said and folded his arms.

"What? I told you to get out of my office."

"Mr. Cruz, I'm giving you 24-hour security until this crisis is over."

"What, you and your seven sons?"

"My seven sons, me, and the cops from Internal Affairs."

I laughed. "Internal Affairs?"

"They're police, too."

"But police don't think so. What are you trying to do? Ruin my rep with the real rank-and-file. No, I'm not taking any security from you."

"Then who? These sidewalk johnny jokers you have around you like flies? When the gangs come, what will they do? Throw a hat at them? None are armed. Gangs, Mr. Cruz, are."

"I'll figure out something."

"What, you and your personal cyborg?"

"My name is Punch Judy! And I'm about to punch you in the head, stupid man!"

"You can go now," I said to him.

"You don't seem to get it, Mr. Cruz. One of the top animal gangs in the city has a contract out on you."

"What?"

"You know what a contract is?"

"Stop being offensive. What are you talking about?"

"Monkey Baker has a contract out on you. That means any—any gang member can collect on it."

"Who or what is Monkey Baker?"

"I know you are quite familiar with his crime organization. Monkey Baker runs the Animal Farm Crime Syndicate."

"I thought—"

"You thought Red Rabbit did, Mr. Cruz? The gang member you killed or left for dead. No, Mr. Cruz, he didn't run it. You have no one to blame, but yourself. You went on national TV and announced to the world that one of the top leaders in his organization was on the payroll of the cops. In the gang world, that's the same as saying he is, too. He has to kill you, or every gang will kill him."

I felt queasy in my stomach all of a sudden.

"What's it going to be, Mr. Cruz? You want to do your perp walk alone, or could you use police protection? I don't care what you say, because we're protecting you. You and I are shackled ankle-to-ankle from this moment forward, you punk. You think I'll let you destroy 40 years of my police career without a fight? You will clear me in the eyes of my people."

"Okay," I said. "We start now. I have a hoverlimo waiting. Let's go pay our respects to the men and women who are convinced you got their loved ones killed." I could see the toughness in Chief's Hub's face soften. "What's wrong? Not so eager to do your unwelcome police protection?"

"My son is right. I should let Monkey Baker have you. If I didn't care more about this city than I hate you, I would."

"Good, because I hate you too, pompous bastard. Maybe, I'll get to see some *real* cops shoot you again."

"Maybe, I'll get lucky and get to see some gang skell punk shoot you. I hear you have quite the problem with strange people shooting at you."

"Yeah, they don't like my hat. Maybe, they'll try to shoot me and hit you instead."

It would have gone on forever, but a smiling PJ said, "Can you two continue your conversation outside? I have a business to run."

We left, and later I learned there was another "high-level" client she wanted me to call, but had forgotten to mention the messages were on my desk. It didn't matter. The calls or meetings wouldn't have made a bit of difference for what came next.

413

On reflection, my combat-drop strategy was majorly flawed. It worked for Flash to drop me off, but what about leaving the building? Out into the rain, we went—me, Chief Hub, and his seven sons. We could hide all we wanted with our hooded dark slickers, but there were many ways to identify a person if they really wanted to. All we heard was...

"Hey, Cruz!"

I recognized the voice. I looked up and saw the Hippo waving and smiling without his animal mask, but with the black airbrushed eye sockets. He walked to me, and I walked to him. It may have been centuries old, but I saw the Godfather when I was a kid with my Pops. I reached him and flicked my wrist.

Pop!

Before he went down, I saw the flash of anger on his face as he realized he wouldn't be able to assassinate me so easily. The cyborg yelled, fell back and crashed to the ground; a burning hole in his chest. Then we saw them. These Hippos, all with their masks on, came out from the shadows with guns blazing.

Civilians scattered as the gang members took positions at one end of the street, and we took cover where we could—close to the tower walls and low. Thank goodness for the rain and the steam from the vents. Hub took his position in front of me and returned fire, like a maniac; I heard two Hippos cry out. His sons followed his lead, but two of his sons ran off. Based on what I was seeing, this was not a coward family and no cop in this city, even a scumbag like Hub, would run away like a scaredy-cat against criminals, no matter how out-gunned. I hoped they had a hovercar somewhere with laser machine guns in the trunk.

I looked up again, and this time, I saw it. People were jumping out of a hovercar onto the buildings. The Hippos had the firepower to hold us, but not overpower us. They were buying time.

"They're stalling for time," I yelled at Hub.

"So are we," he answered back and continued firing.

There are times you see things you've never seen before, and it takes days to process it. The sky traffic above us just stopped and hovercars began descended to the ground. We heard doors opening and saw them. In all my years, I had never seen an entire sky-lane of traffic stop and drop like that. The gunfire from the hovercars almost cut us to pieces right there. It was a miracle we weren't killed outright, and that none of the bullets, laser beams, or laser rounds hit us. We scrambled back as fast as we could into what shadows there were.

Hovercar after hovercar landed, and out came the animal gangs—Jackals, Pigs, Lions, Unicorns, Snakes, Toads, Lizards, and others I couldn't make out. One hovercar zipped to a stop, right above us, with the door already open and a Monkey at a side mounted machine gun. I didn't hesitate and shot him right in the head. He fell over and crashed ten feet to the ground. Another Monkey pushed two others out of the way and jumped onto the machine gun turret. He was dressed differently than the others—they were all in chocolate brown suits; he was in a bright, white-silver one and tie. Was this Monkey Baker, the head of the Animal Farm Crime Syndicate?

I shot at him too, but hit only the turret. An explosion of gunfire erupted from behind me. I physically jumped, startled, and looked back. Chief Hub had a compact machine-gun in his hands. At least, the scumbag was prepared. I looked back to see, who I suspected was Monkey Baker strafed by bullets, jump back into the hovercar, another Monkey fell out to crash to the ground, and then, the vehicle blasted off and away.

One often played Cowboys and Indians as a kid with sonic toy guns or colored paint shooters. Everyone always wanted to be the Cowboys to defeat the Indians. This wasn't that. This was the Battle of Little Big Horn, and I was General Custer, and that meant, I was about to get killed badly with all my men. The barrage of lighted gunfire from these deranged animal masked gang members was overwhelming. We were encircled by neon signs and neon bullets coming at us every which way. There were just too many of them.

"This is the police! Drop your weapons!"

The voice rumbled through the air and seemed to come from the heavens above as if spoken by God. Silver-and-black police "PEACE" officers descended from the sky via their silent jetpacks, like black rain, blitzing them with more intense gunfire than seemed possible.

These gang members had really stepped in it. To us, it seemed like world war with 5,000 of them firing at us seven guys, but now, 500,000 jetpacked police—thousands of points of light—descended from the black sky, firing at them! It was a bloodbath. I was certain that every gang gunman was hit dozens of times by police gunfire, and they were still taking bullets and laser rounds. Bodies collapsed to the ground; their hovercars shot apart and exploding. This wasn't world war; it was the End of the World for the Animal Farm Crime Syndicate. Hub's two sons had brought the Cavalry to the rescue all right, with not a moment to spare. I had never ever, ever, ever seen so many cops in the sky—no one had.

Whoever Monkey Baker was, he was done. His Animal Farm Syndicate was done. The Metro Police would track down every last one, until every last one was dead or in jail. Monkey Baker would not have time to think about me ever again, let alone come after me. A smile crept onto my face as I watched the silver-and-black event before my eyes. A few police incursions like this in key points of the city, and Metropolis would be crime-free...well, for a week, at least.

"How did you learn to shoot so well," one of Hub's sons asked me, almost annoyed by the fact.

"Video games," I answered.

Securing the scene was elevated to an insane new level. The entire street was locked down, and that meant, twenty miles, in either direction, on the ground with a human net of hovering police in the air. I couldn't even comprehend how the coroner's department would clear a body count of this magnitude. Exe said there was a time that criminals were killing 10,000 people a weekend. Such numbers were beyond my ability to grasp. That was too many innocent faces. Hopefully, the cosmic scales had been balanced today.

The standard procedure was done and officers walked to me. The sight of what amounted to a ground armada of silver-and-black peace officers approaching me...I couldn't swallow hard enough, but at least, I knew they were on my side. Chief Hub and sons must have been soiling themselves and I noticed how they got closer and closer to me as the crowd approached.

"You!" It was Wilford G. Jr. He pulled off his half-visor helmet. "We're glad you have a death wish, because that wish will be granted."

"Why do you think we're here?" Hub yelled back. "You jokers weren't providing proper protection."

"Protection? We saved your asses," an officer yelled back.

"If you all hadn't abandoned the city, this would never have happened!"

"Abandoned? Says the man who let his own officers get gunned down," a female officer yelled.

"I had nothing to do with it!"

The officers had engulfed us, and every one of them had their long guns in hand. I could see the sweat pouring down the side of Hub's face. A hovervan descended slowly, and I could see Wilford G. Jr. and the others gesture for the officers to clear a space. The vehicle landed a couple of feet from me, and the door opened. Inside were families—adults and kids from toddlers to teenagers.

"Mr. Cruz," one of the women said. "We've been trying to get you to come to us, but it seems with your busy life, it's better and easier to come to you. My husband was one of the officers killed at the Sweet Street Shootout."

She and the other spouses introduced themselves.

"Why is the murderer here?" one of the women in the hovervan yelled, looking at Wilford G. Jr.

"I am not a murderer," Chief Hub answered back. "I had nothing to do with it."

"Is your Mayor master going to have those Up-Top spaceships try to take over the planet?" asked another widow. "We're going to blast them from the sky."

"I have nothing to do with the Mayor or them, either," Hub answered.

"Tell me, Mr. Cruz," asked one of the widowers, holding his little son's hand, "Are you going to identify everyone involved in this plot? Are you going to tell us the masterminds behind the death of my boy's mother? The mastermind behind the death of all our loved ones?"

"I am," I answered.

"Is he one of them?" he asked, pointing directly at Chief Hub.

If I were evil, I could have lied, and Hub and Sons would never have left that street alive. But I was a good guy, so I couldn't, but it was interesting to feel what true temptation to the dark side felt like. Hub, undoubtedly, was holding his breath. One word from me truly could end his life.

"No, not him," I said. "He's just a scumbag, who wanted to play politics. There's another who's the mastermind. Or the co-mastermind. The criminal animal gang leader, Red, was one. This person is the other half. And their time is coming to an end soon. However, before I concentrate on finishing the job, I must ask: Can you all secure the city first? People are hiding in their homes and businesses. They can't walk the streets in safety. People can't send their kids to school. I know you haven't had a chance to do any tours, but Metropolis is a ghost town. The criminal punks think they run the city, now, and not you. Can you take care of that? I'll take care of my end. Can that happen?" I looked at the widower, holding his son's hand. "This city doesn't need any more widows, widowers, or orphans."

The families in the hovervan and the officers looked at each other.

Wilford G. Jr. spoke up, "We can do that, but not him!" He pointed at Hub.

"I'm no fan of the Chief. He and the Mayor tried to destroy my life, but he saved my life. I don't know if his motives were pure. Probably not, but if he wasn't backing me, I'd be dead, period."

"Let's do what the man says and restore order to the city," Hub said. "If you want to get me, then all you have to do is organize a recall or demand the Mayor replace me or replace the Mayor, but not this."

"This was the only way to break through the cover-up," one of the widows said.

"I don't disagree, but my way would have accomplished the same thing," Hub said.

"Yeah, if we wanted to wait for the next twenty years," another officer said

"It would have taken time, but it would have happened," Hub said back.

"But then, the people responsible are never the ones who pay for misdeeds," Wilford G. Jr. said.

"You want my job?" Hub asked him directly. "We can switch jobs, right now. Say the word."

Wilford's expression said it all. He was not interested, nor was anyone else.

"Being a revolutionary is easy," Hub said. "Running a department of 500,000 men and women in a 50 million supercity is a far different thing. My humble suggestion is we send 90% of the forces to do what the man says and take the remaining 10% with me back to City Hall and get those Up-Top spaceships off our planet! That should be acceptable to everyone, because if there's a possibility of any real violence, City Hall is where that will be. Maybe, you'll get what you want after all, and I'll get shot for real there."

The two sides stared at each other. I had to get the ball rolling.

"Can someone escort me to my hoverlimo?" I asked. "It's not what it sounds like. It's donated. A guy, like me, with a red Ford Pony can't exactly drive around incognito. Let's bring this whole matter to an end and get the bad guy."

It worked. Cops volunteered. I knew the tension wouldn't go away soon, if ever, but at least, the city could get its streets back.

CHAPTER 61

Police Watch

As I sat in the hoverlimo, with Flash at the wheel and two police cruisers following as escorts, I reflected how this whole mess unfolded. Run-Time gave me a simple gig, and it snowballed into this. Since I planned to make this my new permanent career, I hoped this was a once in a lifetime event. I don't think my nerves could handle any repeats.

"Oh, Mr. Cruz?"

"Yeah."

"Mr. Run-Time is sending his security to meet you at the Watch Division."

"The cops are protecting me now."

"You can never have too much security."

I nodded. "After today, never a truer statement was spoken."

We arrived at Police Watch Division, and there was Run-Time's VP, The Mick, waiting. He had a compact machine gun in hand and behind him were no less than a dozen armed men. I exited the elevator capsule, and he spoke into his cupped left hand. He lowered his hand as he approached me, and the two police officers with me.

"I'm leading Mr. Run-Time's additional private security for Mr. Cruz. Everyone calls me The Mick," he said to the officers.

"Officer Break and my partner, Officer Caps."

"If I may suggest a security strategy," The Mick said. "I will maintain a close detail on Mr. Cruz. My men can take positions in the hall and secure the restrooms on the floor. You can maintain security of the main elevators."

Officer Break nodded. "Sounds like a plan."

"Mr. Cruz," The Mick said and gestured me to follow.

I didn't like this and couldn't wait for life to return to normal. Bodyguards were supposed to be an as-needed thing, not a permanent part of life. Politicians, rock stars, and gazillionaires could keep the life. I wanted no part of it.

We arrived.

Exe may have been worried, but she was one of those people with an outgoing demeanor that radiated congeniality. She walked me through the underground watch room of the division. I was being given a tour of a place most people had never and would never see, which seemed strange. The civilian Police Watch Commission was comprised of only civilians to protect civilians, but the civilian population had no oversight over them.

Weeks ago, when I was doing my own informal survey of the Police Watch Commission, I called a random sampling of criminal defense lawyers from the Yellow Pages. I made up a cover-story that I was a victim who wanted to sue the police. They all laughed at me. One lawyer put it succinctly, "Body-cams on police monitored by the civilian Police Watch Commission made the City legally bulletproof." Police brutality criminal cases were nearly impossible to prove, even before the body-cam regime. The main reason wasn't police protecting their own or political cover-ups, but because civilian juries *wanted* police to beat up criminals. But that left the domain of civil cases, which was where trial attorneys lived and, for ages, became filthy rich, suing the police. But, that was a long time ago.

There was the main executive committee of the Police Watch Commission, who maintained their watching duties, but there were tens of thousands of watchers on duty at any given time, manning the body-cam feed from police in the field. Police could not engage in any contact with the public or suspect without an active body-cam interface. It wasn't police procedure; it was law, mandated by the Police Union contract.

Everyone in the City knew someone on the Police Watch Commission, even if they didn't realize the fact. All 500,000 active police in the city were not on the streets at the same time (except for the unfortunate animal gang skells who tried to assassinate me earlier), but even being off-duty, on vacation, or in the station doing work, nearly 100,000 were in the field. And that is, actually, how many police watchers were here at the Division, plugged in.

Exe pointed to an old picture on the wall, just before she introduced me to her colleagues. It was over thirty years old and showed a younger and more slender Exe. Everyone in the photos was there in the room, as she introduced me. There was Cisco, who as a twenty-something pseudo radical, looked rather cool with his ponytail, but as a sixty-something, with practically all his natural hair receding to the point of invisibility, his ponytail looked rather silly—like a seventy-year old with a twenty-year old buxom girlfriend. Let's be age appropriate shall we? There was Mr. Link and Ms. Mosaic. Exe had an afro in her youth, but she let that go a long time past. Ms. Mosaic still had hers, tall, fluffy, and who knows how much time she spent having it dyed black; her eyebrows were natural gray. Mr. Link wore these old zoot suits that I remember wannabe gangsters used to wear, hanging out on the street. They looked synthetic and cheap on them, and looked the same on this old guy, too. Every member of the executive board was a social radical in their youth, but here, they were in their sixties and seventies, still trying to maintain the fiction, except for Exe. It was real back then, when they started, but it was all show now. They were all so booshy with their mansion-sized apartments, multiple hovercars, when they weren't being chauffeured around by hoverlimo, all their kids well-placed in society, their grandchildren attending the best universities. I didn't like fake people, which was one reason I liked Exe. She didn't pretend to be something she wasn't anymore.

"And the President of the Commission, Mr. Stone," Exe introduced last.

"Ah, the thin man," I said.

He laughed. "I'm too thin, Mr. Cruz."

"Let's move to the Watch chambers," Exe directed. "We can't keep Mr. Cruz here all day."

"Yes, Mr. Cruz is Mr. Popularity these days," Mr. Cisco said.

"Tell me, Mr. Cruz," Ms. Mosaic began. "You're a champion of the people, a champion of the cops..."

"An enemy of the politicians and an enemy of the criminals," I said. "But then, I repeat myself."

She liked my little joke and laughed.

"True champions of the people rarely last long without becoming politician or criminal," Cisco said. "What's your views on the megacorporations trying to take over Metropolis, Mr. Cruz?"

I gave him a slight frown. "Don't all your children work for megacorp firms in Silicon Dunes and a few of your grandchildren got megacorp college scholarships?"

Exe quickly jumped in. "Mr. Cruz is here for a tour, not political debates."

"You seem to know a lot about us," Cisco said. "Did your new cop friends share the FBI files on each of us with you?"

I paused for a moment and said, "Yeah."

There was nothing special about the chairs they sat in, maybe some extra padding, but no cup holders or any compartment for a mobile. Each row had six chairs across, and there were six rows in each room. Exe was the last to sit in the front. They all donned black opaque shades and sat back in their chairs. Behind the lenses glowed white; the virtual reality interface was activated. They were plugged into their designated police person.

I stood at the back. Each room had its own army of technicians to monitor and maintain the hardware, and legal aides to consult with every Police Watch Commissioner by headphone, as needed. It all looked so low-tech but all this was the foundation of the Metropolis civil and criminal justice system.

"What brings you to Police Watch?" Mr. Stone asked me when they had their first extended break after 45 minutes in the chair.

We had convened in the break room for refreshments.

"I wanted to see how it all works for myself," I answered.

"Mr. Cruz, we must thank you for getting the police back on the streets. There can be no Police Watch without police."

"The system looks so simple, but I bet it's far more sophisticated than I think."

"It is," he answered. "You're looking at the only full-use digital technology anywhere in Metropolis. Actually, when Police Watch was formed, we were hand-picked to pilot the conversion to digital. Decades later, we're still the only one, but our record is spotless, and none of the city divisions can say the same with their outdated analog tech. We have moved into the new. Do away with the cables and cords for wireless and near-teleport transference. I've been a strong advocate for pushing technological advancement. That's why humans are in space."

"Well, some humans are in space," I said.

"Don't worry about those things, Mr. Cruz. No one can stop the progress for all. They can try, but they always fail."

"The technology Police Watch uses is the same as is used Up-Top."

"That's correct," he said. "That really is the only reason all of Metropolis doesn't use the newer generation technology. Nationalism. They use it, so we won't. That's how low modern politics has become and, unfortunately, the thinking of the average Metropolitan."

"The heart of this whole crisis is where the body-cam tapes went from the shootout in question."

"Yes. Quite the mystery, but I have faith in our techs. Since you're a detective, maybe you can give them some ideas."

"It's funny you say that. I said the same thing."

"Do you have any theories? It's shocking to think that someone at Metro Police or the Mayor's office could break into Police Watch and erase the tapes of that day. A true scandal. They should be fired for such incompetence."

"You know what I think about when new technology comes around? All the new ways criminals will find to exploit it. My girlfriend says I have a very dark view of the sunny things in life, but that's just the way I am. I remember, when I was a child, I read a story that whenever the latest and greatest safes came out, criminals would be the first to buy them in bulk, so they could break it apart and learn everything about it and learn to break into it. If you could break into one, then you could break into them all.

"When I was kid, I used that same principle to get into hovercars. I spent time at hovercar repair shops and the salvage yards. I learned all about cars from the scraps. I learned how to build them from the ground up. Once I understood the basic concepts, I could build any car, from an old junker to a classic, like my Ford Pony.

"The Police Watch's body-cam interface is some kind of technology. Deceptively simple, but it's all digital tech. Easy Chair Charlie told his buddies he'd make enough money to buy his way Up-Top. Easy didn't brag, and he never went anywhere without his wife. So, he was talking an astronomical amount of money times two. That's what made me keep looking at the system over and over again. My OCD tendencies are like that. They won't let me stop, until I get to a resolution. Then I figured it out. Is the system the Police Watch uses fool-proof, hack-proof? That's what Exe was scared of. If it was shown that the system was hacked into, then that would put every past, present, and future case in jeopardy. Lawyers could argue their criminal punk clients didn't do this, and because the system was hacked, it would render all videos inadmissible in court. We'd be back to eye-witness only testimony, which would put the whole court system into chaos."

I could see Exe wasn't smiling as she and other Police Watch people were watching me, quietly, but nervously.

"Well, I'm happy to say one thing."

"What's that?" Stone asked me.

"The interface wasn't hacked."

I could see them all breathe a sigh of relief.

"The system recorded that night perfectly. The incident was even watched live, as it should have been. There were no unauthorized entries, but no recordings of that night were filed. How is that possible?"

"It's not," Stone said. "There are a minimum of two watchers per police team, and every watcher has to sign off on their partners to end their shift, and when their shift is over, the recordings are logged."

"Isn't it funny how we humans say that computers are in error, when in fact, they are doing exactly what we programmed them to do? Then we get mad at them, because we're too dumb to remember what we programmed them to do. The police watch system, even now, isn't faulty or broken. It did exactly what we told it to do."

"We don't understand you, Mr. Cruz," Exe said. "Our techs have been over the system hundreds of times at our direction and on direction of Police One, City Hall; a lot of people want this. This city is holding its breath, until we can find those tapes or determine how they were destroyed."

"Sometimes, humans can't even properly read all the data it collects," I continued. "They can't see the patterns. Some great data people work for the city. They mentored me, when I was a police intern. Looking at the data, sometimes, the patterns are hard to see. You have to stare at it and assimilate all the data over days and weeks to see it. But you know, sometimes, things are so obvious, it's sitting right there in front of you."

"Mr. Cruz, I'm sure you fancy yourself a clever person, but I, for one, am getting bored. What is it you think you found that all of our techs haven't?" Cisco asked.

"You said there has to be two people on the same police watch team to end a session and send the recordings to file?" I asked.

"Yes," Exe answered.

"What if there was only one?"

All of them were thinking. The techs and the legal aides were thinking. Everyone trying to figure out my riddle.

"People," I said. "If you program a computer system not to end a session until two people are plugged into a session and sign off, then you get an error or...it goes into stand-by mode and recordings stay in the resident memory...forever."

"He's right," a tech said. "But that can't be. A shootout of that magnitude would have had as many watchers as police officers. Fifty officers were on the scene that night."

"58," I corrected and looked at the Police Watch President. "When you look at who was logged in as watcher for Officer Bus, it was you. And

Officer Boot, you. Officers Singletree and Azure, you. Everyone was only looking for unauthorized access into the system. They saw the trees and examined each closely, looking for an outside unauthorized user, but no one ever stepped back to see the forest, look at the big picture. How did you manage that, Mr. Stone? You were the designated watcher for all 58 officers on scene at the same time. What was the plan, Mr. Stone? You found an unbelievable, exploitable vulnerability in the system. Sell that knowledge to the Up-Top criminal world? With that, they could break into global banks, raid government general funds; maybe sell to terrorists to crash a space cruiser into a lunar base? They could manipulate the entire City's criminal justice surveillance system through its very own police force. Recordings could be changed, modified, replaced from *within* the system itself. Untraceable. Foolproof."

Stone stared at me, like he was a mannequin.

I said, "Easy was your go-between, but something this big...you couldn't leave him alive, because he could identify you. You couldn't take the chance, especially when he wanted to take his wife and himself to join you in the Up-Top good life."

I pointed at him with a simmering anger. "You killed my friend, and now, you're going to burn for it. Don't bother to run, because there are police and security all over this floor. You thought you were some great master criminal, but you're like every other criminal punk who trips themselves up in the end. Note to self: when you meet your criminal partner, who wears a stupid rabbit mask in a dark alley somewhere, it might be a good idea not to drive your own personal hovercar there, which can be captured on video. There it is, Mr. Stone. What do you have to say, now?"

Say? Mr. Stone did what so many people recently seemed to like doing—he shot me.

"Sir, just remain still," the medic said as I looked up at the ceiling in a haze.

My chest felt like a Hippo had punched me center-mass.

"Your bulletproof vest took most of the blast," she said.

My chest didn't think so. I turned my head and tried to sit up.

"Sir, don't sit up." Despite her objection, I did anyway.

Mr. Stone was lying, not far from me, dead! His eyes wide open and there were bloody marks all over his shirt, a knife sticking out of his belly, and a pool of blood slowly growing around the body.

I looked at the crowd behind the yellow crime tape. On one side were the Police Watch Commissioners, including Exe. They all looked at me quietly, almost indifferently. On the other side, were Wilford G. Jr., Chief Hub, and a whole lot of police. Their expressions were as empty as the Police Watch. Finally, there was City Hall—the Mayor and council members.

The main coroner arrived and looked at Stone's dead body and glanced at me. He noticed my gaze, so he knew I didn't kill him. He looked at the Police Watch, the police, and City Hall. A tiny smirk appeared on his face.

"Junior!" he yelled.

A kid ran to him in medic crime scene attire.

"Junior, it's your lucky day."

"Yes, Mr. Del?"

"You get to be the primary coroner on one of the biggest cases in Metropolis history."

"Really, Mr. Del?"

"Yes, really. Your case, beginning to end. In fact, I have so much confidence in you, I will vacate the scene and let you work," he said and took off his surgical gloves. "Yours will be the only signature on the reports."

"Oh sir, you won't regret this. You won't."

"I know." The main coroner glanced at me before disappearing out the main door. I could hear the commotion of gathering media outside.

I stood to my feet, slowly, as two medics helped me. A Police Watch commissioner was lying dead in a secure Police Watch room. I realized all three groups were wondering what I would do. I started this case getting shot at and ended it by getting shot at. I was officially done. I held my chest and walked to the door.

"Mr. Cruz!" the reporters yelled.

The only thing more disturbing than the city's reporters knowing you by sight was seeing a few wearing T-shirts with your face on it.

"Mr. Cruz, what happened in there?" one asked.

"They say the real mastermind of the Sweet Street Shootout was a Police Watch Commissioner."

"People," I stopped and said. "Metropolis has to heal and get back on its feet. Please let it do that. I followed a lead here and confronted the man. He attempted to shoot me, and he was killed by security. That's it. He and the gang leader were behind it all for what all these criminals are about—money. So please don't write any false stories of grand conspiracies. Two criminals tried to do a crime. They got caught. They got killed. That's it. I'm going home, and you better let the city heal. Now, get out of my way."

The media cleared a path for me as I walked by, holding my chest.

CHAPTER 62

The Mayor

I pretended to be in more pain and anguish than I was, because waiting for me at the Concrete Mama was my new sidewalk johnny army, courtesy of Phishy. The cheers and applauding gave me a headache. Inside my own place was the next bit of madness with my concealed-weapon Ma and my sword-toting Pops. She would mother me to death, which is what all mothers do, so I closed my eyes, from time to time, as she spoke. Finally, they let me go to bed. Dot stopped by, but I was so exhausted that I couldn't move. My body wanted to merge with the covers and bed and never emerge again.

Is this what a real case was like? I wouldn't make it to 40, let alone 92, if there were many more cases like this one. Well, I made it to the end alive and case solved. My next appointment was with sleep.

I really didn't want to go back to the office, but I had to. I had a business to run, and I suspected I'd have more clients than I could handle.

"Remember when I said you had two more high-level clients wanting to see you?" PJ asked me standing in my office.

"The case is over. What does it matter now?"

"He's on his way up."

"What? Who?"

The Mayor came in through the front door without security or his entourage, dressed in casual clothes and a black baseball cap. He saw me standing at the entrance of my office.

"Nice work, Mr. Cruz. You saved the city."

He walked over to PJ's desk and dumped a fat envelope on her desk. "What the city owes you." He smiled, turned, and left.

"What was that about?" I asked.

"He hired you."

"What?"

"He hired you to find out who was behind the body-cam tapes disappearing. I wouldn't take no for an answer."

I saw PJ's bionic arm reaching for the envelope, and I snatched it from her desk. I opened it with PJ's big head peering around my shoulder, as I quickly counted it.

"What's that?"

Inside the envelope was my new gun license. I had never seen a full-use gun license before. With this license, I could possess, carry, even concealed, any weapon known to man. It was signed by none other than Chief Hub, himself. I had asked Wilford G. Jr. to straighten this out for me, and he did. I went back to counting.

"This is a lot of money."

"You have a lot of bills and starving employees, too."

"You, starving." I laughed and pulled out a wad of cash from the envelope. "Here, so you can stop pestering me."

"About time," she said with a smile.

She opened her mobile computer, and I knew for the rest of the day, she'd be shopping online.

"And when will we be, officially, open again?" she asked. "Famous people can't go on vacation."

"I'm not famous, and I can go on vacation whenever I want. We can open on Monday, officially."

Hopefully, I could pick some cases, where I didn't get shot.

CHAPTER 63

The Man From Up-Top

Technically, he was a spaceman. All Up-Top people were space people. They were always in their all-white outfits, and we never knew if that was for some legitimate reason, or if it was just to be the opposite of us.

"You're a Zero-baby?" I asked.

The spaceman sitting in the chair across from my desk smiled. "If that colloquial means I was born in zero-gravity, then yes."

"I didn't mean any offense."

"None taken. We have colloquialisms, too."

"I'm sure you do."

Mr. Seraff was the third and final "high-level" client PJ had for me. I was eager to meet him, even though I had no idea what I was meeting him about. Meeting him meant, officially, all the business that had to do with the Easy Chair Charlie Murder Case was concluded. I liked clear endings to things.

"It was very important for us to meet with you, but—"

"You're with Interpol?"

"Interpol reports to my agency. We're the civilian side of things."

"I don't like Interpol."

He smiled. "I don't suppose you would. Which is why we wanted to meet with you. People seem to misconstrue the actions of off-worlders too often."

"I was not misconstruing anything. Your guy wanted to sacrifice an innocent victim to a kidnapping criminal gang member informant on your payroll. And to be fair, senior members of my own government and police force were going along. You see how things turned out for them. What happened to this guy, who threatened me and my livelihood?"

"Mr. Cruz, the person you're referring to is no longer working for Interpol."

"Where did he go? I bet he was promoted."

"Actually, he's in charge of the security at a local colony school. His career change was not voluntary. Mr. Cruz, Up-Top doesn't believe innocents should be sacrificed in the name of politics, either. People seem to forget; we're all humans."

"What about the spaceships?"

"A prelude to an invasion, Mr. Cruz?"

"I don't believe all that, but you did side with the Mayor and Chief, against the police and people."

"The police and people, how quaint. We were asked by the duly elected leader of one of the largest super-cities in the world to render aid in the face of a city emergency. What should we have done? We came. I can't help what conspiracy theorists and anti-off-worlder bigots say."

"My secretary said you wanted to hire me. Hire me for what, Mr. Seraff? The case is over."

"This case is over, Mr. Cruz. The next one is right around the corner and many more after that. I'm here, because I want to hire you for...access."

"Access? What does that mean? I'm a detective."

"Ever looked at your competition in the Yellow Pages, Mr. Cruz?"

"I have."

"You represent a very unique kind of detective. I'm not sure if even you grasp that, yet. You're not a government detective, not a megacorp detective. Your clients have been government, corporate, and the average citizen on the street. High-class and low-life. How many of your competitors can say they are known by sight by every cop in the city—favorably? Who can call in favors—favors from a vast network of street people across the city? Yes, you are a very unique individual, and we believe it's a relationship worth cultivating."

"For what reason?"

"Insurance against the future. The future rarely is as shiny as people think."

"I can assure you, Mr. Seraff, in a city where it rains 80% of the time, no one here really has a sunny disposition on anything."

"Yes, of course, you're right, Mr. Cruz. Let's just say the retainer I'm leaving is the price of a video-call to be made to you, sometime in the future, and that all you have to do is take the call. Nothing more. No obligation to even take the case."

"I can do that."

"Good. Then my job is done."

He stood from his chair, and he shook my hand. The man seemed to have no muscle strength in his hand. Zero-baby, indeed.

"One other thing, Mr. Cruz. Do you know a Mr. W?"

"No."

"Monkey Baker?"

"Yeah, he tried to have his animal gangs kill me, but the police took care of them."

"Did they get him?"

"No, but he has no men left. Why do you ask?"

"My sources say he's Up-Top."

437

"How?"

"Sadly, we have a criminal world, too. I'd keep an eye and ear out for him. You can never be too careful."

"I don't forget people who shoot at me. It's a personality flaw of mine."

"Good for you. It was a pleasure meeting you, Mr. Cruz. I look forward to our next encounter. The detective who saved Metropolis. I have a spaceship to catch."

I wasn't going to get too worked up about some grown man running around in a monkey mask. He'd get what was coming to him.

It was all so weird. Politicians and spacemen wanting me on their payroll. I would ignore all of them, though I was happy to take the money. I wanted to get back to normal cases. I wouldn't need to solicit reviews anymore. At last glance of my virtual storefront, I had more reviews than the top ten private investigation firms in Metropolis, combined. I wasn't so averse to being franchised after all.

CHAPTER 64

Run-Time

Like every classic hovercar collector in the universe, I was still paranoid about my vehicle. I went stalker crazy when someone scratched it; who knows what creature I'd become if someone damaged it. I had left it in storage all this time. I marked the end of the case when the spaceman walked out my office.

I waited in the Concrete Mama parking bay, expecting to see Flash jet in, but as it came in, I knew it wasn't Flash driving. Not all people drive the same; some have their own idiosyncrasies. Flash was a zippy-driver; this person was a smooth glider. I heard the passenger door click open and I lifted the door.

"Mr. Run-Time," I said to my friend lounging in my driver's seat. "I don't think I've seen you drive, since we were back in high school."

He laughed. "I can assure you I've driven quite a bit since then. I only use the limo or jet for business. When my kids need to go anywhere, it's me, Dad, who gets them there. No drivers allowed for the family hovercar. Get in."

I hopped into my passenger seat and closed the door. It had been a long time since I had the passenger seat vantage point of my own Pony.

"We gave it a complimentary wax and detail."

I looked around and rubbed the dashboard. There was nothing like that new car smell.

"Nice," I said.

"I wanted to chat before life intrudes in again."

"That happens a lot."

"What do you think, Private Investigator, Cruz? At the beginning of this, I bet you never thought it would all unfold as it did."

"I was betting I wasn't even going to get to the end."

"You did. We all did."

"Sometimes, I'll get quiet at my office desk or on the home sofa and wonder what the hell I'd gotten myself into. Then, I'd realize I had a big grin on my face."

Run-Time laughed. "Then life is good. Keep it that way."

"You gave me my first case."

"I gave you your first investigation gig. You got your case on your own. You made the case. No one else would have or could have done what you did. I'm glad I was there to help. Don't forget your friends when you get to the top."

I laughed. "You're the one at the top."

"You're right there with me," he said.

We shook hands and spent almost an hour small-talking about absolutely nothing, which was what friends do.

CHAPTER 65

Dot

"What do you plan to do, Mr. Cruz?"
"I don't know, yet."

Everyone kept asking me that question, when I was in the thick of things, when all I wanted was to be left alone. I remember Exe's conversation with me in Run-Time's office.

"I lived in a time when the crooks had better weapons than the cops. It was no fun at all. I remember hiding in my place, scared of the crooks coming at me, shooting me on purpose to get my stuff, and scared of the neighbors, shooting me by accident. Anarchy only looks cool in the movies; the real thing is far from it. Please, Mr. Cruz, I appeal to your good judgment. You live here; you know the streets. We have to look out for ourselves. No one Up-Top gives a damn. I'm not asking you to do anything illegal. I'm just asking you to keep the full truth to yourself. No one must know. We can't jeopardize the Angel program. I helped it get started when I was a hottie in my twenties. It was controversial at the time. The cops despised us, civvies, watching their every move when they went into action. But a strange thing happened. They grew to love it. They wouldn't go into action without us watching. We changed, too. We saw what the, so-called, good people did. Spitting at them, cursing, provoking them. They became more like us, and we became more like them. It has kept our fragile order intact all this time, but it's still fragile. I can't offer you anything for your cooperation, Mr. Cruz. That would be quid pro quo, and that's illegal. I appeal to your good sense, because we all live in this city together."

Dot took the day off to hang out with me in the office. It was a field trip of sorts, and she brought with her a group of high school fashionistas-in-training. It seemed like every kid in the city wanted to visit Liquid Cool.

I got back from my food run, and PJ yelled at me, "You just missed her. Run to the elevator, and you can catch her."

I dumped the bags of food in her arms and ran to the elevator. Who am I running after? I got a glimpse of Exe as the elevators doors closed. She managed do to a quick wave. I walked back to my office.

"What did she want?"

PJ handed me an envelope.

"What's with all these envelopes?" I tucked the envelope under my arm and focused on the food. We were all starving. PJ grabbed her nouveau-French-whatever and plopped it on her desk. Dot and I took our food into my office.

We set the food on the table in my sitting area.

"Are you going to open it?" Dot asked.

"Oh." I had already forgotten about the envelope.

I walked to my desk and grabbed a letter opener from my front desk drawer and sliced open the top.

Dot joined me at the desk. I opened it and reached in.

It was an official Private Investigation License!

I stared at the document, speechless. It was affirmation that I was legal, and I no longer had to play games.

"Wow, look at the expiration date," Dot said.

The date was 100 years in the future. I had a private investigator license for life.

There was another document in the envelope. It was small, and I glanced at Dot. What could it be?

It was a reissue of my national ID card. Why would they do that? I had to stare at it before I noticed it. My title! It was listed as Private Investigator.

For all my adult life, I was a "laborer." In my eyes, that always meant the same as "human" or "mammal" or "Earthling". It was a constant reminder of failure. Everyone said otherwise, but I could never shake the feeling I was nothing. Laborer was the bare-bones basic occupation designation. You did nothing to get it. The computer assigned it to you, automatically. You had to take an affirmative step to change your occupation designation, which I had never done.

No one cared about names in business. Titles! Metropolis was all about title status—the last prejudice.

The card said I had made it. My new vocation was real and had been rendered as such with the city government for all to see. There it was. I was crying. I didn't even have time to stop myself.

Dot was smiling and gave me a side hug.

"A better life is all I want for me and my girl."

I thought of when I was hiding in that new spot in that secret alley, days after my birthday. How far I had come in such a short time. Run-Time, Prima Donna, and so many others said my ticket would come, and now it had. I touched the tip of my hat as an acknowledgment to my posthumous mentor Wilford G. I'd send copies of the license to Ma and Pops for framing.

There was a major storm brewing outside, but I said to myself that we'd take a half-day off from work to celebrate and stop by the Good Kosher man for a righteous rack of roses, then I'd take Dot out dancing, and no storm would tell us different.

"Oh, my parents want you over for dinner again, soon," Dot said as we walked out of the office. "I can proudly show them your official private eye license. But I don't know what's gotten into them with the planning for the wedding and all. They want to make your favorite burrito. I didn't know you had a favorite burrito."

Thank you for reading!

Dear Reader,

I hope you enjoyed my debut cyberpunk detective novel, *Liquid Cool*.

Can You Write Me a Review?

If you enjoyed *Liquid Cool*, I'd greatly appreciate an honest review on one or more of the following sites:

Reviews are the best way for readers to discover good books. My writer's motto is simple: "Readers Rule!" Thanks so much.

Always writing,

Austin Dragon

CONTINUE THE ADVENTURE

Get Your Next *Liquid Cool* Books!

- *These Mean Streets, Darkly* (Liquid Cool Prequel Short)
- *Liquid Cool* (Liquid Cool: The Cyberpunk Detective Series, Book 1)
- *Blade Gunner* (Liquid Cool, Book 2)
- *NeuroDancer* (Liquid Cool, Book 3)
- *The Electric Sheep Massacre* (Liquid Cool, Book 4)
- *I, Alien Hunter* (Liquid Cool, Book 5)
- *A.I. Confidential* (Liquid Cool, Book 6)

- *Liquid Cool Box Set* (Liquid Cool Prequel and Books 1-3)
- *Liquid Cool Box Set 2* (Liquid Cool: Books 4-6)

Also by Austin Dragon

See all my books in science fiction, horror, and fantasy at: http://www.austindragon.com/books

ABOUT THE AUTHOR

Austin Dragon is the author of the *After Eden* **Series**, including the mini-series, ***After Eden: Tek-Fall***, the classic ***Sleepy Hollow Horrors***, the new epic fantasy adventure ***Fabled Quest Chronicles***, and the cyberpunk detective series, ***Liquid Cool***. He is a native New Yorker, but has called Los Angeles, California home for the last twenty years. Words to describe him, in no particular order: U.S. Army, English teacher, one-time resident of Paris, political junkie, movie buff, Fortune 500 corporate recruiter, renaissance man, dreamer.

He is currently working on new books and series in science fiction, fantasy, and classic horror!

Connect with Austin on social media at:

Website and blog: http://www.austindragon.com

Twitter: https://twitter.com/Austin_Dragon

Pinterest: http://www.pinterest.com/austindragon

Google+: https://google.com/+AustinDragonAuthor

Goodreads: https://www.goodreads.com/ADragon

Other books by Austin Dragon
See all my books at: **http://www.austindragon.com/books**

Printed in Great Britain
by Amazon

76182089R00254